The Pleasure of English Language and Literature

A Festschrift for Akiyuki Jimura

Edited by

Hideshi Ohno
Kazuho Mizuno
Osamu Imahayashi

KEISUISHA
Hiroshima, Japan
2018

The Pleasure of English Language and Literature
A Festschrift for Akiyuki Jimura

First published in 2018

Ohno, Hideshi, 1970-
Mizuno, Kazuho, 1961-
Imahayashi, Osamu, 1964-
The Pleasure of English Language and Literature
A Festschrift for Akiyuki Jimura
Hideshi Ohno, Kazuho Mizuno, and Osamu Imahayashi
Includes Tabula gratulatoria and Curriculum vitae of Akiyuki Jimura
ISBN978-4-86327-462-4　C3098

Copyright © 2018 Hideshi Ohno, Kazuho Mizuno, and Osamu Imahayashi

All rights reserved. No part of this book may be reprinted or reproduced or utilised in any form or by any electronic, mechanical, or other means, now known or hereafter invented, including photocopying and recording, or in any information storage or retrieval system, without permission in writing from Keisuisha Publishing Company.

Printed by
Keisuisha Co. Ltd., 1-4 Komachi, Naka-ku, Hiroshima 730-0041

Printed in Japan

Akiyuki Jimura

The medieval vision through "bodily" and "ghostly" in English devotional prose

Akio Katami   123

James Joyce and a freer flow of consciousness

Shigeo Kikuchi   139

A study of Matthew Bramble's language and epistolary style in *The Expedition of Humphrey Clinker*

Hironobu Konishi   151

Sound symbolism of feminine rhymes in Spenser's *Faerie Queene Book V*

Masaru Kosako   167

Mirrors, reflection and language in *Hamlet*

Fusako Matsuura   183

The world of *Kyng Alisaunder*: A comparison with the Hereford *Mappa Mundi*

Eri Shimamoto Matsuzawa   199

Stylistic analysis of Mansfield's *A Cup of Tea*

Yumi Mizuno   215

Negative declarative *I not say* and negative imperative *Not say* in Modern English

Fujio Nakamura   227

The semantics of Chaucer's speech/thought presentation in *Troilus and Criseyde*: The emergence of conceptual blending

Yoshiyuki Nakao   241

On the use of *lief* in Chaucer

Hideshi Ohno   261

Contents

Reading text analysis tools

Geoffrey Rockwell 277

Some Americanisms in Marryat's land-based novels and other English authors' works

Motoko Sando 293

The usage of intensive adverbs in John Evelyn's *Diary*

Akemi Sasaki 307

The Clerk's Tale: Rewritten Griselda story

Hisayuki Sasamoto 319

Authenticity and consciousness representation in Defoe's *Moll Flanders* and *Roxana*

Eri Shigematsu 335

Palaeographical researches into the Macregol Gospels: the scribe of folio 126r, marginal notes and drawings

Kenichi Tamoto 347

How Caxton translated French verbs of composite predicates by their English equivalents in *Paris and Vienne*: A study on the semantics of verbs along with their collocability with nouns

Akinobu Tani 361

On the adjectives modifying knights in Chaucer: With special references to Troilus

Yue Zhou 375

Curriculum vitae of Akiyuki Jimura 391

Preface

This festschrift is published in honour of Professor Akiyuki Jimura, Emeritus Professor at Hiroshima University, on the occasion of his retirement from the University in March 2016. We would like to express our deep respect for his brilliant career as a scholar and an educator. The essays presented here were contributed by a number of his academic colleagues and his former students at home and abroad, and were refereed by the editors.

Professor Jimura especially loves the language and literary works of Geoffrey Chaucer, although his academic interest and knowledge ranges from Old English to Present-day English to English education. As a distinguished scholar of Chaucer, he has actively participated in many domestic and foreign conferences such as those of the Japan Society for Medieval English Studies (JSMES), the English Literary Society of Japan (ELSJ) and the New Chaucer Society. He has also published a large number of books and articles such as *Studies in Chaucer's Words and his Narratives* (2005), *Chaucer no Eigo no Sekai* (2011), *"General Prologue" to* The Canterbury Tales*: A Project for a Comprehensive Collation of the Two Manuscripts (Hengwrt and Ellesmere) and the Two Editions (Blake [1980] and Benson [1987])* (2008), "Chaucer's Imaginative and Metaphorical Description of Nature" (2013), and "A Computer-assisted Textual Comparison among the Manuscripts and the Editions of *The Canterbury Tales*: With Special Reference to Caxton's Editions" (2016).

He has also made administrative contributions to academic societies especially as President of the English Research Association of Hiroshima (2003-2016), Councillor of JSMES (2005-), Councillor of ELSJ (2011-2015), President of the Chugoku-Shikoku Branch of ELSJ (2011-2015), President of the Western Branch of JSMES (2015-2016), Vice President of JSMES (2016), and President of JSMES (2017-).

In class, he creates a frank atmosphere for academic discussions. He loves making metaphorical and stimulating puns and wordplay, which prompt our efforts to understand their background and, at the same

x Preface

time, endear him to many. As a Chaucerian, "gladly wolde he lerne and gladly teche." In addition, off-campus, he enjoys "mete and drynke" in a friendly atmosphere with his colleagues and students.

We hope that Professor Jimura will find pleasure in reading this Festschrift and also that it will contribute to academic English studies worldwide.

Last but not least, we would like to offer our profound gratitude to Itsushi Kimura, president of Keisuisha Publishing Company.

June 2018
Editors

List of contributors

Manabu Agari
    Associate Professor, Hiroshima Bunkyo Women's University
Hiroji Fukumoto
    Professor, Hiroshima Shudo University
Saoko Funada
    Lecturer, Fukuoka University
Naoki Hirayama
    Associate Professor, Onomichi City University
Masahiro Hori
    Professor, Kumamoto Gakuen University
Tomoko Iwakuni
    Postgraduate Student, Hiroshima University
Yoko Iyeiri
    Professor, Kyoto University
Kazutomo Karasawa
    Professor, Rikkyo University
Akio Katami
    Associate Professor, Aoyama Gakuin University
Shigeo Kikuchi
    Former Professor, Kansai Gaidai University
Hironobu Konishi
    Professor, Hiroshima Bunkyo Women's University
Masaru Kosako
    Professor Emeritus, Okayama University
Fusako Matsuura
    Associate Professor, Okayama Shoka University
Eri Shimamoto Matsuzawa
    Professor, Osaka University of Arts
Yumi Mizuno
    Lecturer, Hiroshima Shudo University
Fujio Nakamura
    Professor, Aichi Prefectural University
Yoshiyuki Nakao
    Professor, Fukuyama University

xii   List of contributors

Hideshi Ohno
        Associate Professor, Hiroshima University
Geoffrey Rockwell
        Professor, University of Alberta
Motoko Sando
        Associate Professor, Wakayama Medical University
Akemi Sasaki
        Associate Professor, Oita University
Hisayuki Sasamoto
        Former Professor, Osaka University of Commerce
Eri Shigematsu
        Postgraduate Student, Hiroshima University
Kenichi Tamoto
        Professor, Aichi University
Akinobu Tani
        Professor, Hyogo University of Teacher Education
Yue Zhou
        Postgraduate Student, Hiroshima University

Tabula gratulatoria

Geoff Hall
>Nottingham, United Kingdom

Terry Hoad
>Cambridge, United Kingdom

Terttu Nevalainen
>Helsinki, Finland

Young-Bae Park
>Seoul, Republic of Korea

Ilse Wischer
>Potsdam, Federal Republic of Germany

Towards the division of the Round Table in the *Morte Darthur*

Manabu Agari

Abstract
With the reservoir of vocabulary enriched by the influx of foreign words such as Latin, Old French and Old Norse, Malory used this favourable situation, making an effective choice of synonymous words. Although Malory has a tendency to use the same words in succession, after the love relationship of Lancelot and Guinevere is uncovered, he substitutes the verb *appeal*, normally used up until then, for its synonymous words. The replaced words seem to have a close connection with the invalidity of the accusations made by Aggravain who wants to disgrace Lancelot's reputation and by Gawain who tries to take revenge on Lancelot for killing his brothers Gareth and Gaheris when Lancelot rescues Guinevere from being burnt at the stake. This essay aims to show that Lancelot's use of synonyms of *appeal* is related to Gawain's charge tinged with abuse and also to the deepening division of The Round Table.

1. Introduction
Malory's *Le Morte Darthur*, as P. J. C. Field observes, is written in chronicle style with abundant stock words and phrases used in spoken English (1971: 57-59). Ordinary words such as *good* and *noble*, which are often encountered in romance do not seem, at first sight, to have any special implications in themselves. Field asserts, however, that "noble knyghtes" is "the most important thematic phrase of the *Morte Darthur*" (p. 75), and Mark Lambert suggests that *noble* has secular implications (1975: 142).[1] Numerous examples of varied implications can be found. D. S. Brewer points out that *worship* is the most important chivalric value, but at the same time plays a decisive role in the disintegration of Arthur's kingdom (1974: 25, 30). Elizabeth Archibald presents a cogent argument about *fellowship* in connection with Malory's ideal of fellowship (1992: 317). Felicity Riddy argues for an association of the word *depart* with a separation of Lancelot and

---

[1] For contemporary readers' possible different reading of this word, see Riddy (1987: 160-62).

Guinevere and the break-up of the Round Table (1987: 145-46).[2]

Turning attention to Malory's style, repetition, one of the character-istics of Malory, gives us the impression of his simple style. Repetition is realised not only with the same words but also with their synony-mous words. Amidst easy access to enriched vocabulary with the influx of Old French and Latin in the Middle Ages, it is worthwhile to examine shades of difference in synonymous words in Malory. Read-ing his text shows that he has a tendency to use the same words in succession, but in the case of words related to *appeal* (meaning "to accuse"), we find an interesting linguistic phenomenon; after a consistent use of *appeal*, it is replaced by its synonymous words. The purpose of this essay, then, is to find what this change in the use of the synonyms implies in Malory.

2. Use of *appeal*

In Malory's text, the most common word belonging to the semantic field of "to accuse" is *appeal*, which is used 15 times out of 24 occurrences. The other examples are *charge* (3), *call* (3), *appeach* (1), *becall* (1) and *deprave* (1).[3] When an official charge is brought, *appeal* is usually used.[4] An appeal is a formal charge brought by an individual in the case of felonies such as murder, assault, robbery, or larceny (Russell 1980: 135-39). The accuser resorted to this procedure to prove the accuracy of the charge by trial by battle (Bellamy 1973: 126). The person accused could choose trial by combat or trial by jury (*Bracton*: 385-86). Although Malory omits a detailed account of the procedure needed for formal charges, his use of *appeal* as a criterion is a useful starting point to discuss the use of its synonymous words.

One day, King Angwysh is summoned to King Arthur's court to find that "Than was sir Blamour de Ganys there that *appeled* the kynge of Irelonde of treson, that he had slayne a cosyn of thers in his courte in Irelonde by treson" (404. 29-32).[5] The narrator in Malory explains the

---

[2] With regard to *depart*, Mann points out "a poignant image of severance, the loss of a fellowship temporarily achieved" (1996: 211).

[3] The numbers in parentheses show the frequency of each word.

[4] *Appeal* is defined as "in *Law*: To accuse of a crime which the accuser undertakes to prove" (*OED*, s.v. *appeal*, v. †1).

[5] Eugène Vinaver, ed., *The Works of Sir Thomas Malory*, 3rd ed., rev. P. J.

Towards the division of the Round Table in the *Morte Darthur*   3

custom of the day that "For the custom was suche tho dayes that and ony man were *appealed* of ony treson othir of murthure he sholde fyght body for body, other ellys to fynde another knyght for hym" (405. 2-5). With regard to this accusation, Tristram was informed by Governayle of the straits King Angwysh was involved in: "how he was somned and *appeled* of murthur" (406. 11-12), and therefore decided to give him assistance.

Before this incident, Angwysh, King of Ireland, had sent his queen's brother Marhault to King Mark of Cornwall to demand the tribute that had not been paid for seven years, but Tristram, King Mark's cousin and representative of Cornwall, defeated him but was seriously wounded by Marhault's envenomed spearhead. Informed by "a witty lady" that his wound would never be healed unless he went to the same country where the venom came, he left for Ireland, arriving at King Angwysh's castle, where he received medical treatment from his daughter La Beale Isode, "a noble surgeon." To repay King Angwysh for the kindness he had received, Tristram offered to undertake trial by combat in his stead. King Angwysh explained the situation he was placed in. When a formal charge is brought, the word used is *appeal*:

> "I shall tyll you," seyde the kynge. "I am assumned and *appleled* fro my contrey for the deth of a knyght that was kynne unto the good knyght sir Launcelot, wherefore sir Blamour de Ganys, sir Bleoberys his brother, hath *appeled* me to fyght wyth hym other for to fynde a knyght in my stede." (407. 11-16)

We may cite another instance of *appeal* used in the episode of the Poisoned Apple. The word occurs when Mador de la Porte makes a formal charge against Queen Guinevere for murdering his cousin Patryse. At a private feast Guinevere held, Pynell intended to kill Gawain by poisoning to take vengeance on him for killing his relative Lamorak. He had some apples poisoned, but Patryse, not Gawain, happened to eat a poisoned apple and died on the spot. Patryse's cousin Mador de la Porte instantly made an accusation against the Queen:

C. Field, 3 vols. (Oxford: Clarendon Press, 1990). Emphasis is added and also will be to the synonyms of *appeal*. Subsequent references to Malory will be to this edition.

4 *Manabu Agari*

> "Thys shall nat so be ended," seyde sir Mador de la Porte, "for here have I loste a full noble knyght of my bloode, and therefore uppon thys shame and dispite I woll be revenged to the utteraunce!"
>
> And there opynly sir Mador *appeled* the quene of the deth of hys cousyn sir Patryse. (1049. 24-29)

When King Arthur, hearing the commotion, came to the scene, Mador "stood stylle before the kynge and *appeled* the quene of treson" (1050. 1-2). After the suspicion against Guinevere was cleared, this incident was inscribed on the tomb of Patryse: "Also there was wrytyn uppon the tombe that quene Gwenyvere was *appeled* of treson of the deth of sir Patryse by sir Madore de la Porte" (1059. 31-33).

We have so far illustrated that when a formal accusation is made, Malory uses *appeal*. What deserves due attention in the way *appeal* and its synonyms occur is that most of the words other than *appeal* make a concentrated appearance in the final tale, beginning to be used from the episode of Guinevere's bedchamber onwards, which incident serves as a trigger to the collapse of Arthur's kingdom.[6]

3. Use of synonyms of *appeal*

On the night when King Arthur is away from his court going out on hunting, Guinevere sends for Lancelot. He comes to her chamber without knowing Aggravain's and Mordred's ruse to capture him. When they are staying together, Aggravain and Mordered leading twelve knights take them by surprise and attempt to break into the chamber, denouncing Lancelot loudly with "Traytor knyght." In order to quell the commotion, Lancelot offers to prove his innocence in the presence of Arthur and the assailants on the following day.

> "I promyse you be my knyghthode, and ye woll departe and make no more noyse, I shall as to-morne appyere afore you all and before the kynge, and than lat hit be sene whych of you all, other ellis ye all, that woll *deprave* me of treson. And there shall I answere you, as a knyght shulde, that hydir I cam to the quene for no maner of male engyne, and that woll I preve and make hit good uppon you wyth my hondys." (1168. 3-10)

---

[6] The other occurrences of *appeal* are: 578. 29; 592. 23; 593. 5; 658. 13; 661. 11; 1086. 18; 1135: 14. There are two synonymous words of *appeal* appearing before this episode. One is *call* (1132. 19) used by Mellyagaunt, which will be dealt with later. The other is *appeach* (579. 73), the implications of which are discussed in Agari (2010).

Towards the division of the Round Table in the *Morte Darthur*   5

It is noteworthy that Malory uses *deprave* ("to accuse": *MED*, s.v. *depraven*, 1. (b)), not the legal term *appeal* because he almost consistently uses *appeal* in the case of making accusations. This word does not appear in the corresponding places of the sources for Tale VIII: there is no equivalent speech in the corresponding portion of the *Mort Artu* (§90), the last part of the Vulgate Cycle.[7] Malory expanded Lancelot's following remark in the stanzaic *Morte Arthur*: "Now know thou wele, Syr Agrawayne, / Thow presons me no more tonyght" (ll. 1852-53).[8] It may be added that the stanzaic poet has Aggravain and his partisans accuse Lancelot as in "Launcelot of tresson they begredde" (l. 1812) just after Lancelot was attacked, not before he kills Agravain and his partisans as in Malory. Though Malory could choose "begredde" ("charge": *MED,* s.v. *bigreden*, v. (b)), his choice was "depraved."

It is likely that Malory made a skilful use of synonymous words belonging to the semantic field of "to accuse" available to him. In the later fifteenth century, *deprave*, derived from Latin, had a central meaning of "to vilify" (*MED*, 1. (a)) along with its derived meaning "to accuse" (*MED*, 1. (b)). The derived meaning, it seems, did not take root at that time, judging from the fact that the *MED* has only two illustrations including the one cited above and that the *OED* has no entry for the subdivided sense "to accuse." Amidst the linguistic circumstance like this, therefore, it makes sense that *deprave*, in addition to the sense "to accuse," could also assume the common sense "to vilify." It is clear that Lancelot did not take the decry made against him as an accusation, as is obvious from his resentful utterance when Aggravain and Mordred demanded loudly that Lancelot come out of the room: "thys shamefull cry and noyse I may nat suffir" (1166. 8-9), or from his speech when he explained to his colleagues about the trap he had escaped: "thys nyght bycause my lady the quene sente for me to speke with her, I suppose hit was made by treson" (1171. 1-3). It is suggestive that Lancelot used *deprave* with a dual sense in the scene where he found the charge against him unfounded. It may be added

---

[7] Jean Frappier, ed., *La Mort Le Roi Artu: Roman du XIIIᵉ Siecle,* 3rd ed. (Genève: Droz, 1964).
[8] P. F. Hissiger, ed., *Le Morte Arthur*: A Critical Edition (The Hague: Mouton, 1975).

6   *Manabu Agari*

that Lancelot's use of *deprave* implies that Aggravain and Mordred, who had "a prevy hate" to Lancelot and Guinevere, perverted their tryst arbitrarily under the pretext of preserving King Arthur's honour, as the etymological meaning of *deprave* "to distort, pervert" (*OED*, s.v. *deprave*) indicates.

The surprise attack by Aggravain and Mordred occasions Arthur's decision to burn Guinevere and then Lancelot's accidental killing of Gawain's brothers Gareth and Gaheris in his rescue of the queen, which inflames Gawain's unabating pursuit of vengeance on Lancelot. Lancelot returns the queen to Arthur through the intercession of the Pope, when he makes a long speech, in which he offers to establish religious houses every ten miles from Sandwich to Carlisle and to pray for the souls of Gareth and Gaheris. Gawain, however, rebuffs Lancelot's generous proposal and calls him names, "thou arte bothe false to the kynge and to me" (1200, 19-20). Lancelot responds to it, saying "And ye, sir Gawayne, woll *charge* me with so hyghe a thynge, ye muste pardone me, for than nedis must I answere you" (1200, 22-24; not in the sources). He uses "charge" again in his earnest request that Gawain not accuse him of treason when Gawain with Arthur's troops advances to France after Lancelot is exiled from Arthur's kingdom: "But as to you, sir Gawayne, if that ye com there, I pray you *charge* me nat wyth treson nother felony, for and ye do, I muste answere you" (1201. 27-29; not in the sources).[9]

Lancelot's avoidance of the legal term *appeal* seems to be related to his view of his killing Gareth and Gaheris and of Gawain's accusation of him. Their deaths could not be helped because Lancelot's rescue of the queen was based on honour, an extremely important chivalric value in Malory.[10] Lancelot explains to Arthur that the rescue of the queen and his subsequent abduction of her were unavoidable because "mesemyth I had loste a grete parte of my worshyp in my knyghthod and I had suffird my lady, youre quene, to have ben brente, insomuche

---

[9] The *MED* defines *charge* as "to accuse, charge" (*MED*, s.v. *chargen*, v. 4. (a)).

[10] Brewer maintains that honour is "the strongest single motivating force" in Malory's world (1974: 25). This value, L. D. Benson says, is also "the central concern of fifteenth-century knights in both fiction and life" (1976: 151).

Towards the division of the Round Table in the *Morte Darthur*   7

as she shulde have bene brente for my sake" (1188. 28-31). Bors also referred to shame, equally as important as honour, when he gave Lancelot advice at the time of Arthur's possible sentencing of the queen to be burnt at the stake: "And also I woll counceyle you, my lorde, that my lady quene Gwenyver, and she be in ony distres, insomuch as she ys in payne for youre sake, that ye knyghtly rescow her; for and ye ded ony other wyse all the worlde wolde speke you shame to the worldis ende" (1171. 26-30).[11]

That honour takes priority is reflected in Lancelot's remark to Gawain that "by Jesu, and by the feyth that I owghe unto the hyghe Order of Knyghthode, I wolde with as good a wyll have slayne my nevew, sir Bors de Ganys, at that tyme" (1189. 17-19). Honour is so important that even if Lancelot anticipated the worst situation: "peradventure I shall there destroy som of my beste fryndis" (1172. 28-29), he had no choice but to carry out the rescue effort.

In addition to the importance of honour, Gawain's accusation cannot be easily justified. Gawain levels a reproach against Lancelot that "thou slewyste hem in the despite of me" (1189. 22-23), which seems to be unfounded. First, after handing over the queen Lancelot speaks to Gawain that "I loved no kynnesman I had more than I loved hym [=Gareth], adding that "I wote well he loved me aboven all othir knyghtes" (1199. 13-18). Second, Gareth's attachment for Lancelot is already made evident: "there was no knyght that sir Gareth loved so well as he dud sir Launcelot; and ever for the moste party he wolde ever be in sir Launcelottis company" (360. 29-31). This, important enough, Gawain knows well in his indignant response to Lancelot: "what cause haddist thou to sle my good brother sir Gareth that loved the more than me and all my kynne?" (1189. 12-13). Third, Gawain's abusive remark, as shown below, seems to be the result of a distorted effusion of his "long-suppressed envy" of Lancelot:[12] "I leve well, false recrayed knyght, for thou haste many longe dayes overlad me and us all, and destroyed many of oure good knyghtes" (1189. 31-33). His accusation escalates to the extent that he exhibits unchivalric

---

[11] For the importance of shame as opposed to guilt in Malory, see Lambert (1975: 176-94).
[12] Kennedy (1985: 208). For a contrary view of Gawain, see Whetter (2008: 137-42).

behaviour, making "many men to blow uppon sir Launcelot, and so all at onys they called hym 'false recrayed knyght'" (1190. 20-22).[13]

We may now refer to scholars' evaluation of Gawain because it will be useful to judge whether Gawain's accusation is justifiable or not. Critical opinion of him is divided and tends towards a negative view of him. Larry Benson puts the heaviest responsibility on Gawain among the four major characters: Arthur, Guinevere, and Lancelot (1976: 241). Helen Cooper asserts that the division of the Arthurian fellowship was caused by Gawain's pursuit of family feud as well as the envy of Mordred and Aggravain (1996: 185). Mark Lambert considers that Gawain's vengefulness is not his innate disposition, but was caused by "an extraordinary situation." But he also criticises Gawain, referring to his "relentless pursuit of revenge" when he refused Lancelot's offer of adequate compensation for his unwitting killing of Gawain's brothers (1975: 215-17).[14] D. S. Brewer even says that Gawain is "half-villain" (1974: 11). On the other hand, a favourable view of him has been put forward by C. D. Benson, who contends that "Gawain's vindictive actions were urged by demand for honour" (1996: 232).[15] K. S. Whetter supports Gawain even more positively, highlighting his chivalric pursuit of familial honour (2008: 137-42).[16]

Admitting the validity of Gawain's adherence to his family loyalties, his excessive rebuke of Lancelot seems to be unreasonable. Lancelot attempts to suspend the hostilities, which Gawain rejects for a reason that goes beyond the bounds of reason, saying that he will retaliate for his three brothers, not two: "thou and I shall never be accorded whyle

---

[13] Lambert calls this kind of shouting "an unchivalric garrulousness" (1975: 190-91). He convincingly discusses the importance of shame in relation to noise (pp. 190-94).

[14] McCarthy regards Gawain's hunger for retaliation as "totally destructive" (1988: 49).

[15] For a detailed discussion of Gawain's familial honour, see C. D. Benson (1983).

[16] For analyses of Gawain made from different viewpoints, see Farrell (2006), who, based on Malory's generic shift from romance to epic, argues for Gawain's epic determination to fight to the death. Shichtman (1984) views Gawain as a figure with many frailties who fails to accomplish chivalric obligations despite his best intentions.

Towards the division of the Round Table in the *Morte Darthur*   9

we lyve, for thou hast slayne three of my brethyrn" (1199. 6-8). We should notice that the brothers Gawain pledged to avenge did not include Aggravain. When Aggravain lost his life in his surprise attack on Lancelot, Gawain assumed a calm attitude to Arthur: "insomuch as I gaff hem warnynge and tolde my brothir and my sonnes aforehonde what wolde falle on the ende, and insomuche as they wolde nat do be my counceyle, I woll nat meddyll me thereoff, nor revenge me nothynge of their dethys" (1176. 2-6). Gawain's inclusion of Aggravain in his retort to Lancelot plainly exposes his irrational voracity for retaliation against Lancelot. It would seem that the immense difficulty with which Lancelot could accept Gawain's unjustifiable accusation led to his avoidance of *appeal*.

Gawain's unreasonable charge against Lancelot continues to emerge at the siege of Benwick as well: "Where arte thou now, thou false traytour, sir Launcelot? Why holdyst thou thyselff within holys and wallys lyke a cowarde? Loke oute, thou false traytoure knyght, and here I shall revenge uppon thy body the dethe of my three brethirne!" (1215. 11-14). Gawain again is accusing Lancelot for killing three of his brothers. Besides, his taunting of Lancelot becomes even more intense with his successive use of the insulting vocative "thou false traytour (knyght)" alongside the scornful simile "lyke a cowarde" used in between. His abusive language is so provocative that Lancelot's entourages urge him to defend himself: "Sir, now muste you deffende you lyke a knyght, othir ellis ye be shamed for ever, for now ye be *called* uppon treson, hit ys tyme for you to styrre! For ye have slepte over longe, and suffirde overmuche" (1215. 18-21; not in the sources).[17]

---

[17] The *MED* cites this illustration, interpreting the word as "to call (sb.) to account, accuse" (*MED*, s.v. *callen*, v. 3. (c)). It does not take the word as a legal term (1. (e)). The *OED* does not label this word as legal (*OED*, s.v. *call*, *v.* †8.). The other example of *call*, originating in Old Norse, occurs in a scene where Mellyagaunt accuses the Queen of having a sexual relationship with one of her knights:

"A ha, madame!" seyde sir Mellyagaunte, "now I have founde you a false traytouras unto my lorde Arthur, for now I preve well hit was nat for nought that ye layde thes wounded knyghtis within the bondys of youre chambir. Therefore I will *calle* you of treson afore my lorde kynge Arthure." (1132.15-

10   *Manabu Agari*

Lancelot is persuaded into taking action, using *charge* as in the case
of the siege at Joyous Gard: "'So God me helpe,' seyde sir Launcelot,
'I am ryght hevy at sir Gawaynes wordys, for now he *chargith* me with
a grete charge. And therefore I wote as well as ye I muste nedys
deffende me, other ellis to be recreaunte'" (1215. 22-25; not in the
sources). The inappropriateness of Gawain's insult seems to be fully
reflected in Lancelot's use of "chargith" and "grete" ("haughty,
insolent": *MED*, s.v. *gret*, 5. (c)). Lancelot declares to Arthur that he
fight in single combat with Gawain. This is probably because
Gawain's unjustified insult has reached the saturation point that
Lancelot loses honour:

> "And now I may no lenger suffir to endure, but nedis I muste deffende
> myselff, insomuch as sir Gawayn hathe *becalled* me of treson; whych
> ys gretly ayenste my wyll that ever I shulde fyghte ayenste ony of youre
> blood, but now I may nat forsake hit: for I am dryvyn thereto as beste
> tylle a bay." (1216. 1-6)[18]

It is evident that Lancelot has decided to fight with Gawain, not readily
but out of necessity, as shown in the above illustration: "but now I may

---

   19; not in *The Vulgate Version of the Arthurian Romances*, Vol. IV, Part II,
   p. 220).

Mellyagraunt's accusation is unfounded because, though it was Lancelot
who slept with the Queen, he accuses one of the wounded knights staying
in the same chamber and also because his accusation is instigated by his
secret desire to hide his crime that he abducted the Queen. It is ironical that
he uses *call* of his own accord, not the legal term *appeal*.

[18] The *Mort Artu* has no equivalent word. The corresponding part of the
stanzaic *Morte Arthur* has the following line: "Launcelot of treson he
becryed" (2774). It could be that Malory averted "becryed" because it
seemed obsolescent: the *MED* has no other citation other than that quoted
above (*MED*, s.v. *becrien*, v. (b)); the *OED* has no entry for this word
except as an instance of the prefix *be-* (*OED*, s.v. *be-*, prefix. 4). We may
add that the stanzaic poet uses a synonymous word of "becryed" in the
episode of the poisoned apple: "Than as Syr Mador loudest spake / The
queen of treson to *bycalle*" (1552-53). It could be that Malory used
"becalled" recalling this episode. The point to be made is that Malory does
not have Lancelot and his colleagues use the legal term *appeal*. Borrowing
words from the sources does not necessarily detract from Malory's
originality. We may note that in writing Tale VIII, Malory "has enough
independence in matter and manner to write in his own way" (Field 1971:
67). See also Vinaver (1990: 1624).

Towards the division of the Round Table in the *Morte Darthur*   11

nat forsake hit: I am dryvyn thereto as beste tylle a bay." After enduring three hours of fierce assault made by Gawain, Lancelot fights back and strikes him down. Despite his defeat, that is, his charge against Lancelot has been proved wrong, Gawain, after his wound has been healed, challenges Lancelot to another combat. Gawain's relentless, unjustifiable vengefulness is reflected in his repeated use of "traytour knyght": "Com forth, thou false traytoure knyght and recrayed"[19] and "Com downe, traytoure knyght" (1219. 1-2, 9). He vaunts of his prowess in a pretentious manner: "I wene this day to ley the as low as thou laydest me" (1219. 12-13). Lancelot responds to him that "ye shall nat thynke that I shall tarry longe, but sytthyn that ye unknyghtly *calle* me thus of treson, ye shall have bothe youre hondys fulle of me" (1219.16-19; not in the sources).[20] Lancelot again defeats Gawain in the second single combat. It is revealing that Lancelot responds to the unacceptability of Gawain's remark with the use of "calle" in combination with "unknyghtly."

The investigation above has revealed that using the synonymous words of *appeal* has much to do with the nature of the charges brought against Lancelot. He stoutly refused to accept the irrational accusations made against him by word and deed. The hostile confrontation caused by Gawain's pursuit of vengeance on Lancelot has created serious fissures between them and among the fellowship of the Round Table as well. Holding the bud of rift and destruction inside the dividing fellowship of the Round Table, the use of the

---

[19] Gawain's harsh language is intensified by the addition of "recrayed." This word, as might be expected, associates the fifteenth-century reader with the meaning of the infinitive form "recray," that is, "To yield in a cowardly manner," and even with the etymological meaning "to yield in a trial by combat" (*OED*, s.v. †*recray*, *v.*). It seems that this word sounds all the more humiliating to Lancelot because he sets so high a value on honour that he could not forbear the idea of being disgraced from being defeated in single combat.

[20] In the *Mort Artu* "apel" is used: «Ha! messire Gauvain, il seroit bien resons que de cest apel que vos avez fet seur moi fusse quites; car bien m'en sui desfenduz vers vos jusques pres de vespres» (*Mort Artu* §157. ll. 12-15). ["Ah! Sir Gawain, it would be very reasonable for me to be acquitted of the accusation you laid on me, because I have defended myself well against you until Vespers"] (*The Death of King Arthur* §157. ll. 10-12).

synonymous words other than the legal term symbolises the confused state of the opposition that is beyond the reach of the law.

4. Conclusion

The linguistic situation in the late fifteenth century seemed favourable to writers with the rich reservoir of vocabulary borrowed from Latin, Old French and Old Norse, in addition to the stock of native words. We may say that Malory used this situation, making a conscious choice of synonymous words. After the private relationship between Lancelot and Guinevere was disclosed, the word *appeal*, until then used regularly, was completely replaced with its synonymous words. Use of the replaced words questioned the validity of the accusations made by Lancelot's accusers, particularly Gawain. Lancelot's avoidance of the legal term in response to Gawain's charge, which has become so abusive and irrational as to be imbued with taunt, represents the chaotic situation where the rule of law has failed to fulfil its proper function. It would be fair to conclude that Malory's use of the synonymous words serves as a contributory factor in making the rupture between Lancelot and Gawain more irreconcilable, and thereby aggravating the division of the Round Table.

References

Agari, Manabu 2010. Semantic change of *appeach* in Late Middle English. *Bulletin of Hiroshima Bunkyo Women's University* 45, 25-34 (in Japanese).

Archibald, Elizabeth 1992. Malory's ideal of fellowship. *The review of English studies* XLIII, 311-28.

Bellamy, John G. 1973. *Crime and public order in England in the Later Middle Ages*. London: Routledge & Kegan Paul.

Benson, C.D. 1983. Gawain's defence of Lancelot in Malory's 'Death of Arthur.' *Modern language review* 78, 267-72.

——1996. The ending of the *Morte Darthur*. In Elizabeth Archibald and A. S. G. Edwards (eds.), *A companion to Malory*, 221-38. Cambridge: D.S. Brewer.

Benson, Larry D. 1976. *Malory's Morte Darthur*. Cambridge, Mass.: Harvard University Press.

Brewer, D.S. 1974. Introduction. In D.S. Brewer (ed.) *Malory: The Morte Darthur: Parts seven and eight*, 2nd ed., 1-36. Evanston: Northwestern University Press.

Cable, James, trans. 1971. *The death of King Arthur.* Harmondsworth: Penguin Books.

Cooper, Helen 1996. The book of Sir Tristram de Lyones. In Elizabeth Archibald and A.S.G. Edwards (eds.), *A companion to Malory*, 183-201. Cambridge: D.S. Brewer.

Farrell, Thomas J. 2006. The clash of genres at the siege of Benwick. *Arthuriana* 16. 2, 88-91.

Field, P.J.C. 1971. *Romance and chronicle: A study of Malory's prose style.* London: Barrie & Jenkins.

Frappier, Jean (ed.) 1964. *La mort le roi Artu: Roman du XIIIᵉ siecle,* 3rd ed. Genève: Droz.

Hissiger, P.F. (ed.) 1975. *Le Morte Arthur: A critical edition.* The Hague: Mouton.

Kennedy, Beverly 1985. *Knighthood in the Morte Darthur.* Cambridge: D.S. Brewer.

Kurath, Hans, *et al.* (eds.) 1956-1999. *Middle English dictionary.* Ann Arbor: The University of Michigan Press.

Lambert, Mark 1975. *Malory: Style and vision in Le Morte Darthur.* New Haven and London: Yale University Press.

Mann, Jill 1996. Malory and the Grail legend. In Elizabeth Archibald and A.S.G. Edwards (eds.), *A companion to Malory*, 203-20. Cambridge: D.S. Brewer.

McCarthy, Terence 1988. *Reading the Morte Darthur.* Cambridge: D.S. Brewer.

Riddy, Felicity 1987. *Sir Thomas Malory.* Leiden: E. J. Brill.

Russell, M.J. 1980. Trial by battle and the appeals of felony. *The journal of legal history* 1. 2, 135-64.

Shichtman, Martin 1984. Malory's Gawain reconsidered. *Essays in literature* 11, 159-76.

Simpson, J.A. & E.S.C. Weiner (eds.) 1989 *The Oxford English dictionary*, 2nd ed. Oxford: Clarendon Press.

Sommer, H.O. (ed.) 1979. *The vulgate version of the Arthurian romances*, Vol. IV, Part II. New York: AMS Press.

Thorne, Samuel E., trans. with revisions and notes 1968. *Bracton: On the laws and the customs of England*, vol. 2. Cambridge, Mass.: The Belknap Press of Harvard University Press.

Vinaver, Eugène, (ed.) 1990. *The works of Sir Thomas Malory*, 3rd ed., rev. P.J.C. Field, 3 vols. Oxford: Clarendon Press.

Whetter, K.S. 2008. *Understanding genre and medieval romance.* Hampshire: Ashgate.

A pragmatic study of tag questions in Shakespeare

Hiroji Fukumoto

Abstract

This paper investigates a quantitative analysis of the polarity and the pragmatic functions of tag questions in Shakespeare. Hoffmann (2006) observes that tag questions came to be used frequently in the late sixteenth century. This period corresponds perfectly with Shakespeare's lifetime. Although tag questions were a new phenomenon in English, Shakespeare makes good use of the various types of tag questions. Among them, it is noted that the frequency of the positive-positive polarity type of the tag questions in Shakespeare is higher than that of other dramatists in the sixteenth century. Furthermore, concerning the pragmatic functions of tag questions, confirmatory tag questions are most favoured in Shakespeare, which is also the most popular type in Present-day English. Attitudinal tag questions are the second most frequent type in Shakespeare. It is concluded that the positive-positive polarity is likely to co-occur with a tag question denoting a speaker's attitude.

1. Introduction

In Present-day English, tag questions are one of the most salient colloquial features and have attracted the interest of many scholars. Therefore, over the past several decades a considerable number of studies have been made on tag questions in Present-day English from various points of view. They include phonological, syntactical, and sociolinguistic studies. Surprisingly enough, however, few studies on tag questions in the history of English have been carried out.

This paper aims to consider the issue of tag questions in Shakespeare. Some scholars have previously discussed the issue (Wikberg 1975, Salmon 1987, Tottie and Hoffmann 2009), but they dealt with only a portion of his plays. Ukaji (1977) deals with all his plays, but does not make a quantitative investigation. This paper, which examines all of Shakespeare's plays, explores a quantitative analysis of the polarity and the pragmatic functions of tag questions. First, I will deal with the polarity of tag questions from a syntactical viewpoint. Second, I will discuss their pragmatic functions.

2. Previous studies

Before going to the discussion of tag questions in Shakespeare, let us first consider when tag questions first occurred in the history of English. Hoffmann (2006) regards an example in a play written in 1497 as the first example of tag questions in English.

> [M]y research retrieved only a single instance from texts that were written before the year 1550. The earliest tag question—dating from 1497—is displayed in (12):
>
> (12) Than thay have some maner gettynge By some occupacione, have thay? (Henry Medwall: *Fulgens and Lucrece*, 1497)
>
> Hoffmann (2006: 39-40)

In addition, he mentions that the second oldest example in his data is found in the early 1550s. Figure 1 shows the historical development of tag questions based on his data.

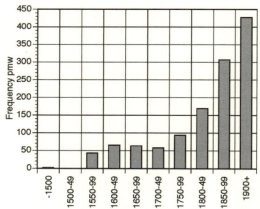

Figure 1. Tag questions in the English Drama Collection
(Hoffmann 2006: 39)

As shown in Figure 1, there is no example of tag questions from 1500 to 1549. This fact is a bit strange, because Hoffman finds one example before 1500. Therefore, we can only assume from this figure that regular use of tag questions began around 1550. In other words, it can safely be said that tag questions began to appear more frequently in Shakespeare's lifetime (1564-1616).

2.1. Polarity of tag questions in Shakespeare

Wikberg (1975: 129) examines the question of tag questions, using 22 plays of Shakespeare and finds 44 examples of tag questions in all. Tottie and Hoffmann (2009: 151-52) also deal with 22 plays and point out that there are 40 examples of tag questions in Shakespeare. Table 1 shows the distribution of the polarity types in Shakespeare according to their studies.

Table 1. Distribution of polarity types of the tag questions in 22 plays of Shakespeare

Polarity Type	Positive-Negative	Negative-Positive	Positive-Positive	Negative-Negative
Wikberg (1975)	75%	7%	18%	0%
Tottie and Hoffmann (2009)	73%	5%	22%	0%

Wikberg (1975) and Tottie and Hoffmann (2009) investigate the same number of plays in Shakespeare, but the plays they use are different and therefore the number of the polarity types is different. As is clear in Table 1, we find that the most frequent tag type is positive statement + negative tag in Shakespeare, while there are no examples of negative statement + negative tag. From this table, we can find the general tendency about the polarity of the tag questions in Shakespeare, because their results are almost the same. However, both studies deal with only 22 plays of Shakespeare and therefore we cannot see an overall picture of the tag questions in Shakespeare.

2.2. Pragmatic functions of tag questions

Holmes (1995: 80-83) divides the functions of tag questions in Present-day English into the following four types: epistemic modal, challenging, facilitative, and softening. This classification exerts a great influence on the later studies and some scholars modify the functions and formulate the new classification so that they can adapt them to their data.

Among them, Tottie and Hoffmann (2009: 141-44) set up the new classification to apply to the analysis of the historical data. They focus on the tag questions from 1550 to 1650, which was the first century since tag questions emerged and they divide the pragmatic functions into four types: confirmatory, challenging, attitudinal, and hortatory. They define the four types as follows. Confirmatory tag questions clearly seek and receive answers of a hearer and do not have any strong affective functions. They usually occur in turn-final position. Challenging tag questions suggest peremptory or aggressive atmosphere of a speaker and they are used when a speaker tries to provoke someone to a quarrel and so do not expect and do not receive answers of a hearer. Attitudinal tag questions are used to express a speaker's attitude and are not turn-final but appear in the middle of long turns and do not seem to expect an answer. Hortatory tag questions have directive functions through use with an imperative.

It is important to note that it is difficult to draw a clear line among these four categories. Tottie and Hoffmann state that "It is important to keep in mind that the pragmatic functions of tag questions form a continuum and that functions overlap and shade into one another" (Tottie and Hoffmann 2009: 141). After careful thought, however, I will follow their classification in this paper, because this seems to be the best classification in analysing the older data.

3. Polarity types in Shakespeare

In this section, I will discuss the polarity types of tag questions in Shakespeare. We find 89 examples of tag questions in total in 37 plays of Shakespeare. This means that on average, tag questions occur 2.4 times a play in Shakespeare. Compared to the frequency of tag questions in Present-day English, this number may sound quite small. However, as mentioned above, since tag questions came to be used in Shakespeare's time, such a small number seems reasonable. Tottie and Hoffmann (2009: 136) examines the polarity types of tag questions in the sixteenth-century British dramas, as shown in Table 2.

Table 2. Distribution of polarity types in sixteenth-century British drama

Polarity Type	Positive-Negative	Negative-Positive	Positive-Positive	Negative-Negative
Sixteenth-century drama (N=136)	68%	15%	17%	0%

(Tottie and Hoffman 2009: 136)

Based on this classification, I classified all examples of tag questions in Shakespeare. Table 3 shows the distribution of the polarity types in Shakespeare.

Table 3. Distribution of polarity types in Shakespeare

Polarity Type	Positive-Negative	Negative-Positive	Positive-Positive	Negative-Negative
Shakespeare (N=89)	61%	9%	30%	0%

By comparing Table 2 and Table 3, we find that both tables show the positive-negative type to be the most predominant, and that there are no instances of the negative-negative type. In Table 2, the positive-positive type accounts for 17 %, while the type increases to 30% in Table 3. This means that Shakespeare used the positive-positive type more often than other dramatists in the sixteenth century.

We will discuss the examples of the types according to the classification.

3.1. Positive—Negative

We shall first look more carefully into the positive-negative type. This is the most common tag type in Shakespeare as well as dramatists in the sixteenth century.

Some examples are:

(1)   You serve Octavius Caesar, do you not? (JC 3.1.276)

(2)   'T was you that kill'd young Rutland, was it not? (3H6 2.2.98)

(3)   I think it is good morrow, is it not? (1H4 2.4.524)

(4)   2. Lord: A servant only, and a gentleman
           Which I have sometime known.
       Count: Parolles, was it not? (AW 3.2.84-85)

As is seen above, in this type, the negative particle *not* is always at the end of the sentence after a subject in a tag question. We cannot find the contracted form like *don't you* in Shakespeare, which is often seen in Present-day English.

As in (4), there are some cases where both a subject and a verb are deleted in the main clause and a noun phrase is followed by a tag question. The ellipsis tends to occur when a subject is a pronoun and a verb is a *be*-verb in the main clause.

3.2. Negative—Positive

Contrary to the positive-negative type, there are cases where an affirmative tag question follows a negative sentence. Concerning the negative-positive type, there are only seven examples in Shakespeare. This type is extremely uncommon, compared to the positive-negative type mentioned above. In this type, a speaker is somehow confident of the negation of the proposition, but wants to make certain of the truth of the proposition by asking a hearer.

(5) You have not the Book of Riddles about you, have you?
(MWW 1.1.201-02)

(6) You have not heard of the proclamation, have you? (MM 1.2.93)

(7) Helen was not up, was she? (Troilus 1.2.49)

3.3. Positive—Positive

In Shakespeare, a positive tag construction sometimes occurs after a positive sentence, which is very rare in Present-day English. This type accounts for 30% in Shakespeare and it is remarkable that Shakespeare uses this type more frequent than other dramatists. Salmon (1987: 55) points out that "certain tag questions can imply irony, annoyance or impatience . . . These attitudes may be indicated by positive + positive, or negative + negative."

(8) You use me well, Master Ford, do you? (MWW 3.3.202)

(9) She writes so to you? doth she? (CYM 2.4.105)

(10) Maria: Madam, there is at the gate a young gentle-man much desires to speak with you.
Olivia: From the Count Orsino, is it? (TN 1.5.99-101)

(11) Prithee come; will you? (Oth 4.1.168)

In (9), it is interesting that the verb in the main clause takes a third person singular -*s*, but the ending changes to -*th* in the tag question. In Early Modern English, there were two forms of the inflection ending for the third person present singular: *s* and *th*. It is clear from this example that both forms were used freely without distinction in those

A pragmatic study of tag questions in Shakespeare 21

days.

(10) is the type where a subject and a verb are omitted and a prepositional phrase is followed by a positive tag question. In (11), an imperative is followed by a tag question *will you*. This rule is true in Present-day English.

3.4. Negative—Negative
There is no instance of this type of tag question in Shakespeare's plays.

4. Pragmatic functions of tag questions in Shakespeare
In this section, let us move to the pragmatic functions of tag questions in Shakespeare. It goes without saying that tag questions have a variety of pragmatic meanings according to their context in the same way as questions. The primary function of a tag question, as we can expect, is to seek information toward a hearer, but besides this, various functions can be observed in a tag question. As mentioned in 2.2., Tottie and Hoffmann (2009) classified the functions of tag questions into four types and divided the examples of Shakespeare and Ben Jonson, as shown in Table 4.

Table 4. Pragmatic functions of tag questions in 17 plays of Shakespeare and 4 plays of Jonson

	Confirmatory	Challenging	Attitudinal	Hortatory
Shakespeare	75%	13%	8%	5%
Jonson	57%	25%	7%	11%

(Tottie and Hoffman 2009: 153)

In accordance with their pragmatic characteristics, I classified all examples of the tag questions in Shakespeare, as shown in Table 5.

Table 5 Pragmatic functions of tag questions in all plays of Shakespeare

	Confirmatory	Challenging	Attitudinal	Hortatory
Shakespeare	70%	16%	10%	4%

When we compare Table 4 with Table 5, we see that the ratios of pragmatic functions in Shakespeare are quite similar, though the number of the challenging type is a little higher in Ben Jonson. In Shakespeare, confirmatory tag questions are the most frequent type, which is the same in Present-day English. According to this classification, I will investigate each type of pragmatic function in Shakespeare.

4.1. Confirmatory

Confirmatory tag questions are used when a speaker seeks information or agreement toward a hearer. In Shakespeare, this type is the most predominant.

Examples include:

(12) Shallow: I dare say my cousin
          William is become a good scholar. He is at Oxford
          still, is he not?
     Silence: Indeed, sir, to my cost. (2H4 3.2.9-12)

(13) Titus: Come, come, thou'lt do my message, wilt thou not?
     Boy: Ay, with my dagger in their bosoms, grandsire.
                                              (TIT 4.1.117-18)

(14) Buckingham: This is All Souls' Day, fellow, is it not?
     Sheriff: It is, my lord. (R3 5.1.10-11)

(15) Polonius: So by my former lecture and advice
          Shall you my son. You have me, have you not?
     Reynaldo: My lord, I have. (Ham 2.1.64-66)

(16) Phebe: I'll write to him a very taunting letter,
          And thou shalt bear it; wilt thou, Silvius?
     Silvius: Phebe, with all my heart. (AL 3.5.134-36)

In these examples, tag questions are used to ask for a confirmation from a hearer. This is supported by the fact that responsive words like *indeed* and *ay* occur in the replies of the hearers.

In (14) and (15), the hearers answer with the echo sentences like *it is* and *I have* respectively in order to give the agreement to the tag questions. In (12) - (15), we find that the hearers reply to the tag questions, using the vocatives, *sir, grandsire* and *my lord*. This means from these vocatives that this type of the tag questions are more likely to be used when a superior speaks to a subordinate. In (13) and (16), *thou is* used as a subject in the main sentence and is followed by *wilt thou* in the tag question. In these examples, the pragmatic function may be confirmatory, but we can assume that the function of request is expressed, particularly because in (16) the hearer agrees by using the phrase *with all my heart*.

4.2. Challenging

Challenging tag questions occur when a speaker speaks provocatively or with an aggressive tone and it is usual that a second person pronoun *thou* is used in the tag question, because *thou* is a pronoun which can be used when a speaker criticizes somebody.

(17) Thersites: Thou canst strike, canst thou? A red murrion a' thy
       jade's tricks!
     Ajax: Toadstool! learn me the proclamation. (Troilus 2.1.19-21)

(18) Hostess: [The page attacks her]
       Thou wo't, wo't thou? thou wo't,
       wo't ta? Do, do, thou rogue! do, thou hempseed!
     Page: Away, you scullion! you rampallian! (2H4 2.1.57-59)

(19) 1. Sail: Slack the bolins there! --Thou wilt not, wilt
       thou? Blow, and split thyself. (PER 3.1.43-44)

In (17), Thersites abuses Ajax, using a tag question, because he was beaten by him. In (18), a page strikes a hostess, and then the hostess speaks to the page with a lot of curse words. She uses *thou* to a page, while the page uses *you* instead of *thou* to the hostess. Here *wo't* is a variant form of *wilt*, which is the second person singular form of an auxiliary *will*.

4.3. Attitudinal

Attitudinal tag questions are employed when a speaker expresses an attitude like anger, delight, sorrow or impatience.

(20) Baptista: Katherina, you may stay,
       For I have more to communicate with Bianca. *Exit.*
     Katherina: Why, and I trust I may go too, may I not?
       What, shall I be appointed hours, as though (belike)
       I knew not what to take and what to leave? Ha! *Exit.*
                                      (Shrew 1.1.100-04)

24 *Hiroji Fukumoto*

(21) Mrs. Ford: You use me well, Master Ford, do you?
Ford: Ay, I do so. (MWW 3.3.202-03)

(22) Ford: Old woman? What old woman's that?
Mrs. Ford: Why, it is my maid's aunt of Brainford.
Ford: A witch, a quean, an old cozening quean!
Have I not forbid her my house? She comes of
errands, does she? (MWW 4.2.170-74)

In (20), Katherina uses a tag question when her father Baptista orders her to stay outside. She becomes irritated, because she wants to go into her house with her father. Her irritation is strengthened by the exclamatory words like *why* and *ha*. In (21), Mrs. Ford is suspected of dishonesty by her husband and so does not think that her husband treats her well. Then she denies her dishonesty by speaking ironically with a tag question. In (22), Mr. Ford uses a tag question impatiently, because an old woman whom he forbids to enter his house is at his house.

It follows from these examples that the attitudinal type tends to co-occur with a positive statement + positive tag construction. Shakespeare uses these tag questions skilfully in order to allude to his characters' attitudes.

4.4. Hortatory

Tottie and Hoffmann (2009: 144) state that hortatory tag questions have directive functions and occur with imperative sentences. As we have seen in Table 5, this type of tag questions is the least frequent in Shakespeare.

(23) Iago: Will you sup there?
Cassio: Faith, I intend so.
Iago: Well, I may chance to see you; for I would
very fain speak with you.
Cassio: Prithee come; will you?
Iago: Go to; say no more. (Othello 4.1.164-69)

(24) Brutus: I prithee, Strato, stay thou by thy lord.
Thou art a fellow of a good respect;
Thy life hath had some smatch of honor in it.
Hold then my sword, and turn away thy face,
While I do run upon it. Wilt thou, Strato?
Strato: Give me your hand first. Fare you well, my lord.
(JC 5.5.44-49)

As is seen from these examples, the tag questions *will you* and *wilt thou* are appended after the imperative respectively. This rule is the same as that in Present-day English. In (23), Cassio asks Iago to come later with a tag question. It is interesting that this imperative co-occurs with *prithee*, which is a politeness marker. Cassio opens the sentence with *prithee*, which is a compound word of *pray* and *thee*. The pronoun *thee* is a friendly form of second person pronouns, but the pronoun changes into *you* in the tag question, which is a polite form. This expression denotes Cassio's strong feeling that he wants Iago to come see him. In (24), Brutus also uses *I prithee* at the beginning of his speech. Then Brutus asks his servant Strato to hold his sword. By adding the tag *wilt thou* to an imperative, we can understand Brutus's serious feeling.

5. Conclusion

This paper has discussed the polarity and the functions of the tag questions in Shakespeare from a quantitative viewpoint. We find 89 examples of the tag questions in 37 plays of Shakespeare. First, concerning the polarity of tag questions, the most popular type is the positive statement + negative tag and accounts for 61%. The positive-positive polarity is 30% and it is notable that Shakespeare uses the type more frequent than other dramatists in the sixteenth century.

Second, we have seen the pragmatic functions of the tag questions in Shakespeare according to the classification of Tottie and Hoffmann (2009). When we classified into four types, the most popular is confirmatory tag questions (70%). It is remarkable that attitudinal tag questions are the second most frequent type. It is concluded that this is because the positive-positive polarity tends to co-occur with a tag question denoting a speaker's attitude.

References

Evans, G. Blakemore (ed.) 1997. *The Riverside Shakespeare*. 2nd edition. Boston: Houghton Mifflin.
Hoffmann, Sebastian 2006. Tag questions in early and late Modern English: Historical description and theoretical implications. *Anglistik*. 17(2) 35-55.
Holmes, Janet 1995. *Women, men and politeness*. Harlow: Longman.

Kopytko, Roman 1995. Linguistic politeness strategies in Shakespeare's plays. In Andreas H. Jucker (ed.) *Historical pragmatics: Pragmatic developments in the history of English.* Amsterdam: John Benjamins. 515-40.

Salmon, Vivian 1987. Elizabethan colloquial English in the Falstaff plays. In Vivian Salmon and Edwina Burness (eds.) *A reader in the language of Shakespearean drama.* Amsterdam: John Benjamins. 37-70.

Tottie, Gunnel and Sebastian Hoffmann 2006. Tag questions in British and American English. *Journal of English linguistics.* Vol. 34. No. 4. 283-311.

Tottie, Gunnel and Sebastian Hoffmann 2009. Tag questions in English: The first century. *Journal of English linguistics.* Vol. 37. No. 2. 130-61.

Ukaji, Masatomo 1977. Tag questions in Shakespeare. *Studies in English linguistics.* No. 5. 265-80.

Wikberg, Kay 1975. *Yes-no questions and answers in Shakespeare's plays: A study in text linguistics.* Acta Academiae Aboensis, Ser. A. Humaniora. Vol. 51:1. Åbo: Åbo Akademi.

Charles Dickens's personification and style: With a special focus on the first-person narrative perspectives

Saoko Funada

Abstract
This paper aims to discuss Dickens's frequent and effective use of metaphor and metonymy observed in two texts: *David Copperfield* and *Great Expectations*, focusing on how a huge number of descriptions of things as humans are created chiefly from the first-person narratives. That is, it is a crucial key to investigate how both heroes (i.e. David and Pip) frequently tend to personify dismal appearances of the surroundings largely in negative contexts so that lifeless objects or natural phenomena such as houses, plants and mist may appear more vigorous and powerful in the narrators' eyes. Additionally, this paper puts a focus on Dickens's device of attributing human emotions and powers to inanimate objects or to non-human living creatures through the conceptual metaphor analysis so as to highlight the analogical correlations between the two referents—the *topic* and the *vehicle*. In bringing to light how we communicate and process the meanings of Dickens's metaphorical/metonymical expressions, my paper gives further analysis of the lexical forms and the data of frequency regarding descriptions of animated artefacts or natural phenomena.

1. Introduction
In reading Dickens, one finds his successive use of figurative expressions such as simile, metaphor or metonymy by which a large variety of people are described as animal species or artificial objects by means of *dehumanisation*, while inanimate objects are animated as if human beings by the device of *humanisation*.[1] His focus on these rhetorical devices is reflected by his so precise or minute observations of the distinctive personalities of characters or the attributes of artificial substances, that his linguistic style is constantly elaborate or rich in

---

[1] The terms *dehumanisation* and *humanisation* are used by Fawkner (1970: 73), who analyses Dickens's converse processes by which human characters are dehumanised as animals or artificial substances, whilst artefacts or natural objects are described as if human beings. In my paper, I also use a term *personification* or *animation* instead of *humanisation* to refer to his method of animating objects or personifying non-human living creatures, for the author is fond of using it as a significant means of representing various non-human entities through metaphor.

humour and vividness. Thus, most of his tropes include unique symbolical expressions, giving the readers colourful images of characters or objects described from every angle or aspect. However, his main concern regarding his rhetorical device presented by his figures of speech, is to not only give detailed descriptions of their physical appearances or natural attributes but also reflect that the author's/the hero's inner emotion or attitude towards the surroundings can largely influence their life and fortune. Above all, in *David Copperfield* and *Great Expectations*, he attempts to evoke an association between a human being and a non-human living being or object in the reader's mind by attributing human emotions and powers to animals/inanimate objects so as to reflect the author's/the heroes' emotions or thoughts toward his social surroundings. This technique of Dickens is of great value to him in representing how closely the conceptual correlations between human beings and non-human living creatures/artificial substances are established in the author's narrative eyes. In this way, the chief concern of my paper is to investigate the linguistic mechanisms of various Dickensian metaphors and metonymies by shedding light on their forms, techniques and mental processes underlying the conceptual relationship between two different things—human beings and non-human living creatures/objects—that are compared in context, and also elucidate the roles and purposes of his figurative descriptions.

1.1. Previous studies on Dickens's converse processes
According to Brook (1970:13), Dickens's language and narrative style, aiming at a strong emotional appeal, was highly regarded in the nineteenth century and above all, metaphor is one of Dickens's powerful and unique stylistic features. In addition, other scholars such as Van Ghent (1967) and Meier (1982) refer to Dickens's effective use of humanising and dehumanising devices. Meier (1982: 9) focuses attention on these particular converse processes in Dickens as characteristic of his style, and a feature that has been widely recognised as a hallmark of his writing. Her study of animation and mechanisation[2] suggests that the effect of both techniques is not merely an embellishment of

---

[2] Instead of a term *dehumanisation*, I also use another term *mechanisation* that Meier (1982) is fond of using, to refer to Dickens's favourite method of dehumanising people into either animals or objects.

description but a symbolisation of the animated objects or inhuman qualities of particular characters, as she focuses on the more profound aspects of the topic:

> This device of animation and mechanisation proves to be extremely versatile within Dickens's literary work. Its scope of function ranges from mere embellishing description to the point where animated objects actually become agents and seem to take an active part in the plot; while its stylistic quality and literary expression extends from flippantly burlesque comedy to the profoundest depth of symbolic meaning.
>
> (Meier 1982: 9)

Moreover, Reed (2010: 73) mentions Dickens's use of animation performed in order to create descriptions beyond reality, for he remarks as follows: "Dickens consciously employed the device of personification or animation to create a literature that feels free to exceed the limits of realism and to stimulate a similar kind of animating activity in his readers." In the process of reading Dickens's prose, he also focuses on the visionary power of the author's narrative style and discovers that his definition by metaphor of certain qualities of things leads the reader to visualise the scene in his or her minds' eye, as he further adds: "personification is a striking manifestation of a fanciful mind, and thus an endorsement for Dickens's preferred mode of narrating" (Reed 2010: 77).

2. Devices of Dickens's personification
2.1. Grammatical patterns

In order to understand Dickens's figurative style, we will examine metaphorical expressions in his stories and see his devices of personification with various forms. Despite the simple structures compared with a simile using *like* or *as*, the metaphorical device in his novels plays a significant role in delineating particular features of objects elaborately or fancifully. As for Dickens's metaphors, Alter (1996) mentions the author's fantastically witty representation of the scenes or persons as well as the fertility of his metaphorical imagination that leads us, the readers, to recognise his dense vision of the world that surrounds him. Therefore, if we apply all the classifications of metaphorical forms presented by Ikeda (1992), Goatly (1997) and Sukagawa (1999), the following six types of forms can be found, namely as in Types I to VI.

Type I: (Det.) + N[3]

(1) But there I was; and soon I was at out house, where *the bare old elm-trees wrung their many hands in the bleak wintry air*, and shreds of the old rooks'-nests drifted away upon the wind. (*DC*, 104)[4]

(2) When I had lain awake a little while, those extraordinary voices with which silence teems, began to make themselves audible. The closet whispered, the fireplace sighed, the little washing-stand ticked, and one guitar-string played occasionally in the chest of drawers. At about the same time, *the eyes* on the wall acquired a new expression, and in every one of those staring rounds I saw written, DON'T GO HOME. (*GE*, 362)

Types II: N1 + Copula + N2

(3) He (Mr. Dick) sat in a particular corner, on a particular stool, *which was called "Dick," after him*; here he would sit, with his grey head bent forward, attentively listening to whatever might be going on, with a profound veneration for the learning he had never been able to acquire. (*DC*, 245)

(4) But I thought with dread that it (the tide) was flowing towards Magwitch, and that *any black mark on its surface might be his pursuers*, going swiftly, silently, and surely, to take him. (*GE*, 376)

To start with, Types I and II denote the typical structures of Dickens's noun metaphors most commonly used in his literary works. Type I, the *determiner and noun* form occurs most frequently in *Great Expectations*, while it is less frequent in *David Copperfield*. Instance (1) exhibits the way in which the bare old-elm trees moved their branches or treetops as if they were hands, and the noun phrase *wrung their many hands* is used to imply a sense of anxiety about David's future fate.

Besides, Dickens makes frequent use of the device, especially when artificial objects are described as human beings as in (2). In this example, Pip in a dismal room hears the dreadful voices of some

---

[3] I use some abbreviations in this paper: Det. for determiner, N for noun, Adj. for adjective, Adv. for adverb, Vi for intransitive verb, and Vt for transitive verb.

[4] The letter and number in round brackets after each example refer to the works of Dickens, for example *DC* for *David Copperfield* and *GE* for *Great Expectations*. Also, italics in each quotation are mine to emphasize areas in question.

artificial objects such as a closet, fireplace, washing-stand, and guitar-string, and even sees the eyes on the wall starting at him with a new expression. In this way, the author elaborately and vividly depicts the appearances of these artefacts and exhibits not only Pip's fear of them but his powers of observation. Meier (1982: 36-39) remarks, "the old and even half-decayed houses attract Dickens's imagination more than new buildings, possibly because they have acquired a certain atmos-phere or, as Dickens puts it, a certain personality." In this instance, one can, therefore, notice that the analogy between each of these artificial objects and a human being does not only operate on the physical level, but on a psychological level, for it suggests the hero's pessimistic view of his future and surroundings.

Next, Type II is the form with a copula as in *A is B*. The copula in this case includes verbs such as *be*, *seem*, *appear* and so on. This type is rare in Dickens's personification. Instance (3) describes the way in which at Miss Trotwood's house, there is a particular stool in a partic-ular corner, which is usually occupied by Mr. Dick and which was called *Dick* after him. In this respect, there can be seen a strong resem-blance between the stool and Mr. Dick as a human being, for David finds, out of an analogical mind, in the stool a mirror image of its user.

Type III takes the form of *adjective and noun* as in (5) to (7). Although rare as compared with his other forms of metaphor, this type of adjective metaphor is of great use in symbolically depicting inani-mate objects as if they were human beings by means of personification. Also, it is worth noting that the author is in the habit of using words such as *pale* or *angry* for humanising metaphors in order to symbolise each character's emotion or personal fate through the dismal appear-ances of their surroundings.

Type III: Adj. + N
(5) "Mother will be expecting me," he said, referring to *a pale, inexpressive-faced watch* in this pocket, … (*DC*, 229)

(6) The marshes were just a long black horizontal line then, as I stopped to look after him; and the river was just another horizontal line, not nearly so broad nor yet so black; and the sky was just a row of *long angry red lines* and dense black lines intermixed. (*GE*, 7)

(7) It was like pushing the chair itself back into the past, when we began the old slow circuit round about the ashes of the bridal feast. But, in

the *funeral room*, with that figure of the grave fallen back in the chair fixing its eyes upon her, Estella looked more bright and beautiful than before, and I was under stronger enchantment. (*GE*, 236)

Instance (5) shows a visual resemblance between Uriah Heep and his watch. However, this metonymical expression does not merely convey a visual similarity between them but symbolises Uriah's naturally villainous and inhuman quality. In Dickens's rhetoric, it is clear that the animation created by a character's (especially David's in this example) imagination tells us a great deal about the owner, such as his/her personality, behaviour or state of mind. Next, instance (7) describes the old and grotesque appearance of Miss Havisham collapsed in a chair in a withered bridal dress. Her ghastly figure is so eccentric and fearful to Pip's eye as a child, that Pip portrays her as *a figure of the grave*, describing her room as *a funeral room*. In this context, the terms *grave* and *funeral* are effective in suggesting metaphorically to the reader, that she is near her death.

Type IV: N + Copula + Adj.
(8) I see the red light shining on the sun-dial, and think within myself, "*Is the sun-dial glad*, I wonder, that it can tell the time again?"

(*DC*, 14)

(9) In truth, the wind, though it was low, had a solemn sound, and crept toward the deserted house with *a whispered wailing that was very mournful*. (*DC*, 620)

Also, as in (8) and (9) above, one can see another form of Dickens's adjective metaphor. In instance (8), the sun-dial as a time-indicator, is animated in David's imagination as he looks at it, thinking: "Is the sun-dial glad that it can tell the time again?" Thus, in his eyes, the sun-dial is not merely a technical device that tells the time, but has an emotional feature, for David intends to impute the human attribute (i.e. the adjective *glad* in this context) to the sun-dial so as to display his feelings by using his imagination. Additionally, in Dickens's novels, natural phenomena such as *wind*, *fog*, *mist*, and *water* are often associated with human beings. Example (9) describes the way in which the wind was creeping around the boat-house with a solemn sound. The noun phrase, *a whispered wailing* and the adjective *mournful* include symbolical meanings; they do not merely evoke the dismal atmosphere around the house but symbolically show David's pessimistic view of his life.

Type V: V + Adv.

(10) *The wind sighing around us even more mournfully*, than it had sighed and moaned upon the night when I first darkened Mr. Peggotty's door. (*DC*, 302)

(11) He (Mr. Peggotty) sang a sailor's song himself, so pathetically and beautifully, that I could have almost fancied that *the real wind creeping sorrowfully round the house*, and murmuring low through our unbroken silence, was there to listen. (*DC*, 308)

As examples (10) and (11) indicate, one can see another metaphorical form with the *verb and adverb*. As to (10), intransitive verbs *sigh* and an adverb *mournfully* symbolically represent the hero David's inner feelings towards his surroundings, since he is scared of the wind blowing in the dark. Furthermore, this sentence conveys another meaning: the moaning of the wind suggests that the peaceful household of the Peggottys will eventually be destroyed as David takes his friend Steerforth to Mr. Peggotty's house. Additionally, the author's method of transforming wind into human being as in (11) is worth noting that the *creeping sorrowfully* and *the murmuring low* of the wind contains a symbolical element, as it points, in David's eye, to Steerforth's dismal life and fortune.

Type VI: Vi or Vt[5]

(12) I used to fancy, as I sat by him of an evening, on a green slope, and saw him watch the kite high in the quiet air, that *it lifted his mind out of its confusion*, and bore it (such was my boyish thought) into the skies. (*DC*, 210)

(13) *The gates and dykes and banks came bursting at me through the mist*, as if they cried as plainly as could be, "A body with Somebody-else's pork pie! Stop him!" (*GE*, 16)

(14) I coaxed myself to sleep by thinking of Miss Havisham's, next Wednesday; and in my sleep I saw *the file coming at me out of a door*, without seeing who held it, and I screamed myself awake.

(*GE*, 77)

---

[5] i = intransitive / t = transitive

Moreover, there can be seen yet other types of forms with verbs as in VI. Instance (12) explains the way in which David watches Mr. Dick flying his own kite high up in the air so that it could lift up his spirits too. With regard to Dickens's animation, he is in the habit of attributing human emotions or powers to such an object as this in order to equate it with the owner by metaphor. The next example (13) implies Pip's fear and sense of guilt after he was forced by the convict to bring stolen food for him. As Fawkner (1977: 32) observes, "Pip finds that guilt and terror cause every inanimate object to be animated with reproachful suspicion and alarming wakefulness," from his point of view, the objects such as *gates*, *dykes*, and *banks* appear to threaten and pursue him crying from behind.

2.2. Frequencies

As shown in Table 1, we will examine the frequencies of the six patterns of metaphorical forms on Dickens's personification. First, one can see from the table that the verb metaphors are the most frequent in both novels, as *David Copperfield* includes fifty-four examples, whilst fifty-two examples are found in *Great Expectations*. In other words, verb metaphors in both novels include an enormous number of descriptions of artificial objects associated with human beings. More-over, one can also find that Dickens has a remarkable tendency to make frequent use of the *determiner and noun* form in *Great Expectations* (twenty-three examples), in order to make each appearance of the objects more vivid and colourful. In contrast, the other forms using adjectives or adverbs are less frequent in both novels.

Table 1. The frequency of grammatical forms on Dickens's personification

Types	David Copperfield	Great Expectations
I. (Det.) + Noun	3	23
II. N1+ Copula + N2	1	1
III. Adj. + N	7	6
IV. N + Copula + Adj.	6	4
V. V + Adv.	4	4
VI. Vi or Vt	54	52
Total	75	90

2.3. Humanising terms in Dickens

Table 2 shows various types of humanising terms classified based on word classes, namely noun, adjective, adverb and verb. The animals or natural objects in the round brackets denote the *topic* or *target* domain that leads to create a semantic linkage of the two references— a human as the *vehicle* and a non-human as the *topic*.[6]

Table 2. Humanising metaphors based on word class in *David Copperfield*

Animals	
Nouns	desire (lobsters; crabs; crawfish), look after (rooks; jackdaws)
Adjectives	obliged (star-fish), shy (birds)
Adverbs	slyly (rooks; jackdaws)
Verbs	like (horse), feel (camel; dromedary), possessed (lobsters; crabs; crawfish), pinch (lobsters; crabs; crawfish), know (young birds), think (horse)
Natural objects	
Nouns	wailing (wind)
Adjectives	solemn (wind), mournful (wind), booming (water)
Adverbs	moanfully (wind), sorrowfully (wind)
Verbs	moan (wind), sigh (wind), creep (wind), murmur (wind), whisper (wind), shiver (water), shake (water)

Firstly, regarding *David Copperfield*, animals such as *lobsters*, *crabs*, *crawfish*, *birds*, *rooks* or *jackdaws* are described in association with human activities. As for verbs, one can find some stative verbs such as *like*, *feel*, *know* or *think*, all of which Dickens is fond of using in humanising metaphors, as he tends to attribute human emotions and abilities to non-human living creatures for the purpose of visualising the scene clearly. Next, Dickens also tends to transform natural objects/phenomena such as *wind* or *water* into human beings. As Meier (1982: 103) remarks, "when the natural elements such as wind, rain, and the sea are animated, this device is usually applied in order to parallel or comment on human action and fate," it can be said that

---

[6] In her study of metaphor, Kittay (1987) makes an analysis of metaphor consisting of a conceptual relation between the two referents, *tenor* and *vehicle*, whist Black (1979) identifies the two as *topic* and *vehicle*, respectively.

Dickens's personification has a symbolic significance in understanding the attributes of non-human entities. Further, as Meier (1982: 47) adds, the animation of the wind as if it were a human being involves the display of malign energy which may assume demonic powers when assigned to the wind. Thus, the terms such as *wailing*, *mournful*, *sorrowfully*, *moan*, *sigh*, *murmur* or *whisper* have a symbolic significance because the moaning or wailing of the wind not only resembles that of human beings but also suggests to the reader that the hero is full of awareness of being pursued or threatened by his surroundings in the insentient world.

Moreover, Table 3 shows that Dickens effectively uses the method of depicting abstracts or artefacts as if they were human beings by metaphor, in which case verb forms are frequent. One can find from the table that the author employs the process of transforming artificial objects into human beings more frequently than other processes, and that inanimate objects such as *houses* or *pictures* are analogically related with human beings so that the narrator could reflect the hero's pessimistic view toward his future fate. Most of his personification in this novel appears in negative contexts, as David is badly treated and severely educated in his childhood, which causes him to convey the negative aspects of the social surroundings.

Table 3. Humanising metaphors based on word class in *David Copperfield*

Abstracts	
Adverbs	sternly (immensity; gravity)
Verbs	sported (days), befriend (terms), protect (terms), affect (terms), delight (nature; spirits), find (nature; spirits), drown (love), arrest (glimpse), floor (friendliness), find (tears), frown (immensity; gravity), speak (echoes)

Artefacts	
Nouns	mind (kite), sleep (street)
Adjectives	pale (watch), inexpressive-faced (watch), pale-faced (watch), glad (kite)
Verbs	look upon (room), ring (school bell), look (windows), lift (kite), bear (kite), lean (house), try (house), see (house), look (picture), come (pictures), go (pictures), ring (boat), receive (kite), try (objects), hide (objects), overlook (tower), shake off (street), give (country)

Charles Dickens's personification and style   37

Similarly in *Great Expectations*, one notices from Table 4, Dickens's predilection for perception verbs such as *think*, *wear* or *know* in terms of the animal species, while reporting verbs such as *whisper*, *mutter*, *address*, *moan* or *tell* are frequent regarding natural objects and abstracts identified with human beings.

Table 4. Humanising metaphors based on word class in *Great Expectations*

Animals	
Adjectives	respectful (cattle)
Verbs	think (cattle; pigeons), wear (cattle), stare (cattle), know (fowl)
Natural objects	
Nouns	voices (wind; rain)
Adjectives	angry (sky), right (mists), loud (wind; rain)
Verbs	want (flower-seeds; bulbs), whisper (beans; clover), disclose (mists), assail (wind), tear (wind), mutter (wind)
Abstracts	
Nouns	forelock (time), cutting (time)
Adjectives	pale (afternoon)
Adverbs	in menace (shadows), out of countenance (affairs)
Verbs	want (time), shake (shadows), stick (place), address (rot), moan (rot), whisper (something), throw (fate), raise (fortune), stare (affairs), tell (desolation)

Besides, as Table 5 shows, artificial objects are often humanised with nouns, adjectives and non-stative verbs such as *jump*, *direct*, *play*, *run* or *make*, all of which give a symbolical delineation of Pip's psychological state. Dickens often uses verbs to visualise the scene where lifeless objects may appear more vigorous and powerful in Pip's eye, as the hero's fear or sense of built is symbolically reflected in each description.

Table 5. Humanising metaphors based on word class in *Great Expectations*

Artefacts	
Nouns	eyes (street-lamp; rushlight tower; wax-work; skelton; wall; ship), pursuers (black mark), finger (post), mourning (soot; smoke), head (soot; smoke; ship), penance (soot; smoke), humiliation (soot; smoke), voices (closet; fireplace; washing-stand; guitar-string), expression (wall), rounds (wall), speech (ship), bosom (ship)

Adjectives	emotional (waistcoat), respectful (grounds; dykes; sluices), spasmodic (doors), audible (closet; fireplace; washing-stand; guitar-string)
Verbs	jump (church), reappear (file), direct (post), drown (beer), wear (grounds; dykes; sluices), stare (grounds; dykes; sluices; wall; ship), glare (house), die (red-hot sparks), attire (soot; smoke), undergo (soot; smoke), arise (hat; neck-cloth; waistcoat; trousers; boots), absorb (doorway), lead (church-clocks), accompany (church-clocks), follow (church-clocks), perplex (tobacco), whisper (closet), sigh (fireplace), tick (washing-stand), play (guitar-string), acquire (wall), run (road), sympathise (road), animate (road), encourage (road), freshen (road), make (ship)

3. Conceptual analysis
3.1. Conceptual colligations in metaphor
This section will investigate how to conceive Dickens's personification by shedding light on the reciprocal influence created by the presence of the *topic* and the *vehicle*. The method of explicating the conceptual system of Dickens's metaphor deals with a metaphorical mapping between the two references, which, according to Kövecses (2010: 7), can be established and tightly connected through a conceptual metaphor. As Kövecses (2010: 150) says, metaphorical linguistic expressions suggest the existence of a number of conceptual metaphors in English, and an *Object is Human* metaphor, for example, makes it possible for us to understand the meaning of humanising metaphors such as "the wind sighed around us mournfully," "I saw the file coming at me out of a door," and so on. Additionally, he also remarks, "personification makes use of one of the best source domains we have—ourselves. In personifying nonhumans as humans, we can begin to understand them a little better." Therefore, it will be fundamental for us to examine the conceptual meanings of Dickens's animated metaphors involving the mapping between the two things—non-human entities or things as the *topic* and human beings as the *vehicle*, and thereby conceive them by imputing human characteristics to things.

In Dickens's humanisation, almost all of the non-human entities or things are metaphorically understood in terms of human behaviours or appearances. As Figure 1 exhibits, we thus have two conceptual metaphors: *Abstract Entity is Human* and *Object is Human* to be applied to Dickens's personification. Furthermore, firstly the *Abstract Entity is Human* conceptual metaphor is closely related to personification, and therefore, not only the *Abstract Entity is Human* metaphor but also *Idea/Emotion is Human* and *Words/Language is Human* metaphors contribute to the humanising expressions.

Similarly, the conceptual metaphors *Object/Substance is Human* and *Natural Object is Human* are concerned with Dickens's personification, and thus, we will apply these conceptual metaphors to Dickens's humanising expressions so that we could investigate the conceptual mechanisms of his devices.

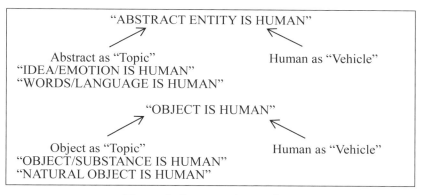

Figure 1. Conceptual metaphors

3.2. Personification as symbolic element: prophetic significance

Further, we will focus on the way inanimate things are humanised based on the symbolic effects. It is important to point out that Dickens employs a variety of nature terms for humanisation; Tables 6 and 7 indicate how each natural object as a *topic* is transformed into a human being as a *vehicle* by metaphor. By looking at the tables, we can see that each natural element such as *wind*, *water* or *mists* are animated in association with a human being, which is one of the author's typical means of personification. Also, verbs such as *moan*, *sigh*, *shiver*, *shake*, *rise*, *assail* or *tear*, and an adjective *booming* derived from a verb *boom*, include symbolical meanings of each character's future fate.

40 *Saoko Funada*

Table 6. *Natural object is human* metaphor in *David Copperfield*

Topic	Symbolical meaning	Natural elements = human beings
wind	David's fate and psychological factor	(15) *The wind came moaning on across the flat* as it had done before. But I could not help fancying, now, that *it moaned of those who were gone.* (*DC*, 137)
wind	Catastrophe of Peggotty's household	(16) *The wind sighing around us even more mournfully, than it had sighed and moaned upon the night when I first darkened Mr. Peggotty's door.* (*DC*, 302)
water	Ham Peggotty's death	(17) *Masses of water shivered and shook the beach with a booming sound*, every shape tumultuously rolled on, as soon as made, to change its shape and place, and beat another shape and place away. (*DC*, 769)

In *David Copperfield*, as the example (16) shows, on the evening when David takes Steerforth down to Yarmouth, he describes the wind as "sighing around us even more mournfully, than it had sighed and moaned upon the night when I first darkened Mr. Peggotty's door." In this sentence, the mournful sighing of the wind is effective in suggesting the reader that Peggotty's peaceful household will be broken up for ever. Similarly, the booming sound of the masses of water, as in (17), has a symbolic significance, as it suggests Ham Peggotty's fatal death on the Yarmouth coast.

Table 7. *Natural object is human* metaphor in *Great Expectations*

Topic	Symbolical meaning	Natural elements = human beings
mists	Pip's fate of his expectations	(18) The village was very peaceful and quiet, and *the light mists were solemnly rising, as if to show me the world.* (*GE*, 157) (19) *The mists had all solemnly risen now, and the world lay spread before me.* (*GE*, 157)
wind	Pip's fate of his expectations	(20) The sound was curiously flawed by the wind; and I was listening, and thinking *how the wind assailed and tore it*, when I heard a footstep on the stair. (*GE*, 309)

In *Great Expectations*, the rising of the mists as in (18) and (19) reflects the rising of Pip's expectations, meaning that the animation of the mists, in this context, plays the part of the hero's life and fortune.

3.3. Personification as analogical element: objects as human personality

In Dickens's personification, the analogy between artificial objects and human beings is apt to convey a variety of particular characteristics of certain people in his novels. Although the animation of artefacts is comic or evokes amusement on a physical level based on the physical correspondences between them that an imaginative spectator might detect, these animated objects mainly reflect the traits or attitudes of their owners or users, as the device suggests to the reader the resemblance between objects and people on a psychological level. In other words, the animation of objects is not merely a general comparison between an object and a human being, but a particular analogy, a psychological bond between them.

Table 8. *Object/subject is human* metaphor in *David Copperfield*

Topic	Analogical feature	Objects = human beings
washing-stand	Mrs. Gummidge's condition	(21) *The washing-stand being ricketty on its three legs, and having a discontented something about it,* which reminded me of Mrs. Gummidge under the influence of the old one. (*DC*, 41-42)
house	David's curiosity	(22) … I fancied *the whole house was leaning forward, trying to see who was passing on the narrow pavement below.* (*DC*, 212)
watch	Resemblance between Uriah Heep and his watch	(23) *A pale, inexpressive-faced watch in this pocket* (*DC*, 229)
stool	Resemblance between Mr. Dick and the stool he sits on	(24) He (Mr. Dick) sat in a particular corner, on a particular stool, *which was called "Dick," after him.* (*DC*, 245)
sun-dial	Self-same feelings of David and the sun-dial	(25) *"Is the sun-dial glad, I wonder, that it can tell the time again?"* (*DC*, 14)

In *David Copperfield*, the animated houses or the other concrete objects tend to acquire a certain personality of the owners, for a psychological bond between the objects and their owner can be established. What is significant is that out of an analogical mind, a child David finds in every object a resemblance to certain characters. In instance (21), as for the interior of houses, David regards his washing-stand as Mrs. Gummidge, on account of "its being rickety on its three legs, and having a discontented something about it." Similarly, as in (22), "the whole house (i.e. Mr. Wickfield's house in Canterbury), leaning forward, trying to see who was passing on the narrow pavement" is attributed to David's curiosity. In addition, Uriah Heep's watch, as in (23), is "pale, inexpressive-faced" as the watch is an exact mirror to Uriah's disposition.

Table 9. *Object/subject is human* metaphor in *Great Expectations*

Topic	Analogical feature	Objects = human beings
tombstones on the graves	Images of resemblance between the tombstones and his parents (by Pip's animistic eyes)	(26) As I never saw my father or mother, and never saw any likeness of either of them (for their days were long before the days of photographs), *my first fancies regarding what they were like, were unreasonably derived from their tombstones.* The shape of the letters on my father's, gave me an odd idea that he was a square, stout, dark man, with curly black hair. From the character and turn of the inscription, "*Also Georgiana Wife of the Above,*" I draw a childish conclusion that my mother was freckled and sickly. (*GE*, 3)
Barnard's Inn	Dismal appearances of the inn associated with Pip's uneasy feelings about his future (by Pip's animistic eyes)	(27) While *To Let To Let To Let, glared at me from empty rooms,* as if no new wretches every came there, and *the vengeance of the soul of Barnard were being slowly appeased* by the gradual suicide of the present occupants and their unholy interment under the gravel. *A frouzy mourning of soot and smoke attired this forlorn creation of Barnard, and it had strewn ashes on its head, and was undergoing penance and humiliation as a mere dusthole.* Thus far my sense of sight. (*GE*, 171)

Charles Dickens's personification and style   43

Also in *Great Expectations*, as (26) indicates, one can see a similar scene at the beginning of the novel, where Pip as a child narrator, creates an image of the appearances of his parents from the inscriptions on their tombstones. In this way, we can recognise the hero's animistic eye.

Additionally, as to the example (27), Pip describes the exterior of the shabby buildings called Barnard's Inn in London, where the hero happened to meet Mr. Pocket, Junior. At first, he thought it to be a hotel kept by Mr. Barnard, but this did not turn out to be true, because when he entered it, he was astonished by the dismal appearance of the sets of chambers affected by rot. By means of metaphor, Dickens gives successive descriptions of every dismal appearance that comes into view as if a human being. Terms such as *glare*, *vengeance*, *appease*, *mourning*, *attire*, *penance* and *humiliation* are related to human emotions, powers and activities. Moreover, Pip's point of view is explicitly reflected in the example, as we can recognise his keen observation and minute descriptions of these artificial substances. Meier (1982: 36-37) focuses on the process by which old and decayed houses are animated as if human beings. As she observes in her study of Dickens's personification, "houses like human beings are subjected to the process of aging," there is a physical analogy between a house and a human being, and what is more, exteriors of houses are alive from Pip's perspective, for they illustrate the child's inner thoughts and emotions towards the external world.

What is significant regarding the animation of non-human entities or things is that it is mostly created by the first-person narrations in both novels. That is, these heroes intend to apply this device in the depiction of a child's mind and his vision of the world. Dickens's animation of objects thus reflects these heroes' views of the characters and the objects that surround them.

Furthermore, we can see some similarities of the plots between the two novels, for in the beginning of these novels both heroes, as narrators, look back on their past days after they go through various hardships in their childhood. In *David Copperfield*, as David is badly treated and severely educated by Mr. and Miss Murdstone in his childhood, he gradually comes to be obsessed with his own guilt and conceives of himself as a prisoner. Similarly in *Great Expectations*, criminality is one of the themes of great importance, for Pip, at the beginning, encounters in a churchyard an escaped convict called Abel Magwitch who threatened him and asked him to bring a file and victuals. After giving the convict the foods stolen from his sister's kitchen, the narrator is overtaken by penitence and starts to describe himself as a *hound* by animalisation. As both heroes are obsessed with a strong sense of guilt in their childhood, they tend to personify dismal appearances of their surroundings in negative contexts, so that they could convey their worldview toward the object world and the human world through their animistic eyes. By so doing, their fortune and fate are symbolically represented by the device.

4. Conclusion

This paper has examined Dickens's metaphorical statements by which various scenes and substances are vividly or symbolically described. Above all, his personification metaphor makes abundant use of verb forms, which can symbolically evoke specific image of what is described, whilst the other word classes like noun, adjective or adverb are less frequent. In other words, the author aims to verbalise his various visions of the surroundings in the stories by depicting the natural attributes or physical appearances of inanimate objects or non-human living creatures as if human beings, achieving this by drawing close analogies between the two things. As his humanising metaphors provide various structures and conceptual meanings to each term, we can conclude that his delineations are constantly rich in humour and vividness, as he is exceedingly aware of the conceptual relationships between objects and people and attempts to give a colourful and vivid depiction of each inanimate object.

Moreover, we can go beyond the linguistic/physical level and deal with the mental structure where we conceive Dickens's personification, mostly in negative contexts, by means of the mapping of the two concepts between the *topic* and the *vehicle*. In *David Copperfield* and *Great Expectations*, the *Abstract Entity is Human* and the *Object is Human* are fundamental conceptual metaphors applicable to Dickens's metaphors involving the comprehension of different properties of different substances in terms of the concept of human being. Thus, Dickens's personification is effective in clearly enunciating his vision of the life-denying society in the novels, and most of his humanising expressions play a role in mirroring both heroes' worldviews of the surroundings through their children's eyes, it is worth noting that Dickens's personification appears with exceedingly high frequency so that he can enrich his expression of his worldview through his unique figurative devices. In this way, the author's/the heroes' imagination and sense of humour are reflected in Dickens's sophisticated use of metaphors.

Texts

Dickens, Charles 1849-50. Nina Burgis (ed.) 1999. *David Copperfield*. The world's classics. Oxford: Oxford University Press.

Dickens, Charles 1860-61. Margaret Cardwell (ed.) 1998. *Great Expectations*. The world's classics. Oxford: Oxford University Press.

References

Alter, Robert 1996. Reading style in Dickens. *Philosophy and literature* 20:1, 130-37. Baltimore: Johns Hopkins University Press.

Black, Max 1979. More about metaphor. In Andrew Ortony (ed.), *Metaphor and thought*. The second edition. Cambridge: Cambridge University Press.

Brook, G.L. 1970. *The language of Dickens*. London: André Deutsch.

Fawkner, Harald W. 1977. *Animation and reification in Dickens's vision of the life-denying society.* Stockholm: Liber Tryck.

Goatly, Andrew 2011. *The language of metaphors*. The second edition. London: Routledge.

Ikeda, Takuro 1992. *Eigo buntairon*. Tokyo: Kenkyusha.

Kittay, Eva F. 1987. *Metaphor: its cognitive force and linguistic structure*. Oxford: The Clarendon Press.

Kövecses, Zoltán 2010. *Metaphor: A practical introduction.* The second edition. Oxford: Oxford University Press.

Meier, Stefanie 1982. *Animation and mechanization in the novels of Charles Dickens*. Bern: Francke.

Reed, John R. 2010. *Dickens's hyperrealism*. Columbus: Ohio State University Press.

Stewart, Garrett 2001. Dickens and Language. In John O. Jordan (ed.), *The Cambridge companion to Charles Dickens*. Cambridge: Cambridge University Press.

Sukagawa, Seizo 1999. *Eigo shikisaigo no imi to hiyu*, 92-112. Tokyo: Seibido.

Van Ghent, Dorothy 1967. The Dickens's world: A view from Todges's. In Martin Price (ed.), *Dickens: A collection of critical essays*. Englewood Cliffs: Prentice-Hall.

Modal auxiliaries of obligation in the *Paston Letters*: With special reference to *shall**

Naoki Hirayama

Abstract
Shall is one of the most frequent modal auxiliary verbs in the *Paston Letters and the Papers of the Fifteenth Century* (Part I). In the text *shall* carries a variety of meanings, such as more objective 'obligation' and more subjective 'prediction.' In this paper, how and in what meaning *shall* is used in the text is investigated in terms of grammaticalization and subjectification. First, as propositional conditions, the person of the subject (first/second/third) and the lexical aspect of the verbs (dynamic/stative) co-occurring with *shall* is focused on. Then, the types of the clauses including *shall* is investigated. Finally, as pragmatic conditions, the social relationships between addressers and addressees, generations of the addressers and addressees, and genre of the documents are considered. In addition, the properties of *shall* are clearly indicated through comparison with *must* and *ought to*. Through the investigation some remarkable examples of *shall* have been found.

1. Introduction
The *Paston Letters*, which is a representative collection of correspondence in the fifteenth century, includes not only the letters sent from, to or between the family members but also a variety of documents such as memorandums, indentures, petitions, and so on.

This paper is an attempt to investigate into the usage of *shall* in the *Paston Letters*, comparing it with two other (quasi-)modal auxiliary verbs, *must* and *ought to*. With this research, the meanings and the usage of *shall* in the fifteenth century are also made clear.

The investigation in this paper is based on 'grammaticalization' (Hopper and Traugott 1993) and 'subjectification' (Traugott 1995) because the variety of meanings of *shall* is considered to be related to the degree of the grammatical development as a modal auxiliary verb and the degree of the addresser's subjective inference. Some features

---

* This article is a revised and enlarged version of the part of the paper read at the 69th General Meeting of the Branch of the Chugoku and Shikoku District of the English Literary Society of Japan held at Ehime University on 29th October, 2016.

of the degrees seem to appear in the sentences where *shall* is used in three levels. Therefore, to investigate the meaning of *shall*, the three levels of conditions are established: the person of the subject (first/second/third) and the lexical aspect of the verb (dynamic/stative) as prepositional conditions, clause types where the auxiliary is included as conditions of clause types, and the relationship between addressers and addressees and genre of the documents as pragmatic conditions.

In this paper, *Paston Letters and Papers of the Fifteenth Century* (part I) edited by Norman Davis (1971) is investigated.

2. Previous studies and research questions
2.1. The development of the meaning of *shall* in *OED*
The historical development of the meanings of *shall* can be seen in *OED*. First, as shown under 1a or 1b, *shall* was originally used as a main verb meaning "to owe money" or "to owe allegiance." Second, it was followed by the infinitive and carried the meaning of obligation or necessity as under 3. Then, co-occurring with second or third person subjects, it came to carry the addresser's volition as under 6. Next, it obtained the meaning and the function of simple future as under 8a. Finally, it came to carry the meaning of the first person subject's simple future as under 8b(a), and then, it expanded its meaning to the first person subject's resolution as under 8b(b).

†1. *trans.* a. To owe (money). *Obs.* (c975)[1]
　　　　　†b. To owe (allegiance). *Obs.* (c1325)
†3. a. In OE. and occas. in ME. used to express necessity of various kinds
　　= 'must', 'must needs', 'have to', 'am compelled to', etc. (c888)
6. In the second and third persons, expressing the addresser's determination to bring about. (a1000)
8. As a mere auxiliary, forming (with present infinitive) the future, and (with perfect infinitive) the future perfect tense.
　a. In OE. *sceal*, while retaining its primary sense, served as a tense-sign in announcing a future event as fated or divinely decreed. (a900)
　b. In the first person, *shall* has, from the early ME. period, been the normal auxiliary for expressing mere futurity, without any adventitious notion.

---

[1]　In this *OED* citation, each number in the brackets indicates the year of the first cited example in each meaning.

(a) Of events conceived as independent of the addresser's volition. (c1200)
(b) Of voluntary action or its intended result. (c1200)

(*OED*, s.v. *shall*, *v*.)

2.2. Traugott (1972)

According to Traugott (1972: 199), *shall* was used as the meaning of (a) obligation or necessity, (b) promise or resolution, and (c) prediction. She points out that (a) obligation or necessity vanished by 1600s and was not used any more. Therefore, the meaning (a) is the one which is not used except in the legal documents in the present-day English (PE).

2.3. *Shall* in ME: Mustanoja (1960)

Mustanoja (1960) explains in detail how *shall* has expanded its meaning in ME. First, how *shall* (along with *will*) has obtained its futurity is mentioned as cited below.

> Originally, of course, both verbs [= *shall* and *will*][2] have independent meanings, expressing obligation and volition. Used in conjunction with other verbs they are gradually reduced to mere modal auxiliaries. Eventually the idea of futurity latent in the notions of obligation and volition becomes predominant. (489)

Furthermore, the reason why *shall* as a main verb has become an auxiliary verb of the future tense is explained.

> … OE *sculan* expresses obligation or constraint. This provides a natural starting-point for the development of this verb into an auxiliary of the future tense because it implies that the action is going to take place independently of the will of the subject. (491)

It is pointed out that *shall* was used as a transitive verb even in Chaucer's *Troilus and Criseyde* in ME as cited below.

> — by the faith I shal Priam of Troie (TC iii 791)
> — *I shal to God and yow* (TC iii 1649) (491 Notes)

It is also explained how *shall* obtained the use of prediction and prophesies in ME.

> *Shall* is often used in ME in all the three persons to indicate that an event

---

[2] Notes in square brackets are mine.

is ordained to take place in accordance with divine will or fate. ... This provides a background for its use in prediction and prophesies. ... From this use there is only a short way to the expression of pure futurity.

(491-92)

An example is cited from the *Paston Letters*, where *shall* is used to show that something is obliged to be done by a contract.

— the Duk of Suffolk and both the Duchessys schal com to Claxton thys day, as I am informyd, and thys next weke he schal be at Cossey

(Paston II 207 [1465]) (492)

2.4. Research questions

Seen from the general view of *OED* and Traugott (1972) and from the specific view of ME in Mustanoja (1960), as shown above, it can be said that the original use of main verb *shall* has influenced the development of *shall* as a modal auxiliary verb. In this paper, how examples of *shall* of obligation remain and how each meaning of *shall* is distributed in the *Paston Letters* will be discussed. The questions can be itemized as shown below.

a. Can any difference be seen in the distribution of the meaning of *shall* according to the sentence elements it co-occurs with, such as the person of the subject, the lexical aspect (dynamic/stative) of the verbs, and so on?
b. Do the types of the subordinate clauses containing the auxiliary verbs affect the distribution of the meaning of *shall*?
c. Do the social relationship between addressers and addressees and genre of the documents affect the distribution of the meaning of *shall*?

3. Methodology

The questions a to c above are highly related to the idea of grammaticalization and subjectification as shown in (1). The categorical change where, for example, *shall* as a main verb gradually gains the function of modal auxiliary verb is known as 'grammaticalization' (Hopper and Traugott 1993). The other change where, for example, *shall* weakens its obligational meaning and at the same time it strengthens the meaning reflecting the addresser's decision or resolution is known as 'subjectification' (Traugott 1995). The two changes are complementary to each other.

(1) Grammaticalization and subjectification
(a) [G]rammaticalization is usually thought of as that subset of linguistic changes through which a lexical item becomes a grammatical item, or through which a grammatical item becomes more grammatical. (Hopper and Traugott 1993: 2)
(b) '[S]ubjectification' refers to a pragmatic-semantic process whereby 'meanings become increasingly based in the speaker's subjective belief state/attitude toward the proposition', in other words, toward what the speaker is talking about. (Traugott 1995: 31)

As indicated in the figure below, in this paper, if *shall* develops its degree of grammaticalization and subjectification, it also develops its subjective meaning as a modal auxiliary verb and expresses the addresser's prediction, mere futurity, or resolution. On the other hand, if *shall* does not develop its degree of grammaticalization and subjectification, it indicates more objective meanings of obligation or necessity.

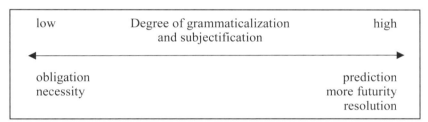

Figure 1. The relation between degree of grammaticalization and subjectification and the meaning of *shall*

The research was conducted as follows. Three groups of checking points were established as in (2): first, propositional conditions such as the person of the subjects, tense of the verbs, and so on, second, the conditions related to the types of the clauses including *shall* such as *I think (that)*-clause, *if*-clause, and so on, and third, pragmatic conditions such as social relationship between addressers and addressees, genre of the documents, and so on. Sentences including *shall* were processed from these points of view.

(2) Conditions to investigate the sentences including *shall*
    1. Propositional conditions
      i) Main clauses
        a) person of the subjects (1st, 2nd, 3rd)
        b) verb tense (present/past)
        c) dynamic/stative verbs
        d) co-occurring modal auxiliary verbs
        e) co-occurring adverbs
      ii) Subordinate clauses
        a) person of the subjects (1st, 2nd, 3rd)
        b) verb tense (present/past)
        c) dynamic/stative verbs
        d) co-occurring modal auxiliary verbs
        e) co-occurring adverbs
    2. Conditions related to the types of the clauses
        a) conjunctions: *wherefore*, *else*, *and*, *or*, etc.
        b) sentence adverbs: *certainly*, *surely*, etc.
        c) position of main and subordinate clauses in the sentences
        d) cognitive main clauses: *I think (that), I suppose (that)*, etc.
        e) added cognitive clauses: *I pray you, if*-clause, *as*-clause, etc.
    3. Pragmatic conditions
        a) social relationship between addressers and addressees
        b) generations
        c) genre

4. Results and discussions

In this section, how *shall* is used is illustrated through the conditions in (2) and some examples are shown. As shown in Table 1, the main addressers of the Pastons are divided into four generations.

Table 1. The members of the Paston family in each generation

Generation	Name
1	William Paston, Agnes Paston
2	John Paston I, William Paston II, Margaret Paston
3	John Paston II, John Paston III, Edmond Paston II, William Paston III, Margery Paston
4	William Paston IV

The family was originally farmers but William of the first generation became a lawyer and had the power of landholding and he gained a large amount of land. Then the family became gentry. In this paper examples found in Part I of the text edited by Davis (1971), which is the collection of the letters written by the Pastons, are investigated.

The statistical data in this paper are limited to the examples in the letters written by William Paston and Agnes Paston of the first generation and John Paston I and Margaret Paston of the second generation.

4.1. The person of the subject

In Table 2 the distribution of the examples of *shall* according to each person of the subject is indicated. In addition, that of *must* and *ought to* is also indicated for a comparison. The data show that all these three auxiliaries tend to co-occur with the third person subjects (*shall*: 64%, *must*: 60%, and *ought to*: 100%). As for the rates of *shall* and *must*, they are the second highest when they co-occur with the first person subjects (*shall*: 21%, *must*: 26%). All of the examples of *ought to* co-occur with the third person subjects.

Table 2. The ratio of *shall*, *must*, and *ought to*, according to the person of the subjects

	shall	*must*	*ought to*	total
1st person	120 (21)	12 (26)	0 (0)	132 (21)
2nd person	82 (14)	7 (15)	0 (0)	89 (14)
3rd person	364 (64)	28 (60)	8 (100)	400 (64)
total	566 (100)[3]	47 (100)	8 (100)	621 (100)

The examples co-occurring with the first person subjects tend to indicate the meaning of resolution rather than obligation. An example is cited in (3), where *shall* clearly expresses the resolution because "yf I may" is an expression of the addresser's desire and intention. This is an example which has greatly developed its degree of grammaticalization and subjectification. On the other hand, (4) is an example which does not carry the addresser's subjectivity but indicates the meaning of obligation. Here, *shall* is in the clause following *how* and the clause is the content of the addresser's assertion "I wote not." In such a clause

---

[3] Each percentage in total (100) is the sum of three percentages above.

54 *Naoki Hirayama*

the auxiliary does not express the subjective meaning.

(3) And, so God help me, I *xal* (= *shall*) exscusse me of myn goyng dedyr (= thither) yf (= if) I may, for I sopose þat I xal redelyer [= more readily] have tydyngys from yow herre dan (= than) I xulde (= should) have þer (= there).[4] (126, 20-21)[5]

(4) The Kyng goth so nere (= near) vs in þis cuntré, both to pooere and ryche, þat I wote [= know] not how we *shall* lyff (= live) but yff [= if not] þe world a-mend. God a-mend it whan his wyll is.
(224, 14-16)

In (5) an example of prediction with the second person subject is cited, where the mother, Margaret, persuades her son, John Paston II, to do something and she tells that he will get good effect if he takes her advice.

(5) I wold ye shuld assay [= ascertain] whedir it be [= is] more profitable for yow to serve me thanne for to serve such masters as ye haue servid afore [= before] this, and that ye fynde moost profitable theraftir (= thereafter) do in tyme to come. Ye haue assayed the werld resonabilly; ye *shall* knowe your-self the bettir heraftir.
(207, 14-17)

In (6) an example with the third person subject expressing mere futurity is cited. In this sentence *shall* includes uncertainty but it does not mean obligation or the addresser's inference. This is an example of *shall* expressing the mere future in the *when*-clause, which is not found in PE.

(6) I pray yow, yf your sor [= injury] be [= is] hol [= healed] and so þat ȝe may indure (= endure) to ryde, wan my fader com to London þat ȝe wol askyn leve and com hom wan (= when) þe hors *xul* be sentte hom a-ȝeyn. (126, 30-32)

In (7) one of the examples of *ought to*, which occurs only with the third person subject, is cited. This quasi-modal auxiliary shows

---

[4] Emphases are mine. Underlines are put to emphasize the elements relevant to each discussion. If the need arises, the present-day spellings are added in round brackets and notes are also added in square brackets if there are no present-day counterparts.

[5] As for the numbers in the brackets following the citations, in this paper, the left ones are the letter numbers and the right ones are the line numbers in the text edited by Davis (1971).

Modal auxiliaries of obligation in the *Paston Letters* 55

obligational meaning included in the more objective clause of giving examples "such … as…." The clause is concerned with the social obligation of paying for the rent.

> (7) Fyrst on the same Satour-day the tenauntys folwyd vppon, and desyryd to haue there catell a-yen, and I awnnsweryd hem yf thay wold do pay <u>such dewtys (= duties) as</u> they *oght for to [= ought to]* pay to you, that then they shold haue there (= their) catell delyueryd a-yen. (182, 6-9)

In this subsection it has been shown that *shall* is used frequently and in a variety of meanings with all the persons of the subjects. An example with highly subjective meaning (the addresser's resolution) with the first person subject is found as shown in (3).

4.2. The lexical aspect of the verbs (dynamic/stative)

Next, as a second condition, the lexical aspect of the verbs is considered. As shown in Table 3, *shall* tends to co-occur with dynamic verbs. In (8) a sentence with two examples is cited. The first *shall* co-occurs with a causative verb "make" and expresses the addresser's resolution of making someone do something. The second one also co-occurs with a dynamic verb "send" and it carries the addresser's volition. On the other hand, in (9) *shall* co-occurring with a stative verb "be" is cited. It is used in an objective clause of *I suppose.* In such an environment, the addresser's subjectivity concerning the proposition increases, so that *shall* expresses the addresser's subjective prediction. In addition, in Table 3, it can be seen that the ratio of *must* co-occurring with stative verbs is higher than that of *shall* with stative verbs. In (10) an example is shown. Here, *must* expresses not only obligation but also the addresser's inference because it co-occurs with what increases the addresser's subjectivity, such as a stative verb "have" and a temporal clause, "tyll it be othere-wyse," expressing unsettled future condition.

Table 3. The frequency of each auxiliary according to the lexical aspect of co-occurring verbs

	shall	*must*	*ought to*	total
dynamic	435 (77)	27 (57)	8 (100)	470 (76)
stative	131 (23)	20 (43)	0 (0)	151 (24)
total	566 (100)	47 (100)	8 (100)	621 (100)

(8) He is owght (= out) at this tyme, and whan þat he comythe home I *shall* make hym make yow a clere bylle of þe receyt of your lyvelod [= property] and Fastolff bothe, and I *shale* send yow a clere bylle of my receytys and also of my paymentys owght (= out) therof ageyn. (172, 10-14)

(9) And [= if] þat had nowte (= not) a (= have) be (= been) ʒe [= you] xul a (= have) be (= been) atte home þis Qwesontyde, and I suppose þat ʒe *xul* be atte home er owte longke [= presently]. (124, 4-5)

(10) And at the reuerens (= reverence) of God, spyde (= speed) youre maters nowe, for it ys to orybell (= horrible) a cost and trobell that we haue now dayly and *most* haue tyll it be othere-wyse. (196, 48-50)

In this subsection it has been shown that *shall* tends to co-occur with dynamic verbs and that in such sentences it expresses the addresser's resolution. Co-occurring with stative verbs, both *shall* and *must* increase their degrees of grammaticalization and subjectification and they express more subjective meanings.

4.3. Clause types containing the auxiliaries
In 4.1 the auxiliaries indicating objective meaning in the clauses of premises which give situations or conditions such as *how*-clause as shown in (4) and *when*-clause as shown in (6) were illustrated. Here, similarly, *shall* in the objective meaning is cited in (11). The auxiliary is included in one of the clauses of premises, which is preceded by *(so) that*, indicating the purpose of (not) doing something. On the contrary, in (12) *shall* increases the addresser's subjectivity, included in the nominal clause preceded by *I trow*. In such a clause, the content of the addresser's subjective prediction is shown. Then in (13) *ought to* expresses objective meaning included in *as*-clause, which refers to a common idea. Although this auxiliary indicates obligation, the degree

Modal auxiliaries of obligation in the *Paston Letters*   57

of that is rather lower than *shall* in the legal documents because the
obligation in (13) is felt by the addresser himself.

(11) ... and I thynk or [= before] ye and I departe þat þe defawte (=
default) schall be knowe (= known) where yt ys, and also that, wyth
yowyr advyse and helpe and myn to-gedyrs (= together), we schall
take some wey þat [= so that] yt *schal* not breke. (226, 11-13)

(12) And I trowe [= I think] ye *xall* be fayne to porveye [= provide]
another man for Symond, for ye hare (= are) nevere the nerer a wysse
(= wise) man for hym. (153, 16-18)

(13) Item, as for yowre sone: I lete yow wete [= know] I wold he dede
wel, but I vnderstand in hym no dispocicion of policy ne (= nor) of
gouernans as man of the werld (= world) *owt to* do, but only leuith
(= lives), and euer hath, as man disolut (= dissolute), with-owt any
prouicion (= provision), ne that he besijth [= consider] hym [=
himself] nothinge to vnderstand swhech (= such) materis (= matters)
as a man of lyuelode [= property] must nedis (= needs) vnderstond.
(73, 6-10)

Here, as one of the points which affect the meaning of the auxiliaries,
clause types including the auxiliaries have been considered. It has been
illustrated that the clause types strongly affect the degrees of the
subjectivity of the auxiliaries, and the meanings of the auxiliaries
change according to such degrees.

4.4. Social relationships between addressers and addressees and genre of the documents

In this subsection how the meanings of the auxiliaries are affected by
social relationships between addressers and addressees and genre of
the documents is considered. In (14) Margaret Paston is giving some
advice to her son John Paston II. She is giving him a reason why he
should not hurry to get married by using the *for*-clause, and in the
clause the obligational *must* is used. Then, as underlined, she instructs
her son what to do next, using the verbs in imperative mood ("labour,"
"be"). Compared to *shall* in obligational meaning, *must* in this
example contains more addresser's judgment.

(14) Also I wuld þat ye shuld not be to (= too) hasty to be maried till ye
were more suere (= sure) of your lyvelode [= property], for ye *must*
remembre what charge ye shall haue, and if ye haue not to mayntene

(= maintain) it, it wull be a gret rebuke; and therfore <u>labour</u> that [=
so that] ye may haue releses of the lordes and <u>be</u> in more suerté of
your lond or than [= before] ye be [= are] maried. (201, 12-16)

In (15) one example of *shall* in an indenture is cited. This is the
contract between John Paston II, who is of the third generation of the
Pastons and called "Sir John Paston," and "Sthephen Kelke," who is a
goldsmith in London. John Paston II mortgages his sixteen soup dishes
to Stephen for 40 pounds.

In the indentures in the *Paston Letters* the subjects are the third
person. Although the verb "selle" is controllable by the subject, *shall*
does not indicate the subject's resolution or his inference. It is used in
the nominal *that*-clause led by "Sthephen graunteth (= grants)," which
indicates that Stephen objectively agree to the following content. This
shall is also in the apodosis of *and [= if]*-clause and it indicates the
obligation when the condition is fulfilled. In addition, although the
next sentence also has *and*-clause, not *shall* but other obligational
phrase "be not bounden" is used in the apodosis as a counterpart of
former *shall*. It is safely said that *shall* here is used in the meaning of
objective obligation because *be bound* in the parallel construction is
an objective expression and it does not carry the addresser's
subjectivity.

(15) INDENTURE PLEDGING PLATE 1470, 07, 08
This endenture (= indenture) made at London the viij (= 8) day of
Julij (= July) the x^{the} (= 10th) yere (= year) of the regne (= reign) of
Kyng Edward the iiij^{the} (= fourth) by-twyxt (= between) Syr (= Sir)
John Paston, knyght, of the on (= one) partye (= party) and Sthephen
Kelke, citeseyne (= citizen) and goldsmyth of London, on the other
partye, bereth (= bears) witnesse þat the said Syr John the day of this
present wrytyng hathe bargained, delyuered (= delivered), and solde
to the forsayd Sthephen xvj potengers [= soup dishes], weying (=
weighing) of Troy weyght xxij li. x vnc (= ounce) of seluer (= silver)
di. [= half] vnc., for xl li. [= pound] of laufull (= lawful) money of
Englond receyued by þe same Syr John for the same bargayne. And
the said <u>Sthephen graunteth (= grants) by this presentes that</u> and [=
if] the said Syr John, his executors or assignez (= assignees), pay or
do to be payed to þe said Sthephen xl li. of laufull money of Englond
by-fore (= before) þe feste of Witsontyde (= Whitsuntide) next
coming (= coming), þat than (= then) the same Sthephen *shall* <u>selle</u>
and delyuer (= deliver) a-yen (= again) to the said Syr John alle the

Modal auxiliaries of obligation in the *Paston Letters*   59

forsaid (= aforesaid) dysshes and potengers of seluer; prouyded (= provided) that, <u>and [= if]</u> the same potengers be [= are] take (= taken) a-wey (= away) by any open robberye (= robbery), that than (= then) þe said Sthephen <u>be not [be not = will not be] bounden (= bound)</u> her-by (= hereby) to þe latter sale or relyueré [= restoration].

In witnesse wher-of (= whereof) the partyes a-bouesayd (= abovesaid) to þis endentures enterchaungeabully (= interchange-ably) haue set to theire (= their) seales (= seals) þe day and yere (= year) a-foresaid (= aforesaid). (251, 1-17)

(16) is an example found in a petition by John Paston I to the chancellor. Here, used in the nominal clause following *ordain that,* two *shall*s strengthen their meaning of obligation.

(16) And also the seid comenauntes [= contract] eftsonis [= afterwards] callid to remembraunce be (= by) the seid Ser John Fastolff, the same Ser John for certeyn consideracions movyng hym, be (= by) his word withowt writyng dischargid your seid besecher of the seid somme of iiij ml (= 4000) mark, desiryng hym so to <u>ordeyn that</u> ich (= each) of the seid monkes or prestes *shull* yerly haue as the prestes of the chauntry (= chantry) of Heylesdon had, and that vij pore (= poor) men *shull* also be founde (= founded) yerly (= yearly) in the seid plase (= place) inperpetuité [= forever] to pray for the sowles abovesayd. (60, 74-81)

In (17) a typical style seen in petitions are cited although there is no *shall* in obligation. In the first sentence, John Paston I entreats and in the second sentence he expresses his resolution because he wants the chancellor to grant his request.

(17) Wherfore please your good and gracious lordship to direct seuerall (= several) writes (= writs) of sub pena (= subpoena) to the seid William and William, chargyng hem (= them) seuerally (= severely) vpon a peyne conuenient to appere (= appear) before your lordship in the Chauncery at a certeyn day be (= by) your lordship to be limityd, to answer to these premisses and to do as right and consiens (= conscience) requirith (= requires). And your seid besecher *shall* pray God for yow. (60, 109-10)

Although (18) and (19) are not cited from a petition, the examples are found in a letter to the man of high position, the Bishop of Winchester. The letter is considered similar to a petition because the addresser John Paston II indicates himself with his name or the third person pronouns. However, in (18) *shall* is not used but hypothetical *should* is used in the object clause of "desyrethe (that)" to ask for a request. In addition, in (19) *ought to*, which expresses obligation based on a common idea, is used. It also co-occurs with "for ij causis (= for two causes)," which gives reasons, and the subjectivity is weakened in such a sentence.

(18) Fyrst (= First), Syr J. P. compleyneth and desyrethe, as he hathe dyuerse (= diverse) tymes dessyred, my lorde to make hym an aquitaunce of m¹m¹m¹m¹ (= 4000) mark whyche myght haue been claymed by vertu (= virtue) of wordes rehersed in the bergayne betwyen Syr J.Fastolf and John Paston, esquiere, fader, &c. ...

Item, he desyrethe hys fefféys (= feoffees) *sholde* be dyschargyd off any entresse (= entries) in any londes þat weer Syr J. Fastolff in Flegge, in as moche as all they excede nott þe valure off l li. yerlye acordyng to þ'endentur (= the indenture). (249, 1-12)

(19) Item, as for the maner (= manor) of Guton, Syr J. Paston thynkythe that he *oweth (= ought)* not *to* assent as yit that [=what] W. Passton shold relese, for ij causis: on for hys penalté for Caster, and þe second fore the entresse off my lorde off Canterbury. (249, 28-31)

In this subsection it has been seen that the degrees of subjectivity of *shall* and other (quasi-)modal auxiliaries in obligational meaning are affected by the social relationships between addressers and addressees and genre of the documents.

5. Conclusion

In this paper *shall* has been considered from prepositional conditions such as the person of the subjects and the lexical aspect of the verbs, the conditions concerning clause types which contain the auxiliary such as *how*-clause and *trow that*-clause, and pragmatic conditions such as social relationship between addresser and addressees and genre of the documents. As the need arises, *must* and *ought to* have been taken into consideration. The findings can be summarized as shown below:

a. Although *shall* co-occurs with first/second/third person subjects and dynamic/stative verbs, it most frequently co-occurs with the third person subjects and dynamic verbs. As shown in (3), when *shall* co-occurs with the first person subject, it tends to express the addresser's subjective resolution. Although *shall* in (4) also co-occurs with the first person subject, it expresses the objective obligation in the *how*-clause. Here, it is safe to say that the degree of subjectivity of *shall* is influenced by not only the propositional elements (subjects and verbs) but also the types of the clauses where the auxiliary occurs.

b. When used in the clauses expressing more objective premises such as *when*-clause or *so that*-clause, *shall* expresses the mere futurity. On the other hand, included in the highly subjective clause such as *I trow (that)*-clause, *shall* also expresses subjective meaning of inference. The clause types including the auxiliaries strongly affect the degrees of the subjectivity of them and the meanings of the auxiliaries change according to such degrees.

c. When the social relationship between addressers and addressees are focused on, *must* in obligational meaning is used in the letter where the mother, Margaret Paston, gives an order to her son, John Paston II, as what he is obliged to do by God. On the other hand, in a contract, *shall* in the meaning of strong obligation and necessity is found. *Shall* in such a meaning is found also in petition when it is used in the clause of obligation such as *ordain that*. Compared with *shall* in contract, *must* in the letter of Margaret is slightly more concerned with the addresser's subjectivity, although it also expresses the obligation.

Text

Davis, Norman. ed. 2004. *Paston letters and papers of the fifteenth century*, part I. Oxford University Press (First published 1971 by the Clarendon Press).

References

Coates, Jennifer 1983. *The semantics of the modal auxiliaries*. London & Canberra: Croom Helm.

Hopper, Paul. J., and Elizabeth C. Traugott 1993. *Grammaticalization*. Cambridge: Cambridge University Press.

Gies, Frances. and Joseph Gies 1998. *A medieval family: The Pastons of fifteenth-century England*. Harper Collins Publishers.

Mustanoja, Tauno F. 1960. *A middle English syntax*, part I. Helsinki: Société Néophilologique.

Shamoto, Tokiko. 1999. *Chusei igirisu ni ikita Paston-ke no josei-tachi: Do-ke shokan-shu kara* (*The women of the Paston family in medieval England: With special regard to the Paston Letters*). Osaka: Sogensha.

Simpson, John A. and Edmund S.C. Weiner 2009 (prepared 1989). *The Oxford English dictionary*, 2nd edition on CD-ROM Version 4.0, Oxford: Oxford University Press.

Traugott, Elizabeth C. 1972. *A history of English syntax*. New York: Holt, Rinehart and Winston, Inc.

Traugott, Elizabeth C. 1995. Subjectification in grammaticalisation. In Dieter Stein & Susan Wright (eds.) *Subjectivity and subjectivisation*, 31-54. Cambridge: Cambridge University Press.

Chronological study of English collocations of -*ly* adverbs

Masahiro Hori

Abstract
The purpose of this article is to discuss the chronological changes and patterns in English-language collocations of -*ly* manner adverbs in fiction from eighteenth to twentieth centuries. Collocational study itself is not novel, but this chronological study of collocation represents a new field of research into the history of the English language. In order to carry out a thorough investigation into this subject, I have made use of *Eighteenth-Century Fiction* on CD-ROM, *Nineteenth-Century Fiction* on CD-ROM, and the *British National Corpus*, as well as the *Oxford English Dictionary on CD-ROM* (2nd edition).

1. Introduction
Just as the study of the English language involves an investigation of phonetic, lexical, grammatical, and semantic change, so also the study of collocations makes possible a clearly defined and precisely stated contribution to historical and chronological approach analysis in descriptive linguistics. Past and present research into the history of the development of the English language generally falls into the following seven categories: (1) phonological changes, (2) spelling changes of words, (3) a simplification of inflection and the loss of grammatical gender and case, (4) increase in vocabulary, (5) syntactic changes, (6) etymology and semantic changes, and (7) dialectal change and diffusion. I would like to insist that a historical approach involving the analysis of chronological changes and patterns of collocation should be added to these research subjects going forward.[1]

1.1. Background to a chronological study of collocations
J. R. Firth, who defined collocation as "the habitual co-occurrence of individual words" (Firth 1951, 1957) and advocated the importance of the study of collocation as a means of investigating semantic statements of meaning in descriptive linguistics, also proposed a historical or chronological approach to collocation:

---

[1] This article is a revised version of "A chronological study of English collocations in fiction from eighteen to twentieth centuries" (2009), which was written in Japanese.

There are many more of the same kind throughout this work [Blake's King Edward the Third], and of course a large number of collocations which have been common property for long periods and are still current even in everyday colloquial. This method of approach makes two branches of stylistics stand out more clearly: (a) the stylistics of what persists in and through change, and (b) the stylistics of personal idiosyncrasies. (Firth 1957: 196)

In "Modes of Meaning" (1951, 1957), he pointed out three research topics in collocational studies: "the study of the usual collocations" (1957: 195), the study of "unique and personal, that is to say, a-normal" collocations (1957: 198), and the chronological study of collocations. With respect to the first topic, "usual collocations," we have many studies performed by research groups mainly related to Birmingham University, which have been led by the late John Sinclair. For example, the studies of Michael Hoey (2005), Susan Hunston (1999, 2002), Michael Stubbs (2001), Bill Louw (1993), Alan Partington (1993), and so on. One of their distinguished achievements has been the production of dictionaries of collocations, or dictionaries containing collocational information.

As to the second topic, "unique and personal" collocations, many articles have so far been published, analysing such areas as the literary collocations of Chaucer, Shakespeare, Woolf, and so on. One such example is the present author's book, *Investigating Dickens' Style: A Collocational Analysis* (2004), which aimed to provide new insight into Dickens' language and style through the corpus-based study of collocation, focusing on not only Dickens's usual collocations but also on his unique and creative use of collocations.

As for the third topic of collocation — "the chronological study of collocations" — satisfactory results have not as yet been produced. For example, in *Historical Linguistics* (Herbert Schendl 2001), part of *Oxford Introductions to Language Study*, a series of brief, clear introductions to the main areas of language study including "Vocabulary change" (Chapter 3), "Grammatical change" (Chapter 4), and "Sound change" (Chapter 5) are discussed in relation to a person's state of mind and societal causation of language change. However, collocation is not mentioned at all. Three books about the history of English published in 2006, *The Oxford History of English* (Oxford), *A History of the English Language* (Cambridge), and *The Handbook of the History of English* (Blackwell) do not contain any discussion of or on collocation from a historical perspective, let alone any chapter devoted to the subject.

However, while materials do exist referring to a chronological study of collocation, it is not investigated as a main research subject. For example, in *The Cambridge History of the English Language*, a seven-volume series, *Volume I: The Beginning to 1066* (405) and *Volume IV: 1776-1997* (33) allude to a collocational change and selectional restrictions. *Volume II: 1066-1476* (451) briefly mentions colligation (grammatical collocation or syntactic pattern of collocation). Moreover, in *Collocational and Idiomatic Aspects of Composite Predicates in the History of English* (Brinton and Akimoto 1999) collocation is not a main subject, but rather chronologically examined from the viewpoint of idiomatization with only the possibility of a synchronic and diachronic study of collocation suggested.

Taking this academic background into account, this present article will focus on the historical and chronological study of collocation. A primary goal of this research is to provide an objective validity for further historical approach of collocation through a chronological analysis of collocation of *-ly* manner adverbs.

1.2. Corpora
In this article I use the following corpora and databases:

(1) *British National Corpus* (BNC)

(2) *Eighteenth-Century Fiction on CD-ROM* (ECF) (Chadwyck-Healey, 1996)
This database comprises the works of 30 of the most influential writers of the British Isles in the eighteenth century. It contains 77 collected works or 96 discrete items.

(3) *Nineteenth-Century Fiction on CD-ROM* (NCF) (Chadwyck-Healey, 2000)
This database contains 250 complete works of prose fiction by 109 authors from the period 1781 to 1901.

(4) *Oxford English Dictionary Online* (OED-Online)
Oxford English Dictionary on CD-ROM, 2nd edition, Macintosh Version (OUP, 1993)

2. Chronological changes in three aspects of collocation

Collocation has three aspects: lexical collocation, grammatical collocation, and semantic collocation. Each aspect can be chronologically discussed. I would like to briefly explain the chronological change occurring in each aspect of collocation by showing a typical example, before continuing with a close examination of the collocations of manner adverbs.

2.1. Lexical collocation

The collocation "completely different" was not found in *Eighteenth-Century Fiction* (ECF) and only one example is found in *Nineteenth-Century Fiction* (NCF). However, there are 50 examples found in twentieth-century fiction within the *British National Corpus* (BNC). Among adverbs co-occurring with the adjective "different" in twentieth-century fiction, the highest-frequency collocation is "very different," the second is "quite different," and the next-highest is "completely different." Therefore, we can say that the collocation of "different" and "completely" began to be frequently used in the twentieth century.

2.2. Grammatical collocation

One of the syntactic features of grammatical collocation is a matter of word order. According to the *OED* the collocation, "Ladies and Gentlemen" was used in reverse word order as "Gentlemen and Ladies" until the middle of the eighteenth century. This can be considered as a change in grammatical collocation.

> 1808 Grose Antiq. Rep. II. 405 All public addresses to a mixed assembly of both sexes, till sixty years ago, commenced *Gentlemen and Ladies*: at present it is *Ladies and Gentlemen*.

2.3. Semantic collocation

The adverb "terribly," meaning "very bad or unpleasantly," could not originally modify adjectives retaining favourable or positive meanings, but the collocation "terribly important" co-occurring with the adjective "important" implying a favourable association is often found in the twentieth century; in the BNC are found 54 examples of this collocation. It is, however, not found in the ECF or NCF. According to the *OED Online*, there are only three examples of the collocation, "terribly important" — one instance in each in the years 1865, 1930, and 1956. This collocational change can be discussed as a semantic expansion of the collocation of "terribly."

3. Collocational changes or persistence of the manner adverbs *fixedly*, *heartily*, and *thoughtfully*

As has so far been observed, chronological changes can be illustrated in terms of lexical, grammatical, and semantic aspects. In this article I will discuss the collocations of some manner adverbs in more detail from a chronological perspective, within the purview of the history of the English language.

The following table shows the frequencies of some main adverbs in eighteenth, nineteenth, and twentieth century-fiction:

Table 1. Frequencies of manner adverbs in 18th, 19th, and 20th century-fiction

	BNC (Imaginative) 19.6 million words		NCF on CD-ROM 41.2 million words		ECF on CD-ROM 12.1 million words	
	Tokens	/ 1 mw*	Tokens	/ 1 mw	Tokens	/ 1 mw
slowly	4,228	215.75	4,514	109.56	137	11.32
quietly	2,603	132.83	2,892	70.19	187	15.45
gently	2,187	111.60	2,573	62.45	439	36.28
softly	1,988	101.44	1,974	47.91	332	27.44
silently	871	44.45	1,152	27.96	90	7.44
angrily	794	40.67	805	19.54	75	6.20
thoughtfully	**582**	**29.70**	**525**	**12.74**	**2**	**0.17**
hastily	549	28.01	2,922	70.92	622	51.40
impatiently	484	24.70	988	23.98	124	10.25
anxiously	424	21.64	1,156	28.06	12	0.99
cheerfully	345	17.60	717	17.40	5	0.41
coolly	295	15.05	659	16.00	78	6.45
hurriedly	295	15.05	616	14.95	1	0.08
gravely	184	9.39	1,358	32.96	180	14.88
solemnly	157	8.07	973	23.62	216	17.85
tenderly	155	7.91	1,017	24.68	386	31.90
earnestly	149	7.90	1,571	38.13	653	53.97
heartily	**97**	**4.95**	**1,283**	**31.14**	**805**	**66.53**
fixedly	**59**	**3.01**	**192**	**4.66**	**11**	**0.91**
timidly	44	2.25	491	11.92	2	0.17

* The "mw" means "occurrence per million words."

68   *Masahiro Hori*

Table 1 presents a list of high-frequency manner adverbs in the Imaginative sub-corpus (fiction) of the BNC, ECF and NCF. Among several interesting points the most obvious is the difference in frequency occurring in each century. In this article I would like to discuss three manner adverbs, *fixedly*, *heartily*, and *thoughtfully* within this chronological framework because they show chronologically interesting collocational features.

In examining each manner adverb, I will first discuss the collocation in the twentieth century, that is, with reference to the BNC, and then follow this with a discussion of the eighteenth and nineteenth centuries.

3.1. Collocations of *fixedly*
3.1.1. British National Corpus (Imaginative: 59 examples): Twentieth-century fiction
There are 59 examples of the word *fixedly* in the Imaginative sub-corpus of the BNC.

(1) Lexical collocation
Fifty eight of the 59 examples modify the following verbs:

> Verbs: stare (40), gaze (8), look (7), focus (1), talk (1), peer (1)

Approximately 70% of the 59 examples of the adverb *fixedly* co-occur with the verb *stare*. We can say that the adverb *fixedly* has a clear tendency of lexical collocation.

(2) Grammatical collocation
Concerning the grammatical collocation of *fixedly*, all apart from one example modify verbs. In all the examples modifying verbs, the collocational pattern "verb + *fixedly* + *at*" is found. The following is typical:

> but Myles stared *fixedly* at him, saying nothing.

(3) Semantic collocation
With respect to the semantic collocation of *fixedly* among 59 examples, apart from one example co-occurring with the adjective *cloudless* and with two verbs *talking* and *focused*, 56 examples of *fixedly* modify verbs meaning an act of seeing, that is to say, *stare*, *gaze*, *look*, and *peer*. Therefore, the semantic collocation of *fixedly* is quite obvious.

Chronological study of English collocations of *-ly* adverbs   69

Was such a collocational tendency of *fixedly* observed even in the eighteenth and nineteenth century?

3.1.2. Eighteenth-century fiction (11 examples)
In a similar way to the collocations of *fixedly* in twentieth-century fiction in the BNC, the collocations of *fixedly* in eighteenth-century fiction are likewise next investigated. There are 11 examples of the adverb in ECF.

(1) Lexical collocation
The verbs that the adverb of manner *fixedly* modifies are as follows:

> Verbs: look (6), gaze (1), eye (1), bend one's eyes (2), be (1)

The adverb *fixedly* most often co-occurs with the verb *look*. In the BNC, in the twentieth century it most often co-occurs with the verb *stare* but the collocation of *fixedly* with *stare* is not found as an eighteenth-century collocation.

(2) Grammatical collocation
As to the grammatical collocation of *fixedly*, all of the 11 examples modify verbs. The collocational pattern of the adverb "verb + *fixedly* + *at*" is used only once, but the collocational pattern "verb + *fixedly* + (*up*)*on*" is used 7 times. Concerning the word order, eight of the 11 examples occur after the verbs. As such, the feature of post-modification of the adverb is already seen in the eighteenth century.

(3) Semantic collocation
With respect to the semantic collocation, 10 of the 11 examples of *fixedly* modify verbs meaning an act of seeing — just as observed in the twentieth century.

3.1.3. Nineteenth-century fiction (192 examples)
In the NCF there are 192 examples of *fixedly*.

(1) Lexical collocation
The verbs the adverb modifies more than three times are follows:

> Verbs: look (114), gaze (29), stare (9), regard (4)

The adverb most often co-occurs with the verb *look* (60%). The collocation of the verb *stare* and the adverb *fixedly*, which was not found in the eighteenth century began to be used in the nineteenth century. Other verbs co-occurring with the adverb are follows:

Other verbs: watched, keep one's eyes, (eyes) gleaming, (eyes) glared, (eyes) nailed, fascinated, disliked, surveyed, etc.

(2) Grammatical collocation
All but six of the 192 examples of the adverb *fixedly* modify verbs. The prepositions after *fixedly* are *at*, *on*, *upon* in order of frequency.

"fixedly at" (80: 42%), "fixedly on"(15: 8%), "fixedly upon" (9: 5%)

With respect to the word order of verbs and *fixedly*, the post-modification is overwhelmingly used (95%).

(3) Semantic collocation
Over 80% of the examples of *fixedly* modify "an act of seeing," which shows the same tendency as in both the eighteenth and the twentieth centuries.

3.1.4. Summary of results for *fixedly*
The chronological investigation of the collocations of the manner adverb *fixedly* leads to the conclusion that the adverb has obvious and consistent collocational tendencies from the eighteenth century through to the twentieth. Regarding the lexical aspect of collocation of the adverb *fixedly*, we can safely say that the adverb has co-occurred with the verb *look* throughout the last three centuries, and that in the twentieth century the co-occurrence with the verb *stare* is more frequently found. From a grammatical aspect, the adverb *fixedly* has been employed to modify verbs, and has formed the collocational pattern "verb + *fixedly* + preposition" through the three centuries. From a semantic aspect, *fixedly* has occurred with verbs expressing an act of seeing.

3.2. Collocations of *heartily*
In a similar way to the chronological examination of collocations of *fixedly*, collocations of the manner adverbs *heartily* and *thoughtfully* are next examined. I will show the collocational data of the adverbs in

each century and briefly explain them, followed by a more involved discussion of each separate statistic datum.

3.2.1. British National Corpus (Imaginative: 97 examples): Twentieth-century fiction

(1) Lexical collocation

> Verbs: say (18), laugh (16), wish (9), eat (8), agree (4), dislike (4), curse (2), slap (2), greet (2)

(2) Grammatical collocation

> (a) A Pattern "verb + *heartily*": say (18: 0), laugh (16: 0), eat (8: 0), curse (2: 0), slap (2: 0)
> > * The pattern "say (18: 0)" means that "say + *heartily*" occurs 18 times while the pattern "*heartily* + say" is not found at all.
>
> (b) B Pattern "*heartily* + verb" : wish (7: 2), agree (3: 1), dislike (3: 1)
> > * The pattern "wish (7: 2)" means that "*heartily* + wish" occurs seven times while the pattern "wish + *heartily*" two times.
>
> (c) Both patterns (A Pattern : B Pattern): None.

(3) Semantic collocation

> "Heartily" (97): verbs expressing action or movement (eg. *laugh*, *say*, *eat*, *curse*, *slap*) (46: 47.4%), verbs expressing feeling or cognition (eg. *wish*, *agree*, *dislike*, *despise*) (13: 13.4%).

3.2.2. Eighteenth-century fiction (805 examples)
(1) Lexical collocation

> Verbs: wish (92), laugh (54), thank (33), eat (31), hate (26), despise (20), pray (18), pity (16), congratulate (17), shake (16), rejoice (14), swear (8)

> Adjectives: sorry (48), glad (26), welcome (24), ashamed (11), weary (10), tired (7), sick (7)

(2) Grammatical collocation

> (a) Pattern A "verb + *heartily*": laugh (52: 2), eat (31: 0), shake (15: 1), swear (6: 2)
>
> (b) Pattern B "*heartily* + verb": hope (10: 0), rejoice (13: 1), congratulate

(15: 2), despise (16: 4), wish (70: 22)

(c) Both patterns (Pattern A : Pattern B): thank (18: 15), hate (14: 10), pray (8: 10), pity (7: 9)

(3) Semantic collocation

Verbs expressing favourable emotions: wish (92), laugh (54), thank (33), pray (18), pity (16), congratulate (17), rejoice (14)

Verbs expressing unfavourable emotions: hate (26), despise (20), swear (8)

Adjectives expressing favourable emotions (50): glad (26), welcome (24)

3.2.3. Nineteenth-century fiction (1,283 examples)

(1) Lexical collocation

Verbs: laugh (246), wish (107), shake (71), thank (49), say (31), despise (24), eat (23), hope (21), congratulate (16), pray (14), hate (7), dislike (6), pity (6)

Adjectives: glad (77), welcome (50), ashamed (31), sorry (23), sick (18), tired (17), weary (3)

(2) Grammatical collocation

(a) Patter A "verb + *heartily*": laugh (246: 3), thank (44: 5), say (29: 2), shake (61: 10), eat (23: 0), congratulate (11: 5)

(b) Pattern B "*heartily* + verb": wish (98: 9), hope (19: 2)

(c) Both patterns (Patter A: Pattern B): pray (7: 7), hate (4: 3), pity (2: 4)

(3) Semantic collocation

Verbs expressing favourable emotions: laugh (246), wish (107), shake (71), thank (49), hope (21), congratulate (16), pray (14), pity (6)

Verbs expressing unfavourable emotions: despise (24), hate (7), dislike (6),

Adjectives expressing favourable emotions: (127): glad (77), welcome (50),

Chronological study of English collocations of -*ly* adverbs   73

Adjectives expressing unfavourable emotions: (92): ashamed (31), sorry (23), sick (18), tired (17), weary (3)

3.2.4. Summary of results for *heartily*

A chronological investigation of the collocations of the manner adverb *heartily* leads to the conclusion that *heartily* shows a very different tendency of collocation when compared with *fixedly*. In particular, *heartily* does not have a consistent collocational tendency throughout the eighteenth to twentieth centuries. The frequency of *heartily* is highest in the eighteenth century and shows a sharp decrease from the nineteenth to the twentieth century. Lexically, it most frequently modifies the reporting verb *say* in the twentieth century, but is not found in ECF. In the nineteenth century, however, it shows a sharp increase. It can be said that *heartily* changed in lexical collocation from the period spanning the eighteenth to twentieth centuries. With respect to grammatical collocation, *heartily* is used in both the pre- and post-modification, that is to say, both before and following verbs in the eighteenth century; but such a grammatical co-occurrence of *heartily* and verbs is not found in the twentieth century. In this sense the grammatical collocation is more fixed in the twentieth century. Concerning its semantic collocation, there is an obvious tendency of co-occurrence with verbs expressing a favourable meaning.

3.3. Collocations of *thoughtfully*
3.3.1. British National Corpus (Imaginative: 582 examples): Twentieth-century fiction

(1) Lexical collocation

say (140: 24.1%), look (61: 10.4%), nod (32: 5.5%), add (27: 4.6%), stare (14: 2.4%), frown (13: 2.1%), gaze (13: 2.1%), regard (13: 2.1%), study (12: 2.1%), narrow (9: 1.5%), watch (9: 1.5%)

(2) Grammatical collocation

(a) Patter A "verb + *thoughtfully*": say (138: 2), look (61: 0), nod (32: 0), added (26: 1), stare (14: 0), frown (9: 4), gaze (13: 0), regard (13: 0), study (12: 0), narrow (9: 0), watch (7: 2)

(b) Pattern B "*thoughtfully* + verb": None.

74   *Masahiro Hori*

    (c) Both patterns (Patter A : Pattern B): None.

(3) Semantic collocation

"Thoughtfully" (582): reporting verbs (175: 30.0%), verbs expressing acts of viewing (100: 17.1%)

3.3.2. Eighteenth-century fiction (2 examples)

(1) I saw with pleasure, as I *thoughtfully went* through the divine pages, that natural religion is the foundation and support of revelation; (Amory's *John Buncle,* Vol. 1, Ch. 8)

(2) "It is difficult to say," *answered* Sir Clement, very *thoughtfully*, ... (Burney's *Evelina*, Vol. 2, Letter 2)

3.3.3. Nineteenth-century fiction (525 examples)
(1) Lexical collocation

say (163), look (70), reply (19), walk (16), repeat (13), sit (11), observe (6), stand (6), remark (5)

(2) Grammatical collocation

(a) Pattern A "verb + *thoughtfully*": say (162: 1), look (63: 7), reply (19: 0), walk (15: 1), repeat (13: 0), sit (11: 0), nod (7: 0), observe (6: 0), stand (6: 0), remark (5: 0)

(b) Pattern B "*thoughtfully* + verb": None.

(c) Both patterns (Patter A : Pattern B): None.

(3) Semantic collocation

Reporting verbs (216): say (163), reply (19), repeat (13), observe (6), remark (5), ask (4), return (4), add (2)

3.3.4. Summary of results for *thoughtfully*
In contrast to the frequency of *heartily*, the manner adverb *thoughtfully* shows a sharp increase from the eighteenth to the twentieth centuries. In the eighteenth century there were only two examples, such as *thoughtfully went* and *answered Sir Clement, very thoughtfully*. In the twentieth century a third of the 582 examples of *thoughtfully* occur with *say* and *look*. In this sense it can be said that *thoughtfully* shows

a more obvious tendency of chronological lexical collocation. Concerning grammatical collocation, in almost all of the examples, *thoughtfully* modifies verbs with post-modification. As for semantic collocation, *thoughtfully* shows an obvious tendency to co-occur with reporting verbs and verbs expressing an act of seeing.

4. Conclusion

Ever since J. R. Firth advocated the importance of the study of collocation in 1951, many impressive accomplishments concerning collocation have been achieved, and collocation has become an important research field in contemporary linguistic studies. Such studies of collocation, however, have focused on only two of the three research topics Firth pointed out in his collocational research, while the third research topic — "the chronological study of collocation" — has received little attention.

The focus of this article was limited to the collocations of the manner adverbs, *fixedly*, *heartily*, and *thoughtfully*. By expanding this approach, the chronological perspective concerning collocations of other adverbs, verbs, nouns, and adjectives will likely yield new understandings in the history of the English language.

Bibliography

Biber, Douglas, Stig Johansson, Geoffrey Leech, Susan Conrad & Edward Finegan 1999. *Longman grammar of spoken and written English*. London: Longman.

Blake, Norman (ed.) 1992. *The Cambridge history of the English language: Volume II 1066-1476*. Cambridge: Cambridge University Press.

Brinton, Laurel J. and Minoji Akimoto (eds.) 1999. *Collocational and idiomatic aspects of composite predicates in the history of English*. Amsterdam: John Benjamins.

Eighteenth-century fiction on CD-ROM 1996. Cambridge: Chadwyck-Healey Ltd.

Firth, J. R. 1951. Modes of meaning. *Essays and studies*. The English Association. 118-49.

Firth, J. R. 1957. *Papers in linguistics, 1934-51*. London: Oxford University Press.

Hoey, Michael 2005. *Lexical priming: A new theory of words and language*. London: Routledge.

76   *Masahiro Hori*

Hogg, Richard (ed.) 1992. *The Cambridge history of the English language: Volume I The Beginnings to 1066*. Cambridge: Cambridge University Press.

Hogg, Richard & David Denison (eds.) 2006. *A history of the English language*. Cambridge: Cambridge University Press.

Hori, Masahiro 1999. Collocational patterns of intensive adverbs in Dickens: A tentative approach. *English corpus studies*, No. 6, 51-65.

Hori, Masahiro 2002. Collocational patterns of *-ly* manner adverbs in Dickens. In Toshio Saito, Junsaku Nakamura & Shunji Yamazaki (eds.), *English corpus linguistics in Japan*, 149-63. Amsterdam: Rodopi.

Hori, Masahiro 2004. *Investigating Dickens' style: A collocational analysis* Basingstoke: Palgrave Macmillan.

Hori, Masahiro 2005. Collocational style in the two narratives of *Bleak House*: A corpus-based analysis. In Carmen Rosa Caldas-Coulthard & Michael Toolan (eds.), *The writer's craft, the culture's technology: Papers from the Poetics and Linguistics Association International Conference, Birmingham 2002*, 225-38. Amsterdam: Rodopi.

Hori, Masahiro 2009. *Introduction to collocation studies in English* (in Japanese). Tokyo: Kenkyusha.

Hori, Masahiro 2009. A chronological study of English collocations in fiction from eighteenth to twentieth centuries. In Masahiro Hori *et al.*, *Chronological study of collocation: A new approach to studies of English and Japanese* (in Japanese), 145-81. Tokyo: Hitsuji Shobo.

Hori, Masahiro 2011. *English collocations learned through exercises* (in Japanese). Tokyo: Kenkyusha.

Hori, Masahiro (forthcoming). In defiance of rules: Unusual collocation and idioms in *The Pickwick Papers*. In Osamu Imahayashi (ed.), *The language and style of Charles Dickens*. Frankfurt: Peter Lang.

Hunston, Susan 2002. *Corpora in applied linguistics*. Cambridge: Cambridge University Press.

Hunston, Susan & Gill Francis 1999. *Pattern grammar: A corpus-driven approach to the lexical grammar of English*. Amsterdam: John Benjamins.

Louw, Bill 1993. Irony in the text or insincerity in the writer? The diagnostic potential of semantic prosodies. In Mona Baker, Gill Francis & Elena Tognini-Bonelli (eds.), *Text and technology: In honour of John Sinclair*, 157-76. Amsterdam: John Benjamin.

Louw, Bill & Mariya Milojkovic 2016. *Corpus stylistics as contextual prosodic theory and subtext*. Amsterdam: Benjamins Publishing

McBride, Christopher 1998. A collocational approach to semantic change: the case of worship and honour in Malory and Spenser. *Language and literature*, Vol. 7, London: SAGE Publications, 5-19.

Chronological study of English collocations of *-ly* adverbs   77

McCarthy, Michael & Felicity O'Dell 2005. *English collocations in use: Advanced*. Cambridge: Cambridge.

Moon, Rosamund 1998. *Fixed expressions and idioms in English: A corpus-based approach*. Oxford: Clarendon Press.

Mugglestone, Lynda (ed.) 2006. *The Oxford history of English*. Oxford: Oxford University Press.

Nineteenth-century fiction on CD-ROM 2000. Cambridge: Chadwyck-Healey Ltd.

Partington, Alan 1993. Corpus evidence of language change the case of the intensifier. In Mona Baker, Gill Francis & Elena Tognini-Bonelli (eds.), *Text and technology: In honour of John Sinclair*, 177-92, Amsterdam: John Benjamins.

Schendl, Herbert 2001. *Historical linguistics (Oxford introduction to language study series)*. Oxford: Oxford University Press.

Sinclair, John 1991. *Corpus, concordance, collocation*. Oxford: Oxford University Press.

Stubbs, Michael 2001. *Words and phrases: Corpus studies of lexical semantics*. Oxford: Blackwell.

The Oxford English Dictionary on Compact Disc, 2nd edn. Macintosh Version. 1993. Oxford: Clarendon Press.

Notes on the tenses
in *The Romaunt of the Rose*-A and the original text

Tomoko Iwakuni

Abstract
Regarding the tenses in the former part of *The Romaunt of the Rose*, it can be seen that Chaucer translated the tenses in it in a way that was faithful to the original text written in Old French. Moreover, it is possible that he used *gan*s and impersonal verbs to express a combination of two past tenses (the preterit / *passé simple* and the imperfect / *imparfait*) in French, which has a different tense system from English. Furthermore, it is suggested that when Chaucer translated the French *subjonctif*, which is not strictly similar to the subjunctive in English, he used not only the subjunctive but also parentheses to show the modality of the *subjonctif* in French.

1. Introduction
1.1. The disparity between English and French
Chaucer himself wrote in *The Prologue to The Legend of Good Women* that he translated *The Romaunt of the Rose* from French into English. *The Romaunt of the Rose*, which was written earlier than *The Legend of Good Women* (1369?), is considered as a work of his early days and a faithful translation from the original octosyllabic *Le Roman de la Rose* in Old French. In this respect, we have to pay attention to the disparity between two languages.

One of the disparities between the original and Chaucer's text is that in tenses or moods. French is one of the Romance languages and has a different tense system from English, which belongs to the Germanic languages. For instance, English did not have the future tense originally. Hence, an auxiliary verb *will* is used to express the future. French, however, which is derived from Latin, has the future tense. In addition, the present form in French has the meaning of both the present and the present progressive. Meanwhile, the past tenses in French include the imperfect (the past as a *sequence*) and the preterit (*passé simple* / the past as a *point*)[1] and the conceptions of the two

---

[1]   The imperfect / *imparfait* is used to express a habit, a continuance of an action and a description in the past (the past as a *sequence*). The preterit /

past tenses do not exist in English. Additionally, the *conditionnel*[2] in French is almost the same as the subjunctive in English, and the *subjonctif*[3] in French is strictly dissimilar from the subjunctive in English.

In this paper I will examine how Chaucer translated Old French, which has different tenses and moods, into Middle English. The following survey is carried out on some scenes in the first part of *The Romaunt of the Rose* -A (lines 1-302 in the Benson edition). The lines correspond to lines 1-292 of the original Old French (the Lecoy edition). I will also consider that "waves" are made in the narrative by a combination of the tenses, based on the argument of Weinrich (1971).

1.2. Preceding studies

Weinrich (1971) suggests that in a frame story in the Middle Ages the imperfect tense and the preterit appear alternately to some degree. In addition, he claims that the combination of the two past tenses has a narrative effect: the preterit has the effect of indicating the foreground and the imperfect has the effect of indicating the background (158). Furthermore, Brinton (1996) indicates that "*Gan* … seems to be a narrative device used in foregrounded clauses to mark salient shifts or turns in the course of events" (77). There are 21 lines including *gan* in *The Romaunt of the Rose*-A. From the survey of the distribution of *gan* in the whole text, Iwakuni (2016) concludes that *gan* has a narrative function as Brinton suggests. Furthermore, Iwakuni points out a high possibility that Chaucer would substitute the combination of *gan* and the past tense for the combination of the preterit and the imperfect in Old French. It has become evident that *gan* is used as one of the devices for translation in that *gan* is placed in the foreground in the narrative (Iwakuni 2016).

---

passé simple is often used in literary language. It is used to express a fact in the past separated from the present (the past as a *point*).

[2] The *conditionnel* is used to express an unreal assumption.

[3] The *subjonctif* is used in an optative sentence, an imperative sentence, a sentence expressing a subjective view. Moreover, it is often used to express an unreal or real supposition in one's mind, feelings or a desire. In Old French, the *conditionnel* and *subjonctif* were not always correctly used.

1.3. The choice of texts

The Romaunt of the Rose by Chaucer consists of Fragments A, B, and C. At present it is concluded that only Fragment A is Chaucer's work. I deal with Fragment A and use the *The Riverside Chaucer* edited by Larry D. Benson (1987) in this paper. For the French version, I use the Lecoy edition in this paper. More than 250 manuscripts of *Le Roman de la Rose* in Old French survive, while only one manuscript of *The Romaunt of the Rose* in Middle English (MS Hunter 409) survives. In the academic arguments from the 19th century to the 21st century, the texts of Méon, Langlois and Lecoy are used and at present the text of Lecoy is mainly used.

2. The correspondence relation between the English and French texts in tenses[4]

2.1. The introductory part of the protagonist narrating dreams

First of all, I examine the opening scene where the protagonist's dreams sometimes come true (ll. 1-20). In the original text in Old French, the preterit[5] (*passé simple*) occurs twice, the indicative present twelve times, the indicative future once and the subjunctive present four times. In Chaucer's text (ll. 1-20) corresponding to the original, the indicative past occurs once, the indicative present seventeen times and the subjunctive present once.

As a first step, I examine the Old French lines. Shading is added to the part of the indicative present and a square is put around the part of the subjunctive present.

Chaucer's lines corresponding to the Old French lines 11-14 are as follows.

(1) Qui c'onques cuit ne qui que die
    qu'il est folor et musardie
    de croire que songes aviegne,
    qui se voudra, por fol m'en tiegne,   (11-14)[6]

---

[4] In this paper the tenses are treated to the exclusion of the infinitive.
[5] When the same verb occurs repeatedly, I count and write the number of times the verb occurs.
[6] cuit = think(s) / die = say(s) / est folor = is foolishness / aviegne = come(s), happen(s) / por fol tiegne = treat(s) as a fool. Some words are glossed ungrammatically to show exactly their meanings in the original.

(2) And whoso *saith* or *weneth* it *be*
    A jape, or elles nycete,
    To wene that dremes after *falle*,
    Let whoso lyste a fol me *calle*.   (11-14)

Concerning the parts in the indicative present, Chaucer only uses the present tense in the corresponding parts. In the lines corresponding to the lines with the subjunctive present (*cuit, die, aviegne, tiegne*[7]) in the original, Chaucer uses the indicative present (*weneth, saith, falle*). Whereas Chaucer uses the subjunctive present *be* in line 11, the indicative present *est* is used in the original line 12. In other words, the indicative in the reporting verb and the subjunctive in the reported speech in Chaucer correspond to the subjunctive in the reporting verb and the indicative in the reported speech in the original. It is probable that Chaucer indicates the subjective view expressed by the subjunctive in Old French by using *be*. In *The Romaunt of the Rose* the protagonist "I" narrates in a first-person narrative. Hence, the view is normally fixed by "I." Then, the subjunctive in Old French shows the modality of "I" that is his viewpoint.

2.2. The scene of the protagonist deciding to write a book on a dream

Next, I examine lines 21-48. In the scene, the protagonist decides to write a book on a dream for Rose.

In the original lines 21-44 corresponding to Chaucer's lines 21-48, the preterit occurs four times, the indicative imperfect four times, the indicative present[8] fifteen times and the subjunctive present four times. In Chaucer's lines 21-48 corresponding to the original lines 21-44, the indicative past occurs six times, the indicative present twenty times and the subjunctive present twice.

I first examine the Old French lines. Shading is added to the part of the indicative present and a square is put around the part of the subjunctive present. The part of the imperfect is underlined and the part of the preterit is double-underlined.

---

[7] *Calle* corresponding to *tiegne* is an infinitive.

[8] In fifteen occurrences of the indicative present, the perfect (*passé composé*) is used in two lines (29, 41). The perfect in lines 29 and 41 means the present. Hence, I considered two uses of *passé composé* as the present.

Notes on the tenses in *The Romaunt of the Rose*-A 83

(3) el point qu'Amors prent le paage
des jones genz, couchier m'aloie
une nuit, si con je sauloie,
et me dormoie mout forment,
et vi un songe en mon dormant
qui mout fu biaus et mout me plot;
mes en ce songe onques riens n'ot
qui tretot avenu ne soit
si con li songes recensoit.   (22-30)[9]

The indicative imperfect occurs for the first time here. The imperfect
and the preterit emerge alternately to some degree after this scene. The
imperfect is used in lines 23-25 and 30. The preterit is used in lines
26-29. Lines 26-29 mean that "I dreamt in my sleeping. It was very
beautiful and pleased me. (All things in the dream) came true (later)."
The subjunctive present is used in the relative clause in line 29. Additionally, lines 29-30 are written in the preterit with the enjambment.

Chaucer uses the indicative present in line 29, which corresponds to
the original line 29 with the subjunctive present.

(4) [...] I *wente* soone
To bedde, as I *was wont* to done,
And faste I *slepte*; and in slepyng
Me *mette* such a *swevenyng*
That *lyked* me wonders wel.
But in that sweven *is* never a del
That it *nys* afterward *befalle*,
Ryght as this drem *wol tel* us alle.   (23-30)

Concerning the other lines in this scene, Chaucer uses the past in lines
23-25 while the original used the imperfect. In Chaucer's line 30 *wol*
is used. Consequently, the future tense in this line does not accord with
the imperfect tense in the original line. From the second half of
Chaucer's line 25 to 27, Chaucer uses the past in the clauses where the
preterit is used in the corresponding original. Concerning line 28,
Chaucer uses the present, not according with the preterit in the original.

---

[9] prent le paage = take the feudal carges for transport / couchier m'aloie = I
went to sleep / sauloie = was accustomed / me dormoie = I slept / vi un
songe = dreamed a dream / fu biaus = was beautiful / plot = pleased /
onques riens n'ot = had not anything at all / avenu ne soit = is not happened
(come) / si con li songes recensoit = like the dream told

Excluding the discordance of the tenses in line 28, Chaucer uses the past in the clauses where the imperfect and the preterit are used in the original. Additionally, from the second half of Chaucer's line 25 to 27, Chaucer uses an impersonal *me mette, lyked*. The two impersonal verbs accord with the preterit *vi, plot* (ll. 26 and 27). Nakao (1972: 297) treats *mete(n)* as one of verbs that show psychological and physical phenomena. In Old French, the verbs *voir, songer, dormier* mean "to dream," although they are not impersonal but personal verbs. However, Chaucer uses *mette* as an impersonal as well as a personal verb in his works. Therefore, it is possible that the impersonal *mette* would give a psychological description in this work. Moreover, the impersonal *mette* focused on the interior of the protagonist "I."

2.3. The scene narrating the season in the dream

Next, I examine the scene in which the protagonist narrates the season in his dream (ll. 49-89). In the corresponding original lines 45-83, the indicative imperfect occurs four times, the indicative present 29 times and the subjunctive present once. In Chaucer's lines 49-89, the indicative past[10] occurs six times, the indicative present 29 times and the future tense once.

I first examine the original lines 45-47. These lines are written in the indicative present and the indicative imperfect. Shading is added to the indicative present. The indicative imperfect is underlined.

> (5) Avis m'<u>iere</u> qu'il <u>estoit</u> mais,
> il a ja bien .v. anz ou mais,
> qu'en may <u>estoie</u>, ce <u>sonjoie</u>,   (45-47)[11]

These lines mean that "it seems to me that it was May. Probably five years ago or so. I was in May in my dream." The following lines in Chaucer correspond to the original lines.

> (6) That it *was* May me *thoughte* tho —
> It *is* fyve yer or more ago —
> That it *was* May, thus *dremed* me,   (49-51)

---

[10] *Had* in "In which that wynter had it set" (62) is used as a part of the pluperfect. However, here I counted *had* as an instance of the indicative past.

[11] m'<u>iere</u> = me thought / <u>estoit</u> = was / li a .v. anz = it has five years / en may <u>estoie</u> = (I) was in May / <u>sonjoie</u> = (I) dreamed

The English text does not have a past tense corresponding exactly to the imperfect tense in the French text. Hence, Chaucer uses the past to correspond to the imperfect in the original. *M'iere* (45) in the original is an impersonal verb. Chaucer faithfully translates it into an impersonal *me thoughte* (49). However, whereas an impersonal verb is not used in the original line 47, Chaucer uses an impersonal *dremed me* in line 51. This may suggest that although the personal pronoun *me* functions as a rhyme word, Chaucer intentionally uses the impersonal verb. For about forty lines after *dremed me* in line 51, almost all the verbs are used in the present. The present verbs produce the effect of the dramatic present. It is quite possible that by putting the impersonal in the past tense in the line switching from the past to the present, Chaucer indicates the change of the scene.

In addition, in spite of some exceptions, both the original lines 45-83 and Chaucer's lines 49-89 are almost all written in the indicative present, showing that Chaucer faithfully translates the tenses in the original.

2.4. The scene of the protagonist going out

In this scene (ll. 90-134), the protagonist wakes up in his dream and goes out. In the original lines 84-128, the preterit appears six times, the indicative imperfect[12] eighteen times and the indicative present three times. In Chaucer lines 90-134 corresponding to the above original lines, the indicative past appears 28 times and the indicative present four times.

In the previous scenes, the present tense is often used. In this scene, however, both the original and Chaucer's text are seldom written in the present, only a few times. Instead, the original is written in the imperfect and the preterit, and Chaucer uses the past tense. In addition, *gan* first occurs in line 95. The subjunctive does not appear from *veille* (51) to *seüst* (167) for over a hundred lines in the original. Based on the argument of Weinrich, who claims that the background and the foreground are produced by the combination of the imperfect and the

---

[12] In the original lines 113-15, the *passé composé* (the pluperfect) is made by compounding the indicative imperfect verbs (*être* or *avoir*) and a past participle.

86   *Tomoko Iwakuni*

preterit, the combination can make the "waves" coming toward and going away from *je*, the protagonist, in the narrative. Moreover, in English, which does not distinguish the imperfect from the preterit, Chaucer may make the "waves" in the narrative by using *gan*s and the past tense.

I look into the original lines 86-96 and Chaucer's corresponding lines 92-102. Shading is added to the part of the indicative present, the part of the imperfect is underlined and the part of the preterit (*passé simple*) is double-underlined.

(7) songai une nuit que j'estoie.
    Lors m'iere avis en mon dormant
    qu'il iere matin durement;
    de mon lit tantost me levé,
    chauçai moi et mes mains lavé;
    lors trés une aguille d'argent
    d'un aguillier mignot et gent,
    si prins l'aguille a enfiler.
    Hors de vile oi talant d'aler
    por oïr des oisiaus les sons,
    qui chantent desus les buissons   (86-96)[13]

(8) Me *thought* a-nyght in my sleping,
    Right in my bed, ful redily,
    That it *was* by the morowe erly,
    And up I roos and *gan* me *clothe*.
    Anoon I wissh myn hondis bothe.
    A sylvre nedle forth I *drough*
    Out of an aguler queynt ynough,
    And *gan* this nedle *threde* anon,
    For out of toun *me list* to gon
    The song of briddes forto here
    That in thise buskes *syngen* clere.   (92-102)

In this scene the preterit and the imperfect alternately occur in the original. In Chaucer's corresponding lines, every verb is in the past tense. To accord with the preterit and the imperfect, the English text uses the past tense because of the difference of the tense system.

---

[13] songai = dreamed / estoire = was / m'iere en mon dormant= me thought in my sleeping / il iere matin = it was morning / chauçai = clothed / trés une aguille d'argent = took a silver needle / prins l'aguille a enfiler = took the needle to thread / oi talant d'aler = had a feeling of going / chantent = sing

First, I examine the original lines 87 and 94 corresponding to Chaucer's lines 92 and 100, in which his impersonal *me thought* (92) corresponds to *m'iere avis* (87). Both are written with an impersonal verb, but the imperfect tense is used in the original line 87, while *me list* (100) in the past tense corresponds to *oi talant* (94), in which *oi* is the preterit form. I looked at the tenses of verbs corresponding to Chaucer's past impersonal verbs in the 302 lines and found that a half of them are in the preterit and the other half are in the imperfect. Therefore, it seems unlikely that Chaucer puts an impersonal verb as a substitute for a preterit (*passé simple*) verb. Additionally, when *list* occurs with the first person pronoun, *list* is always impersonal in Chaucer's works. However, it is assumed that Chaucer combines a past impersonal verb and a past personal verb to avoid putting the past in lines monotonously, that is, it indicates that Chaucer uses the combination of an impersonal verb and a personal verb in place of the combination of the preterit and the imperfect in the original as a means for expressing "waves" in the narrative.

Next, I examine the original lines 90 and 93 corresponding to Chaucer's lines 95 and 99. In Chaucer's lines, *gan* occurs. For instance, *gan me clothe* (95) corresponds to *chauçai moi* (90), in which *chauçai* is a preterit (*passé simple*) form. In *The Romaunt of the Rose*-A, 85 percent of the *gan*s correspond to the preterit (*passé simple*) in the Old French lines (Iwakuni 2016). From this result, there is a high possibility that *gan* has a function of foregrounding and a narrative function as shown in Weinrich (1971: 158) and Brinton (1996: 67-83).

2.5. The scene of the protagonist describing statues of Coveitise and Avarice

First, I examine the scene in which the protagonist describes a statue of Coveitise on the wall (ll. 181-206). In the corresponding lines 169-94 in the original, the preterit (*passé simple*) appears twice, the imperfect once and the indicative present seventeen times. In Chaucer's lines, the indicative past occurs twice and the indicative present fifteen times.

The present tense is used almost entirely in the scene in both texts, whereas the past tense is used in the scene in which the protagonist describes Hate, Felony and Vilany (ll. 135-80 / the original ll. 129-68).

Hate, Felony and Vilany are statues on the outer wall, and Coveitise likewise. Furthermore, the four statues are seen from the protagonist's viewpoint. By using the past in the scene of describing Hate, Felony and Vilany and by using the present in the scene describing Coveitise, the poet creates "waves" in the narrative in the original text. Chaucer may be sensible of the "waves" in the narrative and make use of them. Moreover, after the subjunctive (*subjonctif*) present in the original line 51, the subjunctive does not appear for over 100 lines in the Old French text, until *seüst* and *deüst* in the subjunctive imperfect form appear again in lines 167 and 168. The subjunctive (*subjonctif*) is used in lines 167 and 168, in which the scenes change from the description of Vilany in the past to the description of Coveitise in the present. In addition, *seüst* and *deüst* are used as a couplet with emphasis. In the scenes, the time axis is changed from the past to the present. The addition of the subjunctive (*subjonctif*) expressing a subjective view creates another viewpoint out of the time axis. The subjunctive (*subjonctif*) is arranged impressively as a sign of a scenery shift.

Next, I examine the scene in which the protagonist describes a statue of Avarice (ll. 207-46). In the corresponding lines 195-234 in the original, the preterit appears four times, the indicative imperfect sixteen times, the subjunctive imperfect eight times, the indicative present once and the subjunctive present once. In Chaucer's lines, the indicative past appears twenty times, the subjunctive past five times, the indicative present five times and the subjunctive present once.

Whereas the scene of Coveitise is written in the present tense, the scene of Avarice is written in the past tense. The tense switches again. In the scene of Avarice (ll. 195-234) in the original text, the preterit (*passé simple*) and the imperfect are used alternately to some extent. Hence, it can be said that the "waves" in the narrative are made in this scene as well. Although the preterit and the imperfect are used in combination in the previous scenes, dynamic verbs in the imperfect may be used more often in this scene in order to describe Avarice's mean behavior in the background.

Additionally, the subjunctive (*subjonctif*) is used more often in this scene so as to describe the feelings of Avarice with meanness and to speak of unreal matters. It is likely to be a way of foregrounding in

Notes on the tenses in *The Romaunt of the Rose*-A   89

order to emphasize her feelings more than her behavior. The subjunctive is used eight times between line 221 and 231 in the original text. In these lines given below, a square is put around the parts of the subjunctive present and the subjunctive imperfect. In addition, the subjunctive imperfect is written in bold letters. The indicative imperfect is underlined. The preterit (*passé simple*) is double-underlined.

> (9) car sachiez que mout li **pesast**
> se cele robe point **usast**;
> car s'el **fust** usee et mauvaise,
> Avarice **eüst** grant mesaise
> de robe nueve et grant disete
> avant qu'ele **eüst** autre fete.
> Avarice en sa main tenoit
> une borse qu'el reponoit
> et qu'el nooit si durement
> qu'el **demorast** mout longuement
> avant qu'ele en **peüst** rien treire; (221-31)[14]

Next, I inspect Chaucer's lines 233-43 corresponding to the original lines 221-31. The indicative past is underlined. The subjunctive past is written in bold letters.

> (10) For *certeynly* it **were** hir loth
> To weren ofte that ilke cloth,
> And if it **were** *forwered*, she
> *Wolde have* ful gret necessite
> Of clothyng er she **bought** hir newe,
> Al **were** it bad of woll and hewe.
> This Avarice hild in hir hand
> A purs that heng by a band,
> And that she hidde and bond so stronge,
> Men must abyde wondir longe
> Out of that purs er ther *come* ought. (233-43)

It should be noticed that Chaucer uses the subjunctive in the passages in which the subjunctive (*subjonctif*) occurs in clusters in the original.

---

[14] sachiez = (you) know / li **pesast** = was important to her / **usast** = wore out / **fust** usee et mauvaise= (it) was used and bad / **eüst** mesaise de robe nueve = had suffered for new clothe / **eüst** autre fete = had made another / en sa main tenoit = hold in her hand / reponoit = hid / nooit = knotted, bonded / el **demorast** longuement = she was slowly for a long time / en **peüst** rien treire = could take out nothing from (purse)

90 Tomoko Iwakuni

In the original lines 167 and 168, in the passage changing from the scene of Vilany to the scene of Coveitise, the subjunctive is used. Except for lines 167 and 168, after the subjunctive is used in line 52, the subjunctive does not appear until line 209. In Chaucer's text, the first subjunctive appears in line 221: "Come s'el fust a chiens remese"[15] (209) (= as if she were put with dogs) corresponds to "as she were al with doggis torn" (221). After this line, the subjunctive appears in or around the passage in which the subjunctive (*subjonctif*) appears in the original text. In the original lines 221-26 and 230-31, the subjunctive is used. These lines correspond to Chaucer's lines 233-38 and 243, in which the subjunctive is used to express an unreal supposition.

2.6. The scene of the protagonist describing a statue of Envie
In the scene (ll. 247-302), the protagonist describes the personality of Envie. In the corresponding lines 235-92 in the original, the preterit (*passé simple*) appears twice, the indicative imperfect nine times, the subjunctive imperfect four times, the indicative present eleven times, the subjunctive present four times and the conditional present (*conditionnel présent*) three times. In Chaucer's lines 247-302, the indicative past appears sixteen times, the subjunctive past seven times, the indicative present 23 times, the subjunctive present once and an imperative once. In this scene in which Envie is described as jealous of other people's fortune, the subjunctive and the conditional are often used to express her inner qualities, and tenses change rapidly in the original. Furthermore, the conditional (*conditionnel*) first appears in the original lines 258, 272, and 276. In each line, *voudroit* (in the conditional) (= want, would) is used. *Voudroit* in the original corresponds to *wolde* in Chaucer's lines 270, 284, and 287, where the subjunctive past is used.

---

[15] *Fust*: the subjunctive imperfect.

Notes on the tenses in *The Romaunt of the Rose*-A   91

Table 1. The moods and the tenses in the original lines 235-92 and Chaucer's lines 247-302

Le Roman de la Rose	*The Romaunt of the Rose*
Preterit (*passé simple*) (235-41)	Indicative past (247-51)
	Indicative present (252-54)
Indicative present (242-50)	
	Subjunctive present (255)
Subjunctive present (251)	Indicative present (256-59)
Indicative present (251-56)	
	Subjunctive present (260-61)
	Indicative present (262)
	Imperative (263)
Subjunctive present (256-57)	Indicative present (263-69)
Conditional present (258)	
	Subjunctive past (270)
Subjunctive imperfect (259-60)	Indicative present (270)
	Indicative past (271)
Indicative present (260-69)	Indicative present (272-81)
Indicative imperfect (269)	
Subjunctive present (270-71)	Subjunctive past (282)
	Indicative present (281-83)
Conditional present (272)	Subjunctive past (284-88)
Indicative imperfect (273)	
Subjunctive imperfect (274-75)	
Conditional present (276-78)	
Preterit (*passé simple*) (279)	Indicative past (289-98)
Indicative imperfect (280)	
Subjunctive imperfect (281-82)	
Indicative imperfect (283)	
Subjunctive imperfect (284-85)	
Indicative imperfect (286)	
Preterit (*passé simple*) (287)	
Indicative imperfect (287-92)	
	Subjunctive past (299-300)
	Indicative past (301-02)

92 Tomoko Iwakuni

As shown in Table 1, in this scene the tenses and moods in the original and in Chaucer's text roughly accord with each other. In addition, Chaucer adds parentheses *trustith wel* (263) and *I dar seyn hardely* (270). The former is added to the corresponding original line in the subjunctive.[16] The latter is added to the corresponding original line in the conditional.[17] Moreover, *iwis* (ll. 279,[18] and 281[19]) is inserted in lines with the present. From line 251 to 281 in Chaucer's text, almost all the verbs are in the present. It seems that by adding the narrator's words, the "waves" of the narrative are weakened and strengthened.

3. Final remarks
This paper makes a comparison between *The Romaunt of the Rose*-A and the original text in Old French, concerning tenses and moods. The results of this research are as follows.
(1) Tenses in Chaucer's text generally correspond to those in the original.
(2) In the lines with the conditional in the original, the subjunctive past is used in all the corresponding lines in Chaucer's text.
(3) Chaucer translates the preterit (*passé simple*) and the imperfect into the past form. In addition, he sometimes uses the combination of *gan* or an impersonal verb written in the past and a verb written in the past to express the combination of the two past tenses in Old French.
(4) There is a possibility that Chaucer uses the subjunctive or a parenthesis to express the modality of the subjunctive (*subjonctif*) in the original.

Texts
Benson, Larry D. (ed.) 1987. *The Riverside Chaucer*. 3rd ed. Boston: Houghton Mifflin.

---

[16] *Sachiez que* (= (you) know that): the subjunctive present. "Car sachiez que mout la covient / estre iriee quant biens avient." (250-51) (= because you know that (it) is suitable for her / = (to) be depressed when (it) happens good).

[17] *Voudroit* (= want): the conditional present. "Car certes el ne voudroit mie / que biens venist nes a son pere." (258-59) (= of course she does not want at all / that it went well even for her father).

[18] *Fine* (= finishes): the indicative present. "Envie ne fine nule enre" (267) (= Envy never finishes for a moment).

[19] *Cuit que* (= think that): the indicative present. *Conoissoit* (= knew): the indicative imperfect. "Je cuit que s'ele conoissoit" (269) (= I think that if she knew).

Lecoy, Félix (ed.) 2009. *Le Roman de la Rose par Guillaume de Lorris and Jean de Meun* Tome I. Geneva: Champion.

References

Brinton, Laurel J. 1996. *Pragmatic markers in English: Grammaticalization and discourse functions.* Berlin: Mouton de Gruyter.

Iwakuni, Tomoko 2016. The tense marker in Chaucer's *The Romaunt of the Rose*-A. Unpublished master thesis, Hiroshima University.

Iwakuni, Tomoko 2016. Textual function of *gan* in *The Romaunt of the Rose-A. Hyogen gizyutu kenkyu* [Bulletin of the research center for the technique of representation] 11: 37-56.

Nakao, Toshio 1972. *Outline of English linguistics,* Vol. 9: *History of English II.* Tokyo: Taishukan.

Weinrich, Harald 1971. *Temps.* Verlag: W. Kohlhsmmer.

Interpreting different types of linguistic variation: *hit* and *it* in Middle English*

Yoko Iyeiri

Abstract
Although the pronominal system in English has undergone various changes in its history, the choice of forms in a single user's language tends to be relatively stable, at least in comparison to some other aspects of language, almost hindering intra-textual analyses within the variationist framework. The shift of the third person singular 'it' from *hit* to *it* in later Middle English is a case in point: some texts employ *hit* only, while others *it* alone. This paper shows that it is still possible to find some fifteenth-century texts where both forms are encountered, and that their detailed analyses can reveal the process of the establishment of *it* in the history of English. The distributional pattern of *hit* and *it* in Nicholas Love's *Speculum Vite Cristi* (1494), for example, differs from the situation found in some earlier fifteenth-century English texts, and different patterns reveal different stages of the shift from *hit* to *it*. It is safe to conclude that *hit* was more or less replaced by *it* by the end of the fifteenth century.

1. Introduction
Variation is a presupposed element in language change. It is always involved when language change takes place. Nevalainen & Raumolin-Brunberg (2005: 34) state: "It is hardly an exaggeration to say that the variationist framework has now become one of the standard methods in historical linguistics." They continue: "The variationist approach is based on the assumption that language change does not take place without variation" (p. 34). Indeed, an abundance of studies employ the framework of variation in linguistic analyses, especially in the field of syntax. The fact that syntactic changes are much slower than change in other aspects of language such as phonology and morphology makes the variationist methodology most suitable for syntactic analyses, since relevant syntactic changes are likely to manifest themselves in the form of frequencies.[1] This is applicable to a single user's language,

---

* This paper is in part based upon the work I presented at the FWF-JSPS Joint Seminar 2016, University of Salzburg.
[1] A number of studies have pointed out the difference between syntactic

where syntactic variabilities are likely to be encountered, perhaps reflecting the variabilities of his or her language community.[2]

Phonological, morphological, and lexical variabilities are, by contrast, less clearly visible in individual speakers or texts, although they certainly do exist, when relevant changes are in progress, in the language community. The choice of pronominal forms is, for example, often fairly consistent in a particular person's language. It is well known that Geoffrey Chaucer employs the loan pronoun *they* in the nominative but not in the oblique cases, where he employs forms inherited from Old English like *her* and *hem*. In this manner, his choice of forms for 'they' is consistent, while the environment of late Middle English in general displays variation between forms inherited from Old English and loans from Scandinavian. This is one of the reasons why quantitative methods are not often applied to the variation of pronominal forms used in a particular text.

This paper argues that quantitative analyses at the intra-textual level can, however, be of some significant value even when the variability concerned is fairly restricted, as illustrated by the development of pronominal forms.[3] This is especially the case with Middle English texts, which are extant today in the forms of manuscripts and incunabula (often based upon manuscripts), since their formation involved manual transcription (or type setting) by scribes (or compositors). When the language of the exemplar differs from his own, he can either stick to the forms in the exemplar or translate them into his form. The variability of his decision results in the variability of linguistic forms in the newly prepared text, even if his language does not always

---

changes and those in other aspects of language such as phonology and morphology. See, for instance, Aitchison & Agnihotri (1985: 3) and Mair & Leech (2006: 318).

[2] Bell (1984) refers to the correspondence between the variation in a speech community and the variation of a single speaker in it, saying: "Variation on the style dimension within the speech of a single speaker derives from and echoes the variation which exists between speakers on the 'social' dimension" (p. 151).

[3] Auer & Voeste (2012: 260) point to the general value of intra-textual investigation by saying: "This procedure is particularly useful for the detection of possible internal factors that trigger the choice of a variant."

include variable features. Assuming that detailed analyses of the variability of this kind will highlight the mechanisms involved in relevant language changes, I will discuss in this paper the third person neuter singular pronoun 'it,' and especially the alternation between *hit* and *it* in late Middle English.[4] The form *hit* goes back to Old English, while *it* arises with the dropping of *h* in Middle English. The focus will be placed on intra-textual variability between the two forms (subjective and objective forms only).[5]

2. The variability between *hit* and *it* and some previous studies

Although previous studies discussing the intra-textual variability between *hit* and *it* are not at all numerous, the overall process of the shift from *hit* to *it* in the history of English is known to this day.[6] The *Oxford English Dictionary* (s.v. *it*) attributes the loss of *h* to the Middle English period by saying:

> During the ME. [Middle English] period, *hit* lost its initial *h*, first when unemphatic, and at length in all positions, in Standard Eng.; dialectally, the *h* was preserved to a much later period, esp. in the north; and in Sc. *hit* is still the emphatic, and *it* (*'t*, *'d*) the unemphatic form.

Descriptions on the history of 'it' found in standard references are similar to this. Brook (1958: 126-27), for example, notes the major shift from *hit* to *it* in Middle English and the retention of *hit* until the sixteenth century. *The American Heritage College Dictionary* (p. 737) includes historical as well as dialectal descriptions, as in:

> Early in the history of English, speakers began to drop the *h* from *hit*,

---

[4] I will use the form *hit* as a cover term for all forms with initial *h* (*hit*, *hyt*, etc.) and *it* for all forms without initial *h* (*it*, *itt*, etc.). This practice is followed throughout this paper.

[5] The possessive form 'its' is not considered in this paper because its history involves a separate issue. On the other hand, the form *it self* has been counted as an example of *it* as it always appears with space between *it* and *self*, suggesting that the reflexive form has not been established in the period under analysis. For the gradual and relatively late development of forms with *self* in the history of English, see van Gelderen (2006: 167-68).

[6] Whereas previous studies focusing upon the shift from *hit* to *it* in the history of English are not numerous, the phenomenon of *h*-dropping in general in the history of English has been extensively discussed to this day. See, for example, Scragg (1970) and Milroy (1983).

particularly in unaccented positions, as in *I saw it yesterday*. Gradually, *h* also came to be lost in accented positions, although *hit* persisted in socially prestigious speech well into the Elizabethan period. Some relatively isolated dialects in Great Britain and the United States have retained *h*. But even in such places, *h* tends to be retained only in accented words ... Nowadays, *hit* is fading even in the most isolated dialect communities and occurs primarily among older speakers.

Hence the key period in terms of the shift from *hit* to *it* appears to be late Middle English, in which one would expect the increasing loss of *h*. On the whole, texts tend to display a fairly clear preference for either *hit* or *it* even in the midst of this linguistic change: Tajima (1976: 23-24) notes the consistent choice of *hit* in the Cotton Nero A.x. poems, although he refers to the variability between *hit* and *it* in Chaucer and Langland. While Runde (2010: 273-75) mentions the variability between *hit* and *it* in the Auchinleck manuscript, she also shows that Scribe 1 of the same manuscript employs *it* fairly consistently and Scribe 3 the form *hit*.

One of my earlier publications (Iyeiri 2013) also shows that the Cotton Tiberius version of the *Polychronicon* (Book VI) employs the older form *hit* only, while Caxton's *Polychronicon* (Book VI) chooses *it* at the rate of 96.1%.[7] Iyeiri (2013) also discusses some additional West Midland texts from the late Middle English period, including *St Nicholas*, which displays *it* at the rate of 94.3%, and *St George*, which shows no examples of *hit* and fifteen examples of *it*.

The first task for any intra-textual analysis of the alternation between *hit* and *it* in later Middle English is, therefore, to find a text with reasonable fluctuation between the two forms. Iyeiri (2013) focuses on the first two items in MS Pepys 2125, which display different manners of fluctuation between *hit* and *it* despite the fact that they were transcribed by the same scribe: *Chastising of God's Children* (hereafter *Chastising*) and *Pepysian Meditations on the Passion of Christ* (hereafter simply *Meditations*).[8] As I have found an additional

---

[7] Iyeiri (2013) investigates several fifteenth-century texts, including the two versions of the *Polychronicon*.

[8] The second text, whose edition is more or less ready for publication with the above-cited title (cf. Taguchi & Iyeiri, forthcoming), is referred to as *Meditacion* in Iyeiri (2013), as its title was tentative in 2013.

late Middle English text with an interesting manner of variability between *hit* and *it*, I will first of all conduct an intra-textual exploration of the variation by using this text and then compare and contrast the result with the cases of *Chastising* and *Meditations*. The additional text is Nicholas Love's *Speculum Vite Cristi* (printed by Wynkyn de Worde in 1494). [9] The conclusion of this paper will include some sociolinguistic discussion.

3. The attestations of *hit* and *it* in Nicholas Love's *Speculum Vite Cristi*

As mentioned above, the variability between *hit* and *it* is a characteristic phenomenon in the late Middle English period in general, but not necessarily within a particular single text in the same period. Nevertheless, it is possible to find texts with a reasonable mixture of forms with and without *h*, of which Nicholas Love's *Speculum Vite Cristi*, printed in 1494, is one. Unlike *Chastising* and *Meditations* in MS Pepys 2125, both explored in Iyeiri (2013), Love's *Speculum Vite Cristi* is a printed text, which involves compositors rather than scribes. Although it will eventually be necessary to take into consideration the entire process of the production of the book, examining the influence of the exemplar and the work of the compositor, I will leave this for future opportunities. The present paper will simply concentrate upon the alternation between *hit* and *it* in the text and its possible sociolinguistic implications. The alternation of the two forms itself provides some interesting hints as to the development of *it* in the history of English.

As illustrated by (1) to (3), examples of forms with and without *h* are available in *Speculum Vite Cristi*:[10]

(1) whan *hit* shold be moste wondringe to him   (*Speculum Vite Cristi*)

(2) that *hyt* myght so be spoken or done   (*Speculum Vite Cristi*)

(3) But *it* is a likynge syghte to vs   (*Speculum Vite Cristi*)

(1) and (2) include *hit*, the traditional form with *h*, while (3) illustrates

---

[9] For some details of this text, see Hellinga (2009: 14).
[10] All examples of *Speculum Vite Cristi* in this paper are cited from the *Early English Books Online*. Italics in the citations are mine.

the use of *it*, the newer form which has undergone the dropping of initial *h*. The table below shows the frequencies and proportions of the two forms in *Speculum Vite Cristi*:[11]

Table 1. The occurrences of *hit* and *it* in *Speculum Vite Cristi*

	hit	*it*	Total
Speculum Vite Cristi	66 (8.1%)	751 (91.9%)	817

Table 1 gives the impression that *Speculum Vite Cristi* is another text showing a fairly consistent use of *it* rather than *hit*. The proportion of *it* in the text exceeds 90%. A closer look at the distribution of the two forms in the text, however, reveals that the alternation is worthy of further detailed exploration. The distribution of the limited number of *h*-forms is skewed towards the beginning of the text as displayed in Figure 1:

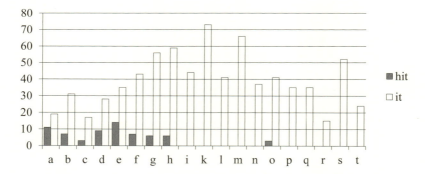

Figure 1. The occurrences of *hit* and *it* in different quires of *Speculum Vite Cristi* (raw frequencies)

As shown in this graph, most examples of *hit* are attested in the first eight quires. In other words, there is a clear intra-textual contrast between the former half and the latter half. It is also noteworthy that

---

[11] The 66 examples of *hit* in this table include nine examples of the variant form <hyt>. Following the practice of this paper, *hit* is used as the representative form throughout (cf. Note 4). By contrast, *it* does not present any orthographic variants in this particular text.

the proportion of the use of *hit* within the total of *hit* and *it* combined is the largest in the first quire. In addition, the fairly restricted occurrences of *hit* in quires f, g and h suggest that the use of *hit* gradually recedes as the text proceeds. To ascertain the exact factors causing this distribution of *hit* and *it* in this text, it is necessary to investigate its textual tradition, which itself is a major project. All one can say at this stage is that it is probably due to the influence of the exemplar and that this influence is particularly strong in the first half of the text. Apparently, the usual form in the compositor's language was *it* rather than *hit*.

Incidentally, there are two rather isolated examples of *hit* in quire o:

(4) For they vnderstode *hit* that tyme   (*Speculum Vite Cristi*)

(5) But whether soo *hit* be in one maner or in other
(*Speculum Vite Cristi*)

It is again difficult to tell the exact reason for the abrupt occurrence of *hit* in this later part of the text. Neither of the examples is encountered in line-final position, and therefore the abundance of space does not seem to be the reason for their occurrence.

In the following sections, I will compare and contrast the intra-textual variability of *hit* and *it* in *Speculum Vite Cristi* with the variability of the same forms in *Chastising* and *Meditations* in MS Pepys 2125 (referring to my earlier work). The discussion will demonstrate that different sociolinguistic implications are involved in different types of intra-textual variability between the two forms.

4. Further discussion on the distribution of *hit* and *it* in *Speculum Vite Cristi*

As shown in the above section, *hit* is attested to a noticeable extent in the first half of *Speculum Vite Cristi*, while it is virtually absent in the latter half of the same text, although the sporadic occurrence of two examples with *h* is attested in quire o. Supposing that the occurrence of *hit* in earlier quires of the text shows the influence of the exemplar, the text displays a fairly clear case of progressive translation. The concept, as described below in the quoted passage from *Linguistic Atlas of Late Mediaeval English* (*LALME*) (I, p. 15), is usually applied to scribes and consequently to medieval manuscripts, but can probably be extended to printed texts such as *Speculum Vite Cristi*:[12]

> For the first few folios or so, he [a scribe] produces a text of which the language is not his own, but that of his exemplar. As he gets used to his copy-text, so he converts with increasing fluency the language of the subsequent text into his own. It may well be that in many such cases what happens is that the scribe moves from copying in a purely visual way to copying via "the mind's ear".

Obviously, the scribe here will correspond to a compositor in the case of printed texts. Unless the virtual disappearance of *hit* in the latter part of the text is attributed to the same feature in the exemplar itself, *Speculum Vite Cristi* illustrates in a way a model case of progressive translation, showing that the *h*-forms of 'it' were no longer part of the active (as opposed to passive) inventory of the compositor's language. Whereas he inherits *hit* from the exemplar at the beginning of the text, he gradually shifts to his own form, namely *it*, in the process of setting the text, eventually reaching, after eight quires, the stage where he consistently employs *it* with two minor exceptions. It is safe to conclude from the distribution of *hit* and *it* in *Speculum Vite Cristi* that the use of *it* was more or less established by the end of the fifteenth century, when this text was prepared, although sporadic examples of *hit* were available mainly as inheritances from exemplars in the contemporary linguistic environment. The form *hit* was probably acceptable but not usual by this stage.

This is interesting, since my earlier study shows that the employment of *it* rather than *hit* was not fully established in the first half of the fifteenth century, though of course the use of *it* had certainly made a significant progress by this time. Iyeiri (2013) carries out a full survey of the occurrences of *hit* and *it* in *Chastising* and *Meditations*, both of which are datable to the period between 1400 and 1450, probably closer to 1400.[13] *Chastising*, where the ratios of *hit* and *it* are

---

[12] *LALME* (I, p. 16) distinguishes a progressive translation from a composite text by saying that the transition is progressive in the former. To draw a line between the two is not always easy in the analysis of texts, though in theory they are both clear concepts. I would consider the gradual loss of *h*-forms in *Speculum Vite Cristi* a case of progressive translation.

[13] For the dating of these two texts, see Iyeiri (2013) and also Taguchi & Iyeiri (forthcoming).

Interpreting different types of linguistic variation 103

around 50% each,[14] illustrates another case of progressive translation, the employment of *it* being increasingly frequent in the latter half of the text. The difference between *Chastising* and *Speculum Vite Cristi* is that in the former the scribe reserves the older form *hit* for special occasions such as sentence-initial positions even after he switches to his own form without *h* (Iyeiri 2013: 345-47). Hence, there exists a stylistic implication in the choice between *hit* and *it* in *Chastising*. This is no longer the case in *Speculum Vite Cristi*, which was prepared about half a century later.

It is also worth mentioning that *Meditations*, which was transcribed by the same scribe as *Chastising*, displays a significantly different situation. Unlike *Chastising*, the use of *hit* or the older form is predominant in *Meditations*, where *hit* accounts for nearly 95% of the relevant examples. It gives only six examples of *it* in total, while it yields 93 examples of *hit*. More interestingly, this text shows the opposite case of progressive translation, in that three of the six examples of *it* are attested on the first page of the text and that *hit* is the form used throughout. Apparently, the scribe introduced his own form without *h* at the beginning of the text as a trial, but he decided to stick to the form in the exemplar after the first page (Iyeiri 2013: 345-47). The different behaviours of the same scribe between *Chastising* and *Meditations* may be ascribable to the difference of the exemplars or the difference in the text types.[15] In any case it is clear from the state of affairs in the two texts that the form *hit* was acceptable and sometimes even a prestigious variant for the scribe, although he used the newer form *it* under usual circumstances. The mixed occurrence of *hit* and *it* in *Chastising* and *Meditations* proves, though in different ways, the fact that there was still a stylistic meaning in the choice of the two forms when they were transcribed.

This is no longer the case with the compositor of *Speculum Vite*

---

[14] In my earlier publication, I understated the number of relevant examples by missing a few, though this does not affect the argument of the paper (Iyeiri 2013). The rectified statistics show that there are 182 examples of *hit* vs. 178 examples of *it* in *Chastising*.

[15] Although both texts are religious, the text type of *Meditations* is probably stricter as a genre, as it describes the life of Jesus Christ.

Cristi, where he shuns the older form with *h* as the text proceeds without hesitation. In fact, *Speculum Vite Cristi* belongs to the same text category as *Meditations*, but a significant gap exists between the two texts in respect of the scribe's or compositor's behaviour towards the *h*-form. This is most likely due to the gap between their dates in transcription or compilation.

Incidentally, in Iyeiri (2013) I investigate *hit* and *it* in *St Nicholas* drawing material from ICAMET, where I do not describe any detailed distributions of the two forms except that the text yields two examples of *hit* (5.7%) and 33 examples of *it* (94.3%). An investigation of this text afresh reveals that one of the two examples of *hit* is found on the first folio, almost marking the beginning of the text, while the other example of *hit* is found towards the end of the text, though not exactly on the last folio. The exceptional occurrence of *hit* in this text is rather difficult to interpret. It is possible that the scribe still reserved the older form *hit* for special occasions, namely at the opening and closing of the text. On the other hand, it is also possible to regard the first *hit* simply as an initial trial case of representing the exemplar form, which the scribe immediately stops, though an exceptional example appears towards the end of the text by accident, as in the case of *Speculum Vite Cristi*. *St Nicholas* goes back to around 1450 according to the dating of it in ICAMET, namely not as old as *Chastising* and *Meditations* but older than *Speculum Vite Cristi*. The linguistic situation in terms of the distribution of *hit* and *it*, especially in terms of where the older form occurs, is also intermediate between the group of *Chastising* and *Meditations* (both going back to the earlier period of the fifteenth century) and *Speculum Vite Cristi* (1494). Judging from all these cases, it is probably safe to conclude that the major shift to the established use of *it* instead of *hit* was reached around the middle of the fifteenth century or thereafter. *Hit* was clearly a relatively unusual form by the end of the fifteenth century.

5. Discussion on sociolinguistic implications and conclusion

Pronominal forms are considered to be relatively stable, at least in comparison to other variabilities such as syntactic variation, within a single author's language even under circumstances where the shifting of forms is in progress.[16] As the above discussion has demonstrated, however, there are some late Middle English texts yielding forms with and without *h* for 'it' in a mixed manner. One of the contributions of the present paper, though modest, is simply to show that *Speculum Vite Cristi*, published in 1494 by Wynkyn de Worde, is another text of this kind. The discussion above has shown that the distribution of *hit* and *it*, when they occur in a mixed manner in a single text, can have some stylistic implications and that their detailed analyses help understand the shift from *hit* to *it* in later Middle English as a whole. *Speculum Vite Cristi* displays a simple case of progressive translation whereby the older form *hit* gradually recedes to be virtually absent in the latter half with only two sporadic exceptions. In the later part of the text, on the whole, the awareness of the compositor no longer affects the choice between *hit* and *it*, perhaps because *hit* was too old-fashioned for him.

The difference between *Speculum Vite Cristi* (1494) and the other three Middle English texts mentioned above (all going back to the fifteenth century) is that the choice of *hit* rather than *it* was still a scribal conscious activity in at least two of the latter three, and probably in all three. The difference seems to derive from the difference in the dates of their production, showing that the use of *hit* was still not unusual in the first half of the fifteenth century as discussed above.

From a sociolinguistic perspective, it is a matter of interest that exemplars are in one way or another functional in showing linguistic norms. They were perhaps different from Modern English norms, which are often linked to the concept of stigmatization, but they clearly contributed to the slowing down of ongoing linguistic changes. This is especially the case with religious texts, where scribes often made an effort to transcribe the text following the exemplars closely. While the introduction of linguistic norms in the real sense is considered to have taken place only in the Modern English period, they certainly did exist in the Middle Ages, though in different ways, when the production of texts usually meant the copying of older texts. In written English at

---

[16] Here I refer to morphological aspects of pronominal forms. The choice of second person singular and plural forms involves matters of discourse. It does vacillate within a single author's language, depending on social settings.

least, language users tended to be aware of their own linguistic behaviours, although it is also true to say that they often translated the language of exemplars into their own as frequently pointed out about medieval scribes.[17] As Milroy (2005) argues, all linguistic changes are social. Irregularities as observed in the four texts explored in the present paper are an annoyance for linguists, but focusing on sociolinguistic aspects of the variability between *hit* and *it* in some Middle English texts, in fact, will adduce additional hints to the understanding of the development of the two pronominal forms in the history of English.

References

Aitchison, Jean & Rama Kant Agnihotri 1985. "I deny that I'm incapable of not working all night": Divergence of negative structures in British and Indian English. In Roger Eaton, *et al.* (eds.), *Papers from the 4th International Conference on English Historical Linguistics, Amsterdam, 10-13 April, 1985*, 3-14. Amsterdam: John Benjamins.

The American Heritage College Dictionary 2002. 4th edition. Boston: Houghton Mifflin.

Auer, Anita & Anja Voeste 2012. Grammatical variables. In Juan Manuel Hernández-Campoy & Juan Camilo Conde-Silvestre (eds.), *The handbook of historical sociolinguistics*, 253-70. Malden: Wiley-Blackwell.

Bell, Allan 1984. Language style as audience design. *Language in Society* 13: 145-204.

Brook, George L. 1958. *A history of the English language*. London: André Deutsch.

Corrie, Marilyn 2006. Middle English: Dialects and diversity. In Lynda Mugglestone (ed.), *The Oxford history of English*, 86-119. Oxford: Oxford University Press.

Duggan, Hoyt N. 1997. Meter, stanza, vocabulary, dialect. In Derek Brewer & Jonathan Gibson (eds.), *A companion to the* Gawain-*poet*, 221-42. Woodbridge: D. S. Brewer.

Early English Books Online. <http://eebo.chadwyck.com/home>. Last accessed August 2017.

van Gelderen, Elly 2006. *A history of the English language*. Amsterdam: John Benjamins.

---

[17] Referring to *LALME* and some *LALME*-related studies, Duggan (1997: 221) states: "Middle English scribes frequently engaged in dialect translation, copying their exemplars not letter for letter but fluently translating from one dialect into their own." This is considered to be particularly common in the fourteenth and fifteenth centuries (Corrie 2006: 102).

Hellinga, Lotte 2009. *Printing in England in the fifteenth century: E. Gordon Duff's bibliography, with supplementary descriptions, chronologies and a census of copies*. London: The British Library.

Iyeiri, Yoko 2013. The pronoun *it* and the dating of Middle English texts. In Michio Hosaka, Michiko Ogura, Hironori Suzuki & Akinobu Tani (eds.), *Phases of the history of English: Selection of papers read at SHELL 2012*, 339-50. Frankfurt am Main: Peter Lang.

LALME = *A linguistic atlas of late mediaeval English*. See McIntosh, Samuels & Benskin (1986).

McIntosh, Angus, Michael L. Samuels & Michael Benskin 1986. *A linguistic atlas of late mediaeval English*. 4 vols. Aberdeen: Aberdeen University Press.

Mair, Christian & Geoffrey Leech 2006. Current changes in English syntax. In Bas Aarts & April McMahon (eds.), *The handbook of English linguistics*, 318-42. Malden: Blackwell.

Milroy, James 2005. Variability, language change, and the history of English. *International Journal of English Studies* 5(1): 1-11.

Milroy, Jim 1983. On the sociolinguistic history of /h/-dropping in English. In Michael Davenport, Erik Hansen & Hans Frede Nielsen (eds.), *Current topics in English historical linguistics*, 37-53. Odense: Odense University Press.

Nevalainen, Terttu & Helena Raumolin-Brunberg 2005. Sociolinguistics and the history of English: A survey. *International Journal of English Studies* 5: 33-58.

Oxford English Dictionary. <http://www.oed.com>. Last accessed August 2017.

Runde, Emily 2010. Reexamining orthographic practice in the Auchinleck manuscript through study of complete scribal corpora. In Robert A. Cloutier, *et al.* (eds.), *Studies in the history of the English language V: Variation and change in English grammar and lexicon: Contemporary approaches*, 265-87. Berlin: Mouton de Gruyter.

Scragg, Donald G. 1970. Initial *h* in Old English. *Anglia* 88: 165-96.

Taguchi, Mayumi & Yoko Iyeiri (eds.) (forthcoming). *Pepysian Meditations on the Passion of Christ: Edited from Cambridge, Magdalene College, MS Pepys 2125*. Heidelberg: Winter.

Tajima, Matsuji 1976. *Gawain*-poet no sakuhin niokeru chusei ninshou daimeishi *hit* no yoho [The neuter person pronoun *hit* in the works of the *Gawain*-poet]. *Linguistic Science* (Kyushu University) 11/12: 23-36.

High feasts in Anglo-Saxon calendars: Contexts for the *Menologium**

Kazutomo Karasawa

Abstract

At the end of the Old English calendar poem *Menologium*, the poet says that his work lists the feasts that must be observed widely in England under the reign of the Saxon king. Its very close prose analogue, called prose *Menologium*, lists a very similar set of feasts. In Anglo-Saxon liturgical calendars, on the other hand, important feasts are often marked in one way or another, but the choice of high feasts considerably differs from calendar to calendar. Yet if we compare all the calendars extant from Anglo-Saxon England, we can see fairly clearly which feasts were widely observed in Anglo-Saxon England since some feasts are marked obviously much more frequently than others. Based on a statistical survey of Anglo-Saxon calendars, I shall provide a list of immovable feasts widely observed in late Anglo-Saxon England. The prose and the verse *Menologium* cover most of the feasts in this list, which shows that they provide a good summary of Anglo-Saxon feasts widely observed in late Anglo-Saxon England.

1. Introduction

Some legal texts imply that there are a set of important feasts which were traditionally observed widely in late Anglo-Saxon England; an example occurs in the laws promulgated during the reign of King Æthelred:[1]

> 14. And sancta Marian freolstide ealle worðian man georne, ærest mid fæstene 7 siððan mid freolse.
>
> §1. 7 to æghwilces apostoles heahtida fæste man 7 freolsige; butan to Philippus 7 Iacobus freolse ne beode we nan fæsten [for þam eastorlian freolse].

---

* This article is a revised version of my paper of the same title read at the 5th International Conference of Language, Culture and Society in Russian/ English Studies held at the Institute of English Studies, School of Advanced Study, University of London on 6 August 2014. I would like to express my thanks to Professors Jane Roberts and Keiko Ikegami for giving me an opportunity to read a paper in this conference. I would also like to thank Professor Eric G. Stanley for presiding over my presentation.

[1] Similar instances are found in VI Æthelred 22.1-4, 23, VIII Æthelred 16, and I Cnut 14.1.

110   *Kazutomo Karasawa*

15. Elles oðre freolsa 7 fæstena healde man georne, swa swa þe heoldon þa ðe betst heoldon.

16. 7 sancte Eadwardes mæssedæg witan habbað gecoran þæt man freolsian sceal ofer eal Englaland on xv kl. Apr.[2]   (VÆthelred 14-16)

"14. And all St Mary's festivals shall be zealously honoured, first with fasting and afterwards with festivity. §1. And at the festival of every apostle there shall be fasting and festivity, except that at the festival of Philip and James we enjoin no fast [because of the Easter festival]. 15. Otherwise, festivals and fasts shall be strictly observed in accordance with the highest standards of the past. 16. And the authorities have decided that St Edward's festival shall be celebrated throughout England on the 18th of March."

Several feasts are specified as in Clauses 14 and 16, but there are *oðre freolsa* "other festivals" which are not specified but must be "strictly observed in accordance with the highest standards of the past." As far as I am aware, it is not known exactly which were high feasts widely observed in those days. However, in many Anglo-Saxon calendars, important immovable feasts are marked in one way or another, and it may be possible to sort out Anglo-Saxon high feasts by comparing those feasts marked in calendars. Thus in this paper, I shall list Anglo-Saxon immovable high feasts, basing myself on the evidence in calendars. In addition to the calendars, the Old English calendar poem *Menologium* uniquely preserved in London, British Library, Cotton Tiberius B.i. and its close prose analogue, the prose *Menologium* recorded in London, British Library, Harley 3271 and Cambridge, Corpus Christi College, MS 422, may provide more clues to solve the problem. In the latter half of this article, I shall compare the feasts mentioned in the prose and the verse *Menologium* with those gleaned from the calendar evidence. In this process, I shall also discuss the nature of the prose and the verse *Menologium* and ask how they are related to each other and to the Anglo-Saxon calendar tradition.

2. High feasts marked in Anglo-Saxon calendars

Twenty seven Anglo-Saxon calendars are extant as listed in the Appendix, and twenty three of them are complete while four are fragmentary (and I exclude the fragmentary ones from my discussion

---

[2] The Old English text and the translation are quoted from Robertson (1925: 84-85).

High feasts in Anglo-Saxon calendars: Contexts for the *Menologium* 111

below).[3] Among the twenty three complete calendars, twenty mark important feasts in various ways as listed here:

Marking by the sign of the cross   (Calendars 4, 6, 13, 24)[4];

Marking by the letter F   (Calendars 7, 9, 19);

Marking by capitals and/or coloured letters
(Calendars 8, 11-13, 17, 18, 20-23, 27);

Marking by metrical entries   (Calendar 5);[5]

Markings by a combination of two or more of these options
(Calendars 7, 9, 13, 19, 24).[6]

Clearly, many calendars mark important feasts in various ways, but none of the twenty calendars mark exactly the same set of feasts. In fact, when consulting only a few calendars, it is difficult to know which feasts were widely held as of primary importance, since some calendars mark them only very sparingly and/or irregularly while others seemingly mark them more or less regularly but always differently from others. The following table indicates how many feasts are marked in each of the extant Anglo-Saxon calendars, and one can see how they differ:

Calendar no.	Marked Feasts	Calendar no.	Marked Feasts
4	36	17	61
5	27	18	53
6	33	19	51
7	34	20	35
8	13	21	54
9	37	22	44
11	32	23	15
12	35	24	41
13	15	25	33
16	12	27	10

---

[3] For details of these calendars, see Rushforth (2008: 18-54), and also Wormald (1934).

[4] Hereafter I shall refer to calendars by the number indicated in the Appendix.

[5] For metrical entries marking high feasts, see Rushforth (2008: 22-23).

[6] Two or more different ways of marking can coexist in one calendar, which is why some calendars are mentioned more than once in this table.

Yet if we compare all the twenty complete calendars, we can see fairly clearly which high feasts were widely observed in Anglo-Saxon England; some feasts are marked obviously much more frequently than others, and those marked more frequently seem more important than others, even if they may not be marked in some calendars. As a result of a statistical survey based on the twenty Anglo-Saxon calendars,[7] it seems that those thirty four feasts listed in the following table are of primary importance in eleventh-century Anglo-Saxon England:

	Feast	Attestations			V Æth	VM	PM
		9-10C	11C	total			
1	Circumcision (1 Jan)	5	11	16	-	+	-
2	Epiphany (6 Jan)	6	10	16	-	+	-
3	Purification (2 Feb)	4	11	15	+	+	+
4	St Mathias (24 Feb)	5	10	15	+	+	+
5	St Gregory (12 March)	5	12	17	-	+	+
6	St Edward the Martyr (17 or 18 March)	1	8	9	+	-	-
7	St Cuthbert (20 March)	4	8	12	-	-	+
8	St Benedict (21 March)	6	8	14	-	+	+
9	Annunciation (25 March)	5	10	15	+	+	+
10	SS Philip and James (1 May)	3	9	11	+	+	+
11	Invention of the Holy Cross (3 May)	5	5	10	-	+	+
12	St Dunstan (19 May)	1	7	8	-	-	-
13	St Augustine of Canterbury (26 May)	5	7	12	-	+	+
14	Nativity of St John the Baptist (24 June)	4	11	15	-	+	+
15	SS Peter and Paul (29 June)	4	9	13	+	+	+
16	St Paul (30 June)	5	9	14	-	-	+
17	St James (25 July)	5	11	16	+	+	+
18	St Laurence (10 Aug)	6	11	17	-	+	+
19	Assumption (15 Aug)	4	14	18	+	+	+
20	St Bartholomew (24 Aug)	3	9	12	+	+	+
21	Decollation of St John the Baptist (29 Aug)	5	8	13	-	+	+
22	Nativity of St Mary (8 Sept)	4	13	17	+	+	+

---

[7] For details about this statistical survey, see Karasawa (2015a: 164-79).

23	St Matthew (21 Sept)	5	9	14	+	+	+
24	Michaelmas (29 Sept)	6	10	16	-	+	+
25	SS Simon and Jude (28 Oct)	5	10	15	+	+	+
26	All Saints' Day (1 Nov)	4	12	16	-	+	+
27	St Martin (11 Nov)	5	10	15	-	+	+
28	St Clement (23 Nov)	5	7	12	-	+	+
29	St Andrew (30 Nov)	6	10	16	+	+	+
30	St Thomas (21 Dec)	5	10	15	+	+	+
31	Christmas (25 Dec)	6	14	20	-	+	+
32	St Stephen (26 Dec)	5	11	16	-	-	-
33	St John (27 Dec)	5	11	16	-	-	-
34	Holy Innocents (28 Dec)	5	10	15	-	-	-

As shown in the third column from the right in this table, the list includes all the fourteen feasts whose strict observance is regulated in V Æthelræd 14-16 quoted above, while it also includes twenty one others. Nearly a hundred other feasts are marked much less frequently,[8] while many feasts are never marked; the high status of the feasts listed here is statistically fairly prominent. However, the feast of St Edward the Martyr (who died in 978) and the feast of St Dunstan (who died in 988) are exceptional in that they are scarcely marked as high feasts in the calendars compiled before the end of the tenth century; because of the late dates of the deaths of these saints, they are established as high feasts only in the eleventh century in accordance with the promulgation of V Æthelred in 1008[9] and the promulgation

---

[8] Among these feasts, the following are marked relatively frequently: Translation of St Judoc (9 Jan, 4x); Conversion of St Paul (25 Jan, 5x); Chair of St Peter (22 Feb, 6x); Resurrection (based on a tradition established in Gaul, 27 Mar, 7x); St Guthlac (11 Apr, 3x); St Ælfeah (19 Apr, 5x); Ascension (forty days after the Gallic Resurrection on 27 Mar, 4/5 May, 4x); St Eadburga (15 June, 3x); St Alban (22 June, 4x); St Ætheldryth (23 June, 3x); St Peter (29 June, 5x); St Swithun (2 July, 5x); Translation and Ordination of St Martin (4 July, 3x); Translation of St Benedict (11 July, 7x); St Kenelm (17 July, 3x); St Christopher (25 July, 4x); St Oswald (5 Aug, 4x); St Adrian (8 Sept, 3x); St Menna (11 Nov, 4x); St Briccius (13 Nov, 4x); Translation of St Benedict (4 Dec, 3x); St Nicholas (6 Dec, 3x); St Anastasia (25 Dec, 3x); St Ecgwin (30 Dec, 3x). For more details, see Karasawa (2015a: 166-79).

[9] For the date of V Æthelred, see Liebermann (1903: 240-41) and Robertson (1925: 84-85).

of I Cnut in the 1020s.[10]

The evidence in the calendars suggests that as far as immovable feasts are concerned, those listed in the table above were widely held as high feasts in the eleventh century, while the two feasts of the later saints are not found in the list of high feasts widely observed by the end of the tenth century.

3. Feasts listed in the prose and the verse *Menologium*

The *Menologium* poet concludes his work with the following words:

> Nu ge findan magon,
> haligra tiida   þe man healdan sceal,
> swa bebugeð gebod   geond Brytenricu
> Sexna kyninges   on þas sylfan tiid.[11]   (*Menologium* 228b-31)
> "Now you can find the feasts of the holy saints that should be observed as far as the command of the king of the Saxons extends over the kingdoms of Britain at this very time."

As shown in the second column from the right in the table of Anglo-Saxon high feasts in the previous section, the verse *Menologium* actually covers most of the high feasts widely observed in late Anglo-Saxon England. Though some consider the criterion for selecting the entries of the poem to be obscure,[12] it seems fairly clear that the poet includes the high feasts widely observed in England under the reign of the Saxon king at the time of composition, as he himself says in the concluding remark. The passage also reminds us of the laws such as those quoted at the beginning of this article, and some scholars actually suggest that the king's command mentioned here may be V Æthelred 14-16.[13] As shown in the table above, however, the *Menologium* mentions neither the feast of St Edward the Martyr nor that of St

---

[10] For the date of I Cnut, see Liebermann (1903: 298-99) and Robertson (1925: 168-69).

[11] The Old English text and its translation are both taken from Karasawa (2015a: 84-85).

[12] For instance, Amodio (2014: 311) writes that "Some of the days highlighted, including the Nativity, the Annunciation, and the Assumption of the Virgin Mary are of obvious importance, but the poet's reasons for selecting the other events and days he does, including the feast of the Circumcision, and the days for saints such as Laurence, Augustine of Canterbury, and Bartholomew, are more obscure."

[13] See Imelmann (1902: 39-40 and 53).

High feasts in Anglo-Saxon calendars: Contexts for the *Menologium* 115

Dunstan, which suggests that it follows the older tradition current before the laws of Æthelred and Cnut were promulgated in the early eleventh century;[14] in fact, these feasts are marked as important feasts in the majority of the calendars compiled in England in the eleventh century.

As also shown in the table above, the same may be said about the prose *Menologium*. Although there are some minor differences in the choice of feasts between the verse and the prose *Menologium*, these two analogues are basically the same in that they provide a list of high feasts current before the end of the tenth century. Both prose and verse *Menologium* omit some high feasts but their omission seems largely based on certain principles. The prose *Menologium* lists all the high feasts except those at Christmastide, i.e. from Christmas (25 December) to the Epiphany (6 January). This may suggest that the compiler of the prose *Menologium* omits the details of Christmastide, which is represented by its core feast, Christmas. By this process, the compiler can focus on the most basic course of the liturgical year for the sake of simplicity (the extant two versions of the prose *Menologium* are both recorded in eleventh-century manuscripts seemingly intended for elementary-level students of grammar and computus).[15] In fact, there are no calendars in which none of the five high feasts after Christmas are marked as high feasts, and it is most probable that the omission of them all in the prose *Menologium* was intentional.

It is also noteworthy that the verse *Menologium* also omits the three high feasts after Christmas, whereas it includes the Circumcision and the Epiphany. The poet seems to follow basically the same principle as that followed by the compiler of the prose *Menologium*. Nevertheless, the poet includes the Circumcision and the Epiphany probably because of a different temporal framework he has introduced into the

---

[14] Based on linguistic, metrical and other features, it has generally been agreed that *Menologium* belongs to the latter half of the tenth century or later. See, for instance, Bredehoft (2009: 125-28) and Karasawa (2015a: 70-72).

[15] The manuscripts in question are: London, British Library, Harley 3271 (s. xi¹), and Cambridge, Corpus Christi College, MS 422 (s. xi med.). For details, see Ker (1957: 309-12 and 119-21), Gneuss (2001: 38 and 77) and Gneuss and Lapidge (2015: 118-19 and 357-59). See also Chardonnens (2007: 24), Hollis (2001: 191), and Scragg (2009: 63).

poem; the temporal framework of the prose *Menologium* is established by the solstices, the equinoxes and the beginnings of the four seasons, whereas the temporal framework of the verse *Menologium* also includes the beginnings of the twelve months.[16] Thus the beginning of January is mentioned in the verse *Menologium*, and in a work listing major feasts, there would be no reason to mention 1 January without mentioning that the Circumcision falls on the same day. Thus the reference to 1 January may have triggered the reference to the Circumcision. And it may have also triggered the reference to the Epiphany, the only other high feast in this period directly related to Christ. This enables the poet to conclude neatly the narrative regarding the earliest days of Christ — that is, he was born, was named Jesus, and was baptized — at the very beginning of the poem.[17] If this is the case, it may also hint that the verse *Menologium* may have come into existence along with a renovation of the template more faithfully followed by the prose *Menologium*, in the process of which the references to the beginnings of the twelve months were added so that the feasts could be located also in the framework of the Roman year.

While the absence of the high feasts in Christmastide can be seen as a deliberate omission as discussed above, both verse and prose *Menologium* show an exceptionally close choice of high feasts to that of Calendar 7 preserved in Oxford, Bodleian Library, Bodley 579,

---

[16] For details about the structures of the prose and the verse *Menologium*, see Karasawa (2007a) and also Karasawa (2015a: 33-39).

[17] As in the case of the prose *Menologium*, the locations of the feasts in the verse *Menologium* are consistently indicated by reference to the intervals between any two consecutive entries, but only once the poet follows a different principle of counting days when locating the feast of the Circumcision; according to his normal way of counting days, it is seven days after Christmas, but here alone he counts in a different way and says it is eight days after Christmas. This is probably because he followed the strong biblical tradition where a male child is circumcised on the eighth day after birth (ex. Genesis 17:12; 21:4). According to Luke 21:4, Christ was also circumcised in accordance with this Jewish custom, and so the poet says the Circumcision is eight days after Christmas. Yet the introduction of a different counting system only here is interesting since it may betray that this part did not belong to the original *Menologium* tradition, which is better preserved in the prose *Menologium*, but was newly introduced by the poet himself. For more information, see Karasawa (2015a: 48-51). See also Karasawa (2007b).

High feasts in Anglo-Saxon calendars: Contexts for the *Menologium* 117

which was compiled between 979 and 987, perhaps at Glastonbury or Canterbury.[18] The affinity between Calendar 7 and the prose *Menologium* is especially close; the only differences between the two are the inclusion of the feast of St Guthlac in Calendar 7, the inclusion of Lammas Day in the prose *Menologium* and the omission of those five feasts in Christmastide in the prose *Menologium*.

The close affinity between Calendar 7 and the prose *Menologium* is chiefly attributed to the fact that Calendar 7 scarcely marks feasts other than those widely observed, but both also share some peculiarities. For instance, both regard the Major Rogation (25 April) as a high feast, although it is not usually treated as such in Anglo-Saxon calendars (apart from Calendar 7, it is marked as a high feast only in Calendar 18). In the majority of calendars, SS Peter and Paul are treated together on 29 June, while both in Calendar 7 and in the prose *Menologium*, they are treated separately on 29 June and 30 June (the same treatment of these saints is to be found only in four other calendars, i.e., Calendars 9, 12, 18 and 25). In addition, though this is not directly related to the topic of this paper, the dates of the solstices and the equinoxes also coincide in Calendar 7 and the prose *Menologium* recorded in Cambridge, CCC MS 422;[19] both always follow the dates according to the original Julian Calendar, which must have come to be outdated by the end of the tenth century. In fact, no other calendars follow this tradition strictly.[20] Thus as far as high feasts and solar turning points are concerned, Calendar 7 and the prose *Menologium* seem to be based on nearly the same way of conceiving the major course of the year.

4. Conclusion

According to the calendar evidence, there used to be, as I have summarised in the table above, thirty two high feasts widely observed in England in the late tenth century, and two more were added in the early

---

[18] For details of this calendar, see Rushforth (2008: 25-26). It is edited in Wormald (1934: 43-55).

[19] The prose *Menologium* recorded in CCCC 422 follows this tradition, while the other version in Harley 3271 has a revised date for the vernal equinox, i.e., 21 March, based on the revised Julian calendar. Yet otherwise, it always adopts the dates based on the original Julian calendar.

[20] The dates of the solar turning points recorded in Anglo-Saxon calendars are summarised in a table in Karasawa (2015a: 181).

eleventh century. Their high status is also verified by the fact that most of them are mentioned in the verse *Menologium*, which the late tenth-century poet himself says is a work listing feasts that had to be observed widely in England. The prose *Menologium*, probably better preserving the *Menologium* tradition, also lists a very similar set of feasts. In comparison with calendars, which considerably differ from one another in the choice of high feasts, the consistency of the prose and the verse *Menologium* with the most basic and general choice is remarkable; apart from Calendar 7 and a few others, there is scarcely any text equally consistent in this respect. However, if we take into account their common reference to the two festivals of less importance, i.e., the Major Rogation and Lammas Day, and also their common absence of reference to the three high feasts after Christmas, the close affinity between the prose and the verse *Menologium* may not be so simple as to allow one to conclude that "it could not be otherwise since both the prose and the verse *menologia* deal only with the major feasts and calendrical events, not with local saints."[21] It is true that they are similar because they summarise basic facts but it is also true that they share multiple peculiarities, including the method of locating feasts by reference to their intervals, the repeated reference to Christmas at the beginning and the end of the whole series of feasts, the omission of the three high feasts after Christmas, and the inclusion of the two seasonal festivals. In fact, there is no other work showing affinities to a similar extent and this may reflect the very close interrelationship between the prose and the verse *Menologium*.

Whether they are directly related or not, the prose and the verse *Menologium* are rare works revealing the most basic course of the Christian year focusing on Anglo-Saxon immovable high feasts. They summarise what is essentials for the English people in general, excluding both minor details and regional peculiarities, such as those differentiating the Latin metrical calendar composed in York from that composed in Ramsey. In this respect, the prose and the verse *Menologium* are quite different from Latin metrical calendars and Old Irish calendar poems, which have sometimes been regarded as Latin and

---

[21] These words are quoted from Stanley (2005: 259).

High feasts in Anglo-Saxon calendars: Contexts for the *Menologium* 119

Old Irish counterparts of the verse *Menologium*.[22] I cannot go into
details regarding this issue here, but their difference is tellingly
reflected in the number of feasts mentioned as summarised in the
following table:[23]

Genre	Works	Feasts
Menologia	Prose *Menologium*	29
	Verse *Menologium*	29
Latin Metrical Calendars	Metrical Calendar of York	65
	Metrical Calendar of Hampson	335[24]
	Metrical Calendar of Ramsey	106
Old Irish Calendar Poems	*Félire Óengusso*	365
	Félire Adamnáin	6
	Énlaith Betha	4[25]

Given that they mention either too many or too few feasts, none of
these Latin or Old Irish works is as neat a summary of widely observed
high feasts as are the prose and the verse *Menologium*.[26]

---

[22] Hennig (1952) regards some Old Irish calendar poems as the Irish
counterparts of the *Menologium*. His view has been quite influential and
its impact upon later studies can be seen, for instance, in Greeson (1970:
87-178), Calder and Allen (1976: 229), Howe (1985: 74-77), Grimaldi
(1988: 14), Richards (2007: 363), and Jones (2012: xxvii). On the other
hand, the *Menologium* has often been compared with Latin metrical calendars as in Imelmann (1902: 40-43), and there have even been attempts to
change the traditional title of the poem to the "Old English Metrical
Calendar" as if to emphasise its close affinity to Latin metrical calendars.
See, for instance, Lapidge (1991: 249-52) and Baker (1999: 312). Hart
(2003: 194) even claims that "the monologist translates and epitomises the
erudite metrical Latin calendar of his house."

[23] The numbers in the following table are based on my own research using
the following editions of these works: Karasawa (2015a), Henel (1934: 71-
91), Wilmart (1934), McGurk (1986), Lapidge (1984), Stokes (1905; repr.
1984), Byrne (1904), and Best and Lawlor (1929). The last two works are
reprinted in Karasawa (2015a: 154-59).

[24] This number does not include the obituaries of King Alfred the Great and
his wife.

[25] In this work, the feasts of the saints are always mentioned for the sake of
the dates, and these dates are given most often in the Roman reckoning.

[26] For more information about this issue, see Karasawa (2015a: 18-32). As
regards the relationship between the *Menologium* and some Old Irish calendar poems, see Karasawa (2015b).

120 Kazutomo Karasawa

Appendix. List of Anglo-Saxon calendars[27]

1	Paris, Biblio. Natio., Latin 10837, 34v-40r	e 8th c	Echternach
2	Nauzenstein near Regensburg, Gräflich Walderdorffsche Biblio., s.n.	mid-8th c	Northumbria
3	Munich, Hauptstaatsarchiv, Raritäten-Selekt 108	729x754	Northumbria or Continent
4	Ox., Bod., Digby 63, 40r-45v	867x892	Northumbria
5	Ox., Bod., Junius 27, 2r-7v	920s	Glaston. or Cant.?
6	Salisbury, Cathedral Library, 150, 3r-8v	969x987	Wilton
7	Ox., Bod., Bodley 579, 39r-44v	979x987	Glaston.? Cant.?
8	Paris, Biblio. Natio., Latin 7229, 3v-9r	1 10th c	Ramsey
9	London, BL, Additional 3751, 2r-3r	1 10th or e 11th c	CC, Canterbury
10	Paris, Biblio. Natio., Latin 10062, 162r-3v	e 11th c	id.
11	London, BL, Arundel 155, 2r-7v	1012x23	id.
12	Rouen, Biblio. Manicipale, Y.6, 6r-11v	1014?x1023?	Peterborough? Canterbury?
13	Camb., Univ. Lib., Kk v.32, 50r-55v	1012x1030	Cant.? Glaston.?
14	London, BL, Cotton Titus D xxvii, 3r-8v	1023x1031	New M., Winchester
15	Camb., Trinity Coll., R.15.32, 15-26	(1036?), 1025x	id.
16	London, BL, Cotton Nero Aii, 3r-8v	1029x46	Leominster
17	Ox., Bod., Douce 296, 1r-6v	1060x1087	Crowland
18	Rome, Vat., Reg. Lat. 12, 7r-12v	3rd quart. 11th c	Bury St Edmunds
19	Camb., CCC 422, 29-40	c. 1061	Sherborne
20	Camb., CCC 9, 3-14	x1062, mid-11th c	Worcester
21	Camb., CCC 391, 3-14	c. 1064	id.
22	Ox., Bod., Hatton 113, iiir-viiiv	1064x1070	id. or Evesham?
23	London, BL, Cotton Vitellius E.xviii, 2r-7v	c. 1060s	New M., Winchester
24	London, BL, Arundel 60, 2r-7v	c. 1073	id.
25	London, BL, Cotton Vitellius A.xviii, 3r-8v	2nd half of 11th c	SW England
26	London, BL, Egerton 3314, 18v-30r	1 11th c, 1083x	CC, Canterbury
27	London, BL, Cotton Vitellius A.xii, 65v-71r	late 11th c	Salisbury

References

Amodio, M.C. 2014. *The Anglo-Saxon literature handbook*. Southern Gate: Wiley.

Baker, Peter S. 1999. OE metrical calendar. In Michael Lapidge, *et al.* (eds.), *The Blackwell encyclopaedia of Anglo-Saxon England*, 312. Oxford: Blackwell.

Best, R.I. & H.J. Lawlor (eds.) 1931. *The Martyrology of Tallaght from the*

---

[27] This list is based on a similar list in Rushforth (2008: 17).

High feasts in Anglo-Saxon calendars: Contexts for the *Menologium* 121

Book of Leinster and MS. 5100-4 in the Royal Library, Brussels, HBS
68. London: Henry Bradshaw Society.

Bredehoft, Thomas 2009. *Authors, audiences and Old English verse*. Toronto:
University of Toronto Press.

Byrne, M. E. 1904. Félire Adamnáin. *Eriu* 1, 225-28.

Calder, D. G. & M. J. B. Allen 1976. *Sources and analogues of Old English
poetry: The major Latin sources in translation*. Cambridge: D.S. Brewer.

Chardonnens, L.S. 2007. London, British Library, Harley 3271: The composition and structure of an Eleventh-century Anglo-Saxon miscellany. In
P. Lendinara, L. Lazzari & M. A. D'Aronco (eds.), *Form and content in
instruction in Anglo-Saxon England in the light of contemporary manuscript evidence*, 3-34. Turnhout: Brepols.

Gneuss, Helmut 2001. *Handlist of Anglo-Saxon manuscripts: A list of manuscripts and manuscript fragments written or owned in England up to
1100*. Medieval and Renaissance Texts and Studies 241. Tempe: Arizona
Center for Medieval and Renaissance Studies.

Gneuss, Helmut & Michael Lapidge 2015. *Anglo-Saxon manuscripts: A bib-
liographical handlist of manuscripts and manuscript fragments written
or owned in England up to 1100*. Toronto: University of Toronto Press.

Greeson, Hoyt St Clair 1970. Two Old English observance poems: *Seasons
for Fasting* and *The Menologium*: An edition. Diss., University of
Oregon, 1970.

Grimaldi, Maria 1988. *Il 'Menologio' poetico anglosassone: introduzione,
edizione, tradizione, comment*. Naples: Intercontinentalia.

Hart, Cyril 2003. *Learning and culture in late Anglo-Saxon England and the
influence of Ramsey Abbey on the major English monastic schools: A
survey of the development of mathematical, medical, and scientific
studies in England before the Norman Conquest*. Medieval Studies 18,
Vol. 2. Lewiston: Edwin Mellen.

Henel, Heinrich 1934. *Studien zum altenglischen Computus*, Beiträge zur
englischen Philologie 26. Leipzig: Bernhard Tauchnitz.

Hennig, John 1952. The Irish counterparts of the Anglo-Saxon *Menologium*.
Mediaeval Studies 14, 98-106.

Hollis, S. 2001. Scientific and medical writings. In P. Pulsiano & E. Treharne
(eds.), *A companion to Anglo-Saxon literature*, 188-208. Oxford:
Blackwell.

Howe, Nicholas 1985. *The Old English catalogue poems: A study in poetic
form*. Anglistica 23. Copenhagen: Rosen Kilde.

Imelmann, Rudolf 1902. *Das altenglische Menologium*. Berlin: E. Ebering.

Jones, Christopher A. (ed.) 2012. *Old English shorter poems*, Vol. 1: Religious and didactic. Cambridge, MA: Harvard University Press.

Karasawa, Kazutomo 2007a. The structure of the *Menologium* and its
computistical background. *Studies in English Literature* 84, 123-41.

Karasawa, Kazutomo 2007b. A note on the Old English poem 'Menologium' line 3b *on þy eahteoðan dæg*. *Notes and Queries*, n.s. 54.3, 211-15.

Karasawa, Kazutomo (ed.) 2015a. *The Old English metrical calendar (Menologium)*. Anglo-Saxon Texts 12. Cambridge: D.S. Brewer.

Karasawa, Kazutomo 2015b. Irish influence upon the Old English poem *Menologium* reconsidered. *Anglia* 133.4, 706-34.

Ker, N. R. 1957. *Catalogue of manuscripts containing Anglo-Saxon*. Oxford: Clarendon Press.

Lapidge, Micheal 1984. A tenth-century metrical calendar from Ramsay. *Revue Bénédictine* 94, 326-69.

Lapidge, Michael 1991. The saintly life in Anglo-Saxon England. In Malcolm Godden & Michael Lapidge (eds.), *The Cambridge companion to Old English literature*, 251-72. Cambridge: Cambridge University Press.

Liebermann, Felix (ed.) 1903. *Die Gesetze der Angelsachsen*, Vol. 1. Halle: Max Niemeyer.

McGurk, Patrick 1986. The metrical calendar of Hampson: A new edition. *Analecta Bollandiana* 104, 79-125.

Richards, Mary 2007. Old wine in a new bottle: Recycled instructional materials in *Seasons for Fasting*. In A. J. Kleist (ed.), *The Old English homily: Precedent, practice, and appropriation*, Studies in the Early Middle Ages 17, 345-64. Turnhout: Brepols.

Robertson, A. J. (ed.) 1925. *The laws of the kings of England from Edmund to Henry I*. Cambridge: Cambridge University Press.

Rushforth, Rebecca 2008. *Saints in English kalendars before A.D. 1100*, HBS 117. London: Henry Bradshaw Society.

Scragg, Donald 2009. Manuscript sources of Old English prose. In Gale R. Owen-Crocker (ed.), *Working with Anglo-Saxon manuscripts*, 61-87. Exeter: Exeter University Press.

Stanley, Eric G. 2005. The prose *Menologium* and the verse *Menologium*. In A. Oizumi, J. Fisiak & J. Scahill (eds.), *Text and language in medieval English prose: A festschrift for Tadao Kubouchi*, 255-67. Frankfurt: Peter Lang.

Stokes, W. (ed.) 1905; repr. 1984. *Félire Óengusso Céli Dé: The Martyrology of Oengus the Culdee*. Dublin: Dublin Institute for Advanced Studies.

Wilmart, A. 1934. Un témoin anglo-saxon du calendrier métrique d'York. *Revue Bénédictine* 46, 41-69.

Wormald, Francis (ed.) 1934. *English kalendars before A.D. 1100*, Vol. 1. London: Henry Bradshaw Society.

The medieval vision through "bodily" and "ghostly" in English devotional prose*

Akio Katami

Abstract

This article explores the medieval vision through the rhetorical effects of a certain type of word pair that combines physical words with spiritual ones in medieval devotional prose. Mysticism is traditionally conceived as the spiritual quest for union with God and the perception of its essential oneness. Initially in this study, the overall frequency and context of physical and spiritual words in Middle English prose and verse are observed by applying a proximity search in an electronic corpus. I suggest that "bodily and ghostly" is an especially important word pair because it was used to represent the oneness of God with humankind.

The higher frequency of "bodily and ghostly" shows that it is an idiosyncratic feature of medieval devotional works. In addition, I would like to emphasize that their insights and deep emotions are condensed into the word pair to imply an intuitive knowledge of spiritual truth. Based on these quantitative findings, this article shows that "bodily and ghostly" is a symbolic representation of mystical consciousness.

1. Introduction

During the medieval period, the Church dominated over all issues concerning sickness, health, life, death and the salvation of individual souls. Thus, bodily and spiritual beings were not only inseparable but also paramount issue at the time of medieval literature. My approach for this paper is, by observing the context and usage of word pairs in mystical writings, to explore the relationships between the soul and the body that together comprise humankind.

Word pairs are stylistic devices which combine related words using "and," for example, "heart and soul," "checks and balances," and "up and down." This usage includes individual stylistic practices as well

---

* This research has its origin in inspiring suggestions from Yoshiyuki Nakao (Hiroshima University Graduate School professor at the time), to whom I wish to express my sincere gratitude. This paper is based on revisions to my presentation at The 26th Japanese Association for Studies in the History of the English Language (April 9, 2016, International Christian University).

124   *Akio Katami*

as binominals which characterize two-element idiomatic collocations. The Middle English mystics whom I focus on—Richard Rolle, Walter Hilton, *The Cloud* author, Julian of Norwich and Margery Kempe— hold a prominent position in the development of English prose.[1] Their works occupy an important but not fully explained position in the history of Middle English prose.

Based on the concept of bodily and spiritual concerns fostered by Plato and Aristotle, spiritual beings are regarded as a phase of bodily existence. It is, therefore, that the body is inseparable from the spirit. In addition to that, in the Fourth Council of Lateran[2] in 1215, the connectedness between bodily and spiritual health is strengthened. In the medieval hospitals, the patients were cured indiscriminately between body and soul throughout the liturgy in the church. Kukita (2014: 4) states as follows:

> Penance and divine forgiveness are indispensable for retrieving physical health. Thus, it was regarded that the recovery of spiritual health would lead to physical health. The disposition assuming a symbiotic relationship between body and soul prevailed in the Christian society before Descartes. A mode of soul was regarded as influential to the body, and the opposite is equally true. By combining medicine and medical treatment with Christianity, the tradition became conventionalized.[3]

On the other hand, what one must notice is that this was also the era of renunciation of the body, as seen in the practices of austerity and

---

[1] Chambers (1932: 102) quotes Allen (1927: 8) to notify the significance of the prose of Richard Rolle that he gives the rare example of a style truly belonging to the Middle Age of English prose. It is reasonable to assert that Rolle's work inherits from the rich national literature before the Norman Conquest. We can see the importance of other mystics. The circulation of as many as sixty-two homiliary manuscripts by Hilton shows a wide range of his audience in the fourteenth and fifteenth centuries. The work by Julian of Norwich is noted as the first prose recorded by a female author. The book of Margery Kempe has value of recourse as the oldest woman autography.

[2] One of five ecumenical councils of the Roman Catholic church held in the Lateran Palace in Rome. The Fourth council condemned the Albigenses as heretical and clarified the Church doctrine on transubstantiation, the Trinity, and the Incarnation.

[3] This quotation was translated from Japanese into English by the author of this paper.

The medieval vision through "bodily" and "ghostly"   125

abstinence. We can observe, in this respect, the quality of the emanci-
pation of the soul from its physical containment.

(1a) is an instance of the words of Jesus addressed to his disciples,
and (1b) is a quotation from the Pauline Epistles. (Italics are mine.)

> (1) a. It is the *Spirit* that quickeneth, the *flesh* profiteth nothing: the
> wordes that I speake vnto you, they are *Spirit*, and they are life.
> *(The Gospel according to S. John*, vi. 63)
> b. For if ye liue after the *flesh*, ye shall die: but if ye through the
> *spirit* doe mortifie the deeds of the *body,* ye shall liue.
> *(Epistle to the Romans*, viii. 13)

What is specified here is that human beings in flesh form are not
qualified to grasp divine truth. In (1a) it is advocated that nothing but
spirit can produce life, and asserts the uselessness of flesh. As for (1b),
the author claims that you do not only live in the body and flesh, but
the spirit. Therefore, to really live, we must live through spirit, not
flesh.

Windeatt (2004: 123) refers to body and soul expressions of Julian
of Norwich and Margery Kempe as follows:

> Julian of Norwich had distinguished between bodily and ghostly sights,
> or sights 'ghostly in bodily likeness'. The *Book* is also careful to specify
> what Kempe perceives in the bodily senses or when sleepy, while by
> contrast what is her most valued experience is emphasized to have been
> seen 'with her ghostly eye'.

It should be noted that Windeatt states that Kempe gains her most
valuable experience by seeing not with her bodily but her ghostly eyes.

Following the seventeenth century, which saw Christian society
becoming divided, medieval views of the body based on mind and
body monism, were considered to be superseded by mind and body
dualism, and the bodily mechanism regarding the body as machine-
like was advocated by Descartes.

But as we see in *Ancrene Wisse,* an anonymous monastic manual
for anchoresses written in the early thirteenth century, spiritual health
took precedence over bodily condition, while religious significance
revolving sickness already strongly reflected this fact. What is advocated in this discipline is fragility of the flesh. And by way of the
bodily suffering, we are purified. This article explores the correlation
between the spiritual or immaterial, and physical part of a human being

126　　　　　　　　　　　*Akio Katami*

in the light of word pairs.

2. Corporeal and incorporeal positional association in Middle English computational corpus

First, we examine the context of corporeal and incorporeal words from the viewpoint of the closeness of occurrence, by using *Corpus of Middle English Prose and Verse*, which compiles 146 volumes of Middle English texts. The proximity search is conducted to find the co-occurrence of two or three words or phrases. As a quite a few number of instances show, there is high frequency of proximity in the position of the corporeal and incorporeal words.

Since it is often the case that there are some spelling variations in Middle English, the modern standard spellings are employed for convenience sake. The numbers in square brackets show frequencies in the corpus. The two distinctive pairs "ghostly and bodily" and "body and soul" will be focused with quotations.

2.1. "ghostly – bodily" [197]

The co-occurrence of "ghostly" and "bodily" is most frequent in number. Let us consider following quotation.

> (2) as woman was made for man & not man for woman, ryght so *bodyly* werkynge was made for *ghostly* & not *ghostly* for *bodyly*. *Bodyly* werkynge goth before & *ghostly* comyth after; ... (*On Mixed Life*)

The writer, Walter Hilton, claims that bodily matters are to serve the spiritual, and not the other way round. He advocates that bodily matters are subordinate to ghostly ones. He claims that you do not only live in the body and flesh, but the spirit. Therefore, to really live, we must live through spirit, not flesh. He advocates that bodily things are subordinate to ghostly ones. Relevant to this point is Geoffrey Chaucer's following quotation.

> (3) And thow schat vndirstonde that marchaundise is in manye maneris / that on is *bodyly* & that othir is *gostely*; that on is honest & lefful; & that othir is dishonest & onleful. (*The Canterbury Tales*)

In (3), a merchandise is divided into two categories, that is "bodily" and "ghostly." Spiritual matters are regarded as lawful, whereas bodily ones occupy the opposite stance.

2.2. "body – soul" [25]

The texts in which "body" and "soul" occur in proximity contain a variety of literary genres outside religious work. For example, (4) is one of the instances from chronicles.

> (4) he shold do fynd iiij tapers to bren perpetuelly Aboute his *body,* þat, for þe extinccion of his *bodely* life, his *soul* may be remembred and lyve in heven in *spirituel* lufe; & also þat he ... (*The Brut*)

The message of the quotation above is that after the extinction of his "bodily" life, his "soul" can be remembered and live in "spiritual" life. Here we can see another dichotomy between the exterior and inner state of people.

Other instances of the proximity search are shown below, with the number of occurrences in the brackets.

> bodily – spiritually [4] / fleshly – ghostly [43] / fleshly – spiritually [1] / flesh – soul [28]

The results are presented by a bar chart which shows the number of occurrences with the proximity search in *Middle English Prose and Verse*.

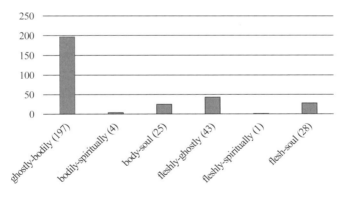

Figure 1.

The highest frequency in the proximity search is "ghostly – bodily" in 197 instances. Since this result is highly relevant to the context of word pairs, further discussion will be presented in Section 4.

3. Carnal and spiritual vocabulary of medieval mystics

In section 2, we found the priority of spirit to flesh in the corpus of Middle English. The same thought is reflected in the mystics we focus on. Hilton advocates in his *The Scale of Perfection* (c.1390-1395) that a soul which longs for knowledge of ghostly things needs first to recognize itself. According to him, the more you seek to find and feel your soul in the way you would feel bodily things, the further you are away from it.

> (5) Hit nedeth to a *soule* that wolde have knowynge of *goostli* thynges, for to have first knowynge of itsilf. For it mai not have knowynge first of a kynde aboven itsilf but yif it have a knowynge of itsilf; and that is whanne the *soule* is so gadred into itsilf, and departed from biholdynge of alle ertheli thynges and fro the use of the *bodili* wittes, that it feelith itsilf as it is in the owen kynde withoute a *bodi*. Thanne yif thou coveite for to knowen and seen thi *soule* what it is, thou schalt not torne thi thought to thi *bodi* for to seken and feelen it, as it were hid withinne in thi *fleschli* herte as thyn herte is hid and hoolden withinne thi *bodi*. Yif thou seke so, thou schalt nevere fynde it in itsilf. The more thou sekest for to fynden and feelen it, as thou woldest feelen a *bodili* thynge, the ferthere thou art therfroo. For thi *soule* is no *bodi*,... (*Scale II*, xxx. 205)

If you desire to know and see what your soul is, you shall not turn your thought into your body to search for it and feel it, as if it were hidden inside your heart. He also advocates that your soul is not your body. Relevant to this point of carnal and spiritual separation, let us consider the following quotation from *A Book of Showings* (c.1395) by Julian of Norwich.

> (6) And of theyse none shalle be perysshyd, for oure kynde, whych is the hyer party, is knytte to god in þe makyng; and God is knytt to oure kynde whych is the lower party in our *flesh* takyng; and thus in Crist oure two kyndys be onyd, ... (*Showings*, lvii. 577-78)

When Christ united the virtues of God with our flesh, our bodies were given sensuality as part of this union. The higher part of our nature was united to God when we were created, and God united himself to our nature in his lower, incarnated form.

Furthermore, what should be noticed is words of Richard Rolle. He expresses confliction and vacillation between the life of heavenly joy and the holy ghost in *Fire of Love*.

The medieval vision through "bodily" and "ghostly"   129

(7) In þis lyfe treuly he is besy to *byrn in fyre* of þe holy goste, & in Ioy
     of lufe takyn & be gode comfortid to be glad. Treuly þe onely parfit
     man in godis lufe hugisly byrns, & qwhils abown hym-self in
     passynge of mynde be contemplacion he is takyn, vnto *þe swete*
     sownd & *heuenly noys* Ioyand he is lyft.
                                                    (*Fire of Love I*, cap. xiv. 30-31)

The phrases like "burning in fire," "sweet melody," and "heavenly
noise" show the parallelism between ghostly and bodily things. Here
we can see the ghostly experiences through the sensuality.

A good place to start to explore word pairs is the context which
causes the parallelism, overlapping, and reciprocality of bodily and
ghostly indications. The next instance is from *The Book of Margery
Kempe* (c.1430). She compares Jesus as a spiritual entity to the pain of
earthly life using a simile.

(8) ... sche sey swech gostly syghtys in hir sowle as freschly and as
     verily as yyf it had ben don in dede in hir bodily sight,...
                                                    (*Book,* lxxix. 190)

These observations direct attention to one of the stylistic devices,
word pairs, which combine related words using a conjunction "and"
and "or." In Section 4, I would like to focus attention on word pairs in
the mystical prose.

4. Word pairs composed of body and spirit in mystical prose

There are not a few valuable inquiries, including binominals, under the
title of word pairs. In the light of recent diachronic approach, Jimura
(2014) investigates the process of idiomatization by focusing on the
paired words[4] "meat and drink" from works of Geoffrey Chaucer to
William Shakespeare. As a synchronic approach in the study of Middle
English, Tani (2008) has brought light to stylistic effect of word pairs
in Chaucer's prose. It assumes English and French bilingualism of the
audience and readers. Concerning the etymology, Katami (2014) refers
to *the Authorized Version* and mystical prose as opposed to Chaucer.
Although the high ratio of word pairs in *the Authorized Version* and
mystical prose are of Anglo-Saxon native origin, they are similar to

---

[4] Jimura uses the term "paired word" as equivalent with "word pairs" in this
    paper.

130   *Akio Katami*

those of Chaucer in stylistic and rhetorical effect.

This article sheds a new light by focusing on word pairs of body and spirit, to see the implicature and significance of the internal world view and the faith of mystics. As space is limited, we shall discuss two types which are worth noting in the peculiarities, "bodily and ghostly" and "body and soul" pairings.

4.1. "bodily and ghostly" / "ghostly and bodily"

Below is the number of occurrences of a word pair with "bodily" and "ghostly."

Table 1. Frequencies of "bodily and ghostly" and "ghostly and bodily"

	bodily and ghostly	ghostly and bodily
Rolle	0 (1)*	0
Hilton	20 (11)	2
Cloud	5 (10)	0
Julian	2	4
Kempe	2	5

* The numbers in the brackets refer to occurrences paired by "or."

Let us consider quotation (9) from *The Scale of Perfection* which describes the ascent of the human soul from sin to perfection. Here we see the integration of body and ghost as shown by the word pair "bodili and goostli."

> (9) A clene herte him bihoveth for to have that schulde prai wel thus, for it is of sich men and women that bi longe travaile *bodili and goostli,* or ellis bi swich smert smytynges of love, as I bifore seide, comen into reste of spirit, so that here affeccioun is turnyd into goostli savoure,... (*Scale I*, xxxii. 63-64)

A pure heart belongs to men and women who through long labour of body and soul come into a restful spirit, so that their affection is turned into spiritual savour.

> (10) He is an ipocrite that cheseth veyn joie of himsilf as the reste and ful delite of his herte, upon this manere wise: whanne a man dooth many good dedes *bodili and goostli*, and aftir is yput to his mynde by suggestioun of the enemye a biholdynge of hymsilf and of his good dedes, how good, how holi he is, how worthi in mennes doom, and

The medieval vision through "bodily" and "ghostly" 131

> hou high in Goddis sight above othere men, he perceyveth this styrynge and resseyveth it wilfulli, for he weneth it be gode and of God in as mykil as it is sooth, for he dooth alle thise good dedes betere thanne othere men. ...that it neer hande ravesschith his mynde out of alle othere thoughtis, bothe *goostli and fleischli*, for the tyme, and settith it in this veyn joie of himsilf as in a reste of his herte.
> (*Scale I*, lix. 97)

The word pair "bodili and goostli" leads the essential of teaching shown by shading, and concludes with a variation of the concept "goostli and fleischli." By the effect of this variation, the valuable concept of unity of body and ghost is highlighted. Here we can see the denial of separation of ghostly things from those of bodily. Let us now extend the observation into *The Cloud of Unknowing* (c.1350).

> (11) For o þing *I telle þee*: it is more profitable to þe helþe of þi soule, more worþi in itself, and more plesing to God & to alle þe seintes & aungelles in heuen — ʒe! and more helply to alle þi freendes, *bodily and goostly,* quik and dede — soche a blynde steryng of loue vnto God for himself, & soche a priue loue put vpon þis cloude of vnknowing... (*Cloud*, ix. 34)

In (11) an illocutionary performative verb "tell" leads the following phrase containing "bodily and goostly." The concept of "bodily" represents *Eros* named by Plato, which urges us to seek after the goodness truth. And therefore, this is an impulse in the spirit to ascend to the god. On the other hand, "ghostly" is *Agape*, a descent of god's love toward human beings. The focal points meeting these two adverse vectors symbolized by "bodily and goostly" signify a feeling of oneness with God.

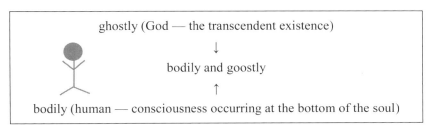

Figure 2.

132   *Akio Katami*

The abstractive spiritual goodness is represented as concrete figure
through the specific bodily action. Consider the following example
from Julian of Norwich.

> (12) ..., truly wyllyng to be with him with al our herte with al our soule
> snd with all our mygte. And than we hate and dyspise oure evyll
> steryng and all that myghte be occasion of synne *gostely and bodely*.
> (*Showings*, lii. 548)

When we truly hope to be with God with all our heart, soul, and physical strength, we can detach ourselves from wickedness. The concept
expressed by "gostely and bodily" is a holistic one and an indispensable and principle idea to have a revelation. Related in the same way
are the clauses in (13) by Margery Kempe. She also suggests insepa-
rability of ghost from body.

> (13) I cry þe mercy, Lord, for alle my childeryn, *gostly and bodily,* and
> for al the pepil in this world that thu make her synnys to me be very
> contricyon as it wer myn owyn synnys, and forgeve hem as I wolde
> that thu forgove me. (*Book II*, x. 251)

She makes plea for God to forgive the sins of her children and
everyone else, as well as herself. The word pair strengthens her wish.
Consider another example in (14).

> (14) So *gostly and bodily* it myth wel ben verifiid he xhal comyn hom in
> safté, not only into þis dedly lond but also into þe lond of leuyng
> men,wher deth xal neuyr aperyn. (*Book II*, ii. 225)

Margery's faithful son passed away suffering from disease after
visiting her house. She thought he left to the grace of the Lord. "Gostly"
symbolizes a house in heaven and "bodily" contrastively represents
Margery's house on Earth.

In the quotations in *The Oxford English Dictionary* (*OED*), there are
two instances of this kind, one is from Hilton's work and another is in
the Scripture. Seeing things from this perspective, we can infer the
contextual relationships of this word pair with Christianity.

4.2. "body and soul" / "soul and body"

Frequencies of another word pair, "body and soul" and "soul and body"
are as follows:

The medieval vision through "bodily" and "ghostly"   133

Table 2. Frequencies of "body and soul" and "soul and body"

	body and soul	soul and body
Rolle	10*	2
Hilton	5(1)**	0
Cloud	7***	0
Julian	0	1
Kempe	1	0

Note: In addition to the items in Table 2, there is one instance of each variant pair as follows:
  * þi body and þi soule
  ** of thi bodi and of thi soule, in bodi and in soule, (an instance in the bracket) in bodi or in soule
  *** in body and in soul

There are many instances in which pronouns and prepositions are attached like, "þi body and þi soule" and "in bodi or in soule." However, they had not been idiomatized as in Modern English yet. In addition to the grammatical aspect, the usage is almost restricted to a certain lexical meaning. Observe the following quotations from Julian and Kempe.

(15) a. that if a man or a woman wer there vnther the brode water, and he myght haue syght of god so, as god is with a man contynually, he shoulde be safe in *sowle and body* [5]... (*Showings,* x. 326)
   b. And so the pepil cesyd and was stille and herd up the sermown wyth qwyet and rest of *body and sowle*. (*Book*, lxviii. 167)

As we see in (15ab), this word pair is used in lexical meaning in the context, not for subjective nor heightened emotion. The modern idiomatic usage such as "The scholar gives body and soul to his research" is not found either. Considering the frequencies in *OED*, there are as many as 68 quotations for "soul and body" and 64 for "body and soul." The result of the most frequent usage among the word pairs in this study indicates that it is used widely not restricted in religious texts.

Mysticism is the belief that direct knowledge of God, spiritual truth, or ultimate reality can be attained through subjective experience. To observe word pairs of mystics, it is noteworthy to draw attention to Underhill. The double underlines represent the concept of "bodily" and the single underlines symbolize that of "ghostly."

---

[5]   In the Slone Manuscript, it is "body and soule."

(16) a. I found that there were two thirsts in me; the one after the creatures to get help and strength there; and the other after the Lord,
the Creator....It was so with me, that there seemed to be two
pleadings in me. ... One day when I had been walking solitarily
abroad and was come home, I was wrapped up in the love of God,
so that I could not but admire the greatness of his love. While I
was in that condition it was opened unto me by the eternal Light
and Power, and I saw clearly therein...But O! then did I see my
troubles, trials, and temptations more clearly than ever I had done.
(Underhill, 1911: 215)

b. When, however, the subconscious intuitions, long ago quickened,
are at last brought to birth and the eyes are opened on new light-
and it is significant that an actual sense of blinding radiance is a
constant accompaniment of this state of consciousness- the storm
and stress, the vague cravings and oscillations of the past life are
forgotten. In this abrupt recognition of reality "all things are made
new": from this point the life of the mystic begins.
(Underhill, 1911: 216)

(16a) is a passage from the diary of George Fox who founded the religious Quaker's society. The shaded parts demonstrate his spiritual
struggle compared to thirsts for water between the transcendental
discordant feelings and his own consciousness. The situation
condensed to a word pair of "bodily and ghostly" symbolizes the unity
of the concrete depiction of God as having a transcendent existence,
and the human being. In (16b), the point to observe is that as highlighted by shading, through the conflict among "ghostly" and "bodily,"
the life of the mystic begins.

5. Conclusion

In the Middle Ages of the recognition that the body and the soul are
one piece, there was a religious view that the soul is located above the
body. However, the binomial relationship such as hendiadys and
emphasizers between the soul and the body depends on the context.
The vocabulary of the spirit and the body are upper and lower relationships and antagonisms in individual contexts, but in a word pair, the
meaning of relationship of the two terms becomes hendiadys like "god
faithful man." The tendency was particularly noticeable in word pairs
of "bodily and ghostly." The crucial thought of mysticism is represented in the word pair of integration with God as a spiritual entity and
self-awareness.

The medieval vision through "bodily" and "ghostly"   135

Initially in this study, the overall frequency and context of physical ("bodily" and "fleshly") and spiritual words ("ghostly," "spiritually," and "soul") in Middle English prose and verse were observed by applying a proximity search in an electronic corpus. The ecstatic state of mind, which is a supreme instance of the close connection between body and soul, has bodily as well as mental results. Since bodily and spiritual beings were closely intertwined in medieval society, an existing religious view was that the spirit precedes bodily existence. We must draw attention to the various instances, however, in which the relationship between the two entities varies depending on their context. In some cases, they may work together as hendiadys or intensifiers. Diachronically, another word pair "body and soul" deserves more than a passing notice. *OED* cites 132 instances of this word pair, but there are no more than two examples of "bodily and ghostly." On the other hand, medieval mystics applied "bodily and ghostly" in 62 instances against "body and soul" 27 times. Moreover, as we saw in the works of Julian and Kempe, "bodily and ghostly" allows more replacement of binomial orders as "ghostly and bodily," unlike "body and soul." The point to observe is that the pair of "bodily and ghostly" is not an unmarked conventional phrase but a marked expression with connotative messages. Though "body and soul" is a parallel pair, "bodily and ghostly" represents concepts where God's view from above and lower view from human eyes meet. From the relationship of the two elements, the thought in mysticism is subjectively expressed in a condensed climax.

Texts
Authorized Version
Pollard, William Alfred. (introduction) *The Holy Bible: An exact reprint in Roman Type, page for page of the Authorized Version published in the year 1611*. Oxford: Oxford University Press, 1985. Rpt. 1995. Terasawa, Yoshio. Tokyo: Kenkyusha.
Richard Rolle
Allen, Hope Emily. (ed.) 1931. *English writings of Richard Rolle hermit of Hampole*. London: The Clarendon Press.
Harvey, Ralph. (ed.) 1896. *The Fire of Love and Meaning of Life or the Rule of Living.* London: Kegan Pole.

Walter Hilton

Bestul, H. Thomas (ed.) 2000. *The Scale of Perfection.* Michigan: Medieval Institute Publications.

Cloud author

Hodgson, Phyllis (ed.) 1944. *The Cloud of Unknowing and the Book of Privy Counselling.* Oxford: Oxford University Press.

Julian of Norwich

Colledge, Edmund, O.S.A. & James Walsh S.J, (eds.) 1978. *A Book of Showings to the Anchoress Julian of Norwich.* Toronto: Pontifical Institute of Medieval Studies.

Margery Kempe

Meech, Sanford Brown. (ed.) 1940. *The Book of Margery Kempe.* Early English Text Society, O.S. 212, Oxford: Oxford University Press.

References

Clark, P.H.John & Rosemary Dorward 1991. *The Scale of Perfection.* New York / Mahwah, Paulist Press.

Corpus of Middle English prose and verse. <http://quod.lib.umich.edu/c/cme/>. Last accessed May 2017.

Inge, William Ralph 1933. *Christian mysticism.* London: Methuen.

Jimura, Akiyuki 2014. Some notes on idiomatic expressions in the history of English: With special reference to 'meat and drink'. In Yoko Iyeiri & Jennifer Smith (eds.), *Studies in Middle and Modern English: historical change*, 115-32. Osaka: Osaka Books.

Katami, Akio 2014. Cyusei ingulando shinpisyugisya no sanbun ni okeru settoku no gihou [Rhetoric for persuasion in medieval English mystical prose]. In Satoshi Kinsui, Hiroyuki Takada & Michi Shiina (eds.), *Rekishi gengogaku no sekai* [Horizons of historical pragmatics: grammaticalization, politeness and speech act], 163-88. Tokyo: Hituzi Syobo Publishing.

Kukita, Yoshikawa, Naoë 2014. *Iryou to sinntai no zushougaku* [Images of medicine, religion and gender in late medieval society]. Tokyo: Chisenshokan.

Kukita, Yoshikawa, Naoë (ed.) 2015. *Medicine, religion and gender in medieval culture,* Cambridge: D.S. Brewer.

Lewis, E. Robert (eds.) 1952-2001. *Middle English Dictionary.* Ann Arbor: University of Michigan Press.

OED = Oxford English Dictionary. <http://www.oed.com>. Last accessed May 2017.

Tani, Akinobu 2008. Chaucer no sanbun sakuhin ni okeru waado-pea shiyou [Word pairs in Chaucer's prose]. In Mitsunori Imai & Hideo Nishimura (eds.), *Kotoba no hibiki* [Words at heart], 89-116. Tokyo: Kaibunsha.

Undwehill, Evelyn 1911. *Mysticism*, London: Methuen.

Wallace, David (ed.) 1999. *The Cambridge history of medieval English literature*. Cambridge, Cambridge University Press.

Watson, Nicholas & Jacqueline Jenkins (eds.) 2005. *The writings of Julian of Norwich: A vision showed to a devout woman and a revelation of love*. Pennsylvania, The Pennsylvania State University Press.

Windeatt, Barry 2004. 'I use but Comownycacyon and Good Wordys': Teaching and *the Book of Margery Kempe*. In Dee Dyas, Valerie Edden & Roger Ellis (eds.), *Approaching Medieval English anchoritic and mystical texts*, 115-28. Cambridge: D.S.Brewer.

James Joyce and a freer flow of consciousness

Shigeo Kikuchi

Abstract

In this article I will focus on how the techniques which James Joyce used to represent his characters' consciousness were elevated to a freer type of representation which flows across the characters' thought boundaries. The stream-of-consciousness writing style, which Joyce used, is a way of writing which covers all the different means used by an author to convey his or her characters' thought processes. In the more mature stage of Joyce's writing career, he created characters whose stream of consciousness flows freely into the consciousness of other characters. I will first discuss the development of Joyce's experiment with this writing technique, and then, after a brief discussion of the ordinary stream-of-consciousness style, I will discuss what I think of this method of writing.

1. Introduction

A character's consciousness can be represented in two main ways, i.e. interior monologue and free indirect discourse, as David Lodge describes in his *The Art of Fiction*:

> There are two staple techniques for representing consciousness in prose fiction. One is *interior monologue*, in which the grammatical subject of the discourse is an "I," and we, as it were, overhear the character verbalizing his or her thoughts as they occur… The other method, called *free indirect style*, goes back at least as far as Jane Austen, but was employed with ever-increasing scope and virtuosity by modern novelists like Woolf. It renders thought as reported speech (in the third person, past tense) but keeps to the kind of vocabulary that is appropriate to the character, and deletes some of the tags, like "she thought," "she wondered," "she asked herself" etc. that a more formal narrative style would require. This gives the illusion of intimate access to a character's mind, but without totally surrendering authorial participation in the discourse.   (Lodge 1992: 43) (Italics in extracts mine throughout.)

Interior monologue presents the scenes around the character directly through his or her consciousness without the use of a narrator, as in Molly Bloom's monologue in *Ulysses*. Free indirect discourse was widely used by modernist writers such as Jane Austen, Virginia Woolf, and, of course, Joyce, but he took a step beyond them.

140 *Shigeo Kikuchi*

2. Joyce's use of interior monologue and free indirect discourse

Interior monologue is defined as "a literary attempt to present the mental processes of a character before they are formed into regular patterns of speech or logical sequence" (*Collins Online Dictionary*). Joyce credited his use of this style to "an obscure French novelist of the late nineteenth century, Edouard Dujardin)" (Lodge 1992: 47-48). It is said that "Joyce had picked up a copy of *Les Lauriers sont coupés* in Tours in March 1903 and it had a significant influence on his use of interior monologue" (James Joyce Centre[1]). In 1922 Joyce told his friend and translator Valéry Larbaud that his inspiration had come from reading Dujardin: "Dans *Les Lauriers son coupés* […] le lecteur se trouve installé, dès les premières lignes, dans la pensée du personage principal, et c'est le déroulement ininterrompu de cette pensée qui, se substituent complètement à la forme usuelle du récit, nous apprend ce que fait ce personage et ce qui lui arrive." (In *Les Lauriers sont Coupés* [...] the reader is installed, from the very outset, in the thought of the principal personage, and it is the uninterrupted development of his thought which completely replaces the usual form of narrative, and tells us what the character does and what happens to him.) (Tumanov 1997: 55) For example, in the following extract from Dujardin's *Les Lauriers sont coupés* (The Laurels Have Been Cut[2]), the italicized part is the monologue uttered inside the narrator's mind:

> — « Vous espérez la toucher ? »
> *Il ricane; il est insupportable. Eh bien, non, elle n'est pas la fille qu'on soupçonnerait. Et quand même!... La rue de Rivoli; traversons; gare aux voitures; quelle foule ce soir; six heures, c'est l'heure de la cohue, en ce quartier surtout; la trompe du tramway; garons-nous.*
> — « Il y a un peu moins de monde sur ce côté droit » dis-je.
>
> (Dujardin, "Les Lauriers sont coupés," Chapter 1)

---

[1] The James Joyce Centre is situated at 35 North Great George's Street, Dublin 1, Ireland (URL: http://jamesjoyce.ie). According to the Centre's web page, it is "dedicated to promoting understanding of the life and works of James Joyce. Set over three floors, the Centre covers Joyce's life and work with a permanent interactive exhibition on *Ulysses*."

[2] It is a story of six hours in the life of a young man who is in love with a young lady. During this "six hours" no adventures occur. The density generally contained in the action of a narrative is here realized in the interior of the hero, Daniel Prince, who speaks to himself. Thirty years before James Joyce, Virginia Woolf and William Faulkner, Edouard Dujardin experiences interior monologue with this romantic figure.

James Joyce and a freer flow of consciousness   141

— «Do you hope to touch her? »
He smirks; he is unbearable. Well, no, she is not the girl everyone suspects her to be. And anyway!... The rue de Rivoli; let's cross; be careful about the cars; What a crowd tonight; six is the rush hour time, in this area above all; the horn of the horse tramway; watch out.
— «It is a little less crowded on the right side » I say.

Dujardin's interior monologue, which is a direct representation of the thoughts of the narrator, who is narrating the story in the first person, continues throughout the text. A typical Joycean interior monologue, such as we find in *Ulysses*, is different from Dujardi's in that the story is narrated by a third-person narrator. The following is from a scene in which Leopold Bloom is about to leave the house in the morning to go to buy a pork kidney (Lodge 1992: 48-49). In this scene Bloom's unspoken monologue appears in the middle of a third-person narration:

> On the doorstep he felt in his hip pocket for the latchkey. *Not there. In the trousers I left off must get it. Potato I have. Creaky wardrobe. No use disturbing her.* She turned over sleepily that time. He pulled the halldoor to after him very quietly, *more*, till the footleaf dropped gently over the threshold, a limp lid. Looked shut. *All right till I come back anyhow.*[3]   (Joyce, *Ulysses*, 55 (Episode 4))

The second method of representing a person's thoughts, i.e. free indirect thought, is used in "Looked shut" in the above passage. As Leech and Short (2007 [1981]: 270-71) say, in free indirect thought the narrator's position is in the present, looking back at the past when the event occurred. In the following examples, the narrator's position outside the person to whom her love is directed renders the person into "him," while the narrator's viewpoint looking back at the past from the present causes the use of the past tense "Did" in [23]:

[21] Does she still love me? (Free Direct Thought: FDT)
[22] He wondered, 'Does she still love me?' (Direct Thought: DT)
[23] Did she still love him? (Free Indirect Thought: FIT)
[24] He wondered if she still loved him. (Indirect Thought: IT)
[25] He wondered about her love for him. (Narrative Report of a Thought Act: NRTA)   (Leech and Short 2007 [1981]: 270-71)

---

[3] All Joyce's texts used are of the 1st edition, which are available online.

142   *Shigeo Kikuchi*

This is why Lodge (1992: 49) argues that the past tense in "Looked" in "Looked shut" above marks the two-word phrase as free indirect style. Joyce's experimental attempt to reveal a character's thoughts, however, began with this writing technique as far back as *Dubliners*.

3. An early stage: free indirect thought
Joyce's first linguistic experiment with representing a character's unspoken thoughts began with free indirect thought, which consists of the representation of a character's thoughts through the narrator's language adopting the character's linguistic style. Jane Austen is acknowledged to be the first English novelist to use this method of expressing a character's thoughts (Burke 2014: 224). Joyce's early attempt to use this technique was in line with Austen's, and was conservative and traditional rather than innovative. We first see him use it in *Dubliners*. In this collection of short stories, Joyce's writing style is very descriptive and one often feels that he gives only the facts of the story, yet in its objective and fact-reporting style there are embryonic traces of his attempts to express his notion of "freer border crossing" in writing.

For example, in the following extract towards the end of "Eveline," Eveline's thoughts are inserted in the form of free indirect thought:

> If she went, to-morrow she would be on the sea with Frank, steaming towards Buenos Aires. Their passage had been booked. *Could she still draw back after all he had done for her?* Her distress awoke a nausea in her body and she kept moving her lips in silent fervent prayer.
>
> (Joyce, "Eveline," *Dubliners*, 48)

Similarly in "A Little Cloud":

> He was beginning to feel somewhat disillusioned. Gallaher's accent and way of expressing himself did not please him. There was something vulgar in his friend which he had not observed before. *But perhaps it was only the result of living in London amid the bustle and competition of the Press.* The old personal charm was still there under this new gaudy manner. And, after all, Gallaher had lived, he had seen the world. Little Chandler looked at his friend enviously.
>
> (Joyce, "A Little Cloud," *Dubliners*, 92)

In the extracts above, the two italicized parts are examples of free indirect thought, and they can be rendered in direct thought as "Can I still draw back after all he has done for me?" and "But perhaps it is only the result of living in London amid the bustle and competition of the Press."

Joyce's use of free indirect discourse in his third-person narration allows the reader to get inside his characters' minds. Free indirect thought, which lacks a main clause such as 'He/She thought that' forming a bridge between the surrounding narration and the narrated thought, was the first stage of his border-eliminating or border-blurring technique of writing.

Free indirect discourse was first used by Austen, so Joyce's use of this technique to blur the demarcation between the surrounding narration and narrated thoughts was not something completely new. However, when we consider other similar border-blurring techniques in Joyce's works after *Dubliners*, we can infer from his use of free indirect thought at this stage that he seems to have become more conscious of thought's crossing of syntactic demarcations in writing.

4. The representation of free thought: the use of a dash instead of quotation marks

In *Dubliners* Joyce used quotation marks to indicate spoken language, but in *A Portrait of the Artist as a Young Man* he used a dash instead, and thus he acquired a new technique to blur verbal demarcations. In the following extract from *Dubliners,* we see that quoted speech is placed in quotation marks, which separate the speech from the reporting clause "said I":

> 'Well, so your old friend is gone, you'll be sorry to hear.'
> 'Who?' *said I.*
> 'Father Flynn.'   (Joyce, "The Sisters," *Dubliners*, 10)

In *A Portrait of the Artist as a Young Man*, Joyce blurred the border between quoted speech and the main clause by the use of a dash, or sometimes with just a comma. In the following extract, the reporting clause "he said" and "Stephen said" are separated from the reported part with only a comma, which is used to indicate a brief pause or separation between one person's utterance and the narration:

144   *Shigeo Kikuchi*

> —Now it is all about politics in the papers, *he said*. Do your people talk about that too?
> —Yes, Stephen said.
> —Mine too, *he said*.   (Joyce, *A Portrait*, 23)

In the above extract, dashes and commas play the role of quotation marks in demarcating reported speech and reporting clauses, and they make the border between the characters' words and the narrator's less clear.

5. The third stage: the use of free direct thought to express an interior monologue

In *Ulysses,* we see Joyce presenting his characters' thoughts (i.e. free direct thought) with neither quotation marks nor commas, as in the following extract:

> *No, mother! Let me be and let me live.*
> —Kinch ahoy!
> Buck Mulligan's voice sang from within the tower.
>   (Joyce, *Ulysses*, 10 (Episode 1))

Virginia Woolf also presented her characters' thoughts without framing devices such as quotation marks. In *To the Lighthouse*, the characters' free thoughts are used as accompaniments to ordinary indirect thoughts. As the character Mrs Ramsey looks round the house, her thoughts begin as free indirect thought, which appears without the main clause "Mrs Ramsey thought" and the conjunction "that," then change to free direct thought or interior monologue with the verbs in the present tense (shown in italics below), before reverting to free indirect thought. The last sentence of the following is a third person narration, and is not Mrs Ramsey's thought:

> FREE INDIRECT THOUGHT ("Mrs Ramsey thought that" is omitted) The mat was fading; the wall-paper was flapping. You couldn't tell any more that those were roses on it. FREE DIRECT THOUGHT (verb in present tense) *Still, if every door in a house is left perpetually open, and no lockmaker in the whole of Scotland can mend a bolt, things must spoil.* FREE INDIRECT THOUGHT ("Mrs Ramsey thought that" is omitted) What was the use of flinging a green Cashmere shawl over the edge of a picture frame? In two weeks it would be the colour of pea soup. (third person narration) But it was the doors that annoyed her; every door was left open. (Woolf, *To the Lighthouse*, 25-6 (Chapter 5)) (explanatory additions and italics mine)

This technique is also used in *Ulysses,* i.e. free direct thought is used to express an interior monologue. In this work Joyce also experimented with a new writing style in which a character's thoughts flow into those of another character. In other words, not only are a character's thoughts portrayed directly, but also they are presented in another character's mind.

6. A new stage of consciousness presentation: A character's consciousness is represented in another character's mind

Ulysses has a scene in which what a character says is verbally repeated in another character's utterance, which actually cannot be what the latter person receives.

Communication takes place between two or more parties and it is successful only if what is thought in one person's mind is transmitted to the other. When we read an exchange between two characters, we naturally assume that what is said by one character is successfully transmitted to the other. This, however, is not always the case. The following exchange, a classroom scene in Episode 2 of *Ulysses*, in which Stephen Dedalus is teaching history to students, deludes the reader into assuming that the utterance by a pupil called Armstrong is successfully transmitted to Stephen and the pupils around him. Stephen asks Armstrong about the death of King Pyrrhus after a battle with the Romans. Armstrong answers thus, which makes his classmates laugh:

> —Pyrrhus, sir? *Pyrrhus, a pier.*
> All laughed. Mirthless high malicious laughter. Armstrong looked round at his classmates, silly glee in profile.
>
> (Joyce, *Ulysses*, 24-25 (Episode 2))

At first reading there seems to be nothing strange in this exchange. We can understand what message is encoded in Armstrong's mind because it is represented before us as words on the page, and we assume it is conveyed to the other pupils and Stephen Dedalus. Armstrong's fellow students and Stephen understand "Pyrrhus" because it has been the topic of their talk. However, we do not expect "a pier" to follow "Pyrrhus" because there is no syntactic or semantic connection whatsoever between "pier" and "Pyrrhus." It is more reasonable to infer

146 *Shigeo Kikuchi*

that what is constructed in the addressee's mind in the fictional world
is only the sound /əpɪə/ or the Irish pronunciation /əpɪər/, and not the
words 'a pier.' As if to prove this, Stephen asks as follows:

> —Tell me now, Stephen said, poking the boy's shoulder with the book,
> what is a pier?
> —A pier, sir, Armstrong said. A thing out in the waves. A kind of
> bridge. Kingstown pier, sir.   (Joyce, *Ulysses*, 25 (Episode 2))

Stephen's "a pier" in his question "what is a pier?" is also only what
is in Armstrong's mind. So Stephen's "a pier" should be only the sound
/əpɪə(r)/. Armstrong's thought is realized in Stephen's mind on the
page and the readers mistake it for what is understood by Stephen and
the other pupils. Because "a pier" is printed on the page, the reader is
misdirected into believing that what Armstrong said has been understood by the other students and Stephen.

Armstrong understands that what he has said is not conveyed to the
others, and this is why he adds an explanation of the word: "A thing
out in the waves. A kind of bridge. Kingstown pier, sir."

When the pupils laugh for the first time, it is because Armstrong's
reply has nothing to do with "Pyrrhus." The second time they laugh,
however, there are a few students who know what the pier means for
the young couples who enjoy dating there:

> Some laughed again: mirthless but with meaning. Two in the back bench
> whispered. Yes. They knew: had never learned nor ever been innocent.
>   (Joyce, *Ulysses*, 25 (Episode 2))

Their second laughter is based upon their understanding of the word
conveyed.

Usually what is thought is never understood by the other characters.
This is not so if it is not what is commonly understood even when it is
verbally expressed. The following extract is from a mystery novel in
which two characters are talking about a murdered woman called
Helen Grehm, whose surname has not been heard correctly by Megs:

> Megs nodded. "We talked some. He seems real interested in some
> woman named Helen. I'm not sure I caught the last name. Graham or
> Grim, I think."
> Eddie's eyes narrowed. "Really?"   (Pease, *The Monkey's Fist*, 112)

Another extract from the same novel reveals the author's concern with the exactness of communication:

> "Who hired Nickles?" asked the chairman.
> "We have a name. Bolles. That's B-O-L-L-E-S. Garland Bolles, and an address on Fifteenth Street here in town."
>
> (Pease, *The Monkey's Fist*, 119)

"Garland" is not spelled out above because this name is quite common.

An uncommon idea is usually left uncommunicated or spelled out as above, or it sometimes used humorously as in the famous "throw away (verbal phrase)–Throwaway (horse's name)" exchange between Leopold Bloom and Bantam Lyons in *Ulysses*.

The contemporary writer Paul Auster does not seem to have any interest in Joyce's way of writing in which thoughts cross the borders of a consciousness, but we can see a similar tendency in his works. His "City of Glass" in his *New York Trilogy* begins with Daniel Quinn, a mystery writer, visiting a character called Paul Auster and introducing himself:

> "Do you have a name?"
> "I'm sorry. Of course I do. Quinn."
> "*Quinn* what."
> "Daniel Quinn."   (Auster, "City of Glass," *New York Trilogy*, 93)

This passage shows that the correct spelling of "Quinn" is conveyed to the interlocutor. Although the name could be spelled "Q-u-i-n" with one *n*, like Harley Quin, a detective created by Agatha Christie, and although this is quite likely since that the "City of Glass" is a detective story, the author does not seem to pay attention to a possible discrepancy between what is said and what is communicated.

A similar example by Joyce is "*It is mine. I paid the rent.*" in Stephen Dedalus's monologue "He wants that key. *It is mine. I paid the rent.* Now I eat his salt bread. Give him the key too." Kenner (1980: 55n-56n) maintains that Mulligan has paid the rent, and the italicized words are a reflection of Mulligan's voice. In the "Pyrrhus, a pier." extract quoted above, Joyce goes one step further in showing a thought crossing from one person's consciousness into that of another.

7. Conclusion

In addition to using conventional orthographical devices for blurring syntactic borders when presenting free indirect thought, Joyce experimented with a new type of consciousness representation which takes place across speakers' consciousness borders, though this technique did not become fully fledged until *Ulysses*.

Shigematsu's (2016) argument regarding the correlation between Daniel Defoe's fictional world and the real world can also be applied to Joyce. Joyce's language and his creation of fictional stories mirror his border-crossing life from Dublin to the European continent, and from one city in Europe to another. The language of *Ulysses* reflects the author's wandering life, in which he kept moving across the boundaries of cities and countries. While living in this way, and influenced by the fact that Ireland was struggling for independence from Britain, he created his own unique writing technique in which a character's thoughts flow more and more freely across the boundaries between characters' minds.

Texts used

Auster, Paul 1987 [1985]. *The New York trilogy*. London: Faber and Faber.

Dujardin, Edouard 2001[1887]. Les lauriers sont coupes. *La Revue Indépendante*. <https://fr.wikisource.org/wiki/Les_Lauriers_sont_coup%C3%A9s/I> (Last accessed 31 July 2017).

Joyce, James 1914. *Dubliners*. London: Grant Richards Ltd. <https://archive.org/stream/dubliners00joycrich#page/n7/mode/2up> (Last accessed 31 July 2017).

Joyce, James 1916. *A portrait of the artist as a young man*. New York: B.W. Huebsch, Inc. <https://archive.org/details/ofartistportrait00joycrich> (Last accessed 31 July 2017).

Joyce, James 1922. *Ulysses*. London: The Egoist Press. <https://archive.org/details/ulysses00joyc_1> (Last accessed 31 July 2017).

Pease, William D. 1996. *The monkey's fist*. New York: Onyx.

Woolf, Virginia 2008 [1927]. *To the lighthouse*. Oxford: Oxford University Press.

References

Burke, Michael 2014. *The Routledge handbook of stylistics*. London and New York: Routledge.

Collins English Dictionary online. <https://www.collinsdictionary.com/dictionary/english/interior-monologue> (Last accessed 31 July 2017).

The James Joyce centre (2014) "On this day...22 July." <http://jamesjoyce.ie/on-this-day- 22-july/> (Last accessed 31 July 2017).

Lodge, David 1992. *The art of fiction.* London: Penguin.

Leech, Geoffrey & Mick Short (2007) *Style in fiction: A linguistic introduction to English fictional prose.* The 2nd ed. London: Pearson Education.

Shigematsu, Eri (2016) Towards authenticity: Narrative techniques for representing consciousness in Defoe's *Moll Flanders* and *Roxana. PALA 2016 Proceedings online.* <http://www.pala.ac.uk/uploads/2/5/1/0/25105678/shigematsu_eri.pdf> (Last accessed 31 July 2017).

Tumanov, Vladimir (1997) *Mind reading: Unframed interior monologue in European fiction.* Amsterdam: Rodopi.

A study of Matthew Bramble's language and epistolary style in *The Expedition of Humphrey Clinker*

Hironobu Konishi

Abstract

The Expedition of Humphrey Clinker (1771) was one of the eighteenth-century readers' favorites. The novel was produced as an epistolary novel. This style had been popular since *Pamela* published in 1740. The popularity is attributed to the letter writing characters' impressive narrations as well as to the comic and romantic plot. The main character is Matthew Bramble. He is a benevolent misanthropist, and his ambivalent personality impresses readers. In this paper, the reader will see Matthew's verbal characterization through his language and epistolary style in the novel. His language is analysed in four points: vocabulary, grammar and speech style, and spelling; his epistolary style, in three: epistolary technique, contrastive expression, and metaphorical expression. After seeing the analyses, Matthew is the very character of sensibility that Smollett created to attempt to achieve popularity among readers in the late eighteenth century.

1. Introduction

Tobias Smollett's last novel *The Expedition of Humphrey Clinker* (henceforward, *Humphrey Clinker*) was published in 1771, one year after his death. Before the novel, Smollett's novels were already popular among English readers in the late eighteenth century. [1] *Humphrey Clinker* is an epistolary novel, presented in the form of letters written by six characters. Lewis M. Knapp (1996: vii) writes, "They all gossip about each other, and they describe their own travelling adventures." The readers enjoy not only the comic and romantic plot of the novel through their letters, but also their unique and ridiculous narrations. William Thackeray was impressed by Smollett's comic powers, saying "The novel of 'Humphrey Clinker' is, I do think, the most laughable story that has ever been written since the goodly art of novel-writing began" (Cunliffe & Watt 1911: 173).

---

[1] *The Adventures of Peregrine Pickle* (1751) and *The Adventures of Roderick Random* (1748) are the fictions the heroine Lydia Languish hurriedly conceals in Act I of Richard Sheridan's *The Rivals* (1775).

It is well known that the successful English epistolary novel began with Samuel Richardson's *Pamela* (1740). Smollett obviously followed Richardson's epistolary style in writing *Humphrey Clinker* so that he might achieve the popularity of the then readers. He probably established his epistolary novel style in writing *Humphrey Clinker*.

Among *Humphrey Clinker*'s pleasing and realistic characters, Matthew Bramble and his nephew Jery Melford write more letters than the other characters because they play a role of giving readers the outline of the novel. This paper is to show Matthew's verbal characterization through his language and epistolary style in the novel.

2. Epistolary form of *Humphrey Clinker*

According to Manfred Görlach (2001: 211), "The domain of letters expanded dramatically in the eighteenth century." A great number of letter-writing guide books were published, and they are careful to give specific rules for letters meant for business, love, consolation, recommendation, etc. Görlach (2001: 211) writes, "Convention relate to address, opening formulas, conclusions and subscription." Epistolary form of a novel was one of the important narrative devices in the eighteenth century. The letters of a novel are written not by one character but by several characters, which establishes multiple points of view. The usual structure of epistolary form is composed of the exchange of correspondence among characters. Norman Page (1973: 47) comments on the important narrative technique of the eighteenth-century epistolary novels as follows:

> In the great eighteenth-century epistolary novels, from *Clarrisa* and *Grandison* to *Humphrey Clinker* and *Evelina*, the letter is the exclusive or principal medium for conducting the narrative, and the effect is of a series of monologues, many of them springing from an immediate dramatic situation, and some of them (like Byron's letters) displaying a carefully-contrived spontaneity which Richardson and his followers felt to be one of the supreme virtues of the medium.

In writing *Humphrey Clinker* in letter form, Smollett surely noticed the great popularity of Samuel Richardson's epistolary novels, and

A study of Matthew Bramble's language and epistolary style   153

followed his technique.[2] In *Humphrey Clinker*, however, all of the letters are outgoing and none are received except one letter from Mr. Wilson to Lydia. The correspondence is one-sided, which is different from Richardson's novels. Smollett's use of this device is associated with his vision that reality is relative. For example, several characters give their own impression of Bath. The differences in their points of view come not only from their different ages but also their temperaments. Smollett does not maintain that any one impression is right or wrong. He just presents different individual responses to the something in order to show that reality exists in this myriad of individual responses. Yukari Kanzaki (1994: 9) writes, "This is the way Smollett understands the reality. The epistolary method in *Humphrey Clinker* is very effective in showing the author's relativistic vision of reality."

"Unlike Richardson," Smollett places the letter-writers' "separate stories into complementary rather than competing relations with one another, which is why they are able to move so credibly toward the novel's harmonious ending" (Beasley 1998: 186-87). Furthermore, Smollett sometimes uses the method to satire the world sharply and ridiculously. For example, Matthew observes and criticizes London as follows:

> (1) The hod-carrier, the low mechanic, the tapster, the publican, the shop-keeper, the pettifogger, the citizen, and courtier, *all tread upon the kibes of one another*: actuated by the demons of profligacy and licentiousness, they are seen every where, rambling, riding, rolling, rushing, justling, mixing, bouncing, cracking, and crashing in one vile ferment of stupidity and corruption—All is tumult and hurry; one would imagine they were impelled by some disorder of the brain, that will not suffer them to be at rest.... In a word, the whole nation seems to be running out of their wits. (88)[3]

All of Smollett's novels are comedies with satiric energy. Here is one impressive instance in which the reader feels the novelist's satire and comedy.

---

[2] About the composition of *Humphrey Clinker*, Knapp (1949: 322) writes, "This novel extension of Richardson's epistolary method, suggested to Smollett by Anstey's *New Bath Guide*, is very successful in effecting narrative variety and in enriching the setting and the characterization."

[3] The text is *The Expedition of Humphrey Clinker* edited by Lewis M. Knapp (1966). The number in parentheses indicates the page number of the text.

3. Matthew Bramble's letters

Matthew is a gouty country squire, and travels with his family from his country Gloucester to Buxton. The journey takes about eight months: from April 2 to November 20. He writes twenty seven letters during his journey, and gives them only to Dr. Lewis, his personal physician and old friend. He may be considered to be one of the main characters of the novel with another, Jery having twenty eight letters. The total number of the letters is eighty three. Thus, chiefly through the eyes of Matthew and his nephew, the reader sees the world of *Humphrey Clinker*. Paul-Gabriel Boucé (1976: 203) writes, "Matthew Bramble is searching for the physical health which will also bring him psychological and moral equilibrium." He writes to his doctor about a variety of his journey experiences as well as his physical condition. *Humphrey Clinker* "is saturated with colorful and authentic details of all sorts of manners, costumes, and food and drink" (Knapp 1949: 32). The other characters also report, in detail, the people, scenery, manners, and incidents that they meet with at every spot of their journey.

Matthew comments on manners, places, and people in England and Scotland. His first letter begins with the passage as follows:

> (2) DOCTOR, THE pills are good for nothing—I might as well swallow snowballs to cool my reins—I have told you over and over, how hard I am to move; and at this time of day, I ought to know something of my own constitution. Why will you be so positive? Prithee send me another prescription—I am as lame and as much tortured in all my limbs as if I was broke upon the wheel: indeed, I am equally distressed in mind and body—As if I had not plagues enough of my own, those children of my sister are left me for a perpetual source of vexation—what business have people to get children to plague their neighbours? (5)

In the above citation (2), Matthew grumbles about his present physical situation to his doctor Lewis writing breathless sequences. According to Boucé (1976: 236), "Bramble uses a solidly negative vocabulary, and the jerky, cantankerous sentences give the impression of a kind of egocentric interior monologue." The citation (2) gives the reader the hint of his character. Also, his personality places him into a variety of troubles, meeting with various people and incidents on the way. During his stay in Bath, he writes about his mind as follows:

(3) IF I did not know that the exercise of your profession has habituated you to the hearing of complaints, I should make a conscience of troubling you with my correspondence, which may be truly called *the lamentations of Matthew Bramble*. (33)

He has such a faint heart as to feel sorry for his doctor who reads his letters. Some of Matthew's letters end with the following such apologetic remarks as follows:

(4) And now, dear Dick, I must tell you for your comfort, that you are the only man upon earth to whom I would presume to send such a long-winded epistle, which I could not find in my heart to curtail, because the subject interested the warmest passions of my heart; neither will I make any other apology to a correspondent who has been so long accustomed to the impertinence of Sept. 30. MATT. BRAMBLE (297)

He shows such respect or esteem for his doctor through this type of apology, which reveals his delicate and sensible nature.

4. Matthew Bramble's personality

Smollett tends to make a caricature of not a few characters of his novels. Matthew is among them. The reader should know he has two mixed personalities: misanthropy and sensibility. Jery writes his impression of his uncle to his friend as follows:

(5) Mr. Bramble's character, which seems to interest you greatly, opens and improves upon me every day.—His singularities afford a rich mine of entertainment: his understanding, so far as I can judge, is well cultivated: his observations on life are equally just, pertinent, and uncommon. He affects misanthropy, in order to conceal the sensibility of a heart, which is tender, even to a degree of weakness. This delicacy of feeling, or soreness of the mind, makes him timorous and fearful; but then he is afraid of nothing so much as of dishonor; and although he is exceedingly cautious of giving offence, he will fire at the least hint of insolence or ill-breeding. (28)

Jery adds that "Mr. Bramble is extravagantly delicate in all his sensations, both of soul and body" (67). Actually Matthew is greatly annoyed with the noise, filth and unhealthiness of the crowd when in Bath and London.[4]

---

[4] Janet Gurkin Altman (1982: 175) writes, "Bramble's letters are marked by

156 *Hironobu Konishi*

Matthew himself admits and sighs over his misanthropy, grumbling about the people in Bath. He writes: "Heark ye, Lewis, my misanthropy increases every day—The longer I live, I find the folly and the fraud of mankind grow more and more intolerable—" (47).

As for Matthew's sensibility, Lydia Melford, Mathew's niece, also writes: "To me, however, he is always good-natured and generous, even beyond my wish. Since we came hither, he has made me a present of a suit of clothes, with trimmings and laces, which cost more money than I shall mention" (94). Jery adds about Matthew's benevolence of giving alms to the poor as follows:

> (6) After a short pause, he said, in a croaking tone of voice, which confounded me not a little, 'Madam, I am truly concerned for your misfortunes; and if this trifle can be of any service to you, I beg you will accept it without ceremony.' So saying, he put a bit of paper into her hand.... (21)

Through their letters, the reader knows Matthew is, what is called, a man of feeling. Thomas R. Preston (1964: 52) comments on Matthew's contradicting personality as follows:

> To some extent, Bramble's peculiar mixture of misanthropy and feeling may be Smollett's idealization of his own personality; in the chronology of Smollett's writings he is also a further development of the splenetic traveler of the *Travels through France and Italy*.

The model of Matthew is Smollett himself. Knapp (1949: 322) writes, "Bramble, who is often the true image of the author's own self." Smollett makes an interesting conversation in the novel concerning the name "Bramble." According to *The Oxford English Dictionary* (1989[2]), the meaning of "bramble" is "A rough prickly shrub, specifically the blackberry bush" (s.v. *bramble*, 1). One day, Matthew is addressed by the duke of Newcastle: "My dear Mr. Brambleberry!" (113). Another day, he replies to the duke's question by saying, "the Blackberry is the fruit of the Bramble—But, I believe, the bishop is not a berry of our bush" (98). Here Smollett does such a word-play as *Bramble* in naming his characters.

---

the repetition of the themes of noise, filth, and health—concerns and repetitions that are natural to an elderly man...."

A study of Matthew Bramble's language and epistolary style   157

5. Language of Matthew
Novel writers use their ingenuity to illustrate the personalities of their novels' characters through the language used by the characters in the novels. The reader will see Matthew's characterization in these four points: vocabulary, grammar, speech style, and spelling.

5.1. Vocabulary
According to Jery's letters in Section 4, Matthew is a benevolent misanthropist. Also, his social position is a country squire. The reader will see his vocabulary reflecting his ambivalent personality and social position.

In the eighteenth and nineteenth centuries, a "squire" could be a designated landowner (possibly of renown) who served as a private legal entity in the local court system. In *Humphrey Clinker*, he is beloved as a sensible and respectable master at his Brambleton-hall in Wales. He is supposed to speak in standard English,[5] and graduated from Oxford, which ensures that he is familiar with classical languages. He often writes a kind inkhorn or technical terms like "constitution" (5) and "valetudinarians" (181). Those words are polysyllabic, and have French or Latin origins. Tabitha Bramble, Matthew's sister, and her maid Win Jenkins cannot write the correct spelling of those words in their letters.

In Matthew's first letter of April 2, he writes to his doctor about his physical condition and requests for his doctor's advice, and the reader sees the medical terms "pills," "physic(s)," and "constitution." Other examples like "stomach and bowel" (141) are frequently found in his letters.

In his letter of May 8, he describes the cause of his swooning at a ball as if he were a doctor as follows:

> (7) ...my swooning was entirely occasioned by an accidental impression of fetid effluvia upon nerves of uncommon sensibility. I know not how other people's nerves are constructed; but one would imagine they must be made of very coarse materials, to stand the

---

[5] N.F. Blake (1981: 108) writes, "The cultivation of a standard English became the mark of a gentleman as outlined in his letter by Lord Chesterfield, who was regarded by many at the time as an authority on such matters."

shock of such a horrid assault. It was, indeed, *a compound of villainous smells*, in which the most violent stinks, and the most powerful perfumes, contended for the mastery. Imagine to yourself a high exalted essence of mingled odours, arising from putrid gums, imposthumated lungs, sour flatulencies, rank arm-pit, sweating feet, running sores and issues, plasters, ointments, and embrocations, hungry-water, spirit of lavender, assafoetida drops, musk, hartshorn, and sal volatile; besides a thousand frowzy steams, which I could not analyse.... (65-66)

In his letter of May 5, he responds to the world of Bath with bewilderment, and describes coffee-house patrons in Bath as follows:

(8) We consisted of thirteen individuals; seven lamed by the gout, rheumatism, or palsy; three maimed by accident; and the rest either deaf or blind. One hobbled, another hopped, a third dragged his legs after him like a wounded snake, a fourth straddled betwixt a pair of long crutches, like the mummy of a felon hanging in chains; a fifth was bent into a horizontal position, like a mounted telescope, shoved in by a couple of chairmen; and a sixth was the bust of a man, set upright in a wheel machine, which the waiter moved from place to place. (54-55)

He sees the world as a reflection of his own valetudinarian temperament: he is hypersensitive to certain objects and his view of the world is eloquently determined by the language of a sick man. Clive T. Probyn (1987: 121) writes, "His [Matthew's] eyes pick out details metamorphosed into grotesque travesties of the normal." Smollett was a doctor in profession, and his medical knowledge and experience help easily create such a scene as above. Occupational backgrounds may give the story of a novel a sense of authenticity and a convincing framework for the strange characters (Boulton 1975: 134).

Matthew's personality, benevolence and misanthropy, appear in several scenes in his letters. He writes about the inconvenience of Bath as follows:

(9) The inconveniences which I overlooked in the high-day of health, will naturally strike with exaggerated impression on the irritable nerves of an invalid, surprised by premature old age, and shattered with long-suffering—But, I believe, you will not deny, that this place, which Nature and Providence seem to have intended as a resource

A study of Matthew Bramble's language and epistolary style   159

> from distemper and disquiet, is become the very center of racket and
> dissipation. Instead of that peace, tranquility and ease, so necessary
> to those who labour under bad health, weak nerves, and irregular
> spirits; here we have nothing but noise, tumult, and hurry; with the
> fatigue and slavery of maintaining a ceremonial, more stiff, formal,
> and oppressive, than the etiquette of a German elector. (34)

He dislikes the manners, places and people that deprive him of
"peace, tranquility and ease." The unbearably awful circumstances
cause his irritation and anger, which finally escalate his misanthropy.
Those circumstances are composed of negative vocabulary like
"irritable," "long suffering," and "distemper and disquiet."

Matthew and his party enjoy the fine view of the Leven and Lough-
Lomond after visiting Glasgow. He admires the beauties of the nature
around the lake as follows:

> (10) We now crossed the water of Leven, which, though nothing near so
> considerable as the Clyde, is much more transparent, pastoral, and
> delightful…. On this side they display a sweet variety of woodland,
> corn-field, and pasture, with several agreeable villas emerging as it
> were out of the lake, till, at some distance, the prospect terminates
> in huge mountains covered with heath, which being in the bloom,
> affords a very rich covering of purple. Every thing here is romantic
> beyond imagination. This country is justly styled the Arcadia of
> Scotland; and I don't doubt but it may vie with Arcadia in every
> thing but climate. (248)

He enjoys "peace, tranquility and ease," visiting the lake. He
admires the area as "the Arcadia of Scotland" and describes it with
positive adjectives like "transparent," "pastoral," "delightful," "sweet,"
"agreeable," "rich," and "romantic." Thus his vocabulary reflects his
personality and his social position, which Smollett elaborately uses to
create characterization in *Humphrey Clinker*.

5.2. Grammar
Matthew usually writes letters following the grammar of spoken
English language. He sometimes expresses irregularly, which is criticized as incorrect expression by the then grammarians. He switches
the second person pronouns *you* and *your* to the archaic pronouns *thou*,
thy and *thee* when he becomes very emotional. He welcomes Humphrey Clinker as his servant. He, while laughing, says, "Foregad! thou

art a complete fellow, I have a good mind to take thee into my family—
Pr'ythee, go and try if thou can'st make peace with my sister—Thou
ha'st given her much offence by shewing her thy naked tail" (84).

Matthew uses archaic forms such as "hath." He often puts the
archaic form "hath" after the relative pronoun *which* like "They look
like the wreck of streets and squares disjointed by an earthquake,
which hath broken the ground into a variety of holes and hillocks" (36).
Other examples are as follows:

> (11) he was obliged to part with his possession, which hath shifted hands
> two or three times since that period (251)/ I perceive that this is the
> place which hath animated the spirit (273)/ in consequence of that
> luxury which our connection with England hath greatly encouraged
> (278)/ so that a friendship ensued among the women, which hath
> continued to this day (326)

About the retention of *-(e)th* in verbal inflection, Görlach (1999:
512) notes it "is a conservative feature rather than a regional one," and
wonders "what extent members of the landed gentry did not care to
adopt standard speech, and possibly cultivated certain local features in
their pronunciation."

Matthew uses the archaic native locative prefix *a-* like "a-foot" in
"those that walk a-foot" (35). Terttu Nevalainen (1999: 383) writes,
"The prefixal element *a-* is a reduced form of the Old English locative
preposition *on, an*." Other examples are "You must know, that now
being a-foot" (54), "YOU ask me, why I don't take the air a-horseback"
(64), "covered a-top" (89) and "nor interrupted, but in a-morning"
(118). Those archaic forms are used in his everyday conversation. His
use of incorrect forms could probably be attributed to his love of
provincial life in spite of his education.

5.3. Speech style

Matthew speaks to others changing his speech style from formal to
informal. Thus, the reader easily knows his attitude. He is a ranked
gentleman who usually meets others politely. In Jery's letter of May
10, his uncle speaks to his old friend reading newspaper: "Mr. Serle,
(resumed my uncle) I beg pardon for interrupting you; but I can't resist
the curiosity I have to know if you received a card on this occasion?"
(68) That speech of his is formal and polite.

A study of Matthew Bramble's language and epistolary style   161

On the other hand, he easily utters foul words like "dunghill" when he is in a rage. In Jery's letter of July 13, he describes Matthew's anger toward English people's arrogant nature: "I despise the insolence of those wretched libellers, which is akin to the arrogance of the village cock, who never crows but upon his own dunghill" (198). His informality makes him use swearing phrases like "what the devil" (141) for expressing himself emotionally. Other examples are "'sdeath" (12), "By Heaven" (64), and "Good Heaven" (45). Those speech items of his are informal and impolite. The changing speech style shows he has such strong feelings as to fail in propriety.

5.4. Spelling

Matthew writes to Dr. Lewis in correct spelling consistently. His sister Tabitha Bramble and her maid Win Jenkins write their letters in bad spelling. This difference makes an impressive contrast between men and women in the eighteenth century. G. H. Vallins (1954: 88) comments on the reason of their spelling difference as follows:

> It is significant that Smollett credits Matthew Bramble (Tabitha's brother) with normal Johnsonian spelling. But the ladies—whether of low rank or high—were traditionally bad spellers. Most of the primers of the period were addressed to various representatives of the lower classes—apprentices and the like-and also to ladies.

However, he sometimes writes in non-standard English spelling when he is in the mood of informality, too. In the letter of April 12, he writes about his sister Tabitha as follows:

> (12) As for that fantastical animal, my sister Tabby, you are no stranger to her qualifications—I vow to God, she is sometimes so intolerable, that I almost think she's the devil incarnate come to torment me for my sins; and yet I am conscious of no sins that ought to entail such family-plagues upon me—why the devil should not I shake off these torments at once?I an't[6] married to Tabby, thank Heaven! nor did I beget the other two: let them choose another guardian: for my part, I an't in a condition to take care of myself; much less to superintend the conduct of giddy-headed boys and girls. (12)

In the above citation (12), the non-standard contraction "an't" is

---

[6] Underlines are mine in this paper.

used twice. The contraction was colloquial or illiterate English instances in the eighteenth century.[7] Other examples of his are: "An't he game, Mr. Gwynn?" (53) "they say as how the very teeth an't safe in your head" (71), "An't you ashamed" (81), and "if the fellow an't speedily removed by Habeas Corpus" (150). He also utters the form in his speech: "An't you ashamed, fellow, to ride postilion without a shirt to cover your backside from the view of the ladies in the coach?" (81). Other illiterate contractions of his are "shan't" and "han't": "I shan't die by water—" (315) and "I han't broke bread" (81). He usually restricts the use of those contradictions in letters and speech, which shows he is a methodical person. He always prefers something equipped with order, propriety, and decorum.[8]

6. Matthew's epistolary style

Humphrey Clinker shows that the epistolary method is a rich source of stylistic variety and contrast. As seen in Section 2, Matthew's sour account of Bath is followed by his niece's gushing praise for the same place. The reader will also see Matthew's characterization through these three points of his epistolary style: epistolary technique, contrastive expression, and metaphorical expression.

6.1. Epistolary technique

The epistolary technique is striking in its variety, as is suggested straight away by the diversity of the ways in which the writers head their letters and the formulas they use in signing them. Matthew follows the eighteenth century's etiquette of writing letters, which shows he is a person of respecting social order.

R. W. Chapman (1963: 147) writes, "The Opening Formula is normally 'Sir,' 'Dear Sir,' and the like." Boucé (1976: 193) writes, "Going only by the mode of address, it would be almost possible to discern the psychological evolution of Matthew Bramble merely from reading the brusque 'Doctor' (5) which softens to 'Dear Doctor' (33)

---

[7] Görlach (2001: 80) writes, "forms like *ha'n't, shan't, can't, mayn't, ben't, an't* (am not) etc. are frequent only in informal texts such as printed plays...."

[8] Matthew dislikes something disordered. For example, he despises the *public* in London, writing "it has no idea of elegance and propriety" (88).

A study of Matthew Bramble's language and epistolary style   163

and expands into a warm 'Dear Dick' (244)." This wealth of technical invention is even more apparent in the opening paragraphs of the letters. The furious denial of the first letter of Matthew's (5-6) contrasts strongly with the much calmer and politer tone of his second letter (11-15).

According to Chapman (1963: 151), "The conclusion is normally some variation on the base 'servant.' 'Your most humble servant' is the commonest.'" It is agreeable that this phrase did not imply any real subservience or even humility in the eighteenth century. Matthew's conclusion is "Dear Lewis, Your affectionate" (6), "Your assured friend" (15), "Dear Lewis, yours ever" (25), "yours" (48), "Dear Dick, yours ever" (57), "Your humble servant" (66), "your always" (90), "your invariable friend" (123), "your unfortunate friend" (146), "Your assured friend" (154), "Dear Lewis, Your affectionate friend and servant" (219), and "Yours invaluably" (331). The number of the conclusion including "servant" is two. Matthew prefers "friend" to "servant" in indicating to Dr. Lewis.

6.2. Contrastive expressions

Matthew often uses contrastive expressions in comparing manners, places, and people with the elaborate use of adjectives. He is often pessimistic especially when confronted with a city suffering from physical, economic and social insanity (Boucé 1976: 195). He loves and admires his country life all the more for his great pessimism. He compares London life with his country life in Brambleton-hall as follows:

> (13) Shall I state the difference between my town grievances, and my country comforts? At Brambleton-hall, I have elbow-room within doors, and breathe a clear, elastic, salutary air—I enjoy refreshing sleep, which is never disturbed by horrid noise, nor interrupted, but in a-morning, by the sweet twitter of the martlet at my window —I drink the virgin lymph, pure and crystalline as it gushes from the rock, or the sparkling beveridge, home-brewed from malt of my own making; or I indulge with cyder, which my own orchard affords; or with claret of the best growth, imported for my own use, by a correspondent on whose integrity I can depend; my bread is sweet and nourishing, made from my own wheat, ground in my own mill, and baked in my own oven.... My sallads, roots, and pot-herbs, my

164 *Hironobu Konishi*

own garden yields in plenty and perfection; the produce of the natural soil, prepared by moderate cultivation. (118-19)

Adjectives such as "refreshing," "sweet," "virgin," "pure," "crystalline," "native," "natural," and "fresh" contribute to the impression of nostalgia for the impeccable purity of a paradisal golden age (Boucé 1976: 212). On the other hand, he speaks ill of London as follows:

(14) Now, mark the contrast at London—I am pent up in frowzy lodgings, where there is not room enough to swing a cat; and I breathe the steams of endless putrefaction; and these would, undoubtedly, produce a pestilence, if they were not qualified by the gross acid of sea-coal, which is itself a pernicious nuisance to lungs of any delicacy of texture: but even this boasted corrector cannot prevent those languid, sallow looks, that distinguish the inhabitants of London from those ruddy swains that lead a country-life—I go to bed after mid-night, jaded and restless from the dissipations of the day—I start every hour from my sleep, at the horrid noise of the watchmen bawling the hour through every street, and thundering at every door; a set of useless fellows, who serve no other purpose but that of disturbing the repose of the inhabitants; and by five o'clock I start out of bed, in consequence of the still more dreadful alarm made by the country carts, and noisy rustics bellowing green pease under my window. (119-20)

The pessimistic adjectives are "frowzy," "endless," "pernicious," "languid," "swallow," "jaded," "restless," "horrid," "useless," "dreadful," and "noisy." Those words make impressive contrast. Matthew's value of his country life is probably Smollett's.

6.3. Metaphorical expressions

The reader finds Matthew criticizes manners, places, and people ironically. Then he usually uses metaphorical expressions. In Bath, he soon dislikes the assembly of fashionable people as well as the resort. He called the people "the polite assemblies of Bath" (66). The reader notices his misanthropy and humour. Other examples of his are "These delicate creatures from Bedfordbury" (37), "what an agreeable task" (48), and "In that case, what a delicate beveridge is every day quaffed by the drinkers" (46).

A study of Matthew Bramble's language and epistolary style   165

Also, he does not hesitate to criticize his relatives ironically, too. He is good at capturing his relatives' distinctive features—Lydia is "a poor good-natured simpleton" (11-12), Tabitha, a "fantastical animal" (12), and Jery, "a pert jackanapes" (12).

Another form of metaphor is simile like "as soft as butter" (12) and "as if she were her own child" (328). The similes "proud as German count," and "as hot and hasty as a Welch mountaineer" (12) are for Jery. The simile "as inflammable as touch-wood" (12) is for Lydia. The examples of *as if-simile* are "as if some Gothic devil had stuffed them altogether in a bag" (36), "as if they were pursued by bailiffs" (88), "as if I was broke upon the wheel" (5), and "as if he was hired to give lectures on all subjects whatsoever" (24). Those metaphorical phrases and clause indicate he is a man of wit.

7. Conclusion

Thus the reader sees Matthew Bramble's personality through his language and style of writing his letters. Matthew is a person of deep feeling and active benevolence, but he hides his feelings behind misanthropy. His language and epistolary style reflect his feelings over his order. In *Humphrey Clinker*, Smollett depicted a very different world from that which dominated his earlier novels. Most of the characters are ruled by varying degrees of sensibility. Smollett is among the writers influenced by the trend of sensibility in the late eighteenth century. Matthew is the very character of sensibility that the author created to attempt to achieve popularity among readers in the late eighteenth century.

Text

Smollett, Tobias 1966. *The Expedition of Humphrey Clinker*, ed. Lewis M. Knapp. London: Oxford University Press.

References

Altman, Janet Gurkin 1985. *Epistolarity: Approach to a form*. Columbus: Ohio State University Press.
Beasley, Jerry C. 1998. *Tobias Smollett: Novelist*. Athens: The University of Georgia Press.
Blake, N.F. 1981. *Non-standard language in English literature*. The language library. London: André Deutsch.

166 *Hironobu Konishi*

Boucé, Paul-Gabriel 1976. *The novels of Tobias Smollett*. London: Longman.

Boulton, Marjorie 1975. *The anatomy of the novel*. London: Routledge & Kegan Paul.

Chapman, R.W. 1963. The formal parts of Johnson's letters. In James Sutherland & F.P. Wilson (eds), *Essays on the eighteenth century*, 147-54. New York: Russell & Russell. Inc.

Cunliffe, J.W. & H.A. Watt (eds.) 1911. *Thackeray's English humorists of the eighteenth century*. Chicago: Scott Foresman and Company.

Görlach, Manfred 1999. Regional and social variation. In Roger Lass (ed.), *The Cambridge history of the English language*, Vol. III., 459-538. Cambridge: Cambridge University Press.

Görlach, Manfred 2001. *Eighteenth-century English*. Heidelberg: Winter.

Kanzaki, Yukari 1994. The epistolary novels: *Clarissa* and *Humphrey Clinker*. *Journal of Osaka Sangyo University Humanities*, No. 80, 1-10. Osaka: Society of Osaka Sangyo University.

Knapp, Lewis M. 1949. *Tobias Smollett: Doctor of man and manners*. New York: Russell & Russell. Inc.

Knapp, Lewis M. 1966. Introduction. In Lewis M. Knapp (ed.), *The expedition of Humphrey Clinker*, by Tobias Smollett, vii-xv. London: Oxford University Press.

Nevalainen, Terttu 1999. Early Modern English lexis and semantics. In Roger Lass (ed.), *The Cambridge history of the English language*, Vol. III, 332-457. Cambridge: Cambridge University Press.

Page, Norman 1973. *Speech in the English novel*. London: Longman.

Preston, Thomas R. 1964. Smollett and the benevolent misanthrope type. *PMLA*, Vol. 79, No. 1, 51-57.

Probyn, Clive T. 1987. *English fiction of the eighteenth century 1700-1789*. London: Longman.

Simpson, J.A. & E.S.C. Weiner 1989. *The Oxford English dictionary*, 2nd ed. Oxford: Clarendon Press.

Vallins, G.H. 1954. *Spelling*. The language library. London: André Deutsch.

Sound symbolism of feminine rhymes in Spenser's *Faerie Queene Book V* *

Masaru Kosako

Abstract
We aim to clarify Edmund Spenser's devices for artistic creativity in the usage of feminine rhymes of *The Faerie Queene Book V*. To attain the aim, we focus on the expressiveness of the unstressed and therefore weakly sounding sylla-bles of feminine endings, particularly with the suffix *-ed* and co-occurring suffixes. On the presupposition that feminine endings are fore-grounded for high-lights with the majority of masculine endings as the background, we are going to show that feminine rhymes in *Book V* convey some types of auditory images at the end of lines, and that these images function as sound symbolism in the interaction with the contexts. We will also show that the images are categorized into five patterns, and that not a few of them are mixed or over-lapped with each other to produce complex and integrated auditory images by virtue of the weak sounds of unstressed syllables of feminine endings.[1]

1. Introduction
1.1. Visual images and auditory images in Spenser's poetry
Spenser's allegory has been discussed in various ways. One of them is in terms of iconicity. Wimsatt (1954) and Graham (1992) discussed "verbal icon," defining it to be a verbal sign which shares the proper-ties or resembles the objects which it denotes. They considered a verbal icon to be a less physical object than a mental image, yet it has a kind of specificity or density that makes it substantial. Aptekar (1969) interpreted Spenser's allegory to be a series of icons, *i.e.* intensely visual images which are interpretations of reality in its met-aphoric and symbolic dimensions.

Besides these visual images, we might also perceive auditory images in the way Spenser uses feminine endings. Auditory images in

---

* The present study is a revised version of "Messages in Feminine Endings in Spenser's *Faerie Queen Book V*" reported on Online Proceedings of PALA 2007.
[1] My former colleague Professor Scott Gardner of Okayama University has kindly read the draft of the present study and given useful pieces of advice, but faults, if any, are all mine.

168   *Masuru Kosako*

Spenser's rhymes, however, have not been discussed so much, at least in my knowledge. So, we are going to deal with them, particularly the expressiveness of the unstressed syllables in feminine endings of *The Faerie Queene* (*FQ*) *Book V* (1596).

1.2. Artistic devices in rhymes of Spenserian stanzas

Book V of *FQ* consists of twelve cantos. The total number of the stanzas in *Book V* is 576, including eleven stanzas of proems. The basic metre in *FQ* is iambic pentametre from the first line to the eighth line, and iambic hexametre (*i.e.* Alexandrine) in the last ninth line. The rhyme scheme is *ababbcbcc*.

According to Harmon (1990: 604-05), most of the rhymes in *FQ* are perfect and single, while there are not a few lines ending with feminine rhymes, whose rhyming syllable is followed by the same unstressed syllable (*e.g.* faces/ places). Harmon adds that there are also "deficient rhymes" such as "stress promotion (*e.g.* daintily/ hye) and redundant rhymes (*e.g.* descendant/ pendant) as well as assonance (*e.g.* brave/ vain) and consonance (*e.g.* sing/ rang)." Harmon mentions that these deficient rhymes are used as "device for avoiding monotony of rhyme and for bringing about two complimentary pleasures of the stanzas: *i.e.* that of constancy and of variety."

1.3. Stylistic approach to rhymes in Spenser

Rhymes in Spenser have long been paid attention as pieces of evidence for conjecturing pronunciation in early modern English.[2]

Contrarily, there are not so many stylistic approaches to Spenser's rhymes. Hamilton (2007: 533) shows some interesting insights into the usage of rhymes in the interaction to contexts in his instructive notes to *FQ*: *e.g.* Artegall, the hero knight for justice in *Book V*, declares equity in judging two brothers' quarrel by "sharing the same 'a' and 'c' rhymes."

Quilligan (1990: 311-26) treated Spenser's and Sidney's masculine and feminine endings, discussing social control in their poems. Kosako (2007: 106-22) examined stylistic features of feminine endings in

---

[2] Gil (1621), Zachrisson (1913), Wyld (1923), Dobson (1968), Strang (1970), Cercignani (1981), and Araki (1993-95), etc.

Radigund episode in *FQ Book V*, with the help of corpora[3]. We are going to expand Kosako (2007) in this study, discussing sound symbolism of feminine rhymes in *Book V*. This study, therefore, may be a piece of research in phonostylistics.

1.4. Pronunciation of suffixes in the Elizabethan period

Feminine rhymes are concerned with the pronunciation of such suffixes as: *-ed, -ie, -ion, -ly (lie), -ent, -ence, -es*, etc. Among others, we are focusing on the suffix *-ed*, and the co-occurring suffixes. It is said that there were varieties in the pronunciation of words in the Elizabethan period, and that syllabification of suffixes was artificial for the sake of metre and rhyme.[4]

According to Görlach (1991: 73), "vowel differences in syllables with secondary stress or in unstressed position, if reflected in spelling at all, are important as the only indication of certain prosodic features in Early Modern English."

1.5. Pronunciation of the suffix *-ed*

Dobson (1968: 880) asserts that "the verbal inflexion *-ed* was still often a separate syllable until the end of the seventeenth century." On the other hand, there are not a few scholars who consider that the suffix *-ed* was not pronounced in speech of the Elizabethan period, while it was deliberately sounded in literary texts, particularly when archaic flavour was aimed at.[5]

Spenser almost always uses the form *-ed* when iambic pentametre (hexametre) requires the syllabic value on the suffix: *e.g.* "In which she noursled him, till yeares he raught" (V i 6), etc., while he uses the form *-'d* or *-d* when metre does not require the syllabic value: *e.g.* "Though also those mote question'd be aright" (V ix 40), etc. We should here remind that Spenser was not thoroughgoing in showing the difference of the syllabic value of suffixes. But, in general, metre or rhyme scheme makes it possible for us to assess the syllabic value: see for example, "Témpred wìth Ádàmánt àmóngst thè sáme" (V i 10)

---

[3] *English Poetry Full-Text Database*, and an e-text of *FQ*.
[4] Wright (1988: 50-51).
[5] Dobson (1968 [1957]: 885-86), Sugden (1936: 102), Kökeritz (1953: 262), Wyld (1956: 06), Wright (1988: 50-51) and Ronberg (1992: 10).

170   Masuru Kosako

and "appeard/ heard/ fared/ stared" (V vii 20). So, as a rule, we can
rely on spellings as the evidence of the syllabic value of suffixes.

2. Method

Considering that majority of Spenserian stanzas end lines with masculine rhymes, it may be possible for us to presuppose that masculine
rhymes constitute the so-called background at the end of lines in *FQ*.
Contrarily, not so many feminine rhymes may be prominent and foregrounded for the purpose of particular highlights. According to
Widdowson (1996: 140), an intuitive awareness of artistic values ultimately depends upon linguistic patterns, which will be made apparent
by investigating the way language is used in a text. So, the prominence
of feminine rhymes is going to be attested by showing patterns in the
way feminine rhymes interact with contexts, particularly focusing on
those with the suffix *-ed*.

We exclude rhymes with non-syllabic suffix *-ed*, such as *appeared/
heard/ fared/ stared* (V vii 20), and those with stress-promoted suffix
-ed, such as *hed/ transfigured/ red/ wondered* (V vii 13). In this way,
we are to show what types of patterns can be categorized in accordance
with auditory images functioning as sound symbolism.[6]

3. Data: Patterns of auditory image

Book V mainly narrates the legend of Artegall or justice. According to
Hamilton (2007: 507-08),[7] all of the seven books of *FQ* include the
motif that "the world hathe lost his youth, and the times beginne to
wax olde." Furthermore, the motif "is treated fully in *Book V*, because
its virtue and justice confront the fallen worlds directly."

How does Spenser lament over the fallen virtue and justice of the
world? Feminine rhymes seem to play not a least part in appealing the
poet's lamentation as well as other related messages, by virtue of the
weakly sounding suffixes. The feminine rhymes with the suffix *-ed* are
categorized into five patterns in accordance with auditory images, as
follows.

---

[6] Leech and Short (2007[2]: 188) and Wales (2001: 363).
[7] The present study is based on the text in Hamilton (2007).

Pattern F-1: The hero knight or a character has forced the opponent to weaken his or her power, capability, or dignity, etc. Hereafter, the pattern is shortened as F-1 (power weakened).

Pattern F-2: A character or a matter is not so strong by nature, or rather weak and fragile by nature, liable to be damaged, or anxious about something. Hereafter, shortened as F-2 (weak by nature).

Pattern F-3: A character (or the narrator) is talking (narrating) a matter with a gentle, tender, and mild tone of voice, to make the hearer (reader) feel empathy, satisfaction, or the like. Hereafter, shortened as F-3 (mild tone).

Pattern F-4: A character (or the narrator) is talking (narrating) a matter with a lamenting tone of voice. Hereafter, shortened as F-4 (lamentation).

Pattern F-5: The narration of a topic has come to the end, and the stage is shifting into another one. Hereafter, shortened as F-5 (stage shifting).

3.1. Pattern F-1: Power weakened

We must note that many instances of F-1 (power weakened) shown below are innately overlapped with F-2 (weak by nature). The pattern F-1 includes physically weakened (or destroyed) image and/or mentally weakened (or disgraced) image.

Pattern F-1: Physically weakened (or destroyed) image
(1) **Talus drowned Munera to destroy her**
After the hero knight, Artegall, defeated cruell Pollente, Artegall's squire, Talus, rent the door of Munera's castle, because Pollente had always been supported by his daughter Munera with her "wicked charmes" (V ii 5). In her castle, "Her selfe then tooke he by the sclender wast, In vaine loud crying, and into the flood Ouer the Castle wall adowne her cast, And there her drowned in the durty mud" (V ii 27). The narration continues into the next stanza. Scansion of the stanza is tried below.

> Ànd lástlỳ áll thàt Cástlè qúite hè rácèd,
> Éuèn fróm thè sóle òf hís fòundátion,
> Ànd áll thè héwèn stónes thèreóf dèfácèd,
> Thàt thére mòte bé nò hópe òf repàrátion,

Nòr mémòrý thèreóf tò ánỳ nátìon,
Áll whìch whèn *Tálùs* thróughlỳ hád pèrfóurmèd,
Sìr *Ártègáll* ùndíd thè éuìll fáshìon,
Ànd wíckèd cústòmes óf thàt Brídge rèfóurmèd,
Whìch dóne, ùntó hìs fórmèr ióurnèy hé rètóurnèd. (V ii 28)

It is noteworthy that the whole lines in this stanza, which depicts Talus's complete destruction of Munera's castle, end lines exclusively with feminine rhymes: "a" and "c" rhymes with the suffix *-ed*, and "b" rhymes with the suffix *-ion*. The weak sounds of these unstressed suffixes resonate well with Talus's thoroughgoing deprivation of Munera's power and destruction of her castle.

Instances with pattern F-1 (physically weakened or destroyed)
Concerning the rest of the instances, the contexts are shown below, together with the rhyming fellows. Notes, if any, are by Hamilton (2007).
(2) Canto i begins with the narration that "euermore some of the virtuous race …with strong hand their fruitfull rancknes (*i.e.* luxuriant growth) did deface..." and "Hercules ... monstrous tyrants with his club subdued" (V i 2: shewed/ subdewed/ endewed).
(3) Artegall's sword excelled all other swords (V i 9: rebelled/ excelled/ quelled).
(4) Artegall "smote" Pollente's head off in water (V ii 19: stayned/ ordayned/ remayned/ contayned).
(5) Talus "down the rock the Giant throwing, in the sea him dround" (V ii 49-50: tumbled/ rumbled/ humbled).
(6) Terpine told Artegall that Radigund tried to hang him after defeating him (V iv 33: atchieued/ belieued/ prieued).
(7) Radigund's shield was forced away by Artegall (V v 8: warded/ garded/ discarded).
(8) Artegall struck Radigund's helmet, and made her fall down (V v 11: prostrated/ vnlaced/ raced).
(9) Talus wounded and slayed many Amazon warriors (V v 19: thondred/ sondred/ encombred/ nombred).
(10) Britomarto destroyed Dolon's sons (V vi 38: fared/ prepared/ scared/ glared).
(11) Mercilla's damsel moved Artegall and Arthur to avenge the evil

Souldan (V viii 24: complained/ disdained/ fained/ mayntained).

(12) The powerful light of Arthur's shield made the Souldan's steeds turn back and run away (V viii 38: burned/ turned).

(13) Belge's sons' "faire blossomes" were blasted by a strong Tyrant's invasion (V x 7: blasted/ tasted/ wasted).

(14) Arthur offered the adventure to defeat Geryoneo (V x 18: arriued/ depriued).

(15) Geryoneo built a chapel and his own idol on the altar, offering the flesh of men in sacrifice (V x 28: framed/ proclamed/ named/ framed).

(16) Arthur came to fight with Gerioneo and defeated him (V xi 7: perceiued/ deceiued).

Instances with pattern F-1 (mentally weakened or disgraced)

(17) Talus "thundred strokes" on the door of Munera's castle "so hideouslie" that he "filled all the house with feare and great vprore" (V ii 22: appeared/ feared).

(18) Artegall revealed that Braggadochio had false imitations. After that, Talus punished Braggadochio, causing him to be disgraced (V iii 39: vncased/ disgraced).

(19) Boaster Braggadochio was deprived of the steed he had stolen, and was forced to go on foot by Artegall (V iii 35 gayned/ disdayned/ ordayned).

(20) Lucy sought to take her own life by drowning herself in the sea, being deserted by her husband (V iv 10: conceyued/ bereaued/ deceaued/ weaued).

(21) The Souldan's wife is exiled to "saluage woods" by Artegall (V ix 2: exyled/ defyled/ despoyled/ foyled).

(22) Zeal, the prosecutor, detailed Duessa's crimes at Mercilla's court (V ix 39: enured/ allured/ procured).

(23) The prosecutor detailed Duessa's crimes, including a plot to overthrow Mercilla (V ix 41: conspyred/ hyred/ inspyred/ aspyred).

3.2. Pattern F-2: Weak by nature

The instances categorized into pattern F-2 (weak by nature) are often overlapped with pattern F-1 (power weakened), because fragile characters are likely to be revealed by others.

(1) **Radigund is love-blinded and not salvage-minded**

Clarinda tries to persuade Artegall to love her queen Radigund. The Amazon maid tells him that "although Radigund scorns the love of men, ... she is not so salvage-minded as to forget herself being begotten of men."[8] Clarinda further informs him of her past love affairs, in which "base love has blinded her proudest heart." It seems relevant for such a love-blinded woman to be narrated with feminine endings. For the lines ending with unstressed weak sounds convey an auditory image that her character is so fragile as to incline towards falling into love. Scansion is tried as follows.

> Thèn whý dòes nót, thòu íll àduízèd mán,
> Màke méanes tò wín thỳ líbèrtíe fòrlórne,
> Ànd trý ìf thóu bỳ fáire èntréatìe, cán
> Mòue *Rádìgúnd*? whò thóugh shè stíll hàue wórne
> Hèr dáyes ìn wárre, yèt (wéet thòu) wás nòt bórne
> Òf Béares ànd Týgrès, nór sò sáluàge mýndèd,
> Às thát, àlbé àll lóue òf mén shè scórne,
> Shè yét fòrgéts, thàt shé òf mén wàs kýndèd:
> Ànd sóoth òft séene, thàt próudèst hárts bàse lóue hàth blýndèd. (V v 40)

The scansion above puts the stress on the auxiliary "can" at the end of the third line to make a masculine ending. Artegall's high probability of moving the Amazone queen to love is enforced by the stressed auxilialy "can." The maid's eagerness in persuading Artegall is also expressed in enjambment which continues from the third to the sixth line. The feminine endings of "c" rhymes (mynded/ kynded/ blynded) may well suggest the maid's tender tone of voice (F-3), trying to lead Artegall to love Radigund. *The English Poetry Full-Text Database* shows that each of these "c" rhymes is only one instance in Spenser. With regard to "kynded," *OED* cites only this instance in the sense "sprung, begotten? *pseudo-arch.*" By the way, the spelling "minded" appears five times only within the line in Spenser, and the spelling "blinded" does four times only within the line as well.[9]

Instances with pattern F-2 (weak by nature)
(2) Pollente's daughter is richly attired and full of pride (V ii 10: attired/ desired).

---

[8] Hamilton (2007: 544).
[9] Kosako (2007).

Sound symbolism of feminine rhymes 175

(3) Hercules, "forgetting warres," "ioyed/ In combats of sweet loue" (V v 24: annoyed/ ioyed/ toyed).

(4) During the night at Dolon's house, Britomart, who is Artegall's love, remained sleepless, brooding and grieving over her beloved's plight (V vi 24: grieued/ relieued/ reprieued). Here Britomart is anxious about her lover.

(5) The villain's garment was worn out and torn to pieces and his locks hung in a shaggy manner (V ix 10: shagged/ ragged/ iagged).

(6) Grandtorto's strokes were directed "with such monstrous" force to Artegall, yet they were not so effective to Artegall. In fact, Grandtorto was soon at a loss because he could not pull his ax out of Artegall's deeply bitten shield (V xii 21: intended/ descended).

Instances with F-2 (weak by nature) overlapped with F-1 (power weakened)

(7) The damsel behaved as if she could easily be spoiled before the villain's den (V ix 9: directed/ abiected/ affected).

(8) Bragaddochio's falsehood was revealed by Artegall (V iii 20: aduewed/ issewed/ shewed/ endewed).

(9) Braggadochio's claim for the steed is disproved (V iii 30: perceiued/ bereaued/ deceaued).

(10) Warned of the warlike men, Amazons swarmed like a cluster of excited bees (V iv 36: warned/ armed/ harmed/ swarmed).

(11) The battle between Artegall and Radigund began first with her bitter strokes, but her strokes were not so powerful, however hard she continued to give the strokes (V v 6: ended/ intended/ rended/ defended).

(12) Artegall yielded to Radigund "of his owne accord" (V v 17: obtayned/ attayned/ gayned).

(13) The ill-natured old Hag, Detraction, sought to deprive men of their good name (V xii 33: conceiued/ perceiued/ bereaued).

3.3. Pattern F-3: Mild tone of voice

(1) **Artegall pronounces his sentence to appease discord**

The stanza cited below, in which Artegall pronounces his sentence to appease the discord between two brothers, has feminine endings at the "b" rhyme positions. Scansion of the stanza is tried below.

176   *Masuru Kosako*

> Whèn hé hìs séntènce thús prònóuncèd hád,
> Bòth *Ámìdás* ànd *Phíltrà* wére dìspléasèd:
> Bùt *Brácìdás* ànd *Lúcỳ* wére rìght glád,
> Ànd ón thè thréasùre bý thàt iúdgemènt séasèd (*i.e.* seized, took legal possession),
> Sò wás thèir díscòrd bý thìs dóome àppéasèd,
> Ànd éach òne hád hìs ríght. Thèn *Ártègáll*
> Whén às thèir shárpe cònténtìon hé hàd céasèd,
> Dèpártèd ón hìs wáy, às díd bèfáll,
> Tò fóllòw hìs óld quést, thè whích hìm fórth dìd cáll. (V iv 20)

Bracidas has had a quarrel with his brother Amidas over the owner-ship of Amidas's island, because "most of Bracidas's island is washed by the sea onto his brother's island."[10] The first line above ends with a masculine rhyme "hád (/ glád)," which, having the stress, accords with Artegall's decisive tone of voice, declaring his sentence to put an end to the two brothers' "sharpe contention." The weak sound of feminine rhyme (*i.e.* displeased) of the second line conveys an audi-tory image that Amidas and his love, Philtra, have such a hopelessly contentious mind by nature. That is characteristic of F-2 (weak by nature), because the couple would not be satisfied with Artegall's reasonable judgement. Here we can perceive the narrator's lamenting tone of voice as well (F-4: lamentation) for their contentious mind.

Bracidas and his lady Lucy, on the other hand, are content with Artegall's decision. The weak sounds of feminine rhymes in the fourth, fifth, and seventh lines (*i.e.* seased/ appeased/ ceased) can be inter-preted to convey the auditory image that Bracidas and Lucy have agreed with Artegal's sentence with a satisfied tone of voice (F-3: mild tone). At the same time, these rhymes convey the auditory image that their quarrel has finally come to the end (F-5: stage shifting). There-fore, this instance has F-2, 3, 4 and 5 mixed and overlapped with one another.

Instances with pattern F-3 (mild tone of voice)
(2) Artegall, as a judge, must have declared his decision with a gentle, tender tone of voice, telling Sangliere and Squire who of two men the lady's real love was (V i 28: perceaued/ reaued).

---

[10] Fukuda in Hamilton (2007: 777).

(3) Artegall's probably mild tone of voice, when forbidding Talus to chastize Hag, is conveyed by feminine endings (V xii 43: deserued/ preserued/ obserued/ swerue). We should note here that "swerue" breaks the rhyme scheme with the suffix -ed. The exceptional choice of masculine rhyme here (*i.e.* "he for nought would swerue/ From his right course") seems to be for the purpose of emphasizing Artegall's resolution to hold his right course.

Instances with F-3 (mild tone of voice) overlapped with F-1 (power weakened)
(4) After Clarinda heard of the queen Radigund's secret love to Artegall, she began to persuade him to love the queen. Her speech abounds with feminine rhymes, which continue into the next stanza. The feminine endings here seem to resonate with Clarinda's tender tone of voice, to make him willing to love her (V v 35: indeuour/ labour/ fauour/ beloued/ behauiour/ roued/ proued).
(5) The narrator (poet) praises Artegall for his firmness in loyalty to his true love Britomart, even when he was enthralled by Radigund (V vi 2: behaued/ craued/ saued/ engraued).
(6) As Prince Arthur slew the three knights near and inside Geryoneo's castle, he received thanks and admiration from Belge (V x 39: greeting/ proued/ weeting/ moued/ behoued/ beloued).
(7) Heralds announced that the winner of the first day's joust was Marinell (V iii 6: wounded/ redounded/ resounded).
(8) When Arthur found no more opponent against his power, he returned to Belge, and told her assuringly what he had done, perhaps with a mild tone of voice (V x 38: issued/ vewed/ shewed).
(9) Clarinda began to soften Artegall's attitudes toward Radigund with her eloquence (V v 36: frowned/ drowned/ swowned/ crowned). Clarinda must have persuaded him with a mild tone of voice.

3.4. Pattern F-4: Lamentation
(1) **Artegall laments woman's fondness**
Artegall persuades Irene to accept her knight's love. A probably gentle tone of voice in his persuasion (F-3) should be accompanied with a lamenting tone of voice (F-4) for a woman's fondness preferring worldly glitter to faithful love (F-2). Scansion is tried below.

178   *Masuru Kosako*

Whý thèn wíll yè, fònd (*i.e.* foolish) Dáme, àttémptèd (*i.e.* seduced) bée
V̀ntó à stràngèrs lóue, sò líghtlỳ plácèd,
Fòr gúiftes òf góld, òr ánỳ wórldlỳ glée (*i.e.* glitter),
Tò léaue thè lóue, thàt yé bèfóre èmbrácèd,
Ànd lét yòur fáme wìth fálshòod bé dèfácèd?
Fíe òn thè pélfe (*i.e.* wealth), fòr whích gòod náme ìs sóld,
Ànd hónòur wíth ìndígnìtíe (*i.e.* disgraceful action) dèbásèd:
Déarèr ìs lóue thèn lífe, ànd fáme thèn góld;
Bùt déarèr thén thèm bóth, yòur fáith ònce plíghtèd hóld. (V xi 63).

Instance with pattern F-4 (lamentation)

(2) The poet seems to be lamenting the unnatural battle between
female warriors, Britomart and Radigund (V vii 29: created/ trans-
lated/ hated).

Instance with F-4 (lamentation) overlapped with F-2 (weak by nature)

(3) Burbon laments women's liability to prefer "golden giftes and
many a guilefull word" (V xi 50: tempted/ consented/ inuented).

Instance with F-4 (lamentation) overlapped with F-1 (power weakened) and F-2 (weak by nature)

(4) Burbon's love was trained amiss to untruth with Grandtorto's
corrupting bribes (V xi 54: obtayned/ detayned/ mis-trayned).

3.5. Pattern F-5: Stage shifting
(1) Radigund disclosed her secret love to Artegall

When Radigund disclosed to the maid her secret love toward Artegall,
the queen had the blush in her face and turned her head to hide it, as
half confounded with a sudden consciousness of shame. For, on one
hand, the queen dreaded it as "shame" to "thrall" her "looser life" to
the enthralled Artegall (V v 29). On the other hand, the "hart-murdring
paine," which derived from her love to him, compelled herself to
disclose her "griefes deepe wound." Scansion is tried below:

Wìth thát shè túrn'd hèr héad, às hálfe àbáshèd
Tò híde thè blúsh whìch ín hèr vísàge róse,
Ànd thróugh hèr éyes lìke súddèn líghtnìng fláshèd,
Déckìng hèr chéeke wìth á vèrmílìon róse:
Bùt sóone shè díd hèr cóuntènánce còmpóse,

Ànd tó hèr túrnìng, thús bègán àgáine;
Thìs gríefes dèepe wóund Ì wóuld tò thée dísclóse,
Thèretó còmpéllèd thróugh hàrt-múrdrìng páine,
Bùt dréad òf sháme mỳ dóubtfùll líps dòth stíll rèstráine. (V v 30)

The feminine "a" rhymes (abashed/ flashed) effectively convey an auditory image how unexpectedly the blush came to her cheek (F-5: stage shifting), with a delicate sound of *-ed* suffix. At the same time, the narration of the Amazon queen fallen in love, who decked her cheek with a rosy vermillion, informs us of her easy inclination to "thrall" her "looser life" to the enthralled Artegall (F-2: weak by nature).

Instances with F-5 (stage shifting)

(2) While Artegall, Talus, and Terpin endured their battle with Amazons, the night came over them (V iv 45: yclowded/ shrowded).
(3) After Britomart defeated Radigund and rescued Artegall from prison, they remained there in the Amazon's city. Britomart regained women's gentleness in the Amazons, who came to adore and obey her as a princess (V vii 42: remained/ rained). Quilligan (1990: 311-26) interprets the feminine endings here in terms of patriarchy.

Instances with F-5 (stage shifting) overlapped with F-2 (weak by nature)

(4) The treasure, which Lucy caught hold of in the sea, brought about the strife between two brothers (V iv 13: contained/ fained/ appertained/ ordained).
(5) Clarinda, betraying Radigund, began to "cast affection" to Artegall (V v 44: sdayned/ gayned/ retayned/ payned).
(6) Radigund, who was waiting for "tydings good" from Clarinda, began to rage at the unexpected ill report (V v 47: perceiued/ conceiued).

Instances with F-5 (stage shifting) overlapped with F-2 (weak by nature) and F-4 (lamentation)

(7) The poet laments the world growing "daily wourse and wourse" (V proem 2: named/ framed).
(8) The poet laments the corruption of "present dayes" (V proem 3 desyred/ outhyred/ admyred).

Instance with F-5 (stage shifting) overlapped with F-1 (power weakened), F-2 (weak by nature) and F-3 (mild tone of voice)

(9) Clarinda began to seek Artegall to love herself (F-1), betraying her queen, probably with a mild tone of voice (F-3). The maid daily told him false stories about the queen (F-2), which shows her unfaithful nature (V v 57: amended/ discommended/ offended/ frended, remayned/ gayned/ contayned). Furthermore, Clarinda's persuasion toward Artegall has shifted the aim from the queen's love to her own love (F-5).

Instance with F-5 (stage shifting) overlapped with F-2 (weak by nature), F-3 (mild tone of voice) and F-4 (lamentation)

(10) Clarinda must be reporting Artegall with a mild (F-3), but false lamenting tone of voice (F- 2 and F-4) that her earnest suit to win his freedom from the queen had failed (F-5) (V v 54: fayned/ gayned).

4. Final remarks

All of the feminine rhymes which end lines with the suffix *-ed* have been examined about *Book V* of *FQ*. The examination is to substantiate our intuition that Spenser might have used them as an artistic device for foregrounding. Thus, five patterns of auditory images, functioning as sound symbolism, have been shown as prominent features for fore-grounding feminine rhymes. We have also shown that not a few of these patterns are mixed or overlapped with each other to produce complex and integrated auditory images by virtue of the weak and delicate sound of the unstressed suffix *-ed*.

Considering that the poet's tone of lamentation for the fallen world is resonating through the whole narration of *FQ*, the patterns of auditory images clarified in *Book V* may be perceived throughout the usages of feminine rhymes in *FQ*, not only those with the suffix *-ed* but also those with other suffixes.

References

Aptekar, Jane 1969. *Icons of justice: Iconography & thematic imagery in Book V of the Faerie Queene*. New York: Columbia University Press.

Araki, Kazuo 1993-95. Eishi kyakuin no kenkyu [Studies in English end-rhymes]. *Bulletin of Kyoto University of Foreign Languages*, No. 41.

Cercignani, Fausto 1981. *Shakespeare's works and Elizabethan pronunciation*. Oxford: The Clarendon Press.

Chadwyck-Healey (comp.) c.1995. *English poetry full-text database*.

Coye, Dale F. 1998. *Pronouncing Shakespeare's words: A guide from A to Zounds*. London: Fitzroy Dearborn Publishers.

Dobson, Eric. J. 1968 [1957]. *English pronunciation 1500-1700*. Second edition. Oxford: The Clarendon Press.

Gabrielson, Arvid 1909. *Rime as a criterion of pronunciation of Spenser, Pope, Byron, and Swinburne*. Uppsala: Almqvist & Wiksells Boktryckeri.

Gil, Alexander 1621. *Logonomia Anglica*. London: rpt. Menston 1969.

Görlach, Manfred 1991. *Introduction to Early Modern English*. Cambridge: Cambridge University Press.

Graham, Joseph F. 1992. *Onomatopoetics: Theory of language and literature*. Cambridge: Cambridge University Press.

Hamilton, Albert Charles, Hiroshi Yamashita, Toshiyuki Suzuki & Shohachi Fukuda (eds.) 2007 [2001]. *Spenser: The Faerie Queene*. Revised second edition. Harlow: Longman-Pearson Education.

Hamilton, Albert Charles (gen. ed.) 1990. *The Spenser encyclopedia*. Toronto: University of Toronto Press.

Harmon, William 1990. Rhyme. In Albert Charles Hamilton (gen. ed.), *The Spenser Encyclopedia*. Toronto: University of Toronto Press.

Hill, Douglas 1980. *The Illustrated Faerie Queene: A modern prose adaptation*. New York: Newsweek Books.

Hollander, John 1988. *Melodious Guile: Fictive pattern in poetic language*. New Haven: Yale University Press.

Kökeritz, Helge 1953. *Shakespeare's pronunciation*. New Haven: Yale University Press.

Kosako, Masaru 2007. Amazon no Joou Radigund no Episode ni-okeru Josei-in [A corpus-based approach to Spenser's *Faerie Queene*: With special reference to feminine endings in the Radigund Episode]. *English Corpus Studies*, No. 14, 106-22.

Leech, Geoffrey Neil 1969. *A linguistic guide to English poetry*. London: Longman.

Leech, Geoffrey Neil & Mick H. Short 2007[2] [1981]. *Style in fiction: A linguistic introduction to English fictional prose*. London: Longman.

OED = Oxford English Dictionary. Second edition on CD-ROM 1989. Oxford: Oxford University Press.

Quilligan, Maureen 1990. Feminine endings: The sexual politics of Sidney's and Spenser's rhyming. In A.M. Haselkorn & B.S. Travitsky (eds.), *The Renaissance Englishwoman in print: Counterbalancing the canon*, 311-26. Amherst: University of Massachusetts.

Ronberg, Gert 1992. *A way with words: The language of English Renaissance literature*. London: Edward Arnold.

Strang, Barbara M.H. 1970. *A history of English*. London: Methuen & Co Ltd.

Sugden, Herbert W. 1936. *The grammar of Spenser's Faerie Queene*. Linguistic Society of America. Philadelphia: University of Pennsylvania.

Verdonk, Peter 2002. *Stylistics*. Oxford: Oxford University Press.

Wales, Katie 2001. *A Dictionary of Stylistics*. Second edition. Longman: Pearson Education.

Widdowson, Henry G. 1996. Stylistics: An approach to stylistic analysis. In Jean Jacques Weber (ed.), *The stylistics reader: From Roman Jakobson to the present*, 138-48. London: Arnold.

Wimsatt, William Kurtz Jr. 1954. *The verbal icon: Studies in the meaning of poetry*. New York: The Noonday Press.

Wright, George T. 1988. *Shakespeare's metrical art*. Berkeley: University of California Press.

Wyld, Henry Cecil 1923. S*tudies in English rhymes from Surrey to Pope*. London: John Murray.

Wyld, Henry Cecil 1956. *A history of modern colloquial English*. Oxford: Basil Blackwell.

Zachrisson, Robert Eugen 1913. *Pronunciation of English vowels 1400-1700*. New York: AMS Press.

Zachrisson, Robert Eugen 1927. *The English pronunciation at Shakespeare's time as taught by William Bullokar*. New York: AMS Press.

Mirrors, reflection, and language in *Hamlet*

Fusako Matsuura

Abstract
The central concern of this paper is to examine the functions of mirror images in the language of *Hamlet,* especially in the use of such rhetorical devices as epanalepsis and antimetabole. Their linguistic structure, which I define as "the language of the mirror," exhibits symmetry, as observed between an object in front of a mirror and its reflection or between reflections projected upon coupled mirrors. Over the course of Shakespeare's life, technical advances in mirror production were in progress, a development considered to generate an epistemological shift at that time. I will discuss what the language of the mirror reflects and how it contributes to deepening the thematic discussion in *Hamlet*.

1. Introduction
William Shakespeare (1564-1616) explores the possibilities of specular images in *Hamlet*.[1] Wright, in his analysis of hendiadys,[2] attributes the dualism in *Hamlet* to diverse mirror images: "The mirrors of other persons, of the clouds, of ghosts; the glass of fashion; the glass of guilt …; even the mirror of art, the play with its Italian murder mirror" (1987: 418). Among all of these, the most notable mirror may be Hamlet's advice to the players:

> Suit the action to the word, the word to the action, with this special observance, that you o'erstep not the modesty of nature. For anything so o'erdone is from the purpose of playing, whose end both at the first and now, was and is, *to hold as 'twere the mirror up to nature*; to show virtue her feature, scorn her own image, and the very age and body of the time his form and pressure.   (3.2.15-20: my emphasis)

Here the notion of theatre as a faithful mirror of life is eloquently praised: the mirror held up to nature is considered to reflect things as they are. However, actual mirror reflection does not correspond to any

---

[1] All citations are from *Hamlet, Prince of Denmark*, the new Cambridge Shakespeare, updated edition, edited by Edwards (2003).
[2] Wright argues that hendiadys depicts "an encounter between two mismatched and incommensurable forces, in open and yet obscure relation to each other, joined yet disparate" (420).

reality: convex mirrors offer a spherical view of the world, embracing manifold perspectives and subject to a degree of distortion, whereas flat mirrors offer a limited and partial image, a framed vision from a single point of view (Melchior-Bonnet 1994: 128; Thorne 2000: 125).

In the age of Shakespeare, there coexisted several sorts of mirrors: even after the glass-makers of Venice had perfected their technique and already produced clear glass mirrors in 1460, steel mirrors[3] as well as glass mirrors were used jointly even into the seventeenth century. The dangers of shipping them made them relatively uncommon, at least in England[4] (Melchior-Bonnet 24; Cook 2010: 49-50; Grabes 1973: 71-73). This means, as Cook (56) points out, "few people would have had experience with a reflection of more than their face," and she is accordingly reluctant to admit any immediate influence of the mirror upon the contemporary epistemic framework, while Melchior-Bonnet (126-29) and Thorne (108) claim the spread of glass mirrors ensured the humanists' new relationship with knowledge about the world and enhanced the objectification or othering of the self.

In the course of European history, from ancient Roman times throughout the Renaissance period, mirrors had embodied the bipolar values of virtue and vice as exemplary and admonitory mirrors respectively. It was not until the twelfth century[5] that the allegories of Prudence[6] and of Pride, Lust and Vanity, started to be personified as a woman holding a glass. These were joined by the allegory of Sight[7] in the thirteenth century. As the use of mirrors for daily grooming spread,

---

[3] The word "glass" is semantically expanded and applied to "a mirror of other materials" (*OED*, s.v. glass, n^1., II. 8b).

[4] In Elizabethan England small convex mirrors were worn decoratively at the waist to check one's appearance (Cook 50).

[5] Glass mirror production was restarted at that time, after having been forgotten since the decline of the Roman Empire.

[6] This symbolisation is based upon Socrates who "urged young people to look at themselves in mirrors so that, if they were beautiful, they would become worthy of their beauty, and if they were ugly, they would know how to hide their disgrace through learning" (Melchior-Bonnet 106; Ono 147), and derives from *Lives and opinions of eminent philosophers* by Diogenes Laertius.

[7] In the seventeenth century, the age of the optical revolution, painters began depicting a man holding an astronomical telescope as an allegory of Sight. See *The allegory of sight* (1615-16) by de Ribera (Ono 178).

the association with Pride, Lust, and Vanity became naturally stronger (Ono 2015: 148-55; Pendergrast 2003: 140-41).

Sight shares these dual symbolic values with the mirror: as the most reliable of our senses, it has equally been blamed for leading us into deception and inducing illusions. This inherent dualism of sight[8] is fully exploited in *Hamlet*: although the prince denies the reliability of seeming, "I have that within which passes show" (1.2.85), he contradictorily resorts to the exterior appearance of things to reach the truth. This is obvious when Hamlet asks Horatio to "Observe my uncle" (3.2.70) to see how he reacts to *The Murder of Gonzago*. In the closet scene, Hamlet emphasises his father's godlike appearance to prove his inner excellence by showing his portraiture to his mother. Hamlet also utilises the dualism of sight to manipulate others: he shows Ophelia such visible signs of madness as disordered attire and lunatic behaviour, expecting her to misread them, to which she responds, focusing merely upon what is visible, "Oh woe is me / T'have seen what I have seen, see what I see" (3.1.154-55). It is not only Ophelia who fails to discern inner truth from outer expression, however. Hamlet also misreads visible signs when he sees Claudius fall to his knees, mistakenly believes the king is at prayer and misses the opportunity for revenge.

2. The mirrors in *Hamlet*
This double-dealing nature of sight significantly influences the language of *Hamlet*. Wright, examining hendiadys in *Hamlet*, points out its resemblances with mirrors and paintings which "mock the reality they pretend to reproduce" (420). Direct references to mirrors and paintings are easily observable in the play, however, what is more worthy of note are the implicit references to mirrors, some of which are rhetorical devices, such as epanalepsis and antimetabole. Interestingly, their component words and phrases are symmetrically arranged,

---

[8] This is also enhanced in the images of theatrical acting and putting on makeup: Polonius advises Ophelia to read a prayer-book while waiting for Hamlet to "colour" her loneliness, "with devotion's visage, / And pious action, we do sugar o'er / The devil himself" (3.1.47-49), which pierces Claudius's conscience, "The harlot check, beautied with plastering art, / Is not more ugly to the thing that helps it / Than is my deed to my most painted word" (3.1.51-53).

reproducing the positional relation between an object in front of a mirror and its reflection, as well as that between reflections projected upon coupled mirrors. I define these rhetorical devices as "the language of the mirror," and will presently discuss their dramatic effect in *Hamlet*, focusing upon what is projected upon their specular surface, and how this influences Hamlet's epistemic development during his search for truth. Firstly, I will give an overview of the direct and indirect references to mirrors, and next proceed with a closer analysis of epanalepsis and antimetabole.

2.1. The direct references to the mirror

Besides the mirror held up to nature, there are two instances of direct reference to the mirror. One is the mirror used as a tool for self-introspection, with which Hamlet forces his mother to "see the inmost part" (3.4.20) of herself; the other is symbolised by the young courtiers, Hamlet and Laertes, both of whom are praised as paragons of the perfect courtier: Hamlet is praised by Ophelia as "The glass of fashion" (3.1.147) and "Th'observed of all observers" (3.1.148), and so is Laertes by Hamlet, as "his semblable is his mirror, and who else would trace him, his umbrage, nothing more" (5.2.110-12).

2.2. The indirect references to the mirror

The indirect allusions to the mirror are variously embedded within the plot of the play, among which the most striking example is the relationship between the characters. In *Hamlet*, the characters are set to each other like coupled mirrors, allowing for a better understanding of themselves by projecting their inner self images onto others (Cook 71). In particular, among the four sons, Hamlet, Laertes, Fortinbras, and Pyrrhus, who all seek vengeance for their fathers' death, Hamlet readily acknowledges his close resemblance to Laertes, "by the image of my cause, I see / The portraiture[9] of his" (5.2.77-78), and adds that "to know a man well were to know himself" (5.2.128). Thorne (125) also argues that almost all the characters are "recruited by Hamlet's imagination and made to reflect different facets of his being," as a mirror wherein Hamlet observes and objectifies himself.

---

[9] See Elam (2017: 201-58) about the use of portraits and pictures in *Hamlet*.

Mirrors, reflection, and language in *Hamlet*   187

The play-within-the-play[10] also serves as a mirror which reflects Claudius's fratricide. Hamlet stages the murder he believes his uncle to have committed, although the nephew[11] of the king is made the murderer.

Polonius offers another allusion to the mirror as a way to reach the truth: he instructs Reynaldo how to spy on Laertes in Paris, "By indirections find directions out" (2.1.64). They contrive to detect the true figure of Laertes by projecting him indirectly onto a notional mirror of fabricated rumours. This kind of indirect usage of a mirror that detects faults is encouraged by Da Vinci (1452-1519) in *A treatise on painting* (1835: 220):

> It will be well also to have a looking-glass by him, when he paints, to look often at his work in it, which being seen the contrary way, will appear as the work of another hand, and will better shew his faults.

Reversed or distorted specular images are thus regarded as indirect reflections of the truth.

More implicit allusions to the mirror are observed in Hamlet's exchanges with the courtiers. In the following quotation, Polonius merely repeats Hamlet's seemingly insane utterances:

HAMLET   Do you see yonder cloud that's almost in shape of a camel?
POLONIUS   By th'mass, and 'tis like a camel indeed.
HAMLET   Methinks it is like a weasel.
POLONIUS   It is backed like a weasel.
HAMLET   Or like a whale?
POLONIUS   Very like a whale.   (3.2.339-44)

Baltrusaitis (1994: 77-80) interprets this passage as a reproduction of "the mirror of clouds." This concept finds its origin in *The clouds* by Aristophanes, wherein Socrates explains how clouds can take up any shape according to what they see below: if clouds see a beastly savage, they mock his appetite by taking the shape of centaurs; when they see a coward they will turn into a deer. Polonius's manner of speaking

---

[10] The stage as a mirror is a ubiquitous metaphor in the Renaissance (Armstrong 2000: 8).

[11] Platt (2009: 160-61) interprets this transposition as a distorted mirror, while Colie (1974: 231) thinks it reveals Hamlet's hidden hostility against Claudius.

serves as a mirror of clouds to reflect his inner hollowness, and so does Osric's:

OSRIC   I thank you lordship, it is very hot.
HAMLET   No believe me, 'tis very cold, the wind is northerly.
OSRIC   It is indifferent cold my lord, indeed.
HAMLET   But yet methinks it is very sultry and hot for my complexion.
OSRIC   Exceedingly my lord, it is very sultry, as 'twere — I cannot tell
how.   (5.2.92-97)

Hamlet is partly responsible for their emptiness. As Colie (223-24) points out, Hamlet has a feeling that "he is mirrored in the distorted characters" around him. In a sense, Hamlet and the Danish courtiers configure a set of coupled mirrors and Hamlet mirrors Polonius, only to mock him:

POLONIUS   My lord, I have news to tell you.
HAMLET   My lord, I have news to tell you.   (2.2.356-57)

Hamlet also mirrors his mother; however, the aim of this mirroring completely differs from the one mentioned above:

GERTRUDE   *Hamlet*, thou hast *thy* father much offended.
HAMLET   *Mother*, you have *my* father much offended.
GERTRUDE   *Come, come*, you *answer* with an idle tongue.
HAMLET   *Go, go*, you *question* with a wicked tongue.   (3.4.9-12)

Repeating his mother's words, he differentiates his viewpoints from hers by inserting antonyms in the identically-structured lines (Kermode 2000: 121). He hereby determines to be an introspective mirror wherein she must see the brutal truth behind her husband's death and also re-examine her incestuous relationship with her brother-in-law.

3. The language of the mirror in *Hamlet*
Along with these references to the mirror, the language of the mirror embodies specular reflections linguistically, especially in such rhetorical devices as epanalepsis and antimetabole. Their component words or phrases are arranged in chiastic symmetry which evokes specular reflections in a mirror or those between coupled mirrors.

3.1. Epanalepsis
Epanalepsis is defined by the repetition of the initial word or words of

a clause or sentence at the end (Mack 2011: 333), which makes the identical elements face each other in a line. In the next quotations, the terms "seems" and "my father" are respectively repeated at the beginning and the end of each line.

> *Seems* madam? nay it is, I know not *seems*. (1.2.76)

> *My father*'s brother, but no more like *my father*
> Than I to Hercules — (1.2.152-53)

> *My father*, methinks I see *my father* — (1.2.184)

Significantly, epanalepsis emphasises the thematic words unfolding the problems which persistently annoy the prince: the repetition of "seems" highlights Hamlet's strong distrust of external seeming, whereas the reiterated "my father" forebodes the appearance of the Ghost in the coming scene.

3.2. Antimetabole (or chiasms)

More complicated mirror-like symmetry is realised in antimetabole,[12] a literary device repeating two words in successive phrases in reverse order (Mack 329). The most evident users of antimetabole are Hamlet and Polonius. For Polonius, it is one of the effective rhetorical devices by which he thinks he can flaunt his quick wit:

> That he is mad, 'tis true; *'tis true 'tis pity*,
> And *pity 'tis 'tis true* — a foolish figure,
> But farewell it, for I will use no art.
> Mad let us grant him then, and now *remains*
> That we find out the *cause* of *this effect*,
> Or rather say, the cause of *this defect*,
> For *this effect defective* comes by *cause*.
> Thus it *remains*, and the remainder thus. (2.2.97-104)

This passage contains two sets of antimetabole use: one (*'tis true* : *'tis pity* :: *pity 'tis* : *'tis true*) in the first and second lines, and the other (*remains* : *cause* : *this effect* : *this defect* :: *this effect defective* : *cause* : *remains*) in the fourth line and thereafter, wherein Polonius completely

---

[12] Joseph (1947: 305) comments that antimetabole is "akin to logical conversion in that it repeats words in converse order, often thereby sharpening their sense."

"loses the thread of his argument" (Jenkins 1982: 241), only to expose his foolishness, contrary to his intention.

Hamlet's use of antimetabole is more closely related to the thematic problems of seeming and inner truth, one of which is demonstrated in his speech where he admires the power of playing, "What's *Hecuba* to *him*, or *he* to *Hecuba*, / That he should weep for her?" (2.2.511-12). In this passage, two perspectives intersect with each other, letting him gaze at the world: the word "Hecuba" represents the theatrical, "he/him" the real world. In the first half of the antimetabole, "*Hecuba* to *him*," Hamlet observes the theatrical world in the mirror of the real world, while in the second half, "*he* to *Hecuba*," he gazes back at the actual world in the mirror of the theatrical world. The use of antimetabole thus verbalises the epistemic process of Hamlet's struggle to see through the actual state of things with double perspectives crossing.[13]

3.2.1. Hamlet and the spies

In his exchanges with other characters, Hamlet employs antimetabole as a linguistic weapon, chiefly against Polonius, Rosencrantz, and Guildenstern, the spies dispatched by Claudius. The same antimetabole also serves as a mirror to reflect the ulterior motives and secrets of the speakers, although the specular images are often so opaque and shadowy that the speakers barely seem to notice their intentions have been exposed. Even Hamlet seems to be oblivious of what his language of the mirror actually reflects. In the next exchanges with Polonius, despite seeming random, the words chosen and arranged by Hamlet correctly shape chiastic symmetry (*actors* : *come* :: *came* : *actor*, and *Capitol* : *Brutus* :: *brute* : *capital*):

> POLONIUS   The *actors* are *come* hither my lord.
> HAMLET   Buzz, buzz!
> POLONIUS   Upon my honour.
> HAMLET   Then *came* each *actor* on his ass —   (2.2.359-62)
>
> [POLONIUS]   I was killed i'th'*Capitol*. *Brutus* killed me.
> HAMLET   It was a *brute* part of him to kill so *capital* a calf there.
>   (3.2.91-93)

---

[13] The similar epistemic process is depicted in Hamlet's advice to the players, "Suit *the action* to *the word, the word* to *the action*" (3.2.15-16).

Mirrors, reflection, and language in *Hamlet*   191

However, this artfully manipulated wording is attended with some danger of betraying his mental sanity. Hamlet himself claims later in the closet scene in front of his mother that such linguistic manipulation could prove his madness exists merely in his craft, "Bring me to the test, / And I the matter will *reword*, which madness / Would gambol from" (3.4.143-45).

Similarly in the next exchange between Hamlet and his schoolfellows, Rosencrantz and Guildenstern, the prince carefully sifts the vocabulary he uses in antimetabole:

> GUILDENSTERN   Why then your *ambition* makes it one; 'tis too
> narrow for your mind.
> HAMLET   O God, I could be bounded in a nutshell, and count myself
> a king of infinite space, were it not that I have bad *dreams*.
> GUILDENSTERN   Which *dreams* indeed are *ambition*, for the very
> substance of the *ambitious* is merely the *shadow* of a *dream*.
> HAMLET   A *dream* itself is but a *shadow*.
> ROSENCRANTZ   Truly, and I hold *ambition* of so airy and light a
> quality that it is but a shadow's shadow.   (2.2.241-49)

Here we see two sets of antimetabole: one is in the first three lines (*ambition* : *dreams* :: *dreams* : *ambition*), and the other is in the latter five lines (*ambitious* : *shadow* : *dream* :: *dream* : *shadow* : *ambition*). If we focus upon the choice of words, it is Guildenstern who completes the first set by embodying "dreams" and "ambition" in his response to the prince, to which Hamlet responds, having his "dream" and "shadow" intersected with those of Guildenstern's. The second set is started by Guildenstern with the word "ambitious" and completed by Rosencrantz with the word "ambitious." Notably, Hamlet excludes "ambition" and "ambitious" from his own speech in both sets. They only appear in the lines of Rosencrantz and Guildenstern, the spies employed by Claudius, as Jenkins (250) points out, to test his theory that Hamlet's distemper is due to frustrated ambition.

Hamlet's exclusion of the words "ambition" and "ambitious" is suspicious enough for Guildenstern to report to the king that Hamlet "with a crafty madness keeps aloof / When we would bring him on to some confession / Of his true state" (3.1.8-10), which verifies Claudius's assumption that he merely "puts on this confusion" (3.1.2).

3.3.2. Hamlet and the female characters

Ophelia and Gertrude are also a trap set for Hamlet to make him probe into his true state. However, when they encounter Hamlet, the language of the mirror projects different facets of the situation, reflecting the vacillating emotional distance existing between Hamlet and each woman. In the following exchange with Ophelia in the nunnery scene, Hamlet's emotional pain is concealed within his moralistic attack on her (Lewis 2017: 37-38):

> HAMLET   That if you be honest and fair, your *honesty* should admit no discourse to your *beauty*.
> OPHELIA   Could *beauty*, my lord, have better commerce than with *honesty*?
> HAMLET   Ay truly, for the power of *beauty* will sooner transform *honesty* from what it is to a bawd, than the force of *honesty* can translate *beauty* into his likeness.   (3.1.107-13)

Here the first set of antimetabole exchanged between Hamlet and Ophelia (*honesty* : *beauty* :: *beauty* : *honesty*) evolves into the second incorporated in Hamlet's response (*beauty* : *honesty* :: *honesty* : *beauty*). Immediately before this, Ophelia greets Hamlet in an excessively rhetorical fashion, "I have remembrances of yours / That I have longed long to re-deliver" (3.1.93-94). Unfortunately for her, Hamlet's ear is quick enough to detect her father's voice behind this wording. It ignites his anger so that he hurls harsh questions at her, "are you honest?" (3.1.103) and "Are you fair?" (3.1.105), to which the bewildered Ophelia carelessly answers by completing the first set of antimetabole. Hamlet responds bitterly in the form of another chiastic symmetry between "beauty" and "honesty." Ophelia's rhetorical wording, mirroring the shadow of her rhetorical father, provokes Hamlet's angry and moralistic antimetabole.

Polonius is an "intruding fool" (3.4.31) for Hamlet, so he remains unconcerned even after murdering him. But the murder of Polonius serves as a turning point for Hamlet, not only stimulating him into action but also offering Hamlet and Gertrude a chance to rebuild their relationship. Hamlet confides in his mother about the reason he killed Polonius and the truth behind his father's death, which subsequently forces Gertrude to introspect on her incestuous relationship with Claudius. The closet scene thus becomes a moment of truth-telling

Mirrors, reflection, and language in *Hamlet*   193

between mother and son. However, Gertrude's bewilderment, together
with her brief response, "What shall I do?" (3.4.181) disappoints and
irritates Hamlet, provoking him into a fresh attack on her, similarly to
what happened to Ophelia. However, the stream of invective helps
Gertrude reassemble herself, a reaction completely different from
Ophelia's. Gertrude pledges to protect him for life in the following set
of antimetabole (*words* : *breath* : *breath* : *life* :: *life* : *breath* : *What
thou hast said to me*):

> Be thou assured, if *words* be made of *breath*,
> And *breath* of *life*, I have no *life* to *breathe*
> What thou hast said to me.   (3.4.198-200)

What makes these lines touch the heart is the way Gertrude individu-
alises the generic "words" and "life" in the first half of the
antimetabole, by linking them, in the second half, to her own life and
to her son's words, hereby embracing his secret. At the beginning of
the next scene, we see Gertrude merely inform Claudius of what she
has seen, "Ah mine own lord, what have I seen tonight!" (4.1.5),
thereby tactically hiding what she has heard from her son. She
purposefully has become a mirror which only offers a partial image of
things as a flat looking-glass does.

3.3.3. Hamlet versus Claudius

After the closet scene, Hamlet must again confront Rosencrantz and
Guildenstern who have come for Polonius's body.[14] He frustrates their
inquiries with a sequence of enigmatic remarks, employing antimetabole to intensify the bitterness of his words, "*The body* is with *the
king*, but *the king* is not with *the body*" (4.2.24). Even to the king, he
sticks to the chiastic wording he has been indulging in, "A man may
fish with the *worm* that hath *eat* of a king, and *eat* of the *fish* that hath
fed of that *worm*" (4.3.25-26), although this provides Claudius further
justification for sending him immediately to England.

Before the voyage to England, Hamlet bids Claudius "Farewell dear
mother" (4.3.45-46) and adds a chiastic passage, "*My mother*. Father
and mother is *man and wife*, *man and wife* is one flesh, and so, *my*

---

[14] Crane (2001: 144) interprets that Polonius's corpse suggestively literalises
the rottenness and inward decay of Denmark.

194   *Fusako Matsuura*

mother" (4.3.48-49).[15] This chiastic line, seemingly meaningless, functions to highlight the deceptive integration Claudius has created in Denmark. The significance of this antimetabole can be verified by examining the king's opening speech in Act 1, Scene 2:

> Therefore our sometime sister, now our queen,
> Th'imperial jointress to this warlike state,
> Have we, as 'twere with a defeated joy,
> With one auspicious and one dropping eye,
> With *mirth* in *funeral* and with *dirge* in *marriage*,[16]
> In equal scale weighing delight and dole,
> Taken to wife;   (1.2.8-14)

Here Claudius deceivingly justifies his marriage to Gertrude, prohibited by cannon law, smoothing over the gap between a sister and a wife, by artfully interposing a variety of oxymoronic integration of "delight and dole" between them (Platt 153; Crane 132). Hamlet's antimetabole is an answer to this speech, mirroring how Claudius has obscured his crime and the divisions he has caused in Denmark, and also serves as a clear declaration that Hamlet is at war with the king. Actually, Hamlet has repeatedly been making insinuating remarks[17] about Claudius's deception, among which the "my mother" speech quoted above proves most effective against the king.

The play-within-the-play is a mirror held up to Claudius to reflect his regicide. Although we are not sure which lines Hamlet has added, we observe Claudius's oxymoronic integration reproduced in the Player King's speech, being incorporated in the following two successive sets of antimetabole (*grief* : *joy* :: *joy* : *grief*, and *grief* : *joys* :: *joy* : *grieves*):

> The violence of either *grief* or *joy*
> Their own enactures with themselves destroy.
> Where *joy* most revels, *grief* doth most lament;
> *Grief joys, joy grieves*, on slender accident.   (3.2.177-80)

---

[15] It also recalls Hamlet's "uncle-father and aunt-mother" (2.2.344-45).

[16] This line also contains a chiastic coupling (Garber 2005: 482).

[17] In his first encounter with Horatio, Hamlet sarcastically comments, "The funeral baked meats / Did coldly furnish forth the marriage tables" (1.2.180-81).

Mirrors, reflection, and language in *Hamlet*   195

In the last scene, these reiterated insinuations against Claudius ultimately crystallize into a deadly "union" (5.2.244), a poisonous pearl which Claudius drops into his cup of wine before toasting Hamlet, and also into a fatal wordplay when Hamlet finally wreaks vengeance upon the king, "Is thy union here? / Follow my mother" (5.2.305-06).

4. Conclusion

The language of the mirror in *Hamlet* reflects how Hamlet reveals the guilt concealed within the Danish court, concurrently mirroring how he plots his vengeance against his uncle, and copes with the traps set for him. However, the following speech of Hamlet, immediately before the duel, demonstrates a new epistemic stage Hamlet has reached:

> There is special providence in the fall of a sparrow. If it be *now*, 'tis not to *come*; if it be not to *come*, it will be *now*; if it be not *now*, yet it will *come* — the readiness is all. Since no man of aught he leaves knows, what is't to leave betimes?   (5.2.192-96)

Interestingly, this line of antimetabole is structured in a twofold chiastic order (*now* : *come* :: *come* : *now* :: *now* : *come*), wherein the second part (*come* : *now*) is used to complete the first set of antimetabole and to start the second set concurrently. This structural overlapping is effective at obscuring the boundary between the present and the future, as a specular image reflected endlessly back and forth between coupled mirrors.

So far Hamlet has struggled to expose the deceptive integration Claudius has so carefully disguised. In this respect, antimetabole, especially with its chiastic symmetry, has been one of his most effective weapons to unmask the incompatibility immanent in Claudius's cover-up. In the speech given above, however, Shakespeare has Hamlet obscure the boundary between the present and the future, although it recalls Claudius's deceptive integration to justify his kingship and marriage with Gertrude. However, it does not endeavour to depict the similarity between the king and the prince, but instead to differentiate between them. It tactfully literalises how Hamlet effaces his deep-seated hostility toward deceptive integration, as is implied in the structural overlapping in the antimetabole. It obscures not only the

196   *Fusako Matsuura*

boundary between the present and the future, but also between any opposing relationships. It moreover embodies the mental state of Hamlet who can finally reconcile with the world, accepting life and death as they are, "There's a divinity that shapes our ends, / Rough-hew them how we will" (5.2.10-11).

References

Armstrong, Philip 2000. *Shakespeare visual regime: Tragedy, psychoanalysis and the gaze*. New York: Palgrave.

Baltrusaitis, Jurgis 1994. *Kagami (Le miroir)*. Atsushi Tanigawa (tr.) Tokyo: Kokushokankoukai.

Colie, Rosalie L. 1974. *Shakespeare's living art*. Princeton: Princeton University Press.

Cook, Amy 2010. S*hakespearean neuroplay: Reinvigorating the study of dramatic texts and performance through cognitive science*. New York: Palgrave Macmillan.

Crane, Mary Thomas 2001. *Shakespeare's brain: Reading with cognitive theory*. Princeton: Princeton University Press.

Da Vinci, Leonardo 1835. *A treatise on painting*. John Francis Rigaud (tr.) London: J.B. Nichols and Son.

Elam, Keir 2017. *Shakespeare's pictures: Visual objects in the drama*. London: Bloomsbury.

Garber, Marjorie 2005. *Shakespeare after all*. New York: Anchor Books.

Grabes, Herbert 1973, 1982. *The mutable glass: Mirror-imagery in titles and texts of the Middle Ages and the English Renaissance*. Cambridge: Cambridge University Press.

Joseph, Miriam, Sister 1947. *Shakespeare's use of the arts of language*. New York: Columbia University Press.

Kermode, Frank 2000. *Shakespeare's language*. New York: Farrar, Straus and Giroux.

Lewis, Rhodri 2017. *Hamlet and the vision of darkness*. Princeton: Princeton University Press.

Mack, Peter 2011. *A history of Renaissance rhetoric 1380-1620*. Oxford: Oxford University Press.

Melchior-Bonnet, Sabine 1994, 2001. *The mirror: A history*. New York: Routledge.

Ono, Yoko 2015. Kagami wo miru otokotachi (Men looking into a mirror). In Kiyoo Uemura (ed.) *Shikaku no iconogurafia (Iconography of sight)*. Tokyo: Arina Shobo.

Pendergrast, Mark 2003. *Mirror mirror: A history of the human love affair with reflection*. New York: Basic Books.

Platt, Peter G. 2009. *Shakespeare and the culture of paradox*. Surrey: Ashgate Publishing Limited.

Shakespeare, William 1982. *Hamlet*. Harold Jenkins (ed.), London: Methuen.

Shakespeare, William 2003. *Hamlet, prince of Denmark*, updated edition. Philip Edwards (ed.), Cambridge: Cambridge University Press.

Simpson, John A. & E.S.C. Weiner, prepared 1989, 2009. *The Oxford English dictionary*, second edition on CD-ROM version 4.0. Oxford: Clarendon Press.

Thorne, Alison 2000. *Vision and rhetoric in Shakespeare: Looking through language*. London: Macmillan Press LTD.

Wright, George T. 1987. Hendiadys and *Hamlet*. In Vivian Salmon & Edwina Burness (eds.), *A reader in the language of Shakespearean drama*. Amsterdam: John Benjamins Publishing Company.

The world of *Kyng Alisaunder*:
A comparison with the Hereford *Mappa Mundi*

Eri Shimamoto Matsuzawa

Abstract

Kyng Alisaunder (KA) is an early fourteenth century rhyme verse. In this paper, I will show through a comparison of the Hereford Map, made around the year 1300 and the vocabulary of KA, what a well-educated man in the fourteenth century knew of the world. The editor of KA, G.V. Smithers, argues that the KA poet had high and broad intellect. First, I compare the Map and KA. I compare some episodes and the marvellous peoples of the world, according to the poet's account of Alexander's expedition. I then list the vocabulary of KA: intellectual people, plants, animals, and religion. What the poet offers largely coincides with the Map. His knowledge of the world satisfies the intellectual curiosity of its audience and anticipates the following age of great exploration and the Map also anticipates the following age.

1. Introduction

Kyng Alisaunder (KA) is an early fourteenth century rhyme verse comprising 8,021 lines in couplets. Its main source is *Roman de Toute Cheualerie* (RTC) composed not later than the thirteenth century by one Thomas of Kent.[1] KA begins with the following lines:

B1[2] DJuers is þis myddellerde	"Divers is this world
B2 To lewed men and to lerede	To lewd men and to the learned
B3 Bysynesse care and sorouȝ	Business, care, and sorrow
B4 Js myd man vche morouȝe	Are with men each morning
B5 Somme for seknesse for smert	Some for sickness for sharp pain
B6 Somme for defaut oiþer pouert	Some for default or poverty
B7 Somme for þe lyues drede	Some for dread lives
B8 Þat glyt away so floure in mede	Pass away like flowers in meadow"

The poet then says that the king, the duke, or the noble knight, foolish or wise, each desire some solace in listening a wonderful story in otherwise burdensome lives. Then, he insists that the noble deeds of

---

[1] Smithers (1957: 15).
[2] The number following B is the line number of B text (the Laud MS. in Bodleian Library, Oxford) of *Kyng Alisaunder*, edited by G.V. Smithers. Translations and punctuations are my own unless otherwise noted.

the conqueror of the known world, Alexander the Great (356-323 BCE), who went to the world's edge and saw the wonders, are more delicious than ribaldry or drinking and eating just to fill the stomach.

KA begins with the geographical knowledge of the world, i.e., Europe, Africa, and Asia, and then the names of the months and season. The last crusade ended in 1270. Richard the Lionhearted (1157-99) had set forth on expeditions and managed to return to England. Palmers, "carrying a palm branch or palm leaf as a mark of his or her pilgrimage,"[3] were known to the English people. The emperor of the Yuan Dynasty, Kublai Khan (1215-94), whose mother was a Christian (Nestorian Church), was interested in European Christian countries and sent a goodwill messenger to Philip IV of France and Edward I of England in 1287.[4] The edge of the world was not a mythical place but a place you could go to and come back from.

At the same time, the need for knowledge or information of the world was growing. The earliest English college, Oxford University, had been founded in 1249. There were also several universities in Europe: Salerno (the ninth century) for medical students, Bologna (late in the eleventh century), Paris (1150-70), and so on. Smithers says the KA poet was not in sacred orders[5] but that his intelligence was high and broad: "The extent of reading goes far beyond anything of which the authors of ME. romances normally show any knowledge."[6] The KA poet could read Old French epics and lyrics.[7] He also demonstrates literacy of Latin (B2198, 3511, 5174, 6361, 6378, 6433, 6446). The episodes of KA reflect the poet's knowledge and general learning of his age. He repeats more than ten times that his source of knowledge is books (B149, 3513, 4786, 4809, 5079, 5682, 5727, 5821, 6161, 6182, 6295, 6300, 6508, 6516, 6542, 6779, 6966, 7766). This means that he believes that what he says is true. In this paper, I will show through a comparison of the Hereford Map and the vocabulary of KA how a well learned man of letters in the fourteenth century recognized the world.

---

[3] *OED* (s.v. *palmer*).
[4] Aoki (1997, 2012: 89-90).
[5] Smithers (1957: 60).
[6] Smithers (1957: 60).
[7] Smithers (1957: 58-59).

The world of *Kyng Alisaunder* 201

2. Hereford *Mappa Mundi*
2.1. About Hereford *Mappa Mundi*
(1) T-O map

First, I will explain the Hereford *Mappa Mundi*, or "World Map." The Hereford Map (hereafter the Map) is the centre piece of the Triptych in the Hereford Cathedral in England, which is also famous for its chained library. The author was Richard of Haldingham or Lafford and the language is mostly Latin and some, French. It was drawn on one large sheet of bellum (1.58 x 1.33 meters) around the year 1300. It was made in almost the same year that the original *Kyng Alisaunder* was composed.

At the top of the Map, between the pentagonal frame and the round world, is Jesus Christ surrounded by St. Mary and angels. Above is the East, so the Garden of Eden (the Terrestrial or Earthly Paradise) was at the top of a round shaped (O-shaped) world. Jerusalem is at the centre of the world, which is divided into three parts: Asia, Europe, and Africa. The waters divide the world: The Black Sea, the Aegean Sea, the River Nile, and the Mediterranean Sea. These waters form a T-shape, so these kinds of maps are called T-O maps.

Some other T-O maps give almost the same image of the world: a twelfth century world map by Isidore of Seville, drawn in northern France; the world map of Sawley Abbey, Yorkshire (c.1200); the Psalter world map of 1260s; and the Ebstorf world map of later thirteenth century.

The encyclopaedic information in the Map has multiple sources including *the Bible*, Solinus (third century), *Etymologies* by Isidore of Sevill (c. 560-636), *Orosii Mundi Istoria*, "History of the World by Orosius" by Orosius (flourished 414-17), and others. [8] Westrem (2010) explains the 1,091 episodes marked on the Map (marked with <§>) and translates the Latin of each episode into English with close commentaries. [9] Some episodes have strong similarities to those recounted by the KA poet, though the locations are sometimes very different.

---

[8] Harvey (2010: *Introduction* 67-77).
[9] All the Map's English translation and Latin words marked with <§> are from Westrem (2010).

(2) The word, MORS

Four letters, MORS, "death" are placed like rivet hangers. It seems as if the round-shaped world is suspended from these letters. The first eight lines (B1-8) given above in Introduction are associated with this Latin word.

(3) The man on a horse

At the lower left corner, there is a man on a horse. He gazes at the Map and seems to be going to the Map's world. However, the horse is heading in the opposite direction. A hunter is behind him and there is a French phrase, *"pass avant,"* ("go ahead") just above him but whether he is the speaker of this phrase is not clear, as Westrem observes (§11).

2.2. The Hereford Map and *Kyng Alisaunder*
2.2.1. Protection of this world by Christ

The poet's understanding of this world is doubtlessly that of the Christian conception of the Middle Ages. The phrase *God it woot* "God knows it" is repeated (B3381, 4924, 5430, and so on). These lines reveal the poet's religious mindset that God created this world and saves us from even the most terrifying creatures like the four-eyed *Matiny* people (cf. 2.2.3.2. (6)).

> B6555 God vs shilde alle from shame!

This line follows the description of the *Cataplebas*, a beast (cf. 3.3. (5)) that instantly kills anyone who sees it. This coincides with the Map with Christ at its top, marking the Last Judgement. The phrase, *"Ecce Testimonium [me]um"* ("Behold my witness") on both sides of Jesus Christ (§6) coincides with the phrases of KA, i.e. God knows everything and protects us despite those terrifying creatures. This concept that Christ controls even pagan or monstrous creatures began from Roman age and continued through the Middle Age. Every map mentioned above (2.1. (1)) shows the same view of the world.

2.2.2. The Hereford Map and Alexander

Alexander was not just a military conqueror of Europe, Africa and Asia. After conquering Darius, his strong curiosity led him to search the land for the wonders of the world. Some episodes on the Map are

The world of *Kyng Alisaunder*   203

connected to the expedition of Alexander. Kline shows at least sixty-nine episodes to be related to Alexander's expedition.[10] I will show some episodes on both the Map and KA.

(1) Gog and Magog and the Caspian Gate

Gog and Magog are "evil forces opposed to the people of God."[11] The Map tells as follows (§302): "The island of Terraconta, which the Turks inhabit, of the lineage of Gog and Magog a barbarous and filthy people who eat the flesh of youths and miscarried fetuses."

Alexander, after experiencing the marvels of Asian and India, during which time he lost his most trusted warrior, Perdicas, is told about Gog and Magog (B5938-79). He decides to make a gate using bitumen to shut out Gog and Magog and other terrifying creatures (B6008-6287): "King Alexander has shut all of them/ Worse or better/ They will not come thence, oh no ever/ All until the doomsday" (B6276-79).

These lines correspond to §141 of the Map:

> "[Here are] all kinds of horrors, more than can be imagined: intolerable cold, a constant blasting wind from the mountains, which the inhabitants call 'bizo'. Here are exceedingly savage people who eat human flesh and drink blood, the accursed sons of Cain. The Lord used Alexander the Great to close them off, for within sight of the king an earthquake occurred, and mountains tumbled upon mountains all around them. Where there were no mountains, Alexander hemmed them in with an indestructible wall."

The Antichrist appears on both.

> B6280-85: "Antichrist shall come then and choose vile men by himself. And he shall fell, through the power of inflammation of the skin, all of Alexander's wall downright and lead all these folks out with him to do much harm to all the world."

The Map §142:

> "… Indeed, at the time of Antichrist they will be bursting forth and inflicting persecution on the whole world."

---

[10] Kline (2001: 175).
[11] *Britannica.*

(2) Trees of Sun and Moon (*Abre Sek*)
Alexander reaches India, where *Abre sek*, two "Dry Trees" of Sun and Moon, foretell that Alexander will die by a treacherous act.

B6755   Arbre sek men done hem calle   "Men call them *Abre sek*"

The Map (§76):

Abor Balsami: id est, Arbor Sicca   "The Balsam Tree—that is, the Dry Tree"

They are near the Earthly Paradise, so there are holy scents (cf. 3.2.). Under the Trees are illustrations of the expulsion of Adam and Eve and of an angel, pointing the direction of exile (southward) (§71).

(3) Hercules Columns
Though Alexander saw the Hercules Columns in India (B5573-78): the Map locates them at Gibraltar, at the end of the Mediterranean (§1091).

2.2.3. Marvellous peoples
The marvellous peoples Alexander witnessed are described in three parts: Asia, Africa (Ethiopia), and *Serese*.

2.2.3.1. Marvellous peoples in Asia (B4853-5027, 5259-5280, 5633-61, 5789-94, 6160-65).
(1) People on *Gamgerodes* Island (B4853-80); (2) People of *Patona* (*Polibote*), (B4881-92); (3) People on the hill of *Malleus* (B4893-4906); (4) *Pandea*, where all inhabitants are girls (B4907-18) (The Map §116: "Pandea, a people of Yndia ruled by women"); (5) *Faraugos*, who eat raw and hot meat (B4919-24); (6) *Maritiny,* a fishing people (B4925-32); (7) People creeping like hogs (B4933-36); (8) *Orphani*, who eat their parents for love after they died (B4937-44) (The Map §212: "The Essedones of Scythia live here, whose custom is to accompany their parents' funerals with songs and, having assembled a group of friends, to tear into their parents' bodies with their teeth and to make a solemn feast of animal meat mixed with human flesh, believing it more honourable to be consumed by each other than by worms."); (9) People who creep into the wood and die when they suffer sickness of urine (B4945-52); (10) Hound men (B4953-62); (11)

The world of *Kyng Alisaunder*   205

One-eyed people (B4963-70); (12) People living like palmers (B4971-84); (13) People with wide forchures[12] (B4985-5002); (14) A wise people who stand on one foot all day (B5003-18); (15) People whose colour of hair changes to brown from grey (B5019-27); (16) *Albanyens* (cf. 3.3. (2), B5259-80); (17) The rich people in Hippuri, *Yperoun*, (B5633-54); (18) The *cee-hounde* "sea-hound" people in the east of Hippuri (B5659-60); (19) People looking up the sky all day on one foot (B5789-94); and (20) a people between Egypt and India, who live like *iker*, NICOR "water demon" in Meopante (B6160-65).

The people of *Patona* (2) are very strong, and their king leads 30,000 men on horse, 600 of infantry, and 8,000 elephants to battle. The Map §129 says, "Patna, ..., an extremely powerful people of Yndia, whose king musters 600,000 foot-soldiers and 30,000 cavalrymen and 8,000 elephants into regular military service."

Regarding the one-eyed people (11), §54 says, "In Yndia are Monocules, with a single leg, of extreme swiftness, who when they want to protect themselves from the heat of the sun, shade themselves with the hugeness of their feet." The Map's illustration of these people near the Himalayas (§47) shows them having two eyes, but is similar to the description of the people (11) in KA (B4965-70): "They have an eye and no more/ And a foot to go/ With his foot, when it rains/ Covers his body, and when it shines/ Because his foot is so big/It can cover his body, indeed."

2.2.3.2. Marvellous peoples in Africa (Ethiopia) (B6288-6395, 6402-95)

After Alexander built the Caspian Gate, he sails to Ethiopia to see unfamiliar peoples. (1) *Garamaiten*, the loathliest people (B6294-6303). The Map §888 says, "Here live barbarians: Gaetuli, Natabres, and Garamantes"; (2) *Serbotes* with wide and long forchures (B6304-07). They resemble the Asian people in 2.2.3.1. (13); (3) *Cenophalis*, drinking only the other's milk (B6308-13); (4) *Azachei*, who eat elephants (B6314-19); (5) *Saubaris,* whose king is a dog (B6320-29); (6) Four-eyed *Maritiny* (B6330-39). The Map §976 says, "Marmini Ethiopians have fours eyes"; (7) *Arriophagy*, who eat only panther,

---

[12] The folk of the body (*OED*, s.v. *forchure*).

lion, and venison (B6340-47). The Map §981 says, "Agriophagi Ethiopians eat only the meat of leopards and lions; they have a king whose one [eye] is in his forehead"; (8) Creeping *Artapides* (B6348-55). The Map §966 says, "Himantopods: with fluid movement of the legs they creep along more than walk and they move along with a glide rather than a step"; (9) *Cinemolgris*, whose face is a dog (B6356-63). The Map §442 says, "In this territory are the Cynocephales." According to Wistrem's explanation the *Cynocephales* is a race of humans with the heads of dogs.[13] However, they live in Europe on the Map.

The above nine peoples live in west Ethiopia in KA. (10) *Macrobij* live in the east Ethiopia. They are Christians and live a best life. The city Saba is in the land (B6364-95); (11) An unattractive people without a nose (B6402-13); (12) *Orifine* without a nose, a mouth, teeth, and a tongue on the face. They put a reed into their mouth and soak with the reed to feed themselves (B6414-33). The Map §964 says, "A people with a sealed mouth gets food through a straw." The illustration of this people has a nose; (13) Long-eared *Auryalyn* (B6434-47). The Map §88 says, "[an Asian people, t]he Phaneses[,] are cloaked with their outer ears"; (14) *Garraman*, who look like Martin the Ape (3.3. (4)) (B6448-73); and (15) *Erpe-drake* "Earth-dragon" women growing out of the ground (B6474-95).

2.2.3.3. People in *Sereses* (B7030-78)
Now, Alexander has learned of his time of death, but he continues his martial expedition against the Indian King Porus. The people of *Sereses* live between the valley of Jordan (B7018) and the Caspian Gate. Alexander's army travelled the mountains for seven nights to reach *Sereses*, in upcountry India with a great amount of silk. Smithers explains the *Sereses*, "RTC *seres*; originally of inhabitants of Northern China."[14] The Map §146 says, "the city of Seres." It is located next to "The city of Caspia" (§147).

---

[13] Westrem (2010: 186).
[14] Smithers (1957:216).

The world of *Kyng Alisaunder* 207

3. Vocabulary lists in KA
3.1. Intellectuals
The following list of people are those named by the KA poet:

(1) Cato: Chaucer identifies Cato as a well-known intellectual in *Miller's Tale* 3227: "He knew nat Catoun, for his wit was rude" ("He did not know Cato, for his mind was untutored").[15] Cato is "the supposed author of a collection of Latin maxims studied in the grammar school."[16] The KA poet cites a phrase from Cato as a good teacher (B17): "Other man's life is our preceptor."

(2) Aristotle (384-322 BCE): Aristotle is known as the private teacher of Alexander. The KA poet introduces him as one of the seven masters of Alexander (B667, 3008, 4767).

(3) Ptolemy (100-170): After describing twelve months from March to February and the season, the KA poet says, "whoever wants to see the nature, he must hear Ptolemy"[17] (B65-66).

(4) Authorities on the wonders of the East: St. Isidor of Seville: His *Etymologiae* was the most important glossography. The KA poet introduces him as one authority of the wonders of the East (B4773). Other authorities are as follows: Solomon (B4771), who, the KA poet says, "goes throughout all the world," E Troge (=Eustroge, B4775), St. Jerome (B4777), Magasthenes (c. 350-290 BCE, B4779),[18] Dionysius (otherwise unknown, B4781),[19] and Pompeius Trogus (first century BCE), author of *Historiae Philippicae* (B 4783).

(5) Gaius Julius Solinus: Solinus is described in KA as follows: "The good scholar named Solim [Solinus] has written in his Latin book that hippopotamus is a wonder beast, more than an elephant, indeed" (B5173-75). Solinus (early third century) is the author of *Collections of Memorable Matters*. He took his writings from Pliny the Elder (23-79) and Pomponius Mela (first century). Pliny is the author of *Natural*

---

[15] Cawley (ed.) (1978: 87).
[16] Cawley (ed.) (1978: 87).
[17] "Who-so wil þe nature ysee/ Hij moten yheren Tholome"
[18] Smithers (1957: 124).
[19] Smithers (1957: 124).

208   *Eri Shimamoto Matsuzawa*

History, "an encyclopaedic work of uneven accuracy that was an authority on scientific matters up to the Middle Ages,"[20] though his name is not found in KA.

3.2. Plants

Most plants mentioned in KA are edible and common: APPLE, BROOM, CANEL "cinnamon," CORN, CRAB "apple," CRESS, CUBEB, CUMIN, CYPRESS, FIGER† "fig," GALINGALE "of the ginger family," GINGER, GILLYFLOWER, HAW, HAZE, HIP, LICORICE, MACE, NUT, NUTMEG, OLIVE, OSIER, PEA, PEAR, RAISIN, REED, RIND, SETWALL "the root of the East Indian plant *Curcuma Zedoaria*, (*OED*)," SLOE, and WHEAT. Some appear in a proverb: "Your high fame does not worth a pea" (B5949).

Some spices and herbs are used to describe love and the holy land. Alexander's mother, Olympias, compares her love for her lover, Neptanabus or Amon, to spices: NUTMEG and LICORICE (B428). Alexander notices that the land of *Arbre sek* is holy from the smell of various herbs (B6782-87): NUTMEG, SETWALL, GALINGALE, CANEL, LICORICE, GILLYFLOWER, CUBEB, MACE, GINGER, and CUMIN. Piment (a "wine flavoured with wine and spices," *OED*) is served at rich feasts (B 4171, 7575). Many kinds of herbs and spices were known and used as something precious.

3.3. Animals

There appear various animals, including everyday animals, those for military use, mythical ones, and extremely fierce ones: ADDER, ANT, APE, ASS, BEAST, BIRD, BUZZARD "hawk," BLACK FOWL, BOAR, BUGLE, BUGLE-HORN, BULL, BUZZARD, CADES or CALES‡[21] "a reptile," CAMEL, CAT, CATOBLEPAS "buffalo," CEPHUS, CHASER "horse," CLAW, COW, CRAB, CROCODILE, CULEUVRE† "snake," DEER, DENTIRAUNS (a corruption of *odontotyrannus*[22]), DESTRER, DOLPHIN, DRAGON, DRAG- ONET, DRAKE, DROMEDARY, EEL, EFT "lizard," ELEPHANT, ERNE

---

[20] *Britannica* (s.v. "Pliny the Elder").
[21] ‡: ἅπαξ λεγόμενον.
[22] Smithers (1957: 129).

The world of *Kyng Alisaunder*   209

"eagle," FALCON, FOWL, GOSHAWK, GRAY-BITCH, GREYHOUND, GRIF-
FIN, GRIFHOUND† "hunting-dog," GRIPE "griffin," HART, HEN, HIPPO-
POTAMUS, HOG, HORSE, HOUND, KITE, LEOPARD, LION, MANTICEROS,
MARE, MONOCEROS, MULE, NIGHTINGALE, NICOR "a water-demon,"
OUNCE "lynx." OX, PAD, PALFREY, PANTHER, PARD "panther," PERCH,
PHEASANT, RAVEN, RHINOCEROS, ROTHER, SALMON, SCORPION,
SHEEP, SNAKE, SOMER, SPERVER† "sparrow-hawk," STEED, SWINE,
TIGER, UNICORN, VERMIN, WATER-DOG, WOLF, and WORM.

(1) HIPPOPOTAMUS (B5157): After citing Solinus (cf. 3.1. (5)), the KA
poet continues as follows (B5182-86): "It will eat all fruit, apples, nuts,
raisins and wheat. But men's flesh and men's bone, it loves best of
everything." The hippopotamuses kill many of Alexander's good
retainers in the river.

(2) Asian Beasts (B5201-5446): Alexander and his army start in India,
and they reach Facen[23] (B5043). However, afterwards, they suffer
from thirst and decide to pass over the mountains to reach water. When
they are in the mountains, various strange beasts pester them one after
another: BORE, BEAR, LION, ELEPHANT, TIGER, DRAGON, OUNCE,
LEOPARD (B 5217-19); ADDER, SCORPION, TIGER, ELEPHANT, BEAR
(B5253-55); SCORPION, ADDER, TIGER, ELEPHANT, LION, BEAR
(B5283-85); ADDER (B5319); DRAGON (B5321); DRAGON (B5337);
CRAB (B5358); WHITE TIGER, BULL (B5377); TIGER (B5384); DEN-
TIRAUNS (*odontotyrannus*) (B5407); GREAT FOX (B5424); and BLACK
FOWL (B5435). After Alexander wipes them out, he starts for Bagdad.
    Among these creatures, the twelve footed crabs (B5358) are as big
as wild bores and their shells so hard that the army cannot pierce them
even with steel swords, so they use *fire-bronde* ("a live coal," B5372).
DENTIRAUNS (*odontotyrannus*) are bigger than elephants, with three
horned horse-like heads (B5407-11). The *Albanians* live near the
mountains. They help the Alexander's army. They have indigo-blue
faces and are glassy-eyes that can see like cats' eyes at night (B5261-
67).[24] Their strong hounds are for military use. They give two dogs
(GRIFHOUND) to Alexander (B5275). One kills a lion, and the other

---

[23] "Country of the river Phasis or Rion, which flows into the Black Sea"
(Smithers (1957: 215)).
[24] Then the line B5267 "Of four feet hij habbeþ þe lengþe" continues.

210   *Eri Shimamoto Matsuzawa*

beats off an elephant (B5290-98). The Hereford Map §207 says, "The Albanians have bright gray eye and see more at night."

(3) Further east are the people of Hippri (2.2.3.1. (17)), ADDER with four heads, DRAGON, GRIPE, TIGER and LION (B5657-58). Then, there appear adders bearing precious stones: JACINTH, PYROPE "ruby," CHRYSOLITE "a green-coloured gem," SAPPHIRE, SMARAGD "emerald," and MARGERY† "pearl" (B5673-74).

(4) *Martin ape* (B6454): They are compared to an Ethiopian people (2.2.3.2 (14)). Smithers explains that "this expression, which is not contained in RTC, and of which there is only one other ME. example (in Wyclif), can derive only from animal fables in MDu. [Middle Dutch] or just possibly an early antecedent (no longer extant) of a MDu. version of the *Roman de Renart* [*Reynard the Fox*]."[25]

(5) Egyptian Beasts (B6496-6615): CEPHUS (*cesseus*) whose feet are like those of human beings (B6509), RHINOCEROS, bigger than elephants (B6519); the strongest MONOCEROS with one strong horn (B6529). The Map §433 says that the monoceros is fierce but before a virgin girl it becomes a harmless creature; CATOBLEPA (cf. 2.2.1., B6554); ANT, bigger than greyhounds (B6556). The Map §942 says, "Here enormous ants hoard golden sands"; CROCODILE with treble teeth (B6587); and DOLPHIN, the crocodile-eater (B6604).

(6) Beasts between the Valley of Jordan and the Caspian Sea (B7018-7149): ADDER (B7019), DRAGON with emerald in the mouth (B7020); ADDER, MONOCEROS (B7084); WORM, CALES, MANTICORE (B7085). The Map §157: "Solinus: The manticore is native to Yndia, with a triple set of teeth, the face of a human, yellow eyes, the colour of blood, a lion's body, a scorpion's tail, a hissing voice"; brown and white LION (B7086); BEAR, wild SWINE (B7089); DRAGON (B7090); and CADES, *cades*, which kills more than 30,000 of Alexander's men (B7094).

3.4. Religion
Various religious words appear in KA.

(1) Biblical Words: Abigail (wife of King David), Absolon (son of

---

[25] Smithers (1957: 143).

King David), Antichrist, Babel, Beelzebub, Cain, Christianity, David, Delilah, devil, God, Jesus, Job, St. Mary, Nimrod, Prester John, and other Christian saints.

Though BEELZEBUB (B1682) is a demon that appears in the Bible. Those who believe in BEELZEBUB are dukes of Darius. In the army of Darius, there are also some Christians of PRESTER JOHN (B2585), a legendary Christian ruler in the East.

(2) Greek, Roman, Egyptian and other heathen Gods: Apollo. Atropos, Aeneas, Bacchus, Clotho, Diana, Dido, Hercules, Lachesis, Oedipus, Liber, Ammon, Balat, and Terugaunt.

(3) Non-Christianity or Saracen Words: HEATHEN, MAHOMET, SARA-CEN: Because Alexander was a king before Christ, he is not a Christian but a "Saracen." Alexander says, "Alle shullen abiggen, by Dans Mahouns" ("All should make amend by the name of Don Mahomet" (B3170). He makes offerings and sacrifices to ask for the help of the heaven *on Sarsynes wise* "in a Saracen's manner" (B6152).

However, the meaning of SARACEN is "non-Christian." The poet does not make a strict distinction between Greek or Roman religion and Muslim as in the obsolete definition of this word (*OED*, s.v. *Saracen* †2 a. "A non-Christian, heathen, or pagan; an unbeliever, infidel."). All the *Maritiny* people are identified as Saracen but they believe in Bacchus and Apollo (B 6338-39, cf. 2.2.3.2. (6)).

The Saracen people are not necessarily unenlightened and primitive. The KA poet describes the death of Saracen soldiers as follows: "Many fair heþen lefdy/ Þere last seiȝen her amy" ("Many fair heathen ladies saw their lovers' last time there") (B 1965-66). The sorrow of burying one's lover in war is the same, Christian or heathen. Alexander never does meaningless killing. The poet does not describe non-Christian religion with a fear of the unknown.

(4) The Earthly Paradise: In KA, the word *Paradise* appears in the following lines (seven times): B1500, 5676, 5927, 6199, 6394, 6401, and 6562. The Tigris (B6394) and the Nile (B6562) are waters from the Paradise. The Earthly Paradise is described as follows (B5675-78): "Beyond the dragons, gripes and beast/ Earthly Paradise is right in the East/ Where Almighty God, through his grace/ Formed Adam that was

our father."

The gate of Paradise (§70) is at the top of the east end of the Map. It is in an island enclosed by flames and a wall. Adam, with forbidden fruits in his right hand, and Eve are there (§64 and §65). As in Genesis 2:11-14, four rivers, the Pishon (§68 *Phison*, the Indus River), the Gihon (§69 *Gion*, the Nile River), the Tigris (§67) and the Euphrates (§66)[26], flow from the Terrestrial Paradise.

4. Concluding remarks

KA is a war chronicle that includes the stories of adulterous love affairs and the descriptions of beautiful nature in headpieces, but at the same time it is a brief and intelligible encyclopaedia. The KA poet, in addition to anthropology, fauna, and flora, tells us about geography, mineralogy, and astrology of the Middle Ages. The details in KA and the Map do not coincide, but the worldview is the same in both: Christ protects the world, which has three parts, where the various creatures live.

The wonders of the East had been known since the OE times. The Beowulf Manuscript contains the illustrated *The Wonders of the East*, *The Letter of Alexander to Aristotle*, and so on. These wonders are real as is the Earthly Paradise. Bede says as follows (Bede *Hexaemeron* (Migne *Patrologia Latina* XCI 43):[27]

> "But indeed, whether it [the Earthly Paradise] is there or elsewhere God knows. We only know that there was such a place, and may not doubt but that it was terrestrial—a place indeed most pleasant, shaded with fruitful groves, made fertile by a great spring...."

In the fourteenth century, books and the literacy were becoming the means of knowledge acquisition. The encyclopaedic information of KA was authentic to its the audience. The illustrations in the Map and other sources support this conception of the world. Many maps and books of the age tell us about this world which is generally the same, as was demonstrated in my comparison of KA and the Map.[28] KA's audience believed that they could experience these wonders if they

---

[26] *The Bible*, American Bible Society.
[27] Lascelles and Ker (1936: 32).
[28] *Mandeville's Travels* is also a kind of encyclopaedia.

travelled to Asia and Africa, or in Europe itself. However, even Alexander lost thousands of his men during his exploration. The world was full of danger but the one they believed in. This worldview of KA and other sources in the fourteenth century must have been a motivation that led to the emergence of explorers in the next century. Thus, from the end of the following century, Christian people entered a new era, the Age of Geographical Discovery. They began to go on explorations around to the world like the man in the lower left corner of the Map (cf. 2.1. (3) above). Because of this adventure, the appearance of the world map changed. It became more accurate, but the image of Christ disappeared. Christ protects the mediaeval world of KA, but one could argue that the new adventurers went out to discover the unknown world that Christ does not protect.

References

American Bible Society 1970, 1973. *The Bible.*

Aoki, Tomitaro (trans.) 1997, 2012. *Marco Polo Toho kenbun roku* [Travels of Marco Polo]. Tokyo: Interplay (e-book on BookLive <https://booklive.jp/>). Last Accessed September 2017.

Cawley, A.C. (ed.) 1978. *Chaucer Canterbury Tales.* New York: E.P. Dutton & Co. Inc.

Encyclopædia Britannica <https://www.britannica.com/> Last Accessed September 2017.

Harvey, P.D.A. 2010. *The Hereford Map: Introduction.* London: Folio Society.

Kline, Naomi Reed 2001. *Maps of medieval thought.* Woodbridge: The Boydell Press.

Lascelles, M.M. & N.R. Ker 1936. Alexander and the Earthly Paradise in mediaeval English writings. *Medium Ævum* Vol. 5, No. 1: 31-48.

OED = Oxford English Dictionary <http://www.oed.com/>. Last Accessed September 2017.

Smithers, G.V. (ed.) 1952. *Kyng Alisaunder: Volume I, E.E.T.S. No. 227.* Oxford: Oxford University Press.

Smithers, G.V. (ed.) 1957. *Kyng Alisaunder: Volume II, E.E.T.S. No. 237.* Oxford: Oxford University Press.

Westrem, Scott D. 2010. *The Hereford Map: Commentary.* London: Folio Society.

Stylistic analysis of Mansfield's *A Cup of Tea*

Yumi Mizuno

Abstract

The paper examines the internal deviation of linguistic features, such as parallelism, repetition, elegant variation, and verbal structure, in the short story *A Cup of Tea*. We focus on the two main characters: Rosemary, the protagonist of the story, and Miss Smith, a young beggar, who asks for the price of a cup of tea. The analysis of internal deviation reveals the distinctive contrast between the two characters, and linguistically indicates the three foregrounded places of the story. Among them, especially just before and right at their meeting, various stylistic techniques are used in layers to show Rosemary's mental change.

1. Introduction

In this paper, we trace internal deviation and make observations about the effects produced. According to Leech and Short (2007: 44), departure from the norms of stylistic consistency in a text is defined as internal deviation:

> The recognition that a text may set up its own secondary norms leads to a further conclusion, that features of language within that text may depart from the norms of the text itself: that is, they may 'stand out' against the background of what the text has led us to expect. This is the phenomenon of INTERNAL DEVIATION, which, although it is most striking in poetry, may equally well be observed in prose style.

To explore internal deviation, this paper focuses on these linguistic features: parallelism in 2.1, repetition of the image of light and shade in 2.2, elegant variation in 2.3, and verbal structure in 2.4. The features are selected because of their prominence in this text. The conclusions drawn from the discussions are presented in Section 3.

2. Analysis
2.1. Parallelism

There are two places in the text worth attention for their parallelism. First, let us examine the part of the opening paragraph that describes Rosemary Fell, the protagonist of the story:

216   *Yumi Mizuno*

(1) She was young, brilliant, extremely modern, exquisitely well dressed, *amazingly well read* in the newest of the new books, and her parties were the most delicious mixture of the really important people and ... artists—quaint creatures, discoveries of hers, some of them too terrifying for words, but others quite presentable and amusing. (408)[1]

The sentence above can be conveniently analysed as follows:

Table 1. Grammatical structure of the passage (1)

[1] She was	young	
	brilliant	
[2]	extremely modern	
	exquisitely well dressed	
	amazingly well read	
[3] in	the newest books	of the new books
and her parties were	the most delicious mixture	of the really important people
[4] and artists	quaint creatures	
	discovery of hers	
[5] some of them	too terrifying for words	
but others	quite presentable and amusing	

With respect to grammatical structure, the words and phrases listed above are all similarly constructed. In [1], [2], and [5], the predicates are all adjectives or adjectival phrases; in [3], the nouns, both *books* and *mixture*, are modified by the superlative forms of adjectives and by prepositional phrases; and in [4], both *quaint creatures* and *discovery of hers* are in apposition to *artists*. Here we notice that the pattern of parallelism is maintained in terms of the grammatical structure except in [2], where the pattern is broken by a third: *amazingly well read*. In fact, Rosemary's encounter with Miss Smith is compared to *something out of a novel by Dostoevsky*, and the very idea develops into the action of her bringing Miss Smith back home:

(2) And suddenly it seemed to Rosemary such an adventure. It was like *something out of a novel by Dostoevsky*, this meeting in the dusk. Supposing she took the girl home? Supposing she did do *one of those things she was always reading about* or seeing on the stage, what would happen? It would be thrilling. And she heard herself saying afterwards to the amazement of her friends: "I simply took her home with me," as she stepped forward and said to that dim person beside her: *"Come home to tea with me."* (411)

---

[1]   Italics within quotations by this author. The text used is: *Collected stories of Katherine Mansfield* (1962 edition). London: Constable, pp. 408-16.

Stylistic analysis of Mansfield's *A Cup of Tea*   217

In (2), there is another expression worth attention, in relation to the image of the phrase *amazingly well read*, that is, *one of those things she was always reading about*. Further, we notice the following similar expression in (3), *one's always reading about these things*, which appears when she tries to convince Philip, her husband, to let Miss Smith stay:

> (3)"My darling girl," said Philip, "you're quite mad, you know. It simply can't be done." "I knew you'd say that," restored Rosemary. "Why not? I want to. Isn't that a reason? And besides, *one's always reading about these things*. I decided—" (415)

The expression in direct speech in (3) becomes the grounds for explaining free indirect thought in (12), which will be discussed in 2.4.2. Now let us return to (1). Interestingly, in sentence (1), nothing besides *amazingly well read*, such as *exquisitely well dressed*, *the really important people*, or *artists*, is explicitly mentioned after the opening paragraph. Therefore, this internal deviation *amazingly well read* has special significance and prominence throughout the text.

The other example is:

> (4) She opened a drawer and took out five pound notes, looked at them, put two back, and *holding the three squeezed in her hand*, she went back to her bedroom. (416)

The sentence above can be analysed as follows:

Table 2. Grammatical structure of the passage (4)

[1] She	opened a drawer
and	took out five pound notes,
[2]	looked at them,
	put two back,
[3] and	holding the three squeezed in her hand,
she	went back to her bedroom

The pattern of parallel structure is broken by the use of a participial construction at one place in [3] *holding the three squeezed in her hand.* The climax of this story is created by this deviation, together with another stylistic device, which will be examined in 2.4.2. It is also noted that *the three*, which means "three pound notes, the price of quite a few cups of tea" (Ferrall 2014: 114), reminds us that it was *the price of a cup of tea* that Miss Smith asks for, as in the examples (5) and (6):

218   *Yumi Mizuno*

(5) "M-madam", stammered the voice. "Would you let me have *the price of a cup of tea*?" (410)

(6) Rosemary, laughing, leaned against the door and said: "I picked her up in Curzon Street. Really. She's a real pick-up. She asked me for *the price of a cup of tea*, and I brought her home with me." (415)

2.2 Repetition of the image of light and shade

Throughout the text, we notice that there is a contrast between light and shade. It is clear that a positive image is assigned to Rosemary by such an adjective as *flashing* (409), and a negative image to Miss Smith by *dark* (410), *shadowy* (410), and *dim* (411). Now let us focus on the following two examples of internal deviation, which include both light and shade at the same time. This is the scene where Rosemary is out of the antique shop:

(7) The discreet door shut with a click. She was outside on the step, gazing at the winter afternoon. Rain was falling, and with the rain, it seemed the *dark* came too, spinning down like *ashes*. There was a cold bitter taste in the air, and the *new-lighted* lamps looked sad. Sad were the *lights* in the houses opposite. *Dimly* they *burned* as if regretting something. (410)

We should note that the door in the passage (7) creates a familiar setting and indicates that "the identity of the door in question has already been established" (Trotter 1992: 15). Leech and Short (2007: 102) mention:

The door referred to in Katherine Mansfield's sentence may not have existed, but plenty of other doors, of which we have real experience, do. So from our knowledge of entities and goings-on in the real world, as well as from our knowledge, acquired from the text, of fictional world, we are able to postulate the nature of the fictional world, drawing inferences about matters not directly communicated by the text.

Further, it is obvious that the sentence *The discreet door shut with a click* demarcates a boundary in the text between the scene inside the antique shop and that outside it. Trotter (1992: 17) states:

Rosemary Fell finds herself in the street outside the shop. She has crossed a symbolic threshold, exchanging the security of the shop for the insecurity of the street.

Then what linguistic patterns represent her emotional transition toward insecurity? In (7), Rosemary's insecure feelings are mainly represented by the use of the words related to light and shade, such as *dark*, *ashes*, *new-lighted*, *lights*, *dimly*, and *burned*. Note especially the sentences: *There was a cold bitter taste in the air, and the new-lighted lamps looked sad. Sad were the lights in the houses opposite.* The inversion *Sad were the lights in the houses opposite* is like the symmetry of a mirror image, and reinforces a circularity of sameness like surging waves, suggesting her feelings that the sadness would continue.

The other example is a description of Miss Smith after having tea:

> (8) And really the effect of that slight meal was marvellous. When the tea-table was carried away, a new being, a light[2], frail creature with tangled hair, *dark* lips, *deep, lighted* eyes, lay back in the big chair in a kind of sweet languor, looking at the *blaze*. (414)

In (8), the connotations of *lighted* are surely apt in describing the satisfaction of her appetite, and the word, associated with *blaze*, is foregrounded as opposed to background information such as *dark* and *deep*. Moreover, *sweet* dilutes the negative connotations of *languor* and suggests the enigma of her personality, which will be discussed in 2.3. Thus, the mixture of the images of light and shade indicates the change, whether mentally or physically, of the two characters.

2.3. Elegant variation

In this section, we observe the elegant variation of the two characters of the story. Before the discussion proper, let us consider the connotations of the characters' names to determine their attributes. From the family name *Fell*, we can infer that Rosemary may be cold in disposition, since *Fell* means "shrewd; clever, cunning" (*OED* s.v. *fell*, A. adj.[1], 1. a.) or "fierce, savage; cruel, ruthless; dreadful, terrible, of terrible evil or ferocity; deadly" (*OED* s.v. *fell*, A. adj.[1], 3.). This coincides with

---

[2] We also notice the word *light* in this variation but this is not to be regarded as a positive image since the word is ambiguous. It might mean "bright, shining," but can be reasonably taken as "of little weight" in association with *frail* as "liable to break or be broken." It can also mean "wanton, unchaste" (*OED* s.v. *light*, adj.[1], III.14.b.) in association with *frail* as "morally weak; unable to resist temptation; habitually falling into transgression" (*OED* s.v. *frail*, adj.[3]).

220   *Yumi Mizuno*

the actions of bringing Miss Smith home out of whimsical generosity
and then of impulsively expelling her. On the other hand, the name
Smith has the connotation of belonging to the working classes, in
association with "one who works in iron or other metals; esp. a black-
smith or farrier; a forger, hammerman" (*OED* s.v. *smith*, n. 1.). We also
note that the introduction of Miss Smith's name is deliberately delayed
and she is nameless throughout much of the story.

Now we shall consider the linguistic patterns of elegant variation
with reference to the two characters. There is a clear contrast in the
identities they are given. Rosemary is referred to by means of her name
or pronominal references. On the contrary, we note that the references
to Miss Smith are constantly altered from the beginning to the end.
Pronominal references being excluded, she is referred to as *the girl*
nine times, as *the other* five times, and as *that other* once. Table 3
shows other variants used for Miss Smith.

Table 3. Elegant variation of Miss Smith

[1]	a young girl, thin, dark, shadowy (410)
[2]	a little battered creature with enormous eyes, someone quite young, no older than herself (410)
[3]	that dim person (411)
[4]	the little captive (411)
[5]	this poor little thing (412)
[6]	the thin figure (412)
[7]	poor little thing (412)
[8]	the poor little creature (413)
[9]	a new being, a light, frail creature with tangled hair, dark lips, deep, lighted eyes (414)
[10]	the languid figure (414)
[11]	the listless figure (415)

Here we notice that a great degree of modification is applied to a
description of Miss Smith at two places [2] and [9]: *a little battered*
creature with enormous eyes, someone quite young, no older than
herself; and *a new being, a light, frail creature with tangled hair, dark*
lips, deep, lighted eyes. These two elegant variations are all the more
remarkable for the lengths of their phrases. The former occurs when
Rosemary sees Miss Smith for the first time, as in (9). This variation
forms Rosemary's first impression of Miss Smith, creating

foregrounding:

> (9) "Speak to me?" Rosemary turned. She saw *a little battered creature with enormous eyes, someone quite young, no older than herself,* who clutched at her coat-collar with reddened hands, and shivered as though she had just come out of the water. (410)

The latter occurs when Miss Smith finishes eating, indicating her physical change with the use of *lighted*, as seen in the example (8) in 2.2. Let us note that all the modifiers used have negative connotations except for this elegant variation. However, the modifiers in the last two variations, *languid* in [10] and *listless* in [11], negate her subtle change. Moreover, the two modifiers, associated with *sweet languor* in (8), present her enigmatic image of being indifferent to what is going on around her or what she has to do.

2.4. Verbal structure
2.4.1. Author's voice
Since the basic tenses are either simple past or past progressive tense, deviation from these draws our attention and conveys special meaning to us:

> (10) The girl put her fingers to her lips and her eyes devoured Rosemary. "You're—you're not taking me to the police station?" she stammered.
> "The police station!" Rosemary laughed out. "Why should I be so cruel? No, I only want to make you warm and to hear—anything you care to tell me."
> *Hungry people are easily led.* The footman held the door of the car open, and a moment later they were skimming through the dusk. (411)

In (10), the sentence *Hungry people are easily led*, marked by the present tense of a verb, represents the general opinion towards the poor. It is noteworthy that the ironic voice of the author interrupts the narrative flow, explaining why Miss Smith has no choice but come to Rosemary's home.

2.4.2. Free indirect discourse and free direct discourse
It is intuitively obvious that we understand Rosemary's feelings because the story "moves fluently into and out of her consciousness" (Trotter 1992: 15). This comes partly from the use of free indirect

222   *Yumi Mizuno*

discourse and free direct discourse of Rosemary to show her stream of consciousness:

> (11) *"Charming!"* Rosemary admired the flowers. *But what was the price*? For a moment the shopman did not seem to hear. Then a murmur reached her. "Twenty-eight guineas, madam." *"Twenty-eight guineas."* Rosemary gave no sign. She laid the little box down; she buttoned her gloves again. *Twenty-eight guineas. Even if one is rich...* She looked vague. She stared at a plump tea-kettle like a plump hen above the shopman's head, and her voice was dreamy as she answered: *"Well, keep it for me—will you? I'll..."* (409-10)

In (11), Rosemary admires a little box shown by a shopman in the antique shop. We notice the transitions from direct speech, *"Charming!"* to free indirect speech, *But what was the price*?, further from direct speech, *"Twenty-eight guineas."* to free direct thought, *Twenty-eight guineas. Even if one is rich...*, and back to direct speech, *"Well, keep it for me—will you? I'll...."* Thus, her typical thought flow leads back to direct speech.

Now we shall examine the passage (12) to find any differences:

> (12) *"How extraordinary!"* Rosemary peered through the dusk, and the girl gazed back at her. *How more than extraordinary!* And suddenly it seemed to Rosemary such an adventure. It was like something out of a novel by Dostoevsky, this meeting in the dusk. *Supposing she took the girl home? Supposing she did do one of those things she was always reading about or seeing on the stage, what would happen? It would be thrilling.* And she heard herself saying afterwards to the amazement of her friends: "I simply took her home with me," as she stepped forward and said to that dim person beside her: *"Come home to tea with me."* (411)

In (12), direct speech, *"How extraordinary!"* is followed by free direct discourse, *How more than extraordinary!* and further, by such free indirect thought as *Supposing she took the girl home? Supposing she did do one of those things she was always reading about or seeing on the stage, what would happen? It would be thrilling.* Like (11), her thought flow returns to direct speech, *"Come home to tea with me."* The important thing is that there is a chain of free indirect thought and this thought flow vividly indicates her mental transition toward the indiscretion to bring Miss Smith back home. In sum, this free indirect thought of Rosemary is vital in the story.

Moreover, in contrast to her typical thought flow leading back to direct speech, we have a different mode of thought presentation of Rosemary, that is, a chain of free direct thought at two places. The first is:

> (13) And people hurried by, hidden under their hateful umbrellas. Rosemary felt a strange pang. She pressed her muff against her breast; she wished she had the little box, too, to cling to. Of course, the car was there. She'd only to cross the pavement. But still she waited. *There are moments, horrible moments in life, when one emerges from shelter and looks out, and it's awful. One oughtn't to give way to them. One ought to go home and have an extra-special tea.* But at the very instant of thinking that, a young girl, thin, dark, shadowy— where had she come from?—was standing at Rosemary's elbow and a voice like a sigh, almost like a sob, breathed: "Madam, may I speak to you a moment?" (410)

In (13), the very encounter of the two characters is described. The transition from pure narrative, *But still she waited*, to free direct thought, *There are moments, horrible moments in life, when one emerges from shelter and looks out, and it's awful. One oughtn't to give way to them. One ought to go home and have an extra-special tea.*, clearly shows that Rosemary is utterly insecure in a difficult situation. In fact, this free direct thought is immediately followed by their meeting. Note also that around this passage, various narrative techniques are used to create foregrounding, as in (7), (9), and (12). Secondly, let us consider this passage where exclamation marks are used as many as five times with free direct thought to show Rosemary's great confusion:

> (14) "You absurd creature!" said Rosemary, and she went out of the library, but not back to her bedroom. She went to her writing-room and sat down at her desk. *Pretty! Absolutely lovely! Bowled over!* Her heart beat like a heavy bell. *Pretty! Lovely!* She drew her cheque-book towards her. *But no, cheques would be no use, of course.* She opened a drawer and took out five pound notes, looked at them, put two back, and holding the three squeezed in her hand, she went back to her bedroom. (416)

It is remarkable that, after hearing Philip fascinated by Miss Smith's physical charms, a chain of free direct thought, *Pretty! Absolutely lovely! Bowled over!*, followed by *Pretty! Lovely!*, appears vividly,

224   Yumi Mizuno

showing how chaotic Rosemary's thought becomes. That her mental disorder remains is shown by such free indirect thought as *But no, cheques would be no use, of course*, leading toward the climax, as in (4). Thus, in both (13) and (14), her pattern of thought conveys an insecure and unfulfilled mind, thus appealing to our feelings.

In contrast, Miss Smith's mind is not represented at all. Regarding this, Ferrall (2014: 114) mentions:

> When a working-class woman poses no threat to a higher class woman she is accorded interiority, but when she is a threat she is merely an object in an upper class couple's relationship.

The following examples (15) and (16) clearly indicate that, with the use of *its*, she is an object for both Rosemary and her husband:

(15) "Oh, please,"—Rosemary ran forward—"you mustn't be frightened, you mustn't really. Sit down, and when I've taken off my things we shall go into the next room and have tea and be cosy. Why are you afraid?" And gently she half pushed the thin figure into *its* deep cradle. (412)

(16) He came over to the fire and turned his back to it. "It's a beastly afternoon," he said curiously, still looking at that listless figure, looking at *it*s hands and boots, and then at Rosemary again. (415)

Therefore, no thought presentation of Miss Smith may imply that she is a threat to the relationship between Rosemary and her husband. This reading of Miss Smith coincides with the discussions in 2.2 and 2.3.

3. Conclusion

We have so far explored the internal deviation of linguistic features to discover the effects produced. The analysis reveals that the reason that Rosemary, an upper-class protagonist, commits her indiscretion to bring Miss Smith, a working-class woman, back home is implicit in the very first paragraph. It also shows that the reason that Miss Smith must obey Rosemary's whim is ironically marked by the present tense.

Moreover, the contrast between the two becomes more distinctive through the analysis of internal deviation such as the mixture of the images of light and shade, the elegant variation of Miss Smith and the use of free indirect thought and free direct thought of Rosemary: that is, Rosemary is involved in psychological processes, whereas Miss

Smith is described as indifferent to thinking. In a way, Miss Smith is considered an enigmatic character. At any rate, this contrast may imply that the gap between the rich and the poor cannot be bridged.

In addition, the analysis indicates the three foregrounded places of the story: Rosemary's unfulfilled feelings leading to her encounter with a working-class woman, and further to her indiscretion; the physical change of the woman after eating; and Rosemary's mental struggle, caused by her husband's remarks on the woman's charms, resulting in her determination to expel the woman. Especially just before and right at their meeting, various stylistic techniques are employed to show Rosemary's mental change from security to insecurity, and then to indiscretion.

References

Ferrall, Charles 2014. Katherine Mansfield and the working classes. *Journal of New Zealand literature*, No. 32, 106-20. <http://www.jstor.org/stable/43198606>.

Leech, Geoffrey & Mick Short 2007. *Style in fiction: A linguistic introduction to English fictional prose* (second edition). London and New York: Routledge.

Mansfield, Katherine. *Collected stories of Katherine Mansfield* (1962 edition). London: Constable.

OED = Oxford English Dictionary. <http://www.oed.com>. Last accessed August 2017.

Trotter, David 1992. Analysing literary prose: The relevance theory. *Lingua*, Vol. 87, 11-27.

Negative declarative *I not say*
and negative imperative *Not say* in Modern English*

Fujio Nakamura

Abstract
The purpose of this paper is to demonstrate, based upon not only 130 volumes of diary and correspondence texts but also nine electronic corpora such as the Early Modern English section of the Helsinki Corpus of English Texts and ARCHER 3.1, how the negative form of *I not say* continued to be used in Modern English until its expiration in Present-day English.

Evidence gathered shows that not only the negative declarative (Neg.Decl.) *I not say* but also the negative imperative (Neg.Imp.) *Not say* continued to be used in prose moderately until around 1800. These negative forms were used widely by a variety of people, including the noble and the educated, throughout Britain and Ireland, and in various kinds of documents, formal or informal, academic or non-academic. Since they were employed far less frequently than *I say not*, *I do not say*, *I don't say*, *Say not*, *Do not say* and *Don't say*, the continued use in Modern English should not be overestimated. Jespersen did not include the negation currently in question in that five-stage development theory, which is appropriate.

1. Introduction
1.1. Previous studies and purpose of the present study
Regarding the history of English Neg.Decl. sentences, Jespersen (1917: 9-14; 1940 [1970]: 426-30) has traced the five-stage development as below. Stage I, *Ic ne secge*, was the Old English type. As the negative *ne* was very weak in this proclitic position, another negative particle *noht* was frequently added after the verb. With *noht* becoming *not*, we reached the second stage, *I ne seye not*. This passed into and was the typical form of Middle English. Here *ne* was pronounced with so little

---

* This study is an extracted version of Nakamura (2014). Here, I would especially like to record my appreciation of the useful comments made on earlier drafts of this paper by Professor Alison Carse, Aichi Prefectural University. It was very kind of her to not only provide me with useful information on the history of the English language but also correct stylistic errors in the earlier versions and provide useful feedback. This study was funded by the Japan Society for the Promotion of Science, Grant-in-Aid for Scientific Research, Category C, No. 25370557.

stress and began to take on such qualities of superfluity that it was dropped altogether. *I say not* was thus the third stage of negation. This negative form was at its prime during the fifteenth to seventeenth centuries, gradually going out of use in the course of the eighteenth century, with the exception of certain verbs such as *know, care* and *doubt*. The fourth stage, *I do not say*, which appeared late in the four-teenth century, had a frequency use of less than ten percent for the first hundred years, but its usage steadily increased, until at last its rapid growth in the seventeenth century took predominance over the third stage. Finally, *not*, tending to be weakly stressed in this position, was encliticised to *do*. We thus reached the colloquial negative form *I don't say*.

Furthermore, the negative form of *I not say* was in coexistence with the third and the fourth types, though it is not identified by Jespersen himself in his five-stage transition. On the origin of *I not say*, Partridge (1953: 9) speculates that it originated from Stage I (*Ic ne secge*), while admitting that *not* stemmed from the Old English indefinite pronoun *noht*, not from *ne*. Ukaji (1992) demonstrates that *I not say* originated as a blend sharing the traits of both Stage III and Stage IV during this transition. Iyeiri (2005: 67-69) attempts to show that the form of *not* + V originated via the following process: *naht* + *ne* + V → *not* + *ne* + V → *not* + V, just as *ne* + V + *not* developed into V + *not*. The Partridge's speculation will gain no support among historical grammarians, since *not* did not derive from *ne*. Ukaji's demonstration loses its grounds, considering the fact that *ne* + V appeared prior to Stage III (*I say not*). At present, Iyeiri's is considered very likely to be the most convincing view, even though it requires further relevant examples of *not* + (*ne*) + V in Old English and Early Middle English.

Among references to the diachrony of *I not say*, Puttenham (?1569/?c1585/?1589: 255) demonstrates that *I not say* was "a pardon-able fault" which gave "a pretie grace vnto the speech." Lowth (1762: 79) observes that this usage, which makes "the impropriety of placing the Adverb *not* before the Verb very evident," had "grown altogether obsolete" around the mid-eighteenth century. Poutsma (1928: 102) has almost the same opinion as Lowth. Smith (1933: 79-80) argues that *I not say* is still used in Modern literary (also colloquial) English for contrasting a verb with a preceding one. Partridge (1953: 9) suggests that *I not say* was a very

Negative declarative *I not say* and negative imperative *Not say* 229

common order in sixteenth century verse. Söderlind (1973 [1951]: 218) writes that J. Dryden used *I not say*, though only once, for emphasis. Ellegård (1953: 198) points out that, around 1500-1700, "*not* hardly ever occurred before the finite verb." According to Visser (1969: 1532), *I not say* was "only sporadically" used before 1500, but it became "pretty common in Shakespeare's time." "After c1700 a decline sets in," and in Present-day English *I not say* "is chiefly restricted to poetry." Visser quotes five examples for Late Modern English and one prose example for Present-day English dated c1930. Whereas Tieken (1987: 118) writes that *I not say* was "so rare" in the eighteenth century, and that it would be "characteristic of colloquial language" of the time, she also suspects that this construction may "have been in regular enough use ... to merit condemnation" from Lowth, a prescriptive grammarian. Her latter statement is proved to be true in the conclusion of the present paper.

The *OED²* (s.v. not, *adv.* and *n.²* A. *adv.*, 1b) states that the negative form of *I not say* has been "chiefly poetic." Ukaji (1992: 455) describes that this form "began to appear in the beginning of the fifteenth century, and was rather rare before 1500." It reached its highest point, he continues, "in the times of Shakespeare and Jonson," but in the middle of the eighteenth century it became "virtually obsolete." Ukaji's assertion is based upon a collection of ninety-one examples which occurred over the fifteenth through the eighteenth century. Rissanen (1999: 271) states that *I not say* was "first attested in late Middle English." Despite its rarity in the early sixteenth century, it became "somewhat more common by the end of the century." In the seventeenth century, however, it succumbed to the *do*-negative, "although instances can be found in eighteenth-century texts" and "it survives even later" in non-standard English. According to Rissanen, this usage "may well have been a usage typical of spoken language." Nakamura (2003: 72-73) argues, using examples systemically collected from 130 volumes of diaries and correspondence, that this negative form persisted in seventeenth, eighteenth and even nineteenth century English, even though *I not say* was infrequent, and is not to be overestimated in the history of English negation system compared with *I do not say* / *I don't say* / *I say not*. Iyeiri (2005: 76-77) concludes that *I not say* can be traced back to the Old and Middle English period,

230   *Fujio Nakamura*

and that *I not* (*ne*) *say* was at its peak as early as Old English or early
Middle English. According to her theory, *not* came to take post-verbal
position in the course of time, and *I not say* declined in Middle English
prose, if not in verse, so the strikingly common use of *I not say* in Early
Modern English verse should be regarded as a residual. With regard to
verbs which were used in the form of *I not say*, she states that modal
auxiliaries and forms of *be* and *have* could occur in this negation in
Middle English while they could no longer do this in Early Modern
English.

A brief sketch of the studies above indicates that it is imperative that
the usage currently in question with special regard to post-seventeenth
century English should be investigated, because large-scale historical
studies on this subject do not seem to have been undertaken. Thus, as
a supplement to those previous studies, the present paper seeks to
demonstrate how Neg.Decl. *I not say* and Neg.Imp. *Not say* continued
to be used in Modern English towards their virtual expiration in
Present-day English.

1.2. Texts and electronic corpora examined and research proce-dures

Texts and corpora examined are as follows.[1]

   a. Seventeenth to twentieth century private diaries and personal cor-
      respondence printed in the form of books: 101 collections, 130
      volumes.
   b. Electronic versions of British English texts written between 1351-
      1800, consisting of a heterogeneous assortment of 145 different
      works or documents, such as biographies, chronicles, essays, let-
      ters, novels, proclamations, religious prose, speeches, treatises and
      verse, randomly selected and downloaded in October 2005 from
      the European and American university and organisation websites.
   c. ARCHER 3.1 = *A Representative Corpus of Historical English
      Registers* version 3.1. 1990–1993/2002/2007/2010/2013.
   d. Eight electronic corpora included in Hofland, Knut, Anne
      Lindebjerg and Jørn Thunestvedt (1999) *ICAME Collection of*

---

[1] For details, see Nakamura (2014: 18-22).

Negative declarative *I not say* and negative imperative *Not say*   231

English Language Corpora, 2nd ed., University of Bergen: The HIT Centre: ACE, CEECS, FLOB, HC Diachronic Part, Kolhapur, Lampeter, LOB and Newdigate.

2. Examples of negative declarative *I not say* and negative imperative *Not say* in the present texts and electronic corpora examined

In Section 2, examples of Neg.Decl. *I not say* and Neg.Imp. *Not say* are provided, with a single example for every sentence structure per fifty-year period.

(1) a. In & before 1400
   Neg.Decl. "Subject + *not* + Verb" (2 examples)
   1374-1386 G. Chaucer, *Boece* (OUP), p. 9, and þat þe sterres not apperen vpon heuene. So þat þe nyȝt semeþ sprad vpon erþe.

   b. 1401-1450
   Neg.Decl. "Subject + *not* + Verb" (40)
   1426 J. Lydgate, trans. *Pilgrimage of the Life of Man* (F. J. Furnivall, ed.), 4-5, Thogh I not folwe the wordës by & by, / I schal not faillë teuchyng the substaunce,
   Neg.Decl. "Subject + *not* + *have* + Obj" (2)
   1426 J. Lydgate, 136, I ... nat had ... Halff A repast of suffysaunce
   Neg.Decl. "Subject + *not* + Aux + Verb" (1)
   1426 J. Lydgate, 131, 'ffor what ys worth, or may avaylle, / A feloun herte or hardynesse, / Daunger, despyt or sturdynesse, / Nat may socoure vp-on no syde,
   Neg.Decl. "Subject + *not* + *have* + PP" (1)
   1426 J. Lydgate, 260, Yiff thow nat haddyst, off entent, / fforfetyd hys comaundëment;
   Neg.Decl. "Subject + *not* + *ne* + Verb" (5)
   1426 J. Lydgate, 35, Hys surname I nat ne knew.
   Neg.Imp. "*Not* + Verb" (9)
   1426 J. Lydgate, 22, Yiff thow lyst acqueynted be / With me: tel on thy fantasye, / And the trowthë nat denye.
   Neg.Imp. "*Not* + *be* + Adj." (1)
   1426 J. Lydgate, 81, & nat be shent
   Neg.Imp. "*Thou*/*Ye*/*You* + *not* + Verb" (2)
   1426 J. Lydgate, 8, On my be halff[e] thow not ffaylle / To dresse yt ewyn by entaylle,
   Neg.Imp. "*Not* + *ne* + Verb" (7)
   1426 J. Lydgate, 534-535, Yiff thow mayst spekë, nat ne spare,

c. 1451-1500

Neg.Decl. "Subject + *not* + Verb" (2)

a1471 *English Chronicle*, 93, Send hom, most gracious Lord Jhesu most benygne, / Sende hoom thy trew blode vn to his propre veyne, / Richard duk of York, Job thy seruaunt insygne, / Whom <u>Sathan</u> <u>not</u> <u>cesethe</u> to sette at care and dysdeyne

Neg.Decl. "Subject + *not* + Aux + Verb" (2)

a1471 *English Chronicle*, 99-100, <u>he</u> ... <u>nat</u> <u>wold come</u> in to the parlement tylle he had aunswere therof.

Neg.Decl. "Subject + *not* + Verb + Aux" (1)

a1471 *English Chronicle*, 77, "Wythe wondrethe that <u>reson nat telle can</u>, / Howe a mayde ys a moder, and God ys manne, / Fle reasoune, and folow the woundre, / For beleue hathe the maystry and reasone ys vnder."

Neg.Imp. "*Thou/Ye/You* + *not* + Verb" (1)

1465 M. Paston, *Paston Letters* (N. Davis, ed.), I 298, And as for all youre othere evydens, <u>ye</u> ther <u>not</u> <u>feere</u> as fore the sy3t of hem, for there hath nor shall no man sen hem tyll ye com hom. [?Declarative 'you there not fear']

d. 1501-1550 (No example)

e. 1551-1600

Neg.Decl. "Subject + *not* + Verb" (11)

1598 E. Guilpin, *Skialetheia, or, A Shadowe of Truth, in Certaine Epigrams and Satyres*, Be not wrath, Cotta, that <u>I</u> <u>not</u> <u>salute</u> thee

Neg.Decl. "Subject + *not* + *have* + PP" (1)

1570 R. Ascham, *The Scholemaster*, Book 2, if <u>soch good wittes, and forward diligence</u>, had bene directed to follow the best examples, and <u>not</u> <u>haue bene caryed</u> by tyme and custome

f. 1601-1650

Neg.Decl. "Subject + *not* + Verb" (3)

1636 Anon., *The King and Queenes Entertainement at Richmond*, <u>The Spaniard</u> regarding him <u>not</u> <u>pursues</u> his intention of reading, when on the suddaine the Violin playes a Pavin, at which amaz'd he leaues off reading, the Violin stops, and as soone as he falls to reading againe it begins a Saraband,

Neg.Decl. "Subject + *not* + Passive *be* + PP" (1)

1605 F. Bacon, *The Advancement of Learning*, Book 2, But this I hold fit, that <u>these narrations</u>, which have mixture with superstition, be sorted by themselves, and <u>not</u> <u>be mingled</u> with the narrations which are merely and sincerely natural.

Neg.Imp. "*Not* + Verb" (1)

1609 T. Dekker, *The Guls Horn-Booke*, CHAP. IV, <u>You must</u> <u>not sweare</u> in your dicing: ... Mary, I will allow you to sweat [*sic*_Nakamura; 'sweat' should be 'swear'] privatly, and teare six or seven score paire of cards, be the damnation of some dozen or twenty baile of dice, and forsweare play a thousand times in an houre, but <u>not</u> <u>sweare</u>. Dice your selfe into your shirt: and, if you have a beard that your frind wil lend but an angell upon, shave it off, and pawne that, rather then to goe home blinde to your lodging.

g. 1651-1700

Neg.Decl. "Subject + *not* + Verb" (23)

1670 J. Milton, "The History of Britain, That Part Especially Now Call'd England", *The Works of John Milton*, in Helsinki Corpus, EModE III, CEHIST3B, <u>The</u> (<u>Northumbrians</u>) had a custom at that time, and many hunder'd yeares after <u>not</u> <u>abolish't</u>, to sell thir Children for a small value into any Foren Land.

Neg.Decl. "Subject + *not* + *be* + Adj" (1)

1680 John Hawles, *The English-mans right. A dialogue between a barrister at law and a jury-man. [...]*, Lampeter, LAWA, <u>Your Tenderness</u> <u>not</u> <u>be</u> accessary to any mans being wrong'd or ruin'd, is (as I said) much to be commended.

Neg.Decl. "Subject + *not* + *have* + Obj" (2)

1691 J. Locke, "Some considerations of the consequences of the lowering of interest, and raising the value of money", in the present current of running Cash ... young Men, and those in Want, might not too easily be exposed to Extortion and Oppression; and <u>the dextrous and combining Money Jobbers</u> <u>not</u> <u>have</u> too great and unbounded a Power, to Prey upon the Ignorance or Necessity of Borrowers.

Neg.Decl. "Subject + *not* + Passive *be* + PP" (1)

1670 R. Coke, *A Discourse of Trade*, This puts the Sugar Bakers on new projects, viz., the boiling up of Panellis Sugar to supply and serve instead of loose Lisbon Sugar, which was the principal Commodity returned in lieu of our Bays, Sayes, Searges, and Perpetuanoes, there vended in great quantities, and for want of returns by exchange <u>not</u> <u>be</u> be [*sic*_Nakamura] there <u>obtained</u>, the value principally returned in Lisbon Sugar;

Neg.Imp. "*Not* + Verb" (6)

1697 D. Defoe, *An Essay upon Projects*, "Of the Highways", WHAT I PROPOSE TO DO TO THE HIGHWAYS.—I answer first, <u>not</u> <u>repair</u> them; and yet secondly, <u>not</u> <u>alter</u>

234 *Fujio Nakamura*

them—that is, <u>not</u> alter the course they run; but perfectly build them as a fabric.

h. 1701-1750

Neg.Decl. "Subject + *not* + Verb" (8)

1711 J. Swift, *Journal to Stella*, I 343, <u>I</u> ... have nothing to say to you more, but finish this letter, and <u>not</u> send it by the bell-man.

Neg.Imp. "*Not* + Verb" (1)

1713 Nic. Frog in J. Arbuthnot, *The History of John Bull*, Ch. IX, I tell thee, thou must not so much as think of a composition. [<u>Not</u> think of a composition; that's hard indeed; I can't help thinking of it, if I would.]

i. 1751-1800

Neg.Decl. "Subject + *not* + Verb" (4)

1767 A. Ferguson, *An Essay on the History of Civil Society*, Part 1, Section VIII, 'Shall any one,' says Antoninus, 'love the city of Cecrops, and <u>you</u> <u>not</u> <u>love</u> the city of God?'

Neg.Decl. "Subject + *not* + *have to*-infinitive" (1)

1796 A. Hughes, *Diary*, 95, I be glad <u>the cowes and pigs</u> have got warm sheds to sleep in this weather, and <u>not</u> <u>have to lie</u> in the cold.

Neg.Imp. "*Not* + Verb" (2)

1764 H. Walpole, *Castle of Otranto*, Ch. 4. "Thou art too cruel," said Isabella to Hippolita: "canst thou behold this anguish of a virtuous mind, and not commiserate it?" "<u>Not</u> pity my child!" said Hippolita, catching Matilda in her arms—"Oh! I know she is good, she is all virtue, all tenderness, and duty. I do forgive thee, my excellent, my only hope!"

Neg.Imp. "*Not* + Causative/Perfective *have*" (1)

1759-67 L. Sterne, *The Life and Opinions of Tristram Shandy, Gentleman*, Ch. 1. XXXI, and <u>not</u> <u>have</u> it known!

j. 1801-1850

Neg.Decl. "Subject + *not* + Verb" (2)

1829 G. Crabbe, *Letters and Journals*, 353-354, You tell me I commended the Silence of Mʳ Elwin: <u>I</u> forget but surely <u>not</u> <u>commended</u> *him*: I know nothing of him, but I own that I might be glad of his Silence—let me be rightly Understood: It was *Your* Silence & not his that I wished:

k. 1851-1900

Neg.Decl. "Subject + *not* + Verb" (1)

1858 M. Arnold, *Letters*, I 76, He is an orator of almost the

Negative declarative *I not say* and negative imperative *Not say*   235

> highest rank—<u>voice and manner</u> excellent; perhaps <u>not</u> quite <u>flow</u> enough—not that he halts or stammers, but I like to have sometimes more of a *rush* than he ever gives you.

l. 1901-1950 (No example)

In documents written between 1951 and 2000, six examples with the form of "Subject + *not* + Verb" were discovered. However, in four out of the six examples, this form clearly seems to have been used for rhetorical colouring of the characters' speech in fiction. The examples in (2), for example, are not Pitman's own wording, but quotations from Chapter 4 of *The Flight from the Enchanter* (1956), a novel written by I. Murdoch. Here, she seems to have the usage of *not* + Verb uttered purposefully from the mouths of 'Jan' and 'Stefan,' fictional Polish immigrants in England. The other two examples are in subjunctive or mandative use in which *should* is construed. These facts indicate the virtual expiration of the construction of *not* + Verb in Present-day English.

> (2) 1961 R. Pitman, "Why has this face appeared among the best-sellers?," *The Sunday Express*, 23 July 1961, p. 6, in LOB, Category C (Press: reviews) 11A, 123-34, Occasionally the brothers dance round the mother or prod her with their feet. One cries: "You old rubbish! You old sack! We soon kill you, we put you under floor-boards, <u>you</u> <u>not</u> <u>stink</u> there worse than here!" ... One day Rosa goes to meet the brothers and finds only one of them, Stefan, waiting for her. He takes her to the room where he says: "We make love now, Rosa. It is time." "Your mother!" exclaims Rosa, noticing the old lady's watching eyes. "<u>She</u> <u>not</u> <u>see</u>, <u>not</u> <u>hear</u>," is the reply. The next day Rosa finds only the other brother, Jan, waiting.

3. Overall chronological trends

Based on the distinction of sentence structures, Table 1 is the tabulation of the data for the frequency of Neg.Decl. *I not say* and Neg.Imp. *Not say*. From Table 1, the following three points can be clarified: (a) Neg.Decl. *I not say* occurred most frequently in the first half of the fifteenth century, especially in Lydgate's translation from French, was relatively common in the second half of the seventeenth century but began to decline after 1800; (b) structurally, *not* could stand before a string of Auxiliary + Verb; (c) even the use of Neg.Imp. *Not say* was permitted before 1800.

236 Fujio Nakamura

Table 1. Frequency of negative declarative *I not say* and negative imperative *Not say* based on the distinction of sentence structures

	1351-1400	1401-1450	1451-1500	1501-1550	1551-1600	1601-1650	1651-1700	1701-1750	1751-1800	1801-1850	1851-1900	1901-1950	1951-2000	Total
Neg.Decl.														
S + *not* + V	2	40	2		11	3	23	8	4	2	1		6	102
S + *not* + *be* + Adj							1							1
S + *not* + *have* + Obj		2					2							4
S + *not* + *have to*-infinitive									1					1
S + *not* + Aux + V		1	2											3
S + *not* + V + Aux			1											1
S + *not* + Passive *be* + PP						1	1							2
S + *not* + *have* + PP		1			1									2
S + *not* + *ne* + V		5												5
Neg.Imp.														
Not + V		9				1	6	1	2					19
Not + be + Adj		1												1
Thou/Ye/You + *not* + V		2	1											3
Not + Causative/Perfective *have*									1					1
Not + *ne* + V		7												7
Total	2	68	6	0	12	5	33	9	8	2	1	0	6	152

Due to limitations on space, syntactic and semantic properties of Neg.Decl. *I not say* and Neg.Imp. *Not say* are mentioned briefly. In the texts and corpora examined, Neg.Decl. *I not say* occurred almost evenly between superordinate and subordinate clauses, and more frequently in the indicative mood. Even in the indicative present, the majority of the verbs conjugated with the third person singular subject in their root forms without the inflectional suffix -(*e*)*th* or -(*e*)*s*. In light of the fact that the number and person concord was not strictly adhered to as it is in Present-day Standard English, it is likely that Neg.Decl. *I not say* was not a polite or refined usage, although this usage was used by a number of learned people. Furthermore, Neg.Decl. *I not say* and Neg.Imp. *Not say* continued to be moderately used in prose, without showing a noticeable preference for intransitive or transitive verbs. No syntactic and semantic traits can be attested with the verbs used in these negative forms. These negative forms were used widely by varied individuals (from common folk to the nobility) throughout Britain and Ireland, and in various kinds of documents, whether formal or informal, academic or non-academic, especially before 1800.

4. Use of negative declarative *I not say* and negative imperative *Not say* in the former British Commonwealth of Nations and colonies

Six examples which seemingly have the usage currently in question have been discovered in documents written in American, Australian and Indian English. Four out of the six examples are used for rhetorical colouring of characters' speech in fictional dialogue and drama. The other two examples appear in news reports or short stories published in the press, and are in the subjunctive or mandatory use. Details are omitted in this paper.

5. Conclusion

Based upon the evidence gathered from 130 volumes of diaries and correspondence, 145 electronic British English texts written between 1351 and 1800, ARCHER 3.1 and eight electronic corpora included in ICAME[2], the following conclusions can be drawn:

a. Not only Neg.Decl. *I not say* but also the Neg.Imp. *Not say* continued to be used in prose moderately until around 1800. Their use throughout the eighteenth century seems to have escaped the attention of English historical linguists. Their use in Present-day English is an artificial one used for rhetorical colouring of a character's speech, or, alternatively, a subjunctive or mandative one.

b. These negative forms showed no special preference for tenses and moods, for (in)transitivity and semantic fields of verbs, and for clause-types, i.e. whether they were used in superordinate or subordinate clauses.

c. These negative forms were used widely by a variety of people, including the noble and the educated, throughout Britain and Ireland, and in various kinds of documents, formal or informal, academic or non-academic.

d. Since these negative forms were employed far less frequently than *I say not*, *I do not say*, *I don't say*, *Say not*, *Do not say* and *Don't say*, the continued use in Modern English should not be overestimated. Jespersen did not include the negation currently in question in that five-stage development theory, which is appropriate.

238   *Fujio Nakamura*

These conclusions suggest that statements of the studies referred to in Section 1.1 above deserve reconsideration as below:[2]

The statement of Lowth (1762: 79) seems to be overly generalised and even contrary to the English historical fact, because he writes that Neg.Decl. *I not say* seems to have "now grown altogether obsolete." In the statement of Poutsma (1928: 102), "the middle" should be altered into "the end." The statement of Partridge (1953: 9) seems to be appropriate, although his evidence is comprised of plays written in the form of verse. The comment of Söderlind (1973 [1951]: 218) is not necessarily pertinent to examples outside Dryden. The fact that examples of those constructions did not occur in the Modern English section of that abundant number of the texts examined by Ellegård (1953: 198) is mysterious. Contrary to the statement by Visser (1969: 1532), Neg.Decl. *I not say* was not in sporadic use before 1500. Nor is it restricted chiefly to poetry in Present-day English. The examples occurred in clusters in 1426 Lydgate, and the examples which were gathered from twentieth century documents are all non-verse examples. The statements by Tieken (1987: 118) seem to be appropriate in terms of the results of the present research.

The description in the *OED*[2] (s.v. not, *adv.* and *n.*[2] A. *adv.*, 1b) seems to be indiscriminate and inaccurate. Ukaji (1992: 455) will need a slight modification, because Neg.Decl. *I not say* was not "rare before 1500" and it was not "in the middle of the eighteenth century" but after 1800 that this negative form became almost obsolete. Rissanen's statement (1999: 271) is in agreement with the results of the present research. Nevertheless, it seems that amendment should be made to the following points: in "non-standard English" the form of *not* + Verb survived even later than "the eighteenth century," and it may well have been a usage "typical of spoken language." Analysing the use of Neg.Decl. *I not say* in diaries and correspondence, Nakamura (2003: 72) points out the following: (i) the authors tended to be men of the

---

[2] Regrettably, a question of whether Neg.Decl. *I not say* gave grace to speech, as declared in Puttenham (?1569/?c1585/?1589: 255), could not be attested by the present author, who lacks in native English linguistic intuition. Regarding Smith (1933: 79-80), what he points out is a fact. However, there was hesitation over including that type of example into the construction currently in question, simply because it seems not to function as sentential negation.

Negative declarative *I not say* and negative imperative *Not say*   239

cloth, (ii) the authors were (likely to have been) born and reared in the North, (iii) this type of negation tended to have a contrastive function, and (iv) it often occurred in short business-like sentences. Now that more and more historical documents have been analysed, however, these points have proved to be less relevant, as the conclusions in (3) indicate. This means that the results deduced from research based on 130 volumes of private diaries and personal letters were not sufficiently trustworthy. Iyeiri (2005: 67-69; 76-77) has presented an original and drastic idea regarding the origin of *I not say*. Even though it is desirable that she should provide additional relevant examples of *not* + (*ne*) + V in Old English and Early Middle English, hers is considered to be the most convincing view of the origin. Her discussion of the discontinuities of traits of *not* + V between Old and Middle English and Early Modern English, which she develops in Section 5, however, is not well-grounded in historical fact. Contrary to her expectations, in Early Modern English the form of *I not say* was used not only in superordinate but also subordinate clauses, and forms of *be* and *have* could occur in this negative form.

References

Ellegård, Alvar 1953. *The auxiliary do: The establishment and regulation of its use in English*. Stockholm: Almqvist & Wiksell.

Jespersen, Otto 1917. Negation in English and other languages. Copenhagen. Reproduced in *Selected writings of Otto Jespersen* (Tokyo: Senjo, 1962) 3-151.

Jespersen, Otto 1940. *A modern English grammar on historical principles*, part V. Copenhagen. Rpt. London: George Allen & Unwin, 1970.

Lowth, Robert 1762. A short introduction to English grammar. In Takanobu Otsuka (gen. ed.), *A reprint series of books relating to the English language*, vol. 13, 15-113. Tokyo: Nan'un-do, 1968.

Nakamura, Fujio 2003. Contribution of non-literary texts to history of English research. In Amano Masachiyo (ed.), *Creation and practical use of language texts* (21st Century COE Program, International Conference Series No. 2). Graduate School of Letters, Nagoya University, 67-77.

Nakamura, Fujio 2004. A history of the negative imperative *do* in seventeenth to nineteenth-century diaries and correspondence. Data sheets distributed at the 13th International Conference on English Historical Linguistics, University of Vienna, Austria, 23-28 August 2004.

Nakamura, Fujio 2008. Uncovering of rare or unknown usage: A history of participles/gerunds followed by *not*. Data sheets distributed at the 15th

International Conference on English Historical Linguistics, University of Munich, Germany, 24-30 August 2008.

Nakamura, Fujio 2014. Negative declarative *I not say* in Modern English. Data sheets distributed at the 47th Annual Meeting of the Societas Linguistica Europaea, Adam Mickiewich University, Poland, 11-14 September 2014.

OED[2] = Simpson, John A. (ed.) 2009. *Oxford English dictionary*, Second Edition, on CD-ROM Version 4.0. Oxford: Oxford University Press.

Partridge, Astley C. 1953. *Studies in the syntax of Ben Jonson's plays*. Cambridge: Bowes & Bowes.

Poutsma, Hendrik 1928. *A grammar of late modern English*, Part I, First Half. Groningen: P. Noordhoff.

Puttenham, George [?]1569/[?]c1585/[?]1589. *The arte of English poesie*. Ed. by Gladys D. Willcock and Alice Walker. 1936. Rpt. Cambridge: Cambridge University Press, 1970.

Rissanen, Matti 1999. Syntax. In Roger Lass (ed.), *The Cambridge history of the English language*, vol. III, 1476-1776. Cambridge: Cambridge University Press, 187-331.

Smith, Arvid 1933. Två Bidrag till Engelsk Ordföljd. *Moderna Språk* (Modern Language Teacher's Association of Sweden) 27, 79-82.

Söderlind, Johannes 1951. *Verb syntax in John Dryden's prose*, I. Uppsala. Rpt. Nendeln: Kraus Reprint, 1973.

Tieken-Boon van Ostade, Ingrid 1987. *The auxiliary do in eighteenth-century English: A sociohistorical-linguistic approach*. Dordrecht / Providence: Foris.

Ukaji, Masatomo 1992. "I not say": Bridge phenomenon in syntactic change. In Matti Rissanen, Ossi Ihalainen, Terttu Nevalainen & Irma Taavitsainen (eds.), *History of Englishes: New methods and interpretations in historical linguistics*. Berlin & New York: Mouton de Gruyter, 453-62.

Visser, Fredericus Th. 1969. *An historical syntax of the English language*. Part III, First Half. Leiden: E. J. Brill.

The semantics of Chaucer's speech/thought presentation in *Troilus and Criseyde*: The emergence of conceptual blending*

Yoshiyuki Nakao

Abstract

This paper is an attempt to describe how and why conceptual blending is likely to emerge in Chaucer's speech/thought presentation with reference to *Troilus and Criseyde*. Few studies have been conducted about his speech/thought presentation, and much less about the semantics of it. We have some seminal studies of his speech/thought presentation: Gordon (1960: 104), Pearsall (1984: 23), Fludernik (1993: 93-94, 194-95), (1996: 117-20), Fleischman (1990: 7-10, 79-81, 229) and Moore (2015: 162-79). These studies still remain much to be reconsidered theoretically and semantically. Little or no attention has been paid to the emergence of conceptual blending among the semantics of Chaucer's presentation forms. Here, I have set up a theoretical perspective to distinguish subjectivities involved in Chaucer's narrative performance and made clear types of speech and thought presentation. Based on this method, I have described how and why conceptual blending is likely to emerge in Chaucer's speech/thought presentation.

1. Introduction

Criseyde sees Troilus coming back to Troy in triumph from the window of her house. The narrator represents how she responds to it indirectly, not in a direct speech, as in (1).

(1)   So lik a man of armes and a knyght
        He was *to seen*, fulfilled of heigh prowesse,
        For bothe he hadde *a body* and a might
        To don *that thing*, as wel as hardynesse;
        And ek *to seen* hym in his gere hym dresse,
        So fressh, so yong, so weldy semed he,[1]
        It was an heven upon hym for to see.   (Tr 2.631-37)

---

* This paper is partially based on "Chaucer no waho no imiron: *Toroirasu to Kuriseide* niokeru waho no tajigen kozo" (The Semantics of Chaucer's Speech Presentation: The Multidimensional Structure of Chaucer's Speech Presentation in *Troilus and Criseyde), Studies in Higher Education* (No.4) (Bulletin of University Education Center, Fukuyama University), 2018, pp. 17-36.

[1] Words in italics are mine. Chaucer's texts and the abbreviations of his works are based on Benson (1987).

Is this a neutral narrative devoid of an individual, say, Criseyde's perspective? Or is it filtered through Criseyde? If the latter is the case, is it speech or (covered) thought? This narrative representation may be on the borderline between these presentations by which "conceptual blending"[2] is encouraged to emerge. By this borderline case I am motivated to investigate the mechanism of Chaucer's speech/thought presentation. This paper does not deal with the whole of it, but is narrowed down to describe how and why conceptual blending is likely to be instanced in it.

Troilus and Criseyde is a romance describing the development and collapse of the love between the two lovers with the Trojan War as backdrop. The scenes there are noticeably and substantially limited to the bedchambers within the characters' houses. The story is devoted not to battle scenes as seen in the *Romance of Guy of Warwick* but to psychological experiences with which Troilus and Criseyde are involved. How the characters and even the narrator in a story experience, evaluate and describe the events through their speech and thought plays a significant role.

The events are filtered through characters who observe and describe them. The narrative parts are not necessarily objective, but influenced by a character's unique perspective. Furthermore, we also have even a "virtual" narrator in the story, not present in the text but working with shifting and integrated perspectives. In *Troilus and Criseyde* the characters' and the narrator's subjectivities are not only distinguished but also combined with each other in complex ways. Chaucer's speech/thought presentation is not limited to a single subjectivity but open to a dynamic interaction of subjectivities bringing about complex relationships, the outcome of which is conceptual blending. Therefore, there remains much research to be done on the semantics of Chaucer's

---

[2] Fauconnier and Turner (2002: 27): "While dogs, cats, horses, and other familiar species presumably must do perceptual binding of the sort needed to see a single dog, cat, or horse, human beings are exceptionally adept at integrating two extraordinarily different inputs to create emergent structures, which result in new tools, new technologies, and new ways of thinking." This conceptual blending can be applied to the emergence of speech/thought presentation open to alternative subjectivities/perspectives. Free Indirect Speech is, for instance, susceptible of the narrator's as well as a character's view of an event they experience.

speech/thought presentation. Here I will set up a theoretical perspective to distinguish subjectivities involved in Chaucer's narrative performance and make clear types of speech and thought presentation. Based on this method, I will describe how and why conceptual blending is likely to emerge in Chaucer's speech/thought presentation.

2. Previous scholarship

Few studies have been conducted about Chaucer's speech/thought presentation, and much less about the semantics of it. Gordon (1960) and Pearsall (1984) are seminal in highlighting that some psychological narrative parts are filtered through Criseyde's perspective. In her historical analysis of speech/thought presentation Fludernik (1993) deals with medieval English texts including Chaucer. She is insightful enough to point out that Chaucer used FIS (Free Indirect Speech) as early as in the late fourteenth century. According to Fludernik (1996), *Troilus and Criseyde*'s primary concern is with psychological experiences of the characters, not war. So how to distinguish between speech/thought presentation should be more of the focus. Fleischman (1990) clarifies the relationship between medieval orality and tense with particular regard to speech/thought presentation. But her exemplifications are limited to medieval French texts. Moore (2015) discusses how to identify speech elements in medieval English texts including Chaucer, the Gawain-poet, and Langland. She also investigates how reporting verbs are varied by their reported contents, and how to make interpretations based on unpunctuated manuscripts although with little classification of speech/thought presentation. These studies still remain to have much to offer theoretically and semantically.

3. Method

I will consider Chaucer's speech/thought presentation from two standpoints: one refers to the conceptual structure underlying his speech/thought presentation, a hierarchical structure of subjectivities in his narrative performance, and the other refers to linguistic structures of how they are realized, i.e. types of his speech/thought presentation such as indirect speech, direct speech, etc.

3.1. A hierarchical structure of subjectivities in his narrative performance

From a communicative point of view, Chaucer's performance of narrative stories is not one-dimensional but multidimensional with the roles of alternative subjectivities on the stages. In his performance the roles of these subjectivities are first divided between reality space (stage) and fictional space (stage). The subjectivity of reality space is structured by Chaucer the writer and also by his audience/reader. Fictional space is divided into three subdivided stages. At the top stage I set up a virtual meta-linguistic subjectivity called view-shifting "I" and the reader who is expected to access him. The view-shifting "I" has a bird's eye view of fictional space, and can fluctuate between and integrate the varying subjectivities of the narrator and characters. The middle stage is the narrator and the narratee. This narrator is not only neutral in perspective with little distance from the view-shifting "I," but also filtered through his own evaluation of an event or those subjectivities ascribed to the characters. The bottom stage is between characters. A character's subjectivity is the most limited. Through the dialogue between the addresser (subjectivity) and the addressee (subjectivity) are performed alternative story lines. Where different story lines are performed overlapping, conceptual blending is likely to emerge.

Figure 1 shows a hierarchical structure of subjectivities and the story lines they produce. This is based on Leech and Short (1981: 216) but slightly revised for this research. The story lines in Figure 1 are apparently fixed by choosing one of the subjectivities from the bottom stage to the top, but in actual fact they are likely to be blended involving complex subjectivities like the narrator and a character.

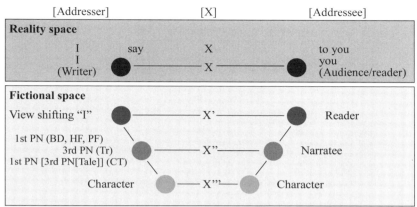

Notes: 1. The series of X indicate the story lines to be inferred between addresser and addressee. The story lines are not made exactly in the same way between addresser and addressee. So, I use not "communicated," but "inferred."
2. The story lines X, X', X", X'" show that there can be discrepancies between them.
3. Cf. For the discourse levels of the *Canterbury Tales*, see Pakkala-Weckström (2010: 230): Level 1=Author: Chaucer, Level 2=Narrator: Chaucer the Pilgrim, Level 3=The pilgrims, Level 4=The characters in the pilgrims' tales.

Figure 1. A multidimensional structure of alternative subjectivities and the story lines they produce

3.2. Types of speech/thought presentation

The above conceptual blending will be made clear and described according to a gradient structure of speech/thought representation. For this structure I will apply Fleischman (1990: 229) [after Short 1982: 184] in Figure 2. Fludernik (1993: 311) added two others regarding the narrator's control: PN=Pure narrative (action, background description plus evaluative commentary by the narrator) and NP=Narrated perception (description replaced by evocation of character's perception). The underlying structure of Chaucer's narrative performances (Figure 1) and types of the representation of speech/thought (Figure 2 + PN and NP) are complementary to each other, and constitute the framework for describing the emergence of conceptual blending in Chaucer's speech/thought presentation.

	Character apparently in control ◄──────────►			Narrator apparently in control		
Speech presentation:	FDS	DS	FIS	IS	NRSA	NRA
Thought presentation:	FDT	DT	FIT	IT	NRTA	NRA

Examples:

> DS/T (direct S/T): She said/thought, "I really like it here in Berkeley."
> IS/T (indirect S/T): she said/thought that she really liked it there in Berkeley.
> FDS/T (free direct S/T): I really like it here in Berkeley.
> FIS/T (free indirect S/T): She really liked it here in Berkeley.
> NRS/TA (narrator's report of an S/T act): She expressed/pondered her pleasure at being in Berkeley.
> NRA (narrator's report of an act): She liked Berkeley a lot.

Figure 2. The representation of speech and thought (After Short 1982: 184)

4. Data and discussion

Troilus and Criseyde has more parts of speech/thought presentation directly through characters than those indirectly through the narrative [Appendix A]. The latter, however, is not necessarily neutral, but is likely to be filtered through the characters. I will focus on three significant events in *Troilus and Criseyde* which the three principal characters are involved to experience: first the narrator's description of Criseyde's response to Troilus's coming back to Troy in triumph in Book II, second a conversation between Troilus and Pandarus upon Criseyde's coming back to Troy in Book V, and third the narrator's description of what dream Troilus dreams and how sceptic of Criseyde's betrayal in Book V.

4.1. The narrator and Criseyde

When she is likely to experience an event hurting her honour, Chaucer tends to let the narrator describe it with some opacity. However, when she is likely to behave in character for her status as a lady of the court, Chaucer tends to let her describe it directly more realistically than she actually does. In (2) when she is told by Pandarus that Troilus loves her, Criseyde is embarrassed and is hesitant as to whether to accept it or not. Whether she immediately shows love to him or not will affect her honour. She sees Troilus coming back to Troy in triumph from the window of her house. The narrator describes how she responds to it indirectly.

The semantics of Chaucer's speech/thought presentation   247

(2)   So lik a man of armes and a knyght
        He was *to seen*, fulfilled of heigh prowesse,
        For bothe he hadde *a body* and a might
        To don *that thing*, as wel as hardynesse;
        And ek *to seen* hym in his gere hym dresse,
        So fressh, so yong, so weldy semed he,
        It was an heven upon hym for to see.   (Tr 2.631-37)

Is this a neutral and objective narrative, the so-called PN, or speech or thought filtered through Criseyde, that is, FIS/T? According to which subjectivity we emphasize, we can bring about different story lines. Speech-like whispering and covered thought are too similar to be distinguishable. The view-shifting "I" is not limited to either way, but can fluctuate between the two different subjectivities: the narrator's neutrality [PN] and the Criseyde's own subjectivity [FIS/T].

Table 1. Criseyde's response to Troilus's coming back to Troy in triumph: PN or FIS/T

	PN	FIS/T
to seen	for people	for Criseyde
body	body trained as a knight	body sexually attractive
might	military power	sexual power
that	referential: knightly	deictic: sexual
thing	fight	sexual action
fresh	young and fresh (knight)	sexually strong (man)
weldy	vigorous (knight)	powerful enough to control a woman
semed	to people	to Criseyde
an heven	a great joy[3]	a sexual ecstasy

In terms of FIS/T the construction "so ... that" is reflective of how Criseyde accumulates as much evidence as possible in order to justify her action which might hurt her honour. We have an equivalent example in Tr 3.918-24.

The *OED* quotes this *weldy* as the earliest instance with the meaning of "capable of easily 'wielding' one's body or limbs" but with no sexual implication. With this implication Hanna III (1971) merits special

---

[3] The *MED* (s.v. heven) quotes this example in 1b. Fig. (b) a supremely blissful experience.

attention although dealing with an alliterative poem.[4]

    (3)   Hanna III (1971: 44): "welden a woman"
          In alliterative poetry the phrase *welden a woman* has a very specific
          sense not recognized by O.E.D., 'to have sexual knowledge of a
          woman.'
              Ho was þe worþiest wight þat eny welde wolde;
              Here gide was glorious and gay, of a gressegrene.
                  (*The Awntyrs off Arthure at the Terne Wathelyn*, 365-66)
          Note: Ho=a lady lufsom of lote ledand a kniȝt (My addition)
                 (*The Awntyrs off Arthure at the Terne Wathelyn*, 345)

If the adjective *weldy* implies this, Criseyde's perspective is likely to underlie it as part of FIS/FIT.

This rare word *weldy*, is filtered through scribes. According to Windeatt (1984), they replace it with a more general word *worthy*.

    (4)   Tr 2.636   weldy]worþi   GgH3H5JRCxW

The other manuscripts including the authentic Cp use *weldy*. This scribal conversion is likely to alter FIS/T to a neutralized presentation PN. Root's (1952) edition only adopts *worthy*. He does not seem to consider this lexical choice in terms of speech/thought presentation.

4.2. Troilus and Pandarus

Troilus is most frequently seen in using DT of all the participants (DT is mostly judged by the following pattern '[subject] + thought " … "' according to Benson (1987)).[5] His speeches are varied by apostrophe, songs, philosophical debates. He is likely to escape from the real world through imagination, enough to reach a philosophical plane.[6] His orientation of thought is extended from DT to IT to FIT. On the other hand, Pandarus working as a bridge between Troilus and Criseyde speaks mostly in DS and is the least likely to use DT/IT/FIT.[7]

Troilus and Criseyde achieve a climax of love in Book III. However, this does not continue long. In Book IV it is determined by the Trojan

---

[4] For the detailed discussion, see Nakao (2012: 52-53, 104-05, 225-27).

[5] Appendices B, C, and D.

[6] Troilus is likely to be devoted to inner debates coming on some occasions close to Boethian arguments of such as love (Tr 3.1744-71) and predestination and free will (Tr 4.958-1078).

[7] Appendices B and D.

The semantics of Chaucer's speech/thought presentation   249

Parliament that Criseyde is sent to the Greek camp for a prisoner exchange. She decides to go to the Greek camp promising Troilus to come back to Troy within ten days. In Book V she is sent to the Greek camp. He is hoping against all probability for her coming back to Troy. On the tenth and last day, Troilus and Pandarus wait for her return to Troy on the siege to divide Troy and the Greek camp. They see something coming towards them. They see exactly the same thing. But what does it look like to Troilus? And how about to Pandarus?

> (5) And at the laste he torned hym and seyde, ...   (Tr 5.1146)
>
> "We han naught elles for to don, ywis.
> And Pandarus, now woltow trowen me?
> Have here my trouthe, *I se hire! Yond she is!*
> Heve up thyn eyen, man! Maistow nat se?"
> Pandare answerde, "Nay, so mote I the!
> Al wrong, by God! What saistow, man? Where arte?
> *That I se yond nys but a fare-carte.*"   (Tr 5.1156-62)

This is exactly DS. Troilus sees "hire/she=Criseyde." But Pandarus instantly modifies it to "fare-cate." Troilus applies to it a courtly ideal concept (non-betrayal Criseyde). Here, concept leads to perception, not the other way. Pandarus is critically detached enough to call a spade a spade. Both of them are sensitive to one thing, and not the other, of the potentials of this event. These two distinct story lines may induce the view-shifting "I" to integrate them with a new story line "merchandise," to borrow a cognitive linguistic term with a "merchandise" as a schema. The "fare-carte" leads metonymically to "merchandise," and "Criseyde" leads metaphorically to "merchandise" because she is in fact the object of "the bartering process between Greeks and Trojans," which Brown (2007: 309) insightfully points out. This "merchandise" is extended to Chaucer the writer in the reality space: he was involved in the Hundred Years' War where prisoners might have been bartered between England and France, and worked as a controller at Aldgate from 1974 to 1986 where commodities were bartered between England and the Continent.[8]

The above four different story lines based on the four different subjectivities are restructured according to Figure 1 as shown in Figure 3.

---

[8] For the detailed discussion of this, see Nakao (2015: 361).

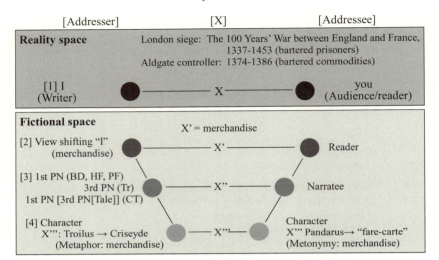

Figure 3. Conceptual blending: merchandise

4.3. The narrator and Troilus

Criseyde does not come back to Troy as she has promised Troilus. Sceptical of her fulfilling her promise, he dreams that a boar and Criseyde embrace and kiss. In (6) we find varieties of speech/thought presentations are juxtaposed without any definite boundaries. This includes a hierarchical extension from PN to IT to NRA to FIT like Chinese boxes.

(6) So on a day he leyde hym doun to slepe,
And [PN][9] *so byfel that* yn his slep [IT] *hym thoughte*
That in a forest faste he welk to wepe
For love of here that hym these peynes wroughte;
And up and doun as he the forest soughte,
[NRTA within IT] *He mette* he saugh a bor with tuskes grete,
That slepte ayeyn the bryghte sonnes hete.

And [NRTA or FIT/NP] *by this bor, faste in his armes folde,*
Lay, kyssyng ay, his lady bryght, Criseyde.
[PN] For sorwe of which, whan he it gan byholde,
And for despit, out of his slep he breyde,
And loude he cride on Pandarus, and seyde:
[DS] "O Pandarus, now know I crop and roote.
I n'am but ded; ther nys noon other bote.   (Tr 5.1233-46)

---

[9] Types of speech/thought presentation are shown in square brackets.

The example is initiated by PN [byfel], suggesting the occurrence of a significant event. This is soon followed by Troilus's IT [hym thought] where the experience he thought is indirectly described. Followed by IT is NRTA [he mette] with the visualized description of a boar in his dream. The next stanza continues this present stanza by beginning with "And." Does this show a simple continuation of the clause content of "he mette"? Or is the thought presentation shifted to FIT with more interactive or deictic characteristics or perhaps more perceptively or visually to NP with no clear linguistic analysis? Immediately after comes PN describing Troilus's sorrow and his waking up from his dream. This PN is immediately slipped into Troilus's DS upon Pandarus where Troilus's consulting of his dream with Pandarus is highlighted. The boundaries between one speech/ thought presentation and another is so low that they may easily alternate and blend into one another. We have a hierarchy of thought presentation in Figure 4.

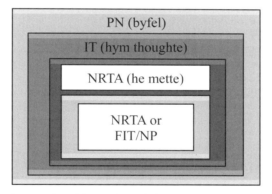

Figure 4. A hierarchy of thought presentation

Let us concentrate on FIT/NP.

(7) And by this bor, faste in his armes folde,
     Lay, kyssyng ay, his lady bryght, Criseyde.   (Tr 5.1240-41)

This narrative passage is open to a continuation of NRTA or FIT/NP, different subjectivities according to degrees of "narrator apparently in control." The difference between FIT and NP is degrees of verbalization: the former tends to be verbalized while the latter tends to be less verbalized. According to which subjectivity to emphasize, speech/

252   *Yoshiyuki Nakao*

thought presentation types are easily variable, bringing about different story lines. Table 2 is a summary of this.

Table 2. Troilus's dream (boar and Criseyde embracing and kissing each other)

Tr 5.1240-41	NRTA	FIT/NP
this bor	referential=the boar in the preceding stanza "*He mette* he saugh a bor with tuskes grete," (Tr 5.1238)	deictic=the boar present in the immediate situation (I-mode=interactional mode of cognition)[10]
word order	inversion due to metrical adjustment/information focus	Troilus's mental scanning
folde	verbalisation of "embracing" (trying to make clear who is the agent/patient of "embracing")	pre-verbalised (analogue) state of "embracing"
ellipsis: kyssyng	descriptive=municipal kissing	deictic=indistinguishable state of confusion
aspect: kyssyng	descriptive=progressive action	deictic=synchronizing the kissing action
Content of *his* in "his lady bright, Criseyde"	referential: the boar (*this bor*)	deictic: Troilus Cf. 5.1247: Troilus's DS, "My lady bright, Criseyde"

In Boccaccio's *Il Filostrato*, the narrator says a boar is eager to please Cressida, and that she feels comfortable with it.

(8)   E poi appresso gli parve vedere
           Sotto a' suoi piè Criseida, alla quale
           Col grifo il cor traeva, ed al parere
           Di lui, Criseida di cosí gran male
           Non si curava, ma quasi piacere
           Prendea di ciò che facea l' animale,
           Il che a lui sì forte era in dispetto,
           Che questo ruppe il sonno deboletto.   (Fil 7.24.1-8)
           (And then afterward it seemed to him that he saw beneath its feet Cressida, whose heart it tore forth with its snout. And as it seemed, little cared Cressida for so great a hurt, but almost did she take

---

[10] See Nakamura (2004: 33-48) for I-mode (Interactional mode of cognition) and D-mode (Displaced mode of cognition). The I-mode shows the speaker's experiencing of an event with such a vivid sensory perception that it is actually present in the immediate situation 'I-here-now.'

The semantics of Chaucer's speech/thought presentation   253

> pleasure in what the beast was doing. This gave him such a fit of
> rage that it broke off his uneasy slumber.)[11]

Boccaccio is more in the narrator's control, being conceptually verbalized [NRTA] than Chaucer, who is less in the narrator's control, suggesting Troilus's confusion in a less conceptualized or verbalized
mode [FIT/NP] (cf. I-mode). It is noticeable that the switch of speech/
thought presentation seems to have occurred between Chaucer and his
original *Filostrato*.

In the case of NP, Troilus is engaged in pre-conceptual or perceptual
(visual) stage of cognition, as is mentioned in Table 2. His cognition
is limited to analogue,[12] not linguistically digitalized.[13] Instead, in the
case of NRTA, the narrator tries to verbalise it for the sake of the audience. The characteristics of NP are significantly filtered through the
scribes and editors. They are encouraged to verbalize the deictic or
analogue characteristics. The scribes try to make clear who is the
agent/patient of embracing while editors are further trying to make
clear the agent/patient of kissing by their added punctuations of the
ambiguous action, in contradistinction of which Chickering's (1990)
unpunctuating Chaucer is worth special attention.

> (9) Tr 5.1240
>   Manuscripts variation:
>   **his**: AClH4; hir: DGg (hyre) H1R (hyr) S1S2Th (her); **omission**
>   H2H3PhCx (CpDgH5 lack this line)
>   Editions variation:
>   **his**: Robinson, Barney (Benson), Skeat, Baugh, Warrington,
>   Howard (note. The image is of Criseyde held by and kissing the
>   boar); **hir/her**: Root, Donaldson, Fisher, Pollard

Regarding editions, we find the difference of punctuations before and
after "kissing."

> (10) Tr 5.1241 punctuation of editions:
>   a. Windeatt (his); Donaldson/Fisher (her)
>   Lay kissing ay his lady bright, Criseyde

---

[11] The text of *Il Filostrato* is based on Griffin and Myrick (1978). Fil is the
abbreviation of this work.

[12] The term "analogue" is used to mean that an event is perceived along a
continuum or as a holistic image.

[13] The terms "digitalized" is used to mean that an event is restricted to discrete
choices rendering it describable with words.

    b. Baugh (his)
       Lay, kissing ay his lady bright, Criseyde
    c. Robinson/Barney (his); Root/Pollard (her)
       Lay, kissing ay, his lady bright, Criseyde

In the case of 10a, with no pause after *Lay*, and with stress on kissing and Criseyde, we are encouraged to interpret Criseyde as the agent of kissing, who is end-focused due to the S-V inversion. In the case of 10b, with pause after *Lay*, reading *kissing ay his lady bright* at a breath, we are encouraged to have an illusion that the agent of kissing is a boar and Criseyde is a patient. In the case of 10c, with a comma before and after kissing, we are encouraged to interpret that a boar and Criseyde are cooperatively engaged in the kissing with no differentiation between agent and patient. Every variant is Chaucer's, and every variant is not Chaucer's. The truth is in between, which may be ascribed to the view-shifting "I." For details of metalinguistic ambiguity, see Nakao (2012: 363-61).

    The scribal variations of (7) are shown for instance in Figures 5, 6, and 7.

Figure 5. Troilus's dream of a boar and Criseyde's embracing and kissing Cl (Campsall (Pierpoint Morgan Library)), 111r: 'in his armes folde' Benson 1987: 1176. Book V 1233-74 Cp omits six stanzas; text from Cl (in 1272, Cl alone reads *compleyne*, rest *to pleyne*).

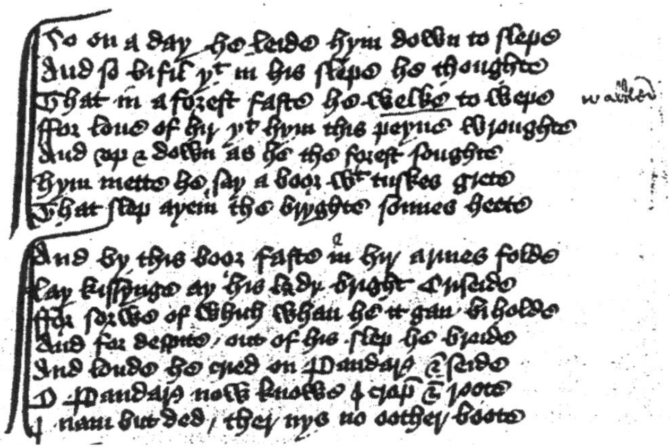

The semantics of Chaucer's speech/thought presentation   255

Figure 6. A boar and Criseyde's embracing and kissing
St. John's College MS, 110v: 'in hir armes folde'

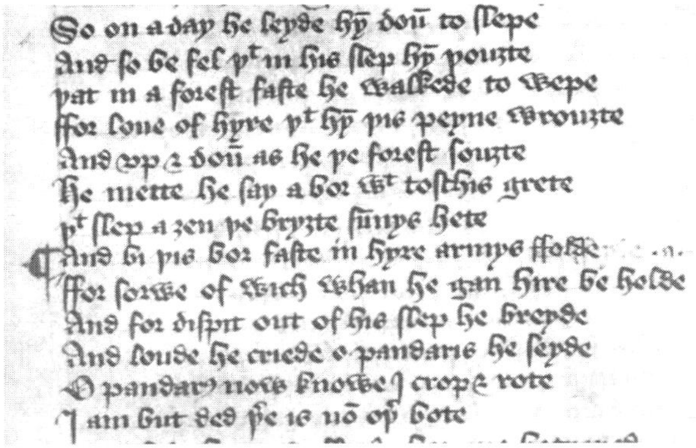

Figure 7. A boar and Criseyde's embracing (their kissing part is ignored)
Cambridge University Library MS GG.4.27, 120v: 'in hyre armys ffolde'

5. Conclusion

I have set up a hierarchical structure of distinguishing subjectivities involved in Chaucer's narrative performance (Figure 1) and made clear types of speech and thought presentation (Figure 2) according to Fleischman (1990) slightly supplemented by Fludernik (1993). Through this framework, I have described how and why conceptual blending is likely to emerge in Chaucer's speech/thought presentation.

I have analysed three examples: conceptual blending of the narrator and Criseyde (PN or FIS/T) (5.1), of Troilus and Pandarus + the view-shifting "I" in fictional space and Chaucer the writer in reality space (two DSs + "merchandise" as a schema) (5.2), and of the narrator and Troilus with a series of speech/thought presentations like Chinese boxes (PN→IT→NRTA→FIT/NP) (5.3). I have noticed, interestingly enough, that NP is filtered through scribes and editors with textual variations with different interpretations. I have activated the view-shifting "I" although textually absent, which I regard as a meta-subjectivity to access conceptual blending. I have many more examples to test my method in *Troilus and Criseyde* while refining its method itself.

References

Baugh, Albert Croll (ed.) 1963. *Chaucer's major poetry.* Englewood, New Jersey: Prentice-Hall.

Beadle, Richard & Jeremey Griffisths (Intro.) 1983. *St. John's College, Cambridge, manuscript L1: A facsimile.* Norman, Oklahoma: Pilgrim Books.

Benson, Larry D. (ed.) 1987. *The Riverside Chaucer: Third edition based on The works of Geoffrey Chaucer edited by F. N. Robinson.* Boston: Houghton Mifflin Company.

Brown, Peter 2007. *Chaucer and the making of optical space.* Bern: Peter Lang.

Chickering, Howell 1990. Unpunctuating Chaucer. *The Chaucer Review* 25 (2): 97-109.

Donaldson, E. Talbot (ed.) 1975. *Chaucer's poetry: An anthology for the modern reader.* New York: The Ronald Press Company.

Fauconnier, Gilles & Mark Turner 2002. *The way we think: Conceptual blending and the mind's hidden complexities.* New York: Basic Books.

Fisher, Jjohn. H. (ed.) 1989. *Complete poetry and prose of Geoffrey Chaucer.* 2nd. edn. New York: Holt, Rinehart and Winston.

Fleischman, Suzanne 1990. *Tense and narrativity: From medieval performance to modern fiction.* Austin: University of Texas Press.

Fludernik, Monika 1993. *The fictions of language and the languages of fiction: The linguistic representation of speech and consciousness.* London and New York: Routledge.

Fludernik, Monika 1996. *Towards a 'natural' narratology.* London and New York: Routledge.

Gordon, Ida L. 1970. *The double sorrow of Troilus: A study of ambiguities in Troilus and Criseyde.* Oxford: Clarendon Press.

Griffin, N.E. & A.B. Myrick (eds. & trs.) 1978. *The Filostrato of Giovanni Boccaccio.* New York: Octagon Books.

Hanna, Ralph III (ed.) 1971. *Auntyrs off Arthure at the Terne Wathelyn.* Manchester: Manchester University Press.

Howard, Donald R. (ed.) 1976. *Geoffrey Chaucer Troilus and Criseyde and selected short poems.* New York: New American Library.

Krochalis, Jeanne (Intr.) 1986. *M.817 (olim Campsall), Pierpont Morgan Library.* Norman, Oklahoma: Pilgrim Books.

Kurath, Hans, Sherman M. Kuhn & Robert E. Lewis (eds.) 1952-2001. *Middle English Dictionary.* Ann Arbor: The University of Michigan Press.

Leech, Geoffrey & Michael Short 1981. *Style in fiction*: *A linguistic introduction to English fictional prose.* London: Longman.

Moore, Colette. 2015. *Quoting speech in early English.* Cambridge: Cambridge University Press.

Nakamura, Yoshihisa (ed.) 2004. *Ninchibunporon II* (Cognitive grammar II). Tokyo: Taishukan.

Nakao, Yoshiyuki 2012. *The structure of Chaucer's ambiguity.* Frankfurt am Main: Peter Lang.

Nakao, Yoshiyuki 2015. Chaucer no *Troirasu to Kuriseide* ni okeru "assege": <houi> (uchi, kyokai, soto) no ninchi purosesu wo saguru ["Assege" in Chaucer's *Troilus and Criseyde*: An exploration into the cognitive process of "enclosure" (inside, boundary, outside)]. In Yuichiro Higashi & Koichi Kano (eds.), *Chaucer and English and American literature: A festschrift for Professor Masatoshi Kawasaki,* 379-58. Tokyo: Kinseido.

Nakao, Yoshiyuki 2018. Chaucer no waho no imiron: *Toroirasu to Kuriseide* niokeru waho no tajigen kozo (The Semantics of Chaucer's Speech Presentation: The Multidimensional Structure of Chaucer's Speech Presentation in *Troilus and Criseyde*), Studies in Higher Education (No.4) (Bulletin of University Education Center, Fukuyama University), 17-36.

Pakkala-Weckström, Mari 2010. Chaucer. In Andreas H. Jucker & Irma Taavitsainen (eds.), *Historical pragmatics*, 219-45. Berlin/New York: De Gruyter Mouton.

Parkes, Malcolm B. & E. Salter (Intr.) 1978. *Troilus and Criseyde Geoffrey Chaucer*: *A facsimile of Corpus Christi College Cambridge MS 61.* Cambridge: D.S. Brewer.

Parkes, Malcolm B. & Richard Beadle (Intr.) 1979. *Poetical works, Geoffrey Chaucer: A facsimile of Cambridge University Library MS GG.4.27. Volume 1.* Cambridge: D.S. Brewer.

Pearsall, Derek 1986. Criseyde's Choices. *Studies in the age of Chaucer: Proceedings* 2: 17-29.

Pollard Alfred W. *et al.* (eds.) 1898. *The works of Geoffrey Chaucer.* (The Globe Edition) London: Macmillan.

Robinson, Fred Norris (ed.) 1957. *The works of Geoffrey Chaucer.* London: Oxford University Press.

Root, R.K. (ed.) 1952. *The Book of Troilus and Criseyde by Geoffrey Chaucer.* Princeton: Princeton University Press.

Short, Michael 1982. Stylistics and the teaching of literature with an example from James Joyce's *Portrait of the Artist as a Young Man*. In Ronald

Carter (ed.), *Language and literature*, 179-82. London: George Allen and Unwin.

Simpson, J.A. & E.S.C. Weiner (eds.). 1989. *The Oxford English Dictionary*. 2nd edition. Oxford: Clarendon Press, 1989.

Skeat, Walter W. (ed.) 1898. *The complete works of Geoffrey Chaucer: Boethius and Troilus.* Oxford: Oxford University Press.

Warrington, John (ed.) 1975. *Geoffrey Chaucer Troilus and Criseyde.* London: J.M. Dent & Sons.

Windeatt, Barry A. (ed.) 1990. *Geoffrey Chaucer Troilus & Criseyde: A new edition of 'The Book of Troilus.'* London: Longman.

Zupitza, Julius (ed.) 1883, 1887, 1891. *The romance of Guy of Warwick: Auchinleck and Caius MSS.* EETS (E.S.) 42 (1883), 49 (1887), 50 (1891).

Appendix A. The frequency of words according to main characters and narrator

	Troilus	Criseyde	Pandarus	Total-character	Narrator
Type	3,718	2,983	4,525	11,226	7,119
Token	11,394	9,032	14,342	34,768	27,820

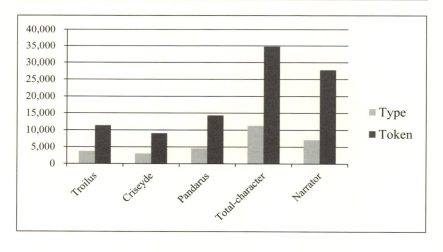

The semantics of Chaucer's speech/thought presentation   259

Appendix B. The words frequency of DT (Direct thought) of main characters according to Books I through V

	T-B1	T-B2	T-B3	T-B4	T-B5
Type	314	25	425	627	613
Token	607	26	840	1,729	1,584
	C-B1	C-B2	C-B3	C-B4	C-B5
Type	0	467	182	216	426
Token	0	1,080	297	377	1,018
	P-B1	P-B2	P-B3	P-B4	P-B5
Type	0	49	0	0	38
Token	0	54	0	0	43

Note: T=Troilus, C=Criseyde, P=Pandarus, B=Book

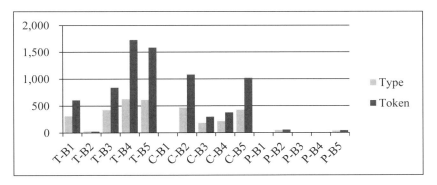

Appendix C. Thought presentation with regard to the verb *thought/thoughte*

	DT	IT (imp)	IT (per)	NRTA
Troilus	5	13	7	3
Criseyde	6	2	4	7
Pandarus	4	2	0	0
Diomede	3	0	1	0

Note: imp=impersonal construction, per=personal construction

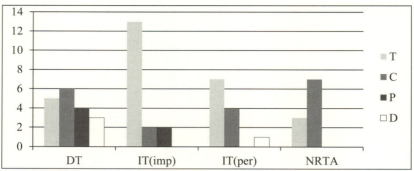

Note: D=Diomede

Appendix D. Speech/thought presentation with regard to the verb *seyde*

	DS	DT	IS	IT	NRSA
Troilus	42	20	13	0	0
Criseyde	27	7	6	0	0
Pandarus	49	4	1	0	0
Diomede	5	2	1	0	1

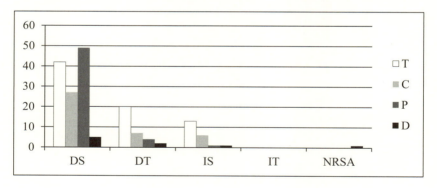

On the use of *lief* in Chaucer*

Hideshi Ohno

Abstract

In Chaucer's time, the word *lief* was sometimes used predicatively with *be* or *have*, the constructions meaning "(someone) had/would rather." Furthermore, the *be* + *lief* and the *have* + *lief* constructions tend to appear in the impersonal and the personal constructions respectively. While several studies have given diachronic descriptions of the *lief* constructions, it appears that a thorough synchronic analysis has not been conducted. This article will, from syntactic and semantic viewpoints, conduct a synchronic analysis on Chaucer's use of the constructions through comparison with data from his contemporaries and from the *Middle English Dictionary*. Specifically, it will treat the questions: "What can the variation between the *be* + *lief* and the *have* + *lief* constructions show?" and "How differently are the *lief* constructions used from its synonymous verbs such as *like* and *list*?" Thus, this article will try to clarify what kind of readings the constructions can allow.

1. Introduction

This article aims to describe the use of the word *lief* in Chaucer's works through some comparison with its synonymous verbs in his works and with *lief* in his contemporaries. According to the *Oxford English Dictionary* (*OED*) (s.v. *lief*, adj. 1.), the word *lief* was originally an adjective, meaning "Beloved, dear, agreeable, acceptable, precious," sometimes used predicatively in comparative phrases such as *liefer was, were, to me, him*, etc. with an infinitival or clausal complement, which means "I/he had rather."

In these phrases, the persons who the pronouns *me* and *him* refer to are psychologically affected by the state expressed by the adjective *lief*, and therefore are called "experiencers.[1]" The experiencers being in the

---

* This article is the revised version of my paper read at Hiroshima Seminar on English Historical Syntax, which was held at Hiroshima University on 3 December 2016. I would like to thank Professor David Denison and the other attendants at the seminar for their valuable comments.

[1] This term is used widely for the impersonal construction as in Crystal (2008: 179). Denison and Cort, who survey *better*, call the persons "beneficiary" (2010: 364).

262   *Hideshi Ohno*

dative case, the phrases are in the impersonal use.[2] On the other hand, with a nominative experiencer or a subject, in other words, in the personal use, the word *lief* means "Desirous, wishful, willing, glad" (*OED*, s.v. *lief*, adj. †2.).

1.1. Previous Studies

Visser states that by the time the *me were liefer* construction "had become obsolescent there occurred six rival constructions: (a) *I were lever*; (b) *I had lever*; (c) *Me had lever*; (d) *I would lever*; (e) *I will rather*; (f) *I would rather*" (1963-73: § 40). Among them, however, Type (d) has its first example in the fifteenth century in his data, and Types (e) and (f) have not *lief* but *rather*. He quotes an example of Type (f) from Chaucer's *Troilus and Criseyde* (*Tr*),[3] but along with Type (e), the *rather* types are smaller in number: only four examples[4] of Type (f) in Chaucer. Therefore, it will be difficult to compare the *lief* and *rather* types in this article.

To classify the examples of *lief* according to a syntactic structure, it is convenient to name the *me were liefer* construction Type (0), which is the oldest, dating from Old English. Thus, this research deals with Types (0), (a), (b), and (c). According to Nakao (1972: 303-04) and Denison and Cort[5] (2010: 354), the mixture or blending of Types (0) and (b) created Types (a) and (c), which became obsolete by the end of the fifteenth century, as shown below:

(0) *me were leofre* (OE – 17th c.) ⎫ (a) *I were lever* (end of 13th c. – end of 15th c.)
(b) *I had lever* (13th c. – 18th c.) ⎬ (c) *Me had lever* (middle of 14th c. – 15th c.)

Other than those mentioned above, van der Gaaf (1904) and Mustanoja (1960) give diachronic descriptions of the *lief* constructions. However, it seems that a thorough synchronic analysis has not been conducted.

---

[2]   Denison calls them "phrasal impersonals" (1990: 125).
[3]   Book 3, line 379.
[4]   *The Canterbury Tales* (*CT*) I 487, IV 1169, *Tr* 3.379, and *The Complaint unto Pity* 46.
[5]   They judge date ranges of *lief* constructions from the evidence of the *OED*, the *Middle English Dictionary* (*MED*), and Visser (1963-73).

2. Overview of data in Chaucer and his contemporaries

This section will demonstrate an overview of the *lief* constructions in Chaucer's works from various syntactic viewpoints.

2.1. Types in Chaucer

In Chaucer's works the word *lief* appears not only in Types (0) to (c) but also in Type (v), in which the verb conjugates clearly not for the experiencer, but for a nominal complement as in (5). We also see Type (w), in which *lief* is juxtaposed with its antonym *loath* without any co-occurring verb or experiencer, i.e. a clipped construction. There are examples of Types (x) and (y) as well, in which *lief* does not co-occur with *be* or *have*, but functions as an adverb by itself. In (7) and (8), the *lief* constructions appear in the pluperfect tense and in the present tense respectively. Additionally, the attributive use of *lief*, Type (z), has plentiful examples, especially in addresses as in (9).

Type (0):
(1)   *Me were levere* a thousand fold to dye. (*Tr* 3.574)[6]

Type (a):
(2)   … I nam no labbe,
        Ne, though I seye, *I nam* nat *lief* to gabbe. (*CT* I 3509-10)

Type (b):
(3)   *He hadde lever* hymself to morder, and dye
                                    (*Legend of Good Women* (*LGW*) 1536)

Type (c):
(4)   … she a doghter hath ybore,
        Al *had hire levere* have born a knave child (*CT* IV 443-44)

Type (v):
(5)   And for the Grekis *weren* me so *leeve*,
        I com myself …   (*Tr* 4.82-83)

Type (w):
(6)   … nevere in my lyf, for *lief ne looth*,
        Ne shal I of no conseil yow biwreye. (*CT* VII 132)

Type (x):
(7)   … she *levere had lost* that day hir lyf (*CT* V 1600)

---

[6] All quotations of Chaucer are from Benson's edition. The emphases are mine.

Type (y):
(8) I *wol* ben he to serven yow myselve,
      Yee, *levere* than be kyng of Greces twelve! (*Tr* 5.923-24)

Type (z):
(9) … Gladly, *leve* nece dere! (*Tr* 2.251)

2.2. Tense and mood

As seen in Section 1.1, Visser (1963-73) uses the simplified forms when describing the types, but the constructions of *lief* appear in various kinds of tense and mood even in Chaucer as shown in Table 1.

Table 1. Tense and mood in which the *lief* constructions occur in Chaucer

	be + lief	*have + lief*
present indicative	+	+
present subjunctive	+	
past indicative	+	+
past subjunctive	+	+
pluperfect subjunctive	+	

Note: In one example of *be + lief* in the past subjunctive, the Hengwrt manuscript has a variant reading: *Hym had leuere* (*CT* I 3541; Manly and Rickert 1940: V 352).

The table shows that compared to the *be + lief* construction, the *have + lief* construction does not have any examples in the present subjunctive. (There is only one example of the *be + lief* construction in the pluperfect subjunctive.)

2.3. Frequency

The frequency of *lief* according to the type is listed in Table 2. This table excludes several examples in which the experiencer is not explicitly shown, or the grammatical case of the experiencer is obscure. For comparison, this article uses the data from Gower's[7] *Confessio Amantis* (*CA*) and from the *MED*.[8]

---

[7] He was "Chaucer's friend and fellow poet" (Gray 2003: 217), and it is inferred that the two poets shared some varieties of the English language.

[8] The present survey utilises the "Corpus of MED quotations" compiled by Petré, from which the quotations from Chaucer's works and *CA* are excluded.

On the use of *lief* in Chaucer   265

Table 2. Frequency of *lief* according to the type

	(0): impersonal + *be*	(a): personal + *be*	(b): personal + *have*	(c): impersonal + *have*
Chaucer	44	1	26	2
Gower	35	1	6	0
MED	184	28	168	24

The table indicates that the three share similar proportions of the types, preferring older Types (0) and (b), with some exceptions in Types (a) and (c).[9]

2.4. Research questions

So far Section 2 has obtained the overview of the *lief* constructions. Here, two questions arise: (1) What can the variation between the *be* + *lief* and the *have* + *lief* constructions show? and (2) How differently are the *lief* constructions used from its synonymous verbs such as *like* and *list*? They will be explained in the next section.

3. Analysis and discussion

3.1. *Be* + *lief* versus *have* + *lief*

This section deals with the research question (1). The variation will be analysed from syntactic points of view shown in Sections 3.1.1 to 3.1.4 below.

3.1.1. Complement type

The *lief* constructions co-occur with nominal, prepositional, infinitival, and clausal complements. However, with a nominal complement, the complement can be regarded as the subject of the sentence, *lief* taking a different construction from those used in questions. Therefore, any examples with this complement are excluded from this survey. In addition, any examples with a prepositional complement are excluded because of the small number of occurrences.

---

[9] For further reference, the analysis of *Paston Letters*, based on Uchioke's concordance, shows that the *be* + *lief* and the *have* + *lief* constructions exclusively take the impersonal and the personal constructions respectively.

266   *Hideshi Ohno*

Table 3. Frequency of *lief* according to the complement type

	Chaucer		Gower		*MED*	
	be	*have*	*be*	*have*	*be*	*have*
implied	2	0	11	1	20	2
infinitival	20	22	12	3	161	154
clausal	8	3	2	1	31	36

Note: This table excludes the examples in which the experiencer is not explicitly shown.

Table 3, which shows the frequency of the examples according to the complement type, indicates that the *be* + *lief* construction takes an implied complement much more frequently as in (10).

(10) And she obeyeth, *be hire lief or looth*. (*CT* IV 1961)

In this case, *lief* is juxtaposed with its antonym *looth* in a concessive clause, and the verb is in the present subjunctive.[10] This use cannot be found in the *have* construction. This means that the type leads to a simplified or clipped form *for lief ne looth* as in (6) above, where Davis, *et al*. gloss the phrase *lief ne looth* as "anything."

3.1.2. Grammatical person of experiencer

This section examines the grammatical persons of the experiencer. According to the Table 4, it cannot be said that they have a correlation with the variation between the *be* + *lief* and the *have* + *lief* constructions.

Table 4. Frequency of *lief* according to the grammatical person of the experiencer

	Chaucer		Gower		*MED*	
	be	*have*	*be*	*have*	*be*	*have*
1st	26	17	7	5	104	112
2nd	4	4	2	0	13	8
3rd	15	14	27	1	96	72

Note: This table excludes the examples in which the experiencer is not explicitly shown.

---

[10] The type is more remarkable in Gower than in Chaucer.

3.1.3. Word order

The data as to the word orders in which the two constructions appear are summarised below.

Table 5. Frequency of the *lief* constructions according to the word order

	Chaucer		Gower		*MED*	
	be	*have*	*be*	*have*	*be*	*have*
VEA	2		10		10	
EVA				1	9	2
EAV			1			
AEV					1	
(*to*)E(*it*)VAX	21	15	12	3	106	160
(*it*)VEAX	5	9	1	2	10	12
AEVX		1	2		49	18
AV(*it*)EX	2				7	
EAVX					8	
XEVA					8	
XVEA					4	

Note: The letters *E*, *V*, *A*, and *X* stand for the experiencer, the verb, *lief*, and the complement, respectively.

Table 5 shows the following:

i. The *be* + *lief* construction takes a larger number of orders, which is the most noticeable in the *MED*.

ii. Both the constructions most frequently take the EVAX order, and they take the VEAX order when they are preceded by adverbs such as *yet* or the formal *it*.

iii. Gower is different from Chaucer in that he uses the VEA order as frequently as the EVAX in the *be* + *lief* construction, and this order appears in a concessive clause as mentioned in Section 3.1.1.

As seen above, minor word orders have something to do especially with the *be* + *lief* construction, but the major order, EVAX, appears in both the constructions. Therefore, the types of word order do not seem closely related to either construction.

3.1.4. Impersonal use versus personal use

It is also necessary to draw focus to the impersonal and personal uses. As seen in Table 2, the *be* + *lief* and the *have* + *lief* constructions are closely related to the impersonal and the personal uses respectively. Even a single person uses the two constructions as shown in (12) and (13) for instance. The Host in *The Canterbury Tales* says, "me were levere" in (12) and "I hadde levere" in (13) with the same phrase of comparison "than a barel ale"[11] and the very similar finite clause complement. Nakamura (1991: 113) denies that the choice of either construction may be caused by geographical or social conditions. It is noteworthy to consider what this difference could mean. The Host has just listened to *The Clerk's Tale* in (12) and *The Tale of Melibee* in (13).

Type (0):
(12) Oure Hooste seyde, and swoor, "By Goddes bones,
     Me were levere than a barel ale
     My wyf at hoom had herd this legende ones! (*CT* IV 1212b-d)

Type (b):
(13) Oure Hooste seyde, "As I am feithful man,
     And by that precious corpus Madrian,
     I hadde levere than a barel ale
     That Goodelief, my wyf, hadde herd this tale!
     For she nys no thyng of swich pacience
     As was this Melibeus wyf Prudence.
     By Goddes bones, whan I bete my knaves,
     She bryngeth me forth the grete clobbed staves,
     And crieth, "Slee the dogges everichoon,
     And brek hem, bothe bak and every boon!" (*CT* VII 1891-900)

Exceptional Types (a) and (c) are found in both the Hengwrt and Ellesmere manuscripts according to Manly and Rickert. A few examples are (2), (4), and (14).[12]

Type (a):
(2)   … I nam no labbe,
     Ne, though I seye, *I nam* nat *lief* to gabbe. (*CT* I 3509-10)

---

[11] This means that the two constructions are the same from the metrical viewpoint.
[12] Although the quotations are from Benson's edition, the two manuscripts share the same constructions with some variations in word form (Manly and Rickert 1940: V 349, 536; VI 294).

On the use of *lief* in Chaucer 269

Type (c):
(4)   … she a doghter hath ybore,
       Al *had hire levere* have born a knave child (*CT* IV 443-44)

(14) I dar wel seyn *hir hadde levere* a knyf
       Thurghout hir brest, than ben a womman wikke (*CT* II 1027-28)

An individual scrutiny may make it possible to say that in (2) the italicised phrase "I nam" is the repetition of the same phrase in the previous line and emphasises that the speaker himself is never a tell-tale or gossip.

It is worth noting that there is an example in which the two manuscripts have different readings as in (15).

(15)   ... "if that *yow be so leef*
       To fynde Deeth, turne up this croked wey (*CT* VI 760-61)

In line 760, the Hengwrt has *yow* while the Ellesmere has *ye* as the experiencer. Whether by accident or design, the Ellesmere manuscript chooses an exceptional construction.

However, we cannot say anything more about the difference between the impersonal and personal constructions from the syntactic points of view.

For comparison, the verbs *like* and *list* (*OED*, s.v. *list*, v.[1]) are mentioned. Although different in part of speech, they belong to the same semantic field as *lief* and have both the impersonal and personal uses in Chaucer's time. The frequency of the two verbs is shown in Table 6. These verbs almost always have the impersonal use, as the *be + lief* construction does.

Table 6. Frequency of *like* and *list* in Chaucer and his contemporaries

		Impersonal	Personal
like	Chaucer	106	1
	Gower	58	2
	Langland	26	2
list	Chaucer	299	8
	Gower	95	6
	Langland	12	0

(Excerpt from Ohno (2015: 11))

270   *Hideshi Ohno*

Ohno (2015: 9-30) points out that although the number of examples is limited, the personal use, especially that of *list*, appears to occur with:

i. a non-finite clausal complement: "thise olde auctours *lysten for to trete*" (*LGW* F 575)

ii. a third-person experiencer

iii. the verb juxtaposed with another personal verb: "whan thei *han* mysaventure, / And *listen* naught to seche hem other cure" (*Tr* 1.706-07)

iv. the experiencer and the verb intervened: "*he* to vertu *listeth* nat entende" (*CT* V 689).

Among them, the second tendency can be seen in other works in Late Middle English and Early Modern English, as Tani names it "person hierarchy" (1997: 59). However, these tendencies do not apply to *lief*.

Therefore, the functions of the two uses should be emphasised. One of the comments on the differences between the two uses was made by Fischer and van der Leek (1983: 351) as follows:

> The difference between (i) [= the impersonal use] and (iii) [= the personal use] is one of volitionality. In (iii) the animate experiencer is nominative subject and therefore the initiator of the 'action' is fully involved in what the verb expresses, whereas in (i) the experiencer, bearing dative or accusative case, is only passively related to what is expressed in the verb.

An assertive adaptation of the idea to all examples of Types (0) and (b) would be misleading, but at the least the idea will allow the following explanation for (12) and (13). In (12) the Host has listened to the tale of Grisilde, who is excessively obedient to her husband, and in (13) he has listened to the tale of Prudence, who is patient with others and excessively cool and collected.[13] Only by looking at his words in lines 1895 to 1900 could we be easily convinced that his wife

---

[13] The two ladies are ideal noblewomen in the era; "Chaucer's Prudence follows the pattern of speech and action Christine de Pizan advises as ideal for a noblewoman in *Le Livre des Trois Vertus*" (Collette 2000: 159) and "Custance, Cecilia, Griselda, and the old hag in the *Wife of Bath's Tale* express elements of the pattern of feminine persuasion delineated in *The Melibee*" (Cowgill 1990: 175).

On the use of *lief* in Chaucer   271

is impatient and violent. His complaint continues until line 1923. Therefore, it is safe to say that the personal use in (13) shows his stronger emotion or wish.

An adaptation of this kind of explanation to Types (a) and (c) may be doubtful or pointless because the common *be* + *lief* construction could be used instead of the exceptional *have* + *lief* construction, and vice versa. However, it can be said that the variation allows the repetition of "I nam" in quotation (2) and that concerning (15) the Ellesmere manuscript makes the speaker feel the stronger rage of the three young men in *The Pardoner's Tale*, who will seek and slay Death.

Next, concerning (4), the *have* + *lief* construction takes the perfect infinitive "have born" as the complement. There is no example of the *be* + *lief* construction with this kind of complement in the data for the present research, Mustanoja (1960), Visser (1963-73), or van der Gaaf (1904). In a kind of counterfactual context, the impersonal *have* + *lief* construction can show the sincere, but helpless wish of Grisilde, whom the pronoun *hire* refers to, for the uncontrollable thing, i.e. the determination of the sex of a baby.

Finally, a tentative interpretation of (14) is that the expression combines the assertion of the speaker, shown by "I dar wel seyn," and the humble behaviour of the woman referred to by *hir*. As the note to Table 1 shows, the Hengwrt manuscript has the other example of Type (c): "Hym had leuere" (*CT* I 3541; Manly and Rickert 1940: V 352), which is also in reported speech. This can infer some correlation between this construction type and the speaker's mental attitude to the propositional content (or what he is conveying).

3.2. *Lief* versus *like/list*

This section deals with the research question (2). It will compare the *lief* constructions and the verbs *like* and *list* from a different point of view. As Table 7 shows, while the verbs usually do not co-occur with comparative or superlative adverbs, *lief* is frequently used in the comparative and superlative. This tendency is more notable in the *have* + *lief* construction than in the *be* + *lief* construction.

272   *Hideshi Ohno*

Table 7. Forms of *lief* in Types (0), (a), (b), and (c)

	be + lief			have + lief			like/list		
	positive	compar.	superl.	positive	compar.	superl.	positive	compar.	superl.
Chaucer	14	28	3	8	27	0	472	2	6
Gower	16	20	4	0	7	0	172	1	1

Note: This table includes the examples in which the experiencer is not explicitly shown, or its case is obscure.

3.2.1. In the comparative

In Chaucer, the comparative expressions of *like* and *list* do not show a choice between two things. One example is quotation (16).

> (16) And, for he was a straunger, somwhat *she*
>   *Likede hym* the bet ...   (*LGW* F 1075-76)

Conversely, the comparative of *lief* does show such a choice, in which one option is often connected to negative or dreadful things, especially to death as shown in (17).

> (17) For, by my trouthe, *me were levere dye*
>   Than I yow sholde to hasardours allye.   (*CT* VI 615-16)

This kind of function can be seen in *had better*[14] and *would rather* in Modern English.

3.2.2. In the positive

Concerning the positive expressions, this section will take *Troilus and Criseyde* as an example, and observe the expressions related to affections or love. Quotations (18)-(21) show the expressions which are related to Criseyde's affections for Troilus, after she fell in love with him at first sight.

> (18) For I sey nought that she so sodeynly
>   Yaf hym hire love, but that *she gan enclyne*
>   *To like hym* first ...   (2.673-75; Narrator)

> (19) *Shal I nat love*, in cas if that me leste? (2.758; Criseyde)

> (20) For *she* was wis, and *loved hym* nevere the lasse (3.86; Narrator)

---

[14] The earliest example of *had better* in the *OED* is in the fifteenth century (s.v. *better*, a. 4. b.).

On the use of *lief* in Chaucer   273

(21) "And nece myn — ne take it naught agrief —
     If that ye suffre hym al nyght in this wo,
     God help me so, *ye hadde hym nevere lief*! (Pandarus→Criseyde)
     That dar I seyn, now ther is but we two.
     But wel I woot that ye wol nat do so;
     Ye ben to wys to doon so gret folie,
     To putte his lif al nyght in jupertie.

     "*Hadde I hym nevere lief*? by God, I weene (Criseyde→Pandarus)
     Ye hadde nevere thyng so lief!" quod she. (3.862-70)

As (18) and (20) show, it is the narrator that uses the verbs *like* and *love*. In (19) Criseyde uses *love* in general terms with no object, although she is thinking of her love for Troilus. She does not use the verbs with any object when she mentions her affections for Troilus. It can be inferred that once she has fallen in love with him, the word sounds straightforward to her as a widow. Instead of *love*, she uses the *have + lief* construction as in (21), although "Hadde I hym nevere lief?" (3.869) and "Ye hadde nevere thyng so lief!" (3.870) reflect Pandarus' words "ye hadde hym nevere lief!" (3.865). On the condition that *love* is straightforward and *like* and *liste* are not usually used in the personal use, the construction with *lief* may be an acceptable way of expressing her affections.

4. Summary

What has been said can be summarised as follows. (1) Even when the four options of expression are available, Chaucer and Gower use *lief* in a historically conservative way with a few exceptions. (2) The idiomatic expression with an implied complement in the present subjunctive in a concessive clause can be found in the *be + lief* construction, and not in the *have + lief* construction. This is a major difference between the two constructions. (3) No syntactic difference can be found between the *be + lief* and the *have + lief* constructions except a choice of the verb. However, semantic and functional viewpoints might enable us to deepen our understanding, especially of the exceptional examples. Finally, (4) a comparison with *like* and *list* shows the difference of *lief* in the usage and function when used in the comparative and positive. In the comparative, the *lief* constructions often appear in the similar context, and some examples in the positive

274 *Hideshi Ohno*

show a certain semantic difference between *lief* and the verbs.

References

Benson, Larry D. (ed.) 1993. *A glossarial concordance to the Riverside Chaucer*, Vol. I. New York: Garland.

Benson, Larry D. (ed.) 2008. *The Riverside Chaucer*, 3rd ed. Oxford: Oxford University Press.

Collette, Carolyn P. 2000. Chaucer and the French tradition revisited: Philippe de Mézières and the good wife. In Jocelyn Wogan-Browne, *et al*. (eds.), *Medieval women: Texts and contexts in late medieval Britain*, 151-68. Trunhout, Belgium: Brepols.

Cowgill, Jane 1990. Patterns of feminine and masculine persuasion in the *Melibee* and the *Parson's Tale*. In C. David Benson & Elizabeth Robertson (eds.), *Chaucer's religious tales*, 171-83. Cambridge: D. S. Brewer.

Crystal, David 2008. *A dictionary of linguistics and phonetics*, 6th ed. Oxford: Blackwell.

Davis, Norman, *et al*. 1979. *A Chaucer glossary*. Oxford: Clarendon Press.

Denison, David 1990. The Old English impersonals revived. In Law S. Adamson, *et al*. (eds.), *Papers from the 5th international conference on English historical linguistics: Cambridge, 6-9 April 1987*, 111-40. Amsterdam/Philadelphia: John Benjamins.

Denison, David & Alison Cort 2010. *Better* as a verb. In Kristin Davidse, *et al*. (eds.), *Subjectification, intersubjectification and grammaticalization*, 349-83. Berlin: De Gruyter Mouton.

Fischer, Olga C.M. & Frederike C. van der Leek 1983. The demise of the Old English impersonal construction. *Journal of linguistics*, 19, 337-68.

Gray, Douglas (ed.) 2003. *The Oxford companion to Chaucer*. Oxford: Oxford University Press.

Kurath, Hans, *et al*. (eds.) 1952-2001. *Middle English dictionary*. Ann Arbor: The University of Michigan Press.

Macaulay, G.C. (ed.) 1900. *The English works of John Gower*. London: Oxford University Press.

Manly, John M. & Edith Rickert 1940. *The text of the Canterbury Tales: Studied on the basis of all known manuscripts*. Chicago: The University of Chicago Press.

Matsushita, Tomonori (ed.) 1998. *A glossarial concordance to William Langland's the vision of Piers Plowman: The B-text*, Vol. I. Tokyo: Yushodo.

Mustanoja, Tauno F. 1960. *A Middle English syntax*, Part I, *Parts of speech*. Helsinki: Société Néophilologique.

Nakamura, Mayumi 1991. Chaucer no hininsho kobun: *lief* niyoru kobun no baai [Chaucer's impersonal constructions: In the case of *lief*]. *Journal of Poole's Junior College*, 31, 107-25.

Nakao, Toshio 1972. *Eigoshi II* [History of English II]. Tokyo: Taishukan.

On the use of *lief* in Chaucer   275

Ohno, Hideshi 2015. *Variation between personal and impersonal constructions in Geoffrey Chaucer: A stylistic approach*. Okayama: University Education Press.

Petré, Peter (comp.) Corpus of MED quotations. <https://perswww.kuleuven.be/~u0050685/Corpus_of_MED_quotations.htm> (17 March 2017).

Pickles, J.D. & J.L. Dawson (eds.) 1987. *A concordance to John Gower's* Confessio Amantis. Cambridge: D.S. Brewer.

Simpson, J.A. & E.S.C. Weiner (eds.) 2009. *The Oxford English dictionary*, 2nd ed. Oxford: Oxford University Press. [CD-ROM]

Tani, Akinobu 1997. One determinant of the choice between the personal and impersonal uses of impersonal verbs *like* and *list* in late Middle English and early Modern English: An inquiry into the possibility of "person hierarchy." *Studies in Medieval English language and literature*, 12, 45-59.

Uchioke, Shinji (ed.) 2004. *A concordance to* Paston Letters. Okayama: University Education Press. [CD-ROM]

van der Gaaf, W. 1904. *The transition from the impersonal to the personal construction in Middle English*. Heidelberg: Carl Winter's Universitäts-buchhandlung.

Visser, F.Th. 1963-73. *An historical syntax of the English language*. Leiden: E.J. Brill.

Reading text analysis tools

Geoffrey Rockwell

Abstract
How has the analysis and mining of texts been imagined in the past? As we develop novel ways of analyzing literature with computers it is useful to ask about the history of analytical projects and tools going back to the *Index Thomisticus* project led by Father Busa starting in the late 1940s. To understand the context and concerns of text analysis tool projects in their time this paper looks at three early text analysis project starting with the *Index* and then Glickman's *PRORA* tool and finally Smith's ARRAS. The theoretical frame of this revisiting of old tools is media archaeology. We can learn more about the concerns of tool developers at the time by looking at projects not considered to be precursors of the online tools we have today. That tells us about the way our analytical imagination has evolved.

1. Introduction

How has text analysis been imagined? As we develop novel ways of analyzing literature it is useful to ask about the tradition of analytical projects and tools. One neglected approach to understanding this tradition in the digital humanities is the reading of the tools developed by humanists. What problems did humanities computing developers think they were addressing with now dated technologies like punch cards, printed concordances and verbose command languages? Whether the analytic functionality is at the surface, as with Voyant Tools, or embedded at deeper levels, as with the Lucene-powered searching and browsing capabilities of the Old Bailey Online, the web-based text analysis tools that we use today are very different from the first technologies developed by computing humanists on mainframes. Following Siegfried Zieliniski's exploration of forgotten media technologies, this paper will look at three forgotten text analysis technologies and how they were introduced by their developers at the time.

Specifically we will:

- Discuss why is it important to recover forgotten tools and the discourse around these instruments,

- Look at how the punch cards used in Roberto Busa's *Index Thomisticus* project (1) were discussed as a way of understanding data entry,

- Look at Glickman's ideas about custom card output from PRORA (2), as a way of recovering the importance of output,

- Discuss the command language developed by John Smith for interacting with ARRAS (3), and

- Conclude with some general reflections on the archaeology of text-analysis tools.

2. Zieliniski and media archaeology

> Cultivating dramaturgies of difference is an effective remedy against the increasing ergonomization of the technical media worlds that is taking place under the banner of ostensible linear progress. (Zielinski 2008: 259)

First a few words about why we want to exhume forgotten tools. Siegfried Zielinski, in *Deep Time of the Media* (2008), argues that technology does not evolve smoothly and that we therefore need to look at periods of intense development and especially at the deadends that get overlooked in order to understand the history of media technology. We learn more about the knowledge embedded in tools if we look away from interactive online tools and try to understand the mainframe environments they replaced.

In particular Zielinksi argues for the value of looking at technologies that are **not** in canonical histories as precursors to "successful" technologies, because they provide insight into the thinking at the time. Concording and early text analysis tools are just such a type of technology. They are generally ignored outside the humanities. They constitute a forgotten branch of information technology history which is why it is worth recovering. Such a branch might look like this:

- 1950s: Ad hoc tools like those used for Busa's *Index Thomisticus*. These were tools developed for specific projects.

- 1970s: Batch concordancers like COCOA and OCP that were developed to be used by many projects, but still on mainframes.

- Late 1980s: Personal computer interactive concordancers like WordCruncher and TACT that could be used by anyone.
- Late 1990s: Web Tools like TACTWeb and HyperPo that could be accessed through the browser.
- 2000s: Specialized data-mining and visualization like Mallet and Gephi that do not try to provide a general-purpose environment.

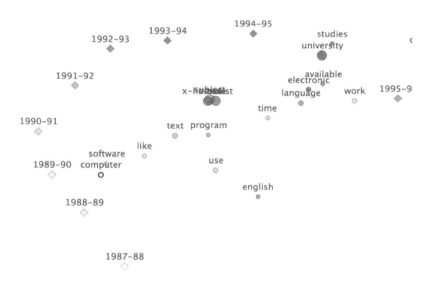

Figure 1. Detail of correspondence analysis scatterplot of 21 years of humanist

What a study of forgotten technologies can help us understand are the opportunities and challenges as they were perceived at the time and on their own terms rather than imposing our prejudices. Zielinski is following Foucault who was suspicious of grand narratives or continuous narratives. The history of tools like that of ideas is punctuated with dramatic shifts or Kuhnian paradigm shifts. It might be compared to Stephen Jay Gould's theory of punctuated equilibrium where periods of stasis (equilibrium) are interrupted (punctuated) by dramatic changes. The history of tools is also that of the infrastructure hidden beneath them (Bowker 2008). In the case of text analysis tools there is first the personal computer (PC) and then the web, both of which dramatically changed not only the interfaces, but how tools are disseminated, and how they were imagined to fit in research practices. The PC and web became infrastructure upon which developers could count. Forgotten works therefore can provide a way into understanding the infrastructure of other periods.

What then are the important text analysis tools? How can we identify the forgotten experiments? A study of the Humanist discussion list using correspondence analysis (Rockwell & Sinclair 2016, Ch. 4) suggests that the development of the web had a marked effect on how humanities computing resources were made available. Computing humanists shifted their focus, no longer talking on Humanist as much about hardware or software.[1] The web allowed humanists to focus on culture rather than the underlying technology. This suggests we want to look at tool development before the web became important in the mid-1990s. Further, a study of articles in the journal *Computers in the Humanities* (CHum) confirmed the shift in focus from the materiality of computing to other issues (Simpson et. al. 2016). This study also provided candidate tools to look at from the software announcements and reviews.

These studies show that from the 1950s until the early 1990s there was significant development around first mainframes and then personal computers. Text analysis and concording development projects feature prominently in the early years of CHum, though many of these have been forgotten with the advent of the web, and as the tools become impossible to run because of changes in computing technologies, despite the considerable investments made at the time. We note that research tools leave little trace other than the ephemera of reviews, catalogues, documentation, manuals, and promotional materials. A tool like the Oxford Concordance Program might have been extensively used, but once it can no longer be used it disappears from sight. Alas, we do not do a very good job of preserving tools, just as we do not do a good job of preserving videogames (Newman 2016). With

---

[1] An online version of this chapter is available at <http://hermeneuti.ca/swallow-flies>.

Reading Text Analysis Tools 281

this loss we lose knowledge of the features of the tools, the challenges they addressed, and the debates around these technologies. In this paper we therefore present three important case studies from the mainframe era that illustrate the thinking behind the first generation of tools. They were chosen so as to help us understand how differently data entry, output, and interaction were thought through before born-digital content, output to wall-sized screens, and interaction on a touch screen.

3. Busa and Tasman on literary data processing

The first case study is about the methods that Father Busa and his collaborator Paul Tasman developed for the *Index Thomisticus*. Busa can hardly be considered a forgotten figure, he is usually discussed as the founder of humanities computing (or digital humanities); but little attention is paid to the specifics of his work, the technologies developed, and what his collaborators, like Paul Tasman of IBM, did. We tend to see Busa in light of our need for a history rather than ask what he and colleagues struggled with.

Father Busa, when reflecting back on the *Index Thomisticus* project justified his technical approach as supporting a philological method of research aimed at recapturing the way a past author used words, much as we want to recapture past development. He argued in 1980 that, "The reader should not simply attach to the words he reads the significance they have in his mind, but should try to find out what significance they had in the writer's mind" (Busa 1980: 83). Concordances could help redirect readers towards the "verbal system of an author" or how the author used words in their time and away from the temptation to interpret the text at hand using contemporary conceptual categories. Concording creates a new text that shows the verbal system, not the doctrine.

To get a sense of what mattered back then we can consider a fascinating paper from 1957 by Paul Tasman's 1957 on "Literary Data Processing" in the *IBM Journal of Research and Development* that focused on how the project prepared the textual data while accounting for human error and other problems. Tasman writes, "It is evident, of course, that the transcription of the documents in these other fields necessitates special sets of ground rules and codes in order to provide for information retrieval, and the results will depend entirely upon the degree and refinement of coding and the variety of cross referencing desired" (1957: 256). In the 1950s data entry for text was new and one of the things they had to do was figure out how to enter unstructured textual data into a computer for processing.

As the Index Thomisticus was not published until much later it is useful to recapitulate the evolution of Busa's concording work as a way of understanding the context. Here are some of the key moments put together by Thomas N. Winter:

- First Busa created a concordance by hand of some 10,000 cards just for "presence" in Aquinas for his dissertation which was defended in 1946. In the dissertation he announced the need for a full concordance.

- In 1949 he visited the United States to try to find the right mechanical information processing technology and ended up convincing Thomas J. Watson of IBM to support the project.

- In 1951 he produced a proof-of-concept machine generated concordance of Aquinas' poetry using IBM punch cards that at the time were limited to 80 characters each.

- In 1954 he started a training school for operators.

- By 1957 he and colleagues like Tasman seemed to have worked out their input process.

- Data entry was not finished until 1969.

The data entry, as far as we can reconstruct it, worked like this:

1. A scholar went through the text and marked the thoughts (logical paragraphs).

2. Then the scholar identified passages that could fit on a card (80 characters is even less that a tweet!).

3. An operator input each phrase with a reference and serial number

4. Another operator input the same phrase on the same card. Should there be a difference this was caught by a checking machine.

5. The cards are then processed to produce word cards and then (word) form cards and on to index entries.

Some of the key things to note are:

- The project was not conceived as one using computers or software, let alone the web or text analysis. It was a concording project that used cards and machines that processing them. It was about data entry onto cards, proofing of cards, transferring of cards from machine to machine, duplicating them, marking them for processing and using electromechanical machines to do the processing of the cards.

- The "programming" in this context was partly in the design of the cards so that various standard sorting, replicating and counting processes get you what you wanted.

- The materiality of the punch cards was what enabled and constrained what could be done. The project as described by Tasman was really about the cards as tokens to be interpreted.

Figure 2. Livia operating a keypunch machine at a demonstration[2]

---

[2] For more on this see Melissa Terras' blog essay at <http://melissaterras.

284 *Geoffrey Rockwell*

It is also important to note that the processing of data at the time was gendered. Scholars tended to be men, keypunch operators women. Julianne Nyhan and Melissa Terras have been digging deeper into data entry for the *Index Thomisticus* project and have presented about how women were trained to be punch card operators (Nyhan & Terras 2017). Terras posted photographs from the Busa archive at the CIRCSE Research Centre, in the Università Cattolica del Sacro Cuore, Milan, Italy. In her Ada Lovelace post Terras quotes Marco Passarotti:

> Once, I was told by father Busa that he was used to choose young women for punching cards on purpose, because they were more careful than men. Further, he chose women who did not know Latin, because the quality of their work was higher than that of those who knew it (the latter felt more secure while typing the texts of Thomas Aquinas and, so, less careful). These women were working on the Index Thomisticus, punching the texts on cards provided by IBM. Busa had created a kind of "school for punching cards" in Gallarate. That work experience gave these women a professionally transferable and documented skill attested to by Father Busa himself.[3]

Julianne Nyhan has traveled to Italy and interviewed a number of the women operators and a book is forthcoming with the title *Uncovering 'hidden' contributions to the history of Digital Humanities: the Index Thomisticus' female keypunch operators*.

In sum, Busa's project is not only about computing technologies of the time, it is also about the people and organizations that enabled the work. To understand the technology properly we need to recover the human and mechanical labour wound through it.

---

blogspot.co.uk/2013/10/for-ada-lovelace-day-father-busas.html>. The image is kindly made available under a Creative Commons CC-BY-NC license by permission of CIRCSE Research Centre, Università Cattolica del Sacro Cuore, Milan, Italy. The original documents pictured in the images are contained in the "Busa Archive," held in the library of the same university. For further information, or to request permission for reuse, please contact Marco Passarotti, on marco.passarotti at unicatt dot it, or by post: Largo Gemelli 1, 20123 Milan, Italy.

[3] Terras, Melissa. "For Ada Lovelace Day — Father Busa's Female Punch Card Operatives." <http://melissaterras.blogspot.co.uk/2013/10/for-ada-lovelace-day-father-busas.html>

4. Glickman on printed interfaces

The second case study we will look at is the development of the PRORA (Programs for Research on Romance Languages) programs developed at the University of Toronto in the 1960s. PRORA was developed by Robert Jay Glickman (Dept. of Italian and Hispanic Studies) and programmed by a then student Gerrit Joseph Staalman (Industrial Engineering) at the University of Toronto. Glickman presented PRORA at the 16th MLA conference in 1965. It was reviewed in the first issue of Computers and the Humanities in 1966 and, with the publication of the *Manual for the Printing of Literary Texts and Concordances by Computer* by the University of Toronto Press, also in 1966 (Glickman & Staalman 1966), it was one of the first academic concording tools to be formally published in some fashion. What is particularly interesting, for our purposes, is the discussion in Glickman's 1965 conference paper (Glickman 1965) and in the *Manual* about alternative ways concordances might be printed for scholarly study. Where Busa and Tasman were developing ways to encode texts to be input and for processing by computers, Glickman was interested in how computers could output new configurations of texts to card-like pages.

In the *Manual* and in the conference paper Glickman included flowcharts of the processes involved. In the manual there is a flowchart that shows the human processes that go into preparing and then coding the text. Again, if you look very closely you will also see that the stick figures of the Scholar and Keypunch Operator are gendered. One lesson we can learn from both Tasman and Glickman is that text analysis is about much more than the tool, algorithm or results. The tools are embedded in human processes that have all the features of social processes from gendered roles to hierarchies of training. To understand the history of text mining we need to think about these processes.

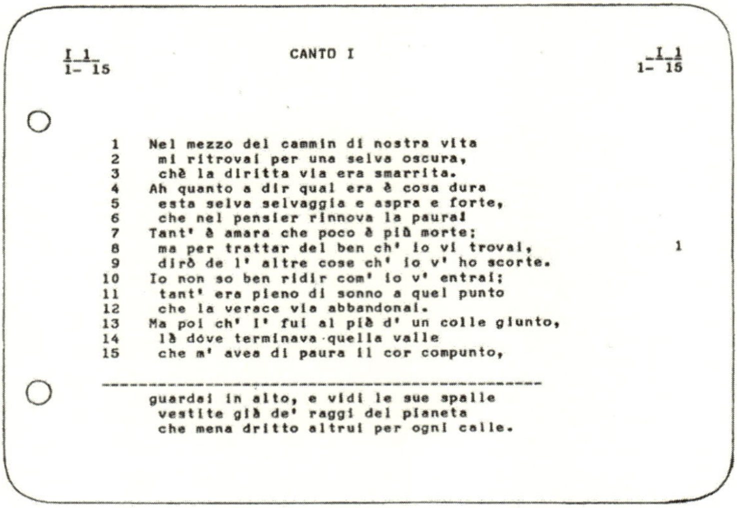

286   *Geoffrey Rockwell*

Figure 3. Output context card

What stands out as unusual is that Glickman was imagining how concordances should be used by scholars without simply reproducing by now traditional layouts. He was, in today's terms, developing alternative visual interfaces for the presentation of results. PRORA was developed so it could print concordances as a combination of small indexes and 5" X 7" CONTEXT CARDS for 2-ring binders (see Figure 3). The idea was that you would look up the word in the index which then points you to the cards that have the word in context. The cards could be taken out and arranged on a surface by users to help with the close reading of the poetic text. He was combining binder technology with computing to re-imagine how you might do close reading with a concordance text on a large surface. This is not so different from the challenge of designing for close reading that Bruno Latour described in his opening keynote at Lausanne in 2014.[4]

Glickman has a caption under two photos he included in both documents that explains his motivation.

---

[4] See Rockwell's conference notes at <http://philosophi.ca/pmwiki.php/Main/DH2014>.

Original editions of Hojas, Nieve, and Rimas; 308 pp. Special Format "concordance edition" contains 329 pp. i.e., instead of being several hundred times longer than the original editions (as would be the case if a traditional concordance format were used), the new "concordance edition" is only 7 % longer than the original editions. Text is reproduced photographically on paper of index card weight for easy handling. (p. 14 of first part)

Note the attention to the material of the cards where he writes about cards of "index card weight." Later on he describes the problem with other concordance outputs that he is correcting.

Since computers were originally designed for scientific applications, little effort was directed toward printing the results in a way that would satisfy the man of letters. Machine reports have therefore appeared without lower-case characters, diacritic marks, and essential punctuation. Understandably, reports printed in this way have been received with toleration, rather than with enthusiasm. (p. 2 of the paper)

He then lists the specific problems he has targeted and they are:

- Excessive bulk
- Insufficient context
- Inflexibility

The problems targeted seem remarkably prescient if one thinks of the attention given to mobile applications today, but that would miss the context he was operating in. Glickman could and did imagine how the printed and output concordance could be redesigned. The software or tool was doubled — there was the tool for making the concordance and the printed concordance which is the tool for interpretation. Despite advances in computing technologies, Glickman was deeply interested in the materiality of the technologies and the opportunities for humans to physically interact with materials.

5. Smith and interaction

Our third example and one of the first text analysis tools designed to support interactive research on the computer was John Smith's ARRAS which stands for Archive Retrieval and Analysis System. In ARRAS Smith developed a number of ideas about analysis that we now take for granted. ARRAS was interactive in the sense that it was not a batch program that you ran for output. It could also generate visualizations and it was explicitly designed to be part of a multi-tasking research environment where you might be switching back and forth between analysis and word processing. Many of these ideas influenced the interactive PC concordancing tools that followed like TACT and WordCruncher from which our modern web-based tools are based. It is the first modern text analysis tool.

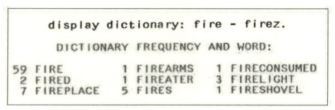

Figure 4. Example of command and output

In this paper, however, we are not going to focus on all the prescient features of ARRAS. Instead we will look at the command language which Smith was so proud of. Very few computing humanists use a command language for text analysis anymore (with the exception of some Unix commandline pipe aficionados); we expect our tools to have graphical user interfaces that provide affordances for direct manipulation. If you need to do something more than what Voyant, Tableau, Gephi or Wordle let you do, then you learn to program in a language like R or Python and use the graphics libraries available. Smith by contrast, spent a lot of time trying to design a natural command language for ARRAS that humanists would find easy to use and this comes through in his publications on the tool (1984 & 1985). Figure 4 shows an illustration from Smith 1984 of a simple command to display the words that show up in the dictionary of words in the text between "fire" and "firez," a now unusual way of doing a truncation search on a list. The frequencies are also shown. (Note that on the computer display they would not be nicely coloured.) Figure 5 shows the command for a concordance for a predefined category (of words related to fire) and some results. Figure 6 shows a distribution graph. It should be noted that Smith was a pioneer in the development of text visualization tools too.

```
CONCORDANCE FOR THE LINEAR CATEGORY, FIRECAT WITHOUT VALUES
ENFLAMING  THEY WERE SECRET AND ENFLAMING BUT HER IMAGE WAS NOT
           ENTANGLED BY THEM.
           92546: P. 232
FIRE       IT WOULD BE NICE TO LIE ON THE HEARTHRUG BEFORE THE
           FIRE, LEANING HIS HEAD UPON HIS HANDS, AND THINK ON THOSE
           SENTENCES.
           1281: P. 4
FIRE       MOTHER WAS SITTING AT THE FIRE WITH DANTE WAITING FOR
           BRIGID TO BRING IN THE TEA.
           1369: P. 4
FIRE       IT WOULD BE LOVELY TO SLEEP FOR ONE NIGHT IN THAT COT-
           TAGE BEFORE THE FIRE OF SMOKING TURF, IN THE DARK LIT
           BY THE FIRE, IN THE WARM DARK, BREATHING THE SMELL OF
           THE PEASANTS, AIR AND RAIN AND TURF AND CORDUROY.
           4485: P. 12
```

Figure 5. Commanding a concordance

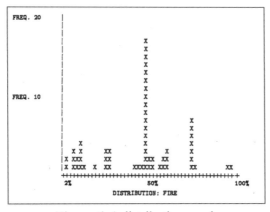

Figure 6. A distribution graph

Command languages were, for a while, the way you interacted with such systems and attention to their design could make a difference. This will not be news to those who started computing on an Apple II or IBM PC with MS DOS. Those fond of Unix will also understand the efficiencies of a well-designed command language. Smith tried to develop a command language that was conversational as he figured that would make it accessible to humanists so that we could use ARRAS to explore "vast continents of literature or history or other realms of information, much as our ancestors explored new lands" (Smith 1984: 31). Close commanding for close analytical reading.

6. Conclusions

In the 2013 Busa Award lecture Willard McCarty called us to look to our history and specifically to look at the "incunabular" years before the web when humanists and artists were imagining what could be done. One challenge we face in reanimating this history is that so much of the story is in tools, standards and web sites — instruments difficult to interrogate the way we do texts. The tools of text analysis and mining provide particular challenges as few can be tried. We have only the documentation in print that surrounded the tools from the manuals to reports in journals. A proper historiography of text analysis and mining has yet to be done to figure out just what we do have.

This paper looks back at one major thread of development — text analysis tools — not for the entertainment of admiring outdated technology, but as a way of recovering ways of thinking about the technologies we are still developing. How will our processes, tools and outputs look in 50 years? More specifically:

- What are the materials of text mining? What are their affordances? How are they part of the "program"? How can we imagine new inputs and outputs?

- How are the tools designed to be embedded in human and social processes? Who is doing what? What relationships are assumed? How could it be different?

- How do we interact with tools? What languages do we use? What is their grammar? How could they be different?

Returning to the study of tools mentioned in *Computing in the Humanities* (CHum) (Simpson et. al. 2016): to study the discourse around tools we went through CHum and identified all the articles, reviews, editorials and notices that mentioned text analysis tools. We used that to create a first list of tools. We then used that list to go back and analyze the entire run of articles in CHum since 1966 to extract a second larger corpus of articles mentioning tools. Wherever we found two tools mentioned in the same article we created a link. Figure 7 shows the tools most mentioned in connection with others. We have inverted the distance so you will then see something that should have occurred to us: the discourse around tools (re)turned around a set of

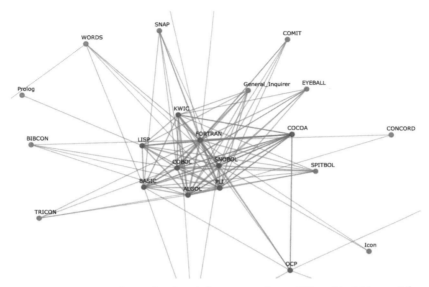

Figure 7. Network graph of tools/languages from CHum Tool Network[5]

preferred programming languages. To understand the history of text analysis tools we now have to go back to a different type of tool upon which the higher order tools were built. We need to understand how programming languages were discussed and what languages were discussed.

> Panelists and participants discussed ... most vigorously of all whether programming should be taught, or only package programs. (Michael Sperberg-McQueen, "Report on ACH/Sloan Foundation Workshop on Teaching 'Computers and the Humanities' Courses." *ACH Newsletter* 8(4), 1986)

An archaeology of tools thus leads us to a debate, which still surfaces to this day, as to whether it is better to teach tools or programming to humanities students.

---

[5] The CHum Network Tool was developed by Ryan Chartier and Amy Dyrbye. See < http://cloud.tapor.ca/viz/network/>.

Bibliography

Bowker, G.C. 2008. *Memory practices in the sciences*. Cambridge, Massachusetts: MIT Press.

Busa, R. 1980. The annals of humanities computing: The index Thomisticus. *Computers and the Humanities*, 14(2), 83-90.

Glickman, R.J. 1965. An integrated series of computing programs for literary research. Typescript of paper. MLA Conference 16, December 27, 1965.

Glickman, R.J. & G.J. Staalman 1966. *Manual for the printing of literary texts and concordances by computer*. Toronto: University of Toronto Press.

Liu, A. 2012. Where is cultural criticism in the Digital Humanities. In Matthew K. Gold (ed.), *Debates in the Digital Humanities*. University of Minnesota Press. Liu's essay is online at <http://dhdebates.gc.cuny.edu/debates/part/11>.

Newman, J. 2012. *Best before: Videogames, supersession and obsolescence*. New York: Routledge.

Nyhan, J. & M. Terras 2017. Uncovering 'hidden' contributions to the history of Digital Humanities: The index Thomisticus' female keypunch operators. Conference proceedings of Digital Humanities 2017, Montréal, Canada, 313-14.

Rockwell, G. & S. Sinclair 2016. *Hermeneutica: Computer-assisted interpretation in the humanities*. Cambridge, MA: MIT Press.

Simpson, J., Rockwell, G., Dyrbye, A. & R. Chartier 2016. The rise and fall tool-related topics in CHum. *Digital Studies/Le champ numérique*, May, 2016. <http://www.digitalstudies.org/ojs/index.php/digital_studies/article/view/313>.

Smith, J.B. 1978. Computer criticism. *Style*, XII(4): 326-56.

Smith, J.B. 1984. A new environment for literary analysis. *Perspectives in Computing*, 4(2/3): 20-31.

Smith, J.B. 1985. *Arras user's manual: TR85-036*. Chapel Hill, NC: The University of North Carolina at Chapel Hill.

Sperberg-McQueen, C.M. 1986. Report on ACH/Sloan Foundation workshop on teaching 'Computers and the Humanities' courses. *ACH Newsletter*, 8(4): 1-2.

Tasman, P. 1957. Literary data processing. *IBM Journal of Research and Development*, 1(3): 249-56.

Winter, T.N. 1999. Roberto Busa, S.J., and the invention of the machine-generated concordance. *The Classical Bulletin*, 75(1): 3-20.

Zielinski, S. 2008. *Deep time of the media: Toward an archaeology of hearing and seeing by technical means*. Cambridge, Massachusetts: The MIT Press.

Some Americanisms in Marryat's land-based novels and other English authors' works

Motoko Sando

Abstract

This paper examines five Americanisms, *ground hog*, *log cabin*, *prairie*, *rapids* and *snake fence*, which appear in Marryat's two later novels, and represent the features of those stories. Most of his novels are nautical fictions and they are usually based on his naval career; however, *The Travels and Adventures of Monsieur Violet in California, Sonora, and Western Texas* and *The Settlers in Canada* are set in the vast wilderness of North America. Furthermore, they include *log cabin* and *snake fence* which Marryat does not mention in *Diary I* and *Diary II*. With the maintenance of principal tradition, various aspects of culture and society reflected on English, which was brought to the New World in the colonial times. With the passage of time, it was Americanised especially on the word level and grew to have many specialties. While *ground hog*, *log cabin* and *snake fence* are coined from familiar existing words, *prairie* and *rapids* are borrowed from French.

1. Introduction

Frederick Marryat is one of the Victorian authors who travelled in North America in the early nineteenth century. However, novel-writing was not his only work; Marryat's life was broadly divided into two parts, as a career of a naval officer and a novelist, and his naval life greatly influenced on his novels. At the age of thirty-eight, he resigned from the Royal Navy in November 1830. After leaving the service, he settled down to a literary career, mainly devoted himself to nautical fictions in the 1830s.

Florence Marryat, the youngest daughter of Frederick, states that her father had "political and professional reasons" for visiting America (Marryat, 1872: Vol. I, 243). When he was in Lausanne, Switzerland, Frederick Marryat finished writing "Diary on the Continent" and closed that diary with the following sentences: "Do the faults of this people [the Swiss] arise from peculiarity of their constitutions, or from the nature of their Government? To ascertain this, one must compare them with those who live under similar institution. I must go to

294   *Motoko Sando*

America, that's decided" (*Olla Podrida*, 207).[1] After travelling the
United States and Canada from 1837 to 1839, Marryat published the
three volumes of diary, *A Diary in America, with Remarks on its
Institutions*, as the first series (hereafter *Diary I*) in October 1839, and
the three additional volumes of *A Diary in America, with Remarks on
its Institutions* (*Part Second*), as the second series (hereafter *Diary II*),
in December 1839. Throughout the texts, Marryat states how he felt
about the new continent and comments on various kinds of peculiar
words and phrases he encountered in North America. Then Marryat
started to write for young generation in the 1840s; *The Travels and
Adventures of Monsieur Violet in California, Sonora, and Western
Texas* (hereafter *MV*), which was published in 1843, and *The Settlers
in Canada* (hereafter *SC*), which was published in 1844, captured
hearts of young readers. Those two stories include many Americanisms; some of them were coined from existing words, others were
adopted from foreign languages and still others were modified to
create new senses.

In this paper, I would like to focus on *ground hog*, *log cabin*, *prairie*,
rapids and *snake fence*, which show the characteristics of *MV* and *SC*,
then examine how they are used by Marryat. I will also pay attention
to other English authors' works and consider whether they reach an
agreement with Marryat on Americanisms.

2. Source texts
2.1. Marryat's *MV* and *SC*
MV is a Marryat's nineteenth novel, and the story is about a son of an
exiled French nobleman, who attacked against the enemies of the
Native American tribe, the Shoshone, also known as Snake Indians. It
depicts his adventures among wild tribes of great western prairies and
the Mormons in the 1830s. As the titles shows, the story is set in
California, Texas as well as Arkansas, Missouri and Illinois. Although
many tribes appear, a farmer in Iowa, a parson, Professor Anthon use
Americanisms.

---

[1]   *Olla Podrida* includes essays which appeared in *The Metropolitan Maga-
       zine*. More than 200 pages consist of travel diary in Europe, "Diary on the
       Continent," which is composed of forty-one chapters and rest of the book
       consists of ten short stories and articles.

SC is a Marryat's twentieth novel, and the story is set in the back-woods of Upper Canada, near Lake Ontario at the end of 1800. Since almost half of the third volume of *Diary II*, four chapters, 185 pages, were devoted to a description of Canada, Marryat had an abundant information about Canada to work on *SC*. It is about the successful adventures of a family, the Campbells, who settled in Canada, in the face of great difficulties such as threats by Red Indians and wild animals. Marryat mainly puts Malachi Bone, a hunter, who used to work as a guide for the English Army, and Martin Super, a trapper and a rough-spoken person, up to speak Americanisms in this story.

2.2. Other English authors' works

In the first half of the nineteenth century, many English travellers visited the United States and wrote about how they felt about the New World. In this paper, I will focus on Frances Trollope, Harriet Martineau and Charles Dickens.

Frances Trollope was strongly influenced by Frances Wright, who had visited the United States twice and founded the Nashoba Community near Memphis, Tennessee. Its utopian community was built for liberating and educating slaves in 1825. Trollope went to America with Wright and her family, then lived there from 1827 to 1831. Unfortunately, the community financially collapsed and Trollope moved to Cincinnati. She took precise notes for publishing her first book and on her return to England, she put out *Domestic Manners of Americans* (hereafter *DMA*) into the world in 1832.

Harriet Martineau is considered to be the first female sociologist. She was interested in observing how democratic philosophies work in the United States, so she made up her mind to stay there. She spent two years living in the United States from 1834 to 1836. After returning to England, she produced *Society in America* (hereafter *SA*) in 1837.[2] Martineau had a positive impression of democracy; however she was concerned how limitedly women were treated and claimed that Americans should improve education system for women.

Charles Dickens visited the United States twice; the first visit in

---

[2] She also published *Retrospect of Western Travel* (1838), however this paper does not cover it.

1842 and the second visit in 1867 to 1868. When he worked on *Master Humphrey's Clock*, Dickens planned to visit either Ireland or America to set in sketches of travel, as stated in his letter addressed to John Forster dated 14th July, 1839.[3] Since he had connections with Washington Irving, wanted to see ideal and free society with his own eyes and looked for some excitement, he travelled the United States and Canada with his wife from January to June 1842, at the age of twenty-nine. After arriving in Boston, he mainly visited in the eastern part of North America. During his journey, Dickens often wrote to Forster, and presented many Americanisms. After he came back to England, he published *American Notes* in 1842.

3. Phrases coined from existing words

As stated by Marckwardt (1958: 85), one of the characteristics of American English is to put words together. Pyles (1952: 12) states that the English language did not have appropriate term for specifying settled areas so that the early colonists instantly arranged words from familiar existing words.

3.1. *Ground hog*

Ground hog is an American marmot, also known as *woodchuck*. According to Motoyoshi (1987: 114), it is one of the zoological Americanisms, which was employed by English authors in the nineteenth century. The first appearance was in 1784 as defined by the *OED* (s.v. *ground-hog*, 2.). "The Groundhog Day" is a national holiday in the United States, celebrated on 2nd February. This custom began among German immigrants in the eighteenth and nineteenth centuries; people predict the arrival time of the spring season whether or not to see *ground hog*'s shadow. The *OED* (s.v. *ground-hog*, 3.) also defines *ground hog* as an American slang denoting "a brakeman," and *ground hog case* as "a desperate or urgent affair."

Marryat refers to *ground hog* once in *Diary I* in order to give details how the Hudson Bay Company traded various animal furs (*Diary I*,

---

[3] House, M. & G. Storey (eds.) 1965. *The Letters of Charles Dickens*, Volume One 1820-1839. The Pilgrim Edition. Oxford: The Clarendon Press, 564.

Vol. I, 205-06). *Ground hog* appears twice in *MV*; Marryat explains about a prairie dog, compared with *ground hog* which is labelled as the animal peculiar to the Northern areas as can be seen in the following quotation:

> (1) The prairie dog is about the size of a rabbit, heavier, perhaps, more compact, and with much shorter legs. In appearance, it resembles the *ground hog*[4] of the north, although a trifle smaller than that animal.
> (*MV*, 75)

According to the next description, *ground hog* is usually inseparable from the great outdoors:

> (2) We had anticipated regaling ourselves with the juicy humps of the buffaloes which we should kill, but although we had entered the very heart of their great pasture-land, we had not met with one, nor even with a *ground-hog*; a snake, or a frog. (*MV*, 214)

It is worth noting that Marryat is the only author who refers to *ground hog*; however, *SC* does not have any usage example and *woodchuck* is used instead:

> (3) "... He has fired and loaded twice as we came back, and has killed this *woodchuck*," continued Martin, throwing the dead animal on the floor. (*SC*, 77)

3.2. *Log cabin*

Since *logs* are broadly used for building in the United States, *log house* appeared in the beginning of colonial times, as early as in the seventeenth century.[5] Romaine (2001: 169) remarks that it was "an early Swedish contribution to the emerging pioneer culture." *Log house* was a popular wooden building in Europe so Swedish settlers brought their ethos. The first citation for *log cabin* was dated in 1770. Motoyoshi (1987: 130) labels *log cabin* as one of the frontier Americanisms which became familiar to British people in the nineteenth century. This term is sometimes associated with Presidents of the United States because the seventh President of the United States, Andrew Jackson, and the sixteenth President of the United States, Abraham Lincoln, were born in *log cabins*. Pyles (1952: 12) comments that *log cabin* acquired a

---

[4]   Italics in each extract hereafter are mine, except for *want* in (18).
[5]   See Mencken (1936[4] [1919]: 115) and Pyles (1952: 12).

political implication due to William Henry Harrison's "the Log Cabin Campaign" in 1840.

As well as *ground hog*, *log cabin* does not appear in *SC*. I found four examples of using *log cabin* only in *MV*. Three of them are used in the descriptive parts of novel (*MV*, 251, 277, 335) and the remaining one is used in additional notes as can be seen in the following quotation:

> (4) A cow is a kind of floating raft peculiar to the western rivers of America, being composed of immense pine-trees tied together, and upon which a *log cabin* is erected. (*MV*, 270)

As for the other English writer, Dickens uses *log cabin* five times in *AN* (133, 151, 158, 159, 169). He describes the sight of Fredericksburg to Richmond in Virginia and adds a parenthetic note in the following quotation:

> (5) The barns and outhouses are mouldering away; the sheds are patched and half roofless; the *log cabins* (built in Virginia with external chimneys made of clay or wood) are squalid in the last degree.
>
> (Dickens, *AN*, 133)

The next example depicts the colony around Harrisburg in Pennsylvania; such a town seemed strange to him:

> (6) Then there were new settlements and detached *log-cabins* and frame-houses, full of interest for strangers from an old country: cabins with simple ovens, outside, made of clay; and lodgings for the pigs nearly as good as many of the human quarters; broken windows, patched with worn-out hat, old clothes, old boards, fragments of blankets and paper ... (Dickens, *AN*, 151)

3.3. *Snake fence*

Mencken (1936[4] [1919]: 145) picks up *snake fence* as one of the most characteristic compounds in Americanisms. Pyles (1952: 12) lists this as one of the new blends which mirror cultural and social circumstance in the New World. The *OED* (s.v. *snake-fence*) labels *snake fence* as North America and defines as "a fence made of roughly split rails or poles laid in a zigzag fashion." As well as *log cabin*, *snake fence* is one of the frontier Americanisms which became widespread in Britain during the nineteenth century.[6] It is also known as *worm fence* or *zigzag fence*. *The American Heritage Dictionary* (s.v. *worm fence, n.*) adds *Virginia fence* and *The Century Dictionary: An Encyclopedic Lexicon of the English Language* (s.v. *fence, n., snake fence*) lists *stake-and-rider fence* as other names.

SC is the only novel in which *snake fence* is applied. Of the six examples, the following quotation is recorded by the *OED* (s.v. *snake-fence*):

> (7) To the westward, and in front of them, were the clearings belonging to the fort, backed with the distant woods: a herd of cattle were grazing on a portion of the cleared land; the other was divided off by a *snake fence*, as it is termed, and was under cultivation. (*SC*, 58)

The following conversation is exchanged by Alfred, the second son of the Campbells, and Malachi, a hunter:

> (8) "What! did he [a bear] climb the *snake-fence?*"
> "Yes, sir, they climb anything; but I have got his tracks, and this night I think that I shall get hold of him, for I shall lay a trap for him."
> (*SC*, 228)

Besides Marryat, Martineau is the only other English author who refers to *snake fence* in her book. She reports about the sight of well-kept New England, which is totally different from other parts of the United States; she seems to be unfavourably impressed by *snake fence*, because she uses two negative sense of adjectives, *ugly* and *hasty*:

> (9) Instead of the ugly, hasty *snake-fence*, there is a neatly built wall, composed of the stones which had strewed the fields ...
> (Martineau, *SA*, Vol. I, 295)

4. Words which are borrowed from the other language
Marckwardt (1958: 21) claims that early settlers encountered plants, animals and even landscapes which were totally different from what they knew, so that new names were required for all those aspects of their life. Mencken (1936[4] [1919]: 104) states that the earliest Americanism was probably brought by Native Americans. According to Romaine (2001: 168), Danish, Dutch, French, German, Russian,

---

[6] See Motoyoshi (1987: 130).

300   *Motoko Sando*

Spanish and Swedish greatly influenced on American English in the
colonial times.

4.1. *Prairie*

Prairie is one of the most common Americanisms. It can be used by
itself or in compounds such as *prairie dog, prairie hen* and *prairie
wolf.* Krapp (1925: Vol. I, 134) points out that *prairie* became more
popular in the early nineteenth century with the opening of the West-
ward migration. It was loaned from French PRAIRIE, meaning
"meadow, grassland." According to *Online Etymology Dictionary* (s.v.
prairie, n.), the Middle English word *prayere* was lost and "re-bor-
rowed" to designate grassland from 1773. Motoyoshi (1987: 107)
remarks that it was borrowed from French people who lived in the
Mississippi and the Saint Lawrence River areas. A *Dictionary of
American English on Historical Principles* (s.v. *prairie*) covers *prairie*
in detail and classifies it into five senses as follows:

> (10) a. A meadow, esp. one alongside a river; a relatively small area of
>   low-lying grassland
>   b. A grass-covered opening in a forest; a savanna
>   c. A level open area about a town, house, etc.
>   d. A broad expanse of level or rolling land in the Indiana, Illinois,
>   and Mississippi Valley country, covered by coarse grass
>   e. An extensive plateau to the west of the Mississippi. In pl.,
>   frequently referring to the entire area between the Mississippi
>   River and the Rocky Mountain.

Prairie State is a nick name for the Illinois. According to the *OED* (s.v.
prairie, b.), the Wisconsin, Iowa and Minnesota are also included
when it is used in plural forms. In the Introduction of *Diary I*, Marryat
states what America is like as follows:

> (11) ... not the young only, but the old, quitting the close-built cities,
>   society, and refinement, to settle down in some lone spot in the vast
>   *prairies*, where the rich soil offers to them the certain prospect of
>   their families and children being one day possessed of competency
>   and wealth. (*Diary I*, Vol. I, 25)

Marryat explains the following towns or places which are located in
prairies; Sandusky in Ohio (*Diary I*, Vol. I, 175); Winnebago in
Wisconsin (*Diary I*, Vol. II, 44); Fort Snelling in Minnesota (*Diary I*,

Vol. II, 108); Texas (*Diary I*, Vol. III, 73). *Diary I* and *Diary II* have the following combinations: *prairie land(s)* (*Diary I*, Vol. I, 175; *Diary I*, Vol. II, 44, 72), *prairie spot* (*Diary I*, Vol. I, 201), *Prairie Fox* (*Diary I*, Vol. I, 206), *prairie flat* and *level* (*Diary II*, Vol. II, 46), *prairie country* (*Diary I*, Vol. II, 49, 137; *Diary I*, Vol. III, 73; *Diary II*, Vol. III, 206), *prairie territory* (*Diary II*, Vol. II, 79). It is interesting to note that Marryat uses positive meaning adjectives for describing *prairie*, "the beautiful *prairie*" (*Diary I*, Vol. II, 66), "a splendid *prairie*" (*Diary I*, Vol. II, 80) and "a charming *prairie* country" (*Diary I*, Vol. II, 137); whereas Dickens was unfavourably impressed by its infertility, as I will see later. According to Florence Marryat (1872: Vol. II, 79), her father brought many *prairie* curiosities such as bear, buffalo, wolf and opossum skins on his return from North America.

Marryat employs *prairie* in both stories. In *SC*, the Surveyor-General explains about the land to Mr. Campbell, whose family plans to settle in; he makes a paraphrase of *prairie* into another expression:

> (12) "... This land, you will observe, Mr. Campbell, is peculiarly good, having some few acres of what we call *prairie*, or natural meadow ..." (*SC*, 35)

MV has the extremely highest frequency of *prairie*; in many cases, it is used as a single word. With regard to living creatures, six compounds are used: *prairie dog(s)* (*MV*, 10, 48, 73, 75, 76, 156, 183, 357), *prairie (horse)-fly* (*MV*, 215, 353), *prairie hen* (*MV*, 236, 356), *prairie ostrich* (*MV*, 356), *prairie tarantula* (*MV*, 150), *prairie wolf* (*MV*, 228, 361, 362). Marryat annotates *prairie wolf* as follows:

> (13) The *prairie wolf* is a very different animal from the common wolf and will be understood by the reader when I give a description of the animals found in California and Texas. (*MV*, 228)

He describes the *wapo*, which lives in a vast field as "small kinds of *prairie ostrich*" (*MV*, 356). As for *prairie tarantula*, Marryat explains it as an "unwelcome customer" at night, and "a large spider, bigger than a good-sized chicken egg, hairy, like a bear, with small bloodshot eyes and little sharp teeth" (*MV*, 150). *SC* does not have any uses of *prairie* for creatures.

I shall leave Marryat and turn to other English authors. *Prairie* is most frequently used by Martineau; she gives an account of the town called Tecumseh in Michigan, and compares *prairie* in the Western areas as follows:

> (14) All that I tasted in Michigan, of *prairie* growth, were superior to those of the west, grown in gardens. (Martineau, *SA*, Vol. I, 238)

Dickens had longed for visiting *prairie*, so he decided to see Looking-Glass Prairie before turning back from St. Louis of Illinois, which was the furthest place of his American travel. In *AN*, he devotes Chapter XIII to report his short trip; at the beginning of the chapter, he states that *prairie* can be pronounced as "*paraaer*," "*parearer*" or "*paroarer*" (*AN*, 174). Dickens expected to feel the briskness brought by the heath of Scotland or downs of England, but unfortunately he was disappointed by its deserted ground:

> (15) It would be difficult to say why, or how—thought it was possibly from having heard and read so much about it—but the effect on me was disappointment. ... There it lay, a tranquil sea or lake without water, if such simile be admissible ... and solitude and silence reigning paramount around. ... It was lonely and wild, but oppressive in its barren monotony. ... It is not a scene to be forgotten, but it is scarcely one, I think (at all events, as I saw it), to remember with much pleasure, or to covet the looking-on again, in after-life.
>
> (Dickens, *AN*, 179-80)

The above examples are chronologically arranged as follows: Martineau's *SA* (1837), Marryat's *Diary I* (1839), Marryat's *Diary II* (1839), Dickens' *AN* (1842), Marryat's *MV* (1843) and Marryat's *SC* (1844).

4.2. *Rapids*

As well as *prairie*, *rapids* was borrowed from the French RAPIDES during the colonial times. First, it was used as an adjective, then it started to be used as a noun in 1765. Pyles (1952: 6) remarks that the early settlers used this word for topographies of the American scenery. *An American Dictionary of the English Language* (s.v. *rapids, n.*) labels *rapids* as follows: "The part of a river where the current moves with more celerity than the common current. *Rapids* imply a considerable descent of the earth, but not sufficient to occasion a fall of the water, or what is called a *cascade* or *cataract*." Marryat gives his impressions of *rapids* at Trenton Falls in New York:

(16) The *rapids* below the Falls are much grander than the Falls them-
     selves; there was one down in a chasm between two riven rocks
     which it was painful to look long upon, and watch with what a deep
     plunge—what irresistible force—the waters dashed down and then
     returned to their own surface, as if struggling and out of breath.

                                                        (*Diary I*, Vol. I, 145)

Other than Trenton Falls (*Diary I*, Vol. I, 147, 156), Marryat refers to
rapids of Oswego in New York (*Diary I*, Vol. I, 157), Sault St. Marie
in Ontario (*Diary I*, Vol. I, 184, 191), Goat Island at the Falls of
Niagara (*Diary I*, Vol. I, 209, 210), the Fox River in Wisconsin (*Diary
I*, Vol. II, 42, 43), and the Falls of St. Anthony in Minnesota (*Diary I*,
Vol. II, 81). The following is the explanation of the bridge in Goat
Island:

> (17) There is a beautiful island, dividing the Falls of Niagara, called Goat
>   Island: they have thrown a bridge across the *rapids*, so that you can
>   now go over. (*Diary I*, Vol. I, 209)

SC has the highest frequency of *rapids*, 9 examples. Two thirds of
them are used in the descriptive parts (*SC*, 1, 56, 197, 228, 231, 232).
One third of them are employed by Malachi (*SC*, 229), Mrs. Campbell
(*SC*, 232) and John, the fourth son of the Campbells:

> (18) "I don't *want* to go down the *rapids*." (*SC*, 232)

In *MV*, both examples refer to the *rapids* of the River Des Moines, a
tributary of the Mississippi River in Iowa (*MV*, 314, 332). Marryat
employs *rapids* in another story of his. The next example is quoted
from his fifteenth novel, *Poor Jack* (hereafter *PJ*), which was
published in 1840. The story is set in Greenwich of London in the early
nineteenth century. The main character, Thomas Saunders, whose
father was a sailor and lost his leg at the Battle of the Nile, was
neglected, but Thomas finally became a wealthy pilot on the Thames
River. The novel describes daily life about low-ranking naval officers
and contains many seamen's side stories. In the following citation,
Thomas's life is explained by an analogy to river and the *rapids* is used
as a metaphor:

> (19) Next it increases in its volume and its power, now rushing rapidly,
>   now moving along in deep and tranquil water, until it swells into a
>   bold stream, coursing its way over the shallows, dashing through the

impeding rocks, descending in *rapids* swift as thought, or pouring its boiling water over the cataract. (*PJ*, 213)

Dickens visited the Niagara Falls from the Canadian side and he was impressed by its splendid power (Dickens, *AN*, 198). He also watched *rapids* on his way to Montreal down the St. Lawrence River:

> (20) In the afternoon we shot down some *rapids* where the river boiled and bubbled strangely, and where the force and heading violence of the current were tremendous. At seven o'clock were reached Dickenson's Landing, whence travellers proceed for two or three hours by stage-coach: the navigation of the river being rendered so dangerous and difficult in the interval, by *rapids*, that steamboats do not make the passage. (Dickens, *AN*, 205)

Prior to Marryat's trip, Trollope visited Goat Island and saw *rapids* (Trollope, *DMA*, 280, 282). The following is the same *rapids* which Marryat described in (16):

> (21) Goat Island has, at all points, a fine view of the *rapids*; the furious velocity with which they rush onward to the abyss, is terrific; and the throwing a bridge across them was a work of noble daring.
>
> (Trollope, *DMA*, 282)

Martineau refers to *rapids* in Fort Gratiot, Michigan:

> (22) A party of squaws, in the Indian encampment, seated on the sands, stopped their work of cleaning fish, to see how we got through the *rapids*. (Martineau, *SA*, Vol. I, 285)

I shall put the previous citations into chronological order: Trollope's *DMA* (1832), Martineau's *SA* (1837), Marryat's *Diary I* (1839), Dickens' *AN* (1842), Marryat's *MV* (1843) and Marryat's *SC* (1844).

5. Final remarks

In the preceding sections, I have focused on Marryat's land-based novels, *MV* and *SC*, and examined *ground hog*, *log cabin*, *prairie*, *rapids* and *snake fence*, which represent the features of those stories. *Ground hog*, *log cabin* and *snake fence* are coined from familiar existing words, whereas *prairie* and *rapids* are borrowed from French. I also observed how those words and phrases were used by other English authors who travelled North America in the early nineteenth century. The results are presented in the Table 1.

Some Americanisms in Marryat's land-based novels 305

According to Table 1, it is reasonable to say that *rapids* is widely accepted by four Victorian authors. On the other hand, *prairie* is highly recognised by Marryat and Martineau, although Trollope never touches on and Dickens gives a disapproving impression on it. In view of the fact that Marryat is the only author who refers to *ground hog*, I may assume that it is a fairly rare animal. As for a building term, the same may be said of *snake fence* and Martineau holds a negative image of it. With regard to Marryat's two novels, it is interesting to note that *ground hog* and *log cabin* occur only in *MV*, while *snake fence* appears only in *SC*. It is also important to keep in mind that Marryat employs *woodchuck* as a substitute for *ground hog* in *SC*. I need further evidence and investigation to suggest that there are obvious regional differences.

Table 1. Americanisms used by Marryat and other English authors

	Marryat				Trollope	Martineau	Dickens
	Diary I (1839)	*Diary II* (1839)	*MV* (1843)	*SC* (1844)	*DMA* (1832)	*SA* (1837)	*AN* (1842)
ground hog	1	0	2	0	0	0	0
log cabin	0	0	4	0	0	0	5
prairie	40	4	218	37	0	40	7
rapids	13	0	2	9	2	1	3
snake fence	0	0	0	6	0	1	0

References

Craigie, William A & James R. Hulbert 1942. *A dictionary of American English on historical principles.* Vol. III. Chicago: The University of Chicago Press.

Dickens, Charles 1970. *American notes.* London: Everyman's Library.

Krapp, George Philip 1925. *The English language in America.* Vol. I. New York: Century.

Marckwardt, Albert H. 1958. *American English.* New York: Oxford University Press.

Marryat, Florence 1872. *Life and letters of Captain Marryat.* 2 vols. London: William Clowes and Sons.

Marryat, Frederick 1839. *A diary in America, with remarks on its institutions.* 3 vols. London: Longman, Orme, Brown, Green & Longmans.

Marryat, Frederick 1839. *A diary in America, with remarks on its institutions* (*Part second*). Vol. II & III. London: Longman, Orme, Brown, Green & Longmans.

Marryat, Frederick 1897. *The works of Frederick Marryat*. Author's limited edition, Vol. XIII (*Olla Podrida*), Vol. XIV (*Poor Jack*), Vol. XVII (*The travels and adventures of Monsieur Violet in California, Sonora, and Western Texas*) and Vol. XXI (*The settlers in Canada*). Boston: Dana Estes.

Martineau, Harriet 1837. *Society in America*. Vol. I, London: Saunders and Otley.

Mencken, Henry Louis 1919, 1936[4]. *The American language: An inquiry into the development of English in the United States*. New York: Knopf.

Motoyoshi, Tadashi 1987. Americanism no 19 seiki Igirisu-Eigo heno shinto. *Tsurumi Daigaku Kiyo Dai 2 Bu Gaikokugo Gaikokugo Bungaku Hen* (24), 105-143.

Online etymology dictionary. <www.etymonline.com>. Last accessed July 2017.

Pickett, Joseph P. (ed.) 2000. *The American heritage dictionary of the English language*. Fourth Edition. Boston: Houghton Mifflin Company.

Pyles, Thomas 1952. *Words and ways of American English*. New York: Random House.

Romaine, Suzanne 2001. Contact with other languages. In John Algeo (ed.), *The Cambridge history of the English language* (Volume VI): *English in North America*, 154-183. Cambridge: Cambridge University Press.

Simpson, J.A. & Edmund S.C. Weiner, prepared 1989. *The Oxford English dictionary*. Second Edition on CD-ROM Version 4.0, 2009, New York: Oxford University Press. [CD-ROM]

Trollope, Frances 1974. *Domestic manners of the Americans*. London: Folio Society.

Webster, Noah 2009. *An American dictionary of the English language*. Republished in Facsimile Edition. Virginia: Foundation for American Christian Education.

Whitney, William Dwight 1980. *The Century dictionary: An encyclopedic lexicon of the English language*. Reprint edition, Vol. V. Tokyo: Meicho-Fukyukai.

The usage of intensive adverbs in John Evelyn's *Diary*

Akemi Sasaki

Abstract
The purpose of this paper is to examine intensive adverbs in John Evelyn's *Diary*, written in the latter half of the seventeenth century, and to consider their usage from syntactic and semantic viewpoints: the variety and the number of occurrences; the *-ly*-suffixed and un-suffixed forms; words collocating with intensive adverbs; and the position of these adverbs in sentences. The investigation clarifies that Evelyn's usage of intensive adverbs in *Diary* was in the process of transitioning towards, but still distinct from, Present-Day English usage. However, it is also observed that his usage was closer to or the same as present-day usage in many aspects. This might reveal some aspects of his progressive stance towards the language.

1. Introduction

The *Diary* of John Evelyn (1620-1706) presents a daily record of events and experiences in his life and in the broader cultural, and religious, and social life in England in the latter half of the seventeenth century. It covers a wide range of topics, such as historically significant events, reports of sermons he heard, the private concerns of his family, his statements about the weather, and his accounts of his travels, both abroad and domestically. His emotional responses to these matters are displayed by various types of expressions; one means he often uses to express an intense surge of emotion is the use of intensive adverbs. This paper focuses on these intensive adverbs and observes his usage of them from syntactic and semantic viewpoints.

In (1), the adverb *greately*, modifying the adjective *desirous*, is used as an intensive adverb; in this case, *greately* intensifies the degree of being desirous, and thus is nearly equivalent to *very*.

> (1) Monsieur Evelyn … was come to Lond: *greately* desirous to see me & his stay so short, that he could not come to me;
>
> (*Diary*, 26 May 1670)

Quirk *et al.* (1985) divide intensive adverbs into subclasses, of which the focus in this study is on two: maximisers, which can denote the upper extreme of the scale, and boosters, which denote a high degree, or a high point on the scale (Quirk *et al.* 1985: 590). There is not a

308 *Akemi Sasaki*

common terminology to refer to these kinds of adverbs among scholars. Bolinger (1972: 18) refers to them as "degree words"; Quirk *et al.* (1985: 567) call them "amplifiers," and Biber *et al.* (1999: 554) call them "amplifiers (or intensifiers)." In this paper, they are referred to as "intensive adverbs." The following sections discuss intensive adverbs in Evelyn's *Diary* from different viewpoints: their variety, parallel forms with/without the *-ly* suffix, collocating words, and syntactic position.

2. The variety of intensive adverbs in Evelyn's *Diary*
Historically, Early Modern English had a wide variety and number of intensive adverbs, as Nevalainen (1999) points out.

> Early Modern English significantly enriches the various adverbial means of expressing speaker attitude to what is being talked about. One of the adverbial categories to be remarkably augmented is boosters, which denote a high degree or a high point on a scale. (Nevalainen 1999: 449)

Peters (1994: 271) further suggests that "the growth of the booster class during Early Modern English, and also the rate of change in the repertoire, are paralleled neither in earlier nor in later periods of English...." In fact, Evelyn frequently uses intensive adverbs to intensify his feelings and descriptions of various moving events. His *Diary* contains 49 intensive adverbs: *absolutely, abundantly, completely, considerably, deeply, desperately, enormously, entirely, exceeding, exceedingly, excessive, excessively, extraordinarily, extraordinary, extravagantly, extreme, extremely, firmly, fully, greatly, grievously, heartily, infinitely, immensely, intolerably, madly, mightily, miraculously, miserably, perfectly, prodigious, prodigiously, really, remarkably, singularly, strangely, stupendously, sufficiently, terribly, totally, truly, undoubtedly, utterly, vastly, vehemently, very, wholly, wonderful,* and *wonderfully*. In the *Diary*, he does not use any specific intensive adverbs very often, but instead employs different intensive adverbs. In addition to this large variety of adverbs, it is worth noting that he gravitates toward relatively new intensive adverbs. According to *OED*, out of the 49 intensive adverbs that appear in the *Diary* as listed above, eight came to have a widely recognized intensive meaning only in the seventeenth or eighteenth centuries: *considerably, desperately, heartily, immensely, prodigiously, remarkable, stupendously,* and *vastly*.

The usage of intensive adverbs in John Evelyn's *Diary*   309

In this respect, a comparison on the use of intensive adverbs in the works of John Bunyan (1628-1688), one of Evelyn's contemporaries, may be of some help. Intensive adverbs found in *The Pilgrim's Progress* (1678-1684) are *absolutely, admirably, bitterly, burning, damnable, dearly, diametrically, desperately, devilishly, delightful, exceeding, exceedingly, extraordinary, extraordinarily, extremely, full, fully, greatly, heartily, highly, loud, mighty, perfectly, pretty, right, sore, sorely, soundly, sufficiently, thoroughly, utterly, wonderful,* and *wonderfully*. Most of these had been traditionally used as intensive adverbs, dating back to Middle English. Thus, compared to Evelyn, Bunyan employs a relatively limited repertoire of relatively established intensive adverbs. Evelyn also exhibits a tendency of advanced usage of other grammatical items; [1] thus, his usage of intensive adverbs may also show his progressive attitude towards the language.

3. The *-ly*-suffixed and un-suffixed forms of intensive adverbs
The focus in this section is on the forms of some intensive adverbs with/without the *-ly* suffix. In Present-Day English, *-ly*-suffixed forms, as in (2), are generally used, whereas in Early Modern English, un-suffixed forms, as in (3), are also used, and both forms (with/without the *-ly* suffix) are commonly found (Nevalainen 1994, 1999; Peters 1994).

(2) I was *exceedingly* drowsy. (*Diary* 31 Jan. 1703)

(3) I was *exceeding* drowsy. (*Diary* 21 May 1699)

A number of intensifiers were regularized towards the beginning of the late Modern English period. The suffix *-ly* was appended increasingly to such short forms as *devilish, dreadful, exceeding, extraordinary,* and *terrible* (Strang 1970: 139) because of the effects of standardization[2] and analogy.[3] According to a search in the *Helsinki Corpus* by

---

[1] For instance, in the "V + NP + plain infinitive construction" in Evelyn's *Diary*, he does retain the older patterns of usage for some verbs, as do his contemporaries; however, such conservative patterns of usage appear much less frequently in his work (Sasaki 2009).

[2] Strang (1970: 139) refers to Robert Lowth's *Short Introduction to English Grammar*:
    Adjectives are sometimes employed as adverbs: improperly, and not agreeably to the genius of the English language. As, "*indifferent* honest, *excellent* well:" Shakespear [sic], Hamlet, "*extreme* elaborate:" Dryden, Essay on Dram. Poet. "*marvellous* graceful:" Clarendon, Life, p. 18. (Lowth 1762/1775: 93)

[3] Nevalainen (1994: 244) mentions that "[s]uch pleonastic forms as *oftenly*

310   *Akemi Sasaki*

Nevalainen (1994: 245), however, "long forms did occur well before the introduction of normative grammars in the eighteenth century, and even before discussions of correctness that took place in the latter half of the seventeenth century." Nevalainen (1994: 256) also points out that the "suffix *-ly* had not fully replaced the zero morpheme in Early Modern English as the standard derivation."

In this paper, six intensive adverbs that have dual forms in the *Diary* are specifically examined: *exceeding, exceedingly*; *excessive, excessively*; *extraordinary, extraordinarily*; *extreme, extremely*; *prodigious, prodigiously*; and *wonderful, wonderfully*. Peters (1994) analysed Early Modern English letters written between 1424 and 1736 and offered concrete evidence for the frequent use of both forms of these adverbs in this period.

3.1. *-ly*-suffixed and un-suffixed forms in Evelyn's *Diary*

In the *Diary,* Evelyn uses both forms of the six sets of intensive adverbs listed above, with some fluctuation, as shown in Table 1: *exceeding, exceedingly*; *excessive, excessively*; *extraordinary, extraordinarily*; *extreme, extremely*; *prodigious, prodigiously*; and *wonderful, wonderfully*.

Table 1. Occurrences of un-suffixed forms and *-ly*-suffixed forms in the *Diary*

	un-suffixed form	*-ly*-suffixed form
exceeding/ly	143	218
excessive/ly	15	16
extraordinary/(i)ly	43	9
extreme/ly	12	44
prodigious/ly	3	7
wonderful/ly	7	21
Total	223	315

As can be seen from Table 1, the *-ly*-suffixed form has an overall higher frequency, but the adverbs have different tendencies: predominance of the *-ly*-suffixed form (*exceedingly, extremely, prodigiously,* and *wonderfully*), predominance of the un-suffixed form (*extraordinary*), and almost equal frequency of both forms (*excessive* and

---

and *soonly* can be found as early as the late fifteenth and early sixteenth centuries, and must be attributed to analogy."

The usage of intensive adverbs in John Evelyn's *Diary*   311

excessively). The choice of forms can be attributed to certain factors, but no one decisive factor for choosing either form can be found in Evelyn's usage, as demonstrated in the comparison of (4) and (5) below:

> (4) Very warm, but *exceedingly* stormy: (*Diary* 18 Dec. 1698)

> (5) *Exceeding* stormy, wett: (*Diary* 25 Dec. 1698)

The entry of quotation (4) was made on December 18, 1698, but refers to the weather on December 24, according to the editor's note. In (4), Evelyn uses the -*ly*-suffixed form to emphasize the adjective *stormy*. In (5), the entry for the next day, however, he uses the un-suffixed form to emphasize the same adjective, *stormy*. These examples clearly demonstrate that both forms of intensive adverbs were used, with no special difference in meaning. Leaving semantics aside, however, the choice of form can be related to syntax. The next sub-section examines the usage from a syntactic point of view.

3.2. Head words modified by intensive adverbs

In this sub-section, head words modified by intensive adverbs in the *Diary* are discussed, and it is determined whether the choice between the two forms is related to the head words, as in Present-Day English.

In the *Diary*, the head words modified by these six sets of intensive adverbs include adjectives, as in (6); adverbs, as in (7); a prepositional phrase, in (8); past participles, as in (9); and verbs, as in (10); the head words in the quotations below are indicated in brackets. The distribution of the types of head word is presented in Table 2.

> (6) Dined at Arundel house, & that Evening, discoursd with his Majestie about Shipping, in which the King was *exceedingly* [skillfull]:
> (*Diary* 11 Nov. 1661)

> (7) I went to St. Paules, to heare Dr. Stanhops first Boylean Lecture which on he performed *exceedingly* [well]. (*Diary* 6 Jan. 1701)

> (8) In this journey went part of the way Mr. Ja: Grahame ..., a Young Gent: *exceedingly* [in love] with Mrs. Dorothy Howard one of the Mayds of honor in our Company: .... (*Diary* 9 July 1675)

> (9) I had ben *exceedingly* [troubled] with a swelling in my throat & neck, which fore-ran the Piles, & had now for 2 Springs indisposd me, ...
> (*Diary* 16 Mar. 1652)

312   *Akemi Sasaki*

(10) I *exceedingly* [admir'd] that sumptuous and most magnificent Church of the Jesuite (*Diary* 4 Oct. 1641)

Table 2. Distribution of head words modified by intensive adverbs: *exceeding(ly)*, *excessive(ly)*, *extraordinary(ily)*, *extreme(ly)*, *prodigious(ly)*, and *wonderful(ly)*

Head word	un-suffixed form	-*ly*-suffixed form
Adjective	215	113
Adverb	8	29
Prep. phrase	0	1
Past participle	0	69
Verb	0	103

As can be seen from the information presented in Table 2, when intensive adverbs modify a prepositional phrase, past participle, or verb, Evelyn exclusively uses -*ly* forms. In this respect, his usage is the same as present-day usage. In contrast, when intensive adverbs modify adjectives, he uses both the un-suffixed and -*ly*-suffixed forms, but prefers the un-suffixed form. Also, he uses both forms to modify adverbs, but shows a preference for -*ly* forms; in Present-Day English, -*ly* forms are used to modify both adjectives and adverbs. Let us examine the situation for each intensive adverb more closely.

Table 3 shows the distribution of head words for each intensive adverb. A slight difference in tendency is discernible, especially when intensive adverbs modify adjectives.

Table 3. Distribution of head words modified by each intensive adverb

	un-suffixed form					-*ly*-suffixed form				
	adj.	adv.	prep. phr.	p.p.	v.	adj.	adv.	prep. phr.	p.p.	v.
exceeding/ly	137	6	0	0	0	62	21	1	50	84
excessive/ly	15	0	0	0	0	12	0	0	0	4
extreme/ly	11	1	0	0	0	27	7	0	7	3
extraordinary/(i)ly	42	1	0	0	0	5	0	0	3	1
prodigious/ly	3	0	0	0	0	4	0	0	0	3
wonderful/ly	7	0	0	0	0	3	1	0	9	8

According to Peters (1994: 284-5), the letter corpora from the seventeenth and eighteenth centuries investigated by him include only "un-

The usage of intensive adverbs in John Evelyn's *Diary*   313

suffixed adverb + adjective" examples, and no example of "-*ly*-suffixed adverb + adjective." The corpora include one example of *exceeding* ("*exceeding* glad"), but no example of *exceedingly*; two examples of *excessive* ("*excessive* cold"), but no example of *excessively*; three examples of *wonderful* ("*wonderful* pretty," "*wonderful* good" and "*wonderful* rich"), but no example of *wonderfully*. Evelyn's *Diary*, however, contains examples of -*ly*-suffixed forms of all the intensive adverbs. The -*ly*-suffixed forms *extremely* and *prodigiously* outnumber their un-suffixed forms; *extremely*, in particular, shows a faster rate of transition towards the -*ly* form. In this respect, Evelyn's usage is close to that in Present-Day English, and his frequent use of the -*ly* forms to modify adjectives might indicate his progressive attitude towards and initiative with regard to the language.

3.3. Collocation

This sub-section is a discussion from a semantic point of view of words that collocate with intensive adverbs in his *Diary*. In Present-Day English, some intensive adverbs have a notable tendency to collocate with certain other words, resulting in certain positive or negative implications. Greenbaum (1970: 83-84) points out, for instance, that "most of the verbs collocating with *utterly* and *completely* have a negative implication, suggesting disapproval, opposition, or failure." Other adverbs have, to greater or lesser degrees, their own distinct tendencies in terms of collocations. In order to ascertain to what extent such tendencies in Present-Day English are established in Evelyn's usage in the *Diary*, words collocating with intensive adverbs in the *Diary* were studied. Overall, there were few similar tendencies in these collocations between Evelyn's usage and present-day usage. It was revealed that most adverbs did not have a marked tendency to co-occur with words in a certain semantic field, but some adverbs did have a slight tendency to do so, as described below.

3.3.1. *entirely*

According to Greenbaum (1970:36), *entirely* tends to occur with *agree*. In the *Diary*, *entirely* occurs with words or phrases that have an implication of obedience, submission, or governance: *give up, obey, submit, in the rebells hands, in his hands*, and *govern*.

314   *Akemi Sasaki*

3.3.2. *greatly*
Greenbaum (1970: 36) reveals that *greatly* tends to co-occur with *admire* and *enjoy*. The *Diary* contains only one example of *greatly* used with *admire*; instead, *greatly* often collocates with words that have a negative implication: *afflicted* (three times), *deplore* (twice), *deface*, *perflex't*, *disoblige*, *destructive*, *indanger*, *disappoint*, *disturb*, and *exasperate*.

3.3.3. *totally*
In the *Diary*, *totally* shows a slight tendency to collocate with words that have a negative implication: *different* (twice), *averse*, *reject*, *decline*, *in ruins*, *discourage*, and *leave off*.

3.3.4. *utterly*
Greenbaum (1979: 83-84) suggests that "most of the verbs collocating with *utterly* … have a negative implication, suggesting disapproval, opposition, or failure." Evelyn shows the same tendency; in the *Diary*, *utterly* collocates with the following words: *lost* (three times), *destroyed* (twice), *false* (twice), *burnt & destroyed*, *burnt*, *ruined*, *demolish*, *take away*, *devastating*, *defaced*, *against the War*, … *which* … *against*, *unlikely*, *ignorant*, *contrary*, *refuse*, *dislike*, *illegal*, and *excluded*.

3.3.5. *wholly*
In the *Diary*, *wholly* occurs with the following words: *mercenarie*, *unfurnished*, *abolished*, *ignorant*, *abandoned*, *unfit*, *decline*, *averse*, *resign*, and *leave off*, all of which have a negative implication.

3.4. The position of intensive adverbs
In this section is examined the position of the 12 intensive adverbs (both un-suffixed and *-ly*-suffixed forms) surveyed in Section 3.1: *exceeding(ly)*, *excessive(ly)*, *extraordinary(ily)*, *extreme(ly)*, *prodigious(ly)*, and *wonderful(ly)*. The adverbs are placed before the head words, as in (11) and (12), which is known as the medial position (M position), or are postposed, as in (13), which is known as the final position (F position). There is no example of adverbs occurring in sentence-initial position in the *Diary*. Table 4 lists where the intensive adverbs occur in the *Diary*: in M position or F position.

The usage of intensive adverbs in John Evelyn's *Diary*   315

(11) I was *exceedingly* <u>sleepy</u>: (*Diary* 23 Mar. 1701) [M position]

(12) drowsinesse *exceedingly* <u>surprized</u> me,

(*Diary* 29 June 1701) [M position]

(13) Sleepe <u>surpriz'd</u> me *exceedingly*: (*Diary* 26 Jan. 1701) [F position]

Table 4. The positions of intensive adverbs: *exceeding*(*ly*), *excessive*(*ly*), *extraordinary*(*ily*), *extreme*(*ly*), *prodigious*(*ly*), and *wonderful*(*ly*)

	Adjective	Adverb	Prep. phrase	Past part.	Verb
M position	328	37	1	69	75
F position	0	0	0	0	28

As is evident from studying Table 4, intensive adverbs modifying adjectives, adverbs, prepositional phrases, and past participles are in M position, without exception. Only when the intensive adverbs modify verbs do their positions vary. Thus, M position is clearly the most common. With regard to the difference in intensifying effect by position, Greenbaum (1970: 31-2) suggests that "it seems intuitively that the intensifying effect is more pronounced when the degree intensifier is in pre-verb position, while the superlative effect is more likely to be present when it is in final position." In the *Diary*, however, there seems to be no difference in meaning between the placement of intensive adverbs in M position or F position, as assumed by the comparison of (12) and (13).

4. Conclusion

In this paper, intensive adverbs in John Evelyn's *Diary* and their usage were examined, the latter in terms of certain aspects: variety, dual forms with/without the -*ly* suffix, collocations, and position. First, it was found that Evelyn uses a variety of intensive adverbs instead of using the same ones repeatedly. Furthermore, brand new intensive adverbs from Evelyn's period were found in relatively large numbers in the *Diary*. Second, it was confirmed that Evelyn uses both the -*ly*-suffixed and un-suffixed forms, without any apparent difference in their meanings. The choice of which of the two forms to use seems to be related to the head words modified by the intensive adverbs. Third, most intensive adverbs in the *Diary* do not have a marked tendency to collocate with words of a certain semantic field, but some (*entirely*, *greatly*, *totally*, *utterly*, and *wholly*) do. Finally, with regard to position, intensive adverbs occur either in medial position (that is, before the head word) or in final position. Only when the intensive adverbs modify verbs does their position vary, but M position remains the most common. There seems to be no difference in intensifying function or meaning between the use of intensive adverbs in M position or F position.

Evelyn's usage of intensive adverbs in the *Diary* is in transition towards present-day usage, and therefore it fluctuates. In many aspects, however, it was observed that his usage is close to or the same as present-day usage. This might lead today's scholarship towards revelations of Evelyn's progressive stance towards the English language and its usage. However, the object of this study is the *Diary* only; to confirm Evelyn's usage of intensive adverbs and his stance towards the language, more comprehensive studies would be required.

Texts
Bunyan, John 1996. *Grace Abounding* and *The Pilgrim's Progress*. Roger Sharrock (ed.). London: Oxford University Press.
Evelyn, John 2000 [1951]. *The diary of John Evelyn*, Vols. II, III, IV, and V. E. S. de Beer (ed.). London: Oxford University Press.

References
Biber, Douglas, Stig Johansson, Geoffrey Leech, Susan Conrad & Edward Finegan 1999. *Longman grammar of spoken and written English*. Harlow: Longman.
Bolinger, Dwight 1972. *Degree words*. The Hague, Paris: Mouton.
Breenbaum, Sidney 1970. *Verb-intensifier collocations in English*. The Hague, Paris: Mouton.
Claridge, Claudia 2011. *Hyperbole in English*. Cambridge: Cambridge University Press.
Fisher, John Hurt, Malcolm Richardson & Jane L. Fisher 1984. *An anthology of Chancery English*. Knoxville: The University of Tennessee Press.
Jespersen, Otto 1961. *A Modern English grammar on historical principles*, Part II. London: George Allen and Unwin.
Hoye, Leo 1997. *Adverbs and modality in English*. London, New York: Longman.
Lass, Roger (ed.) 1999. *The Cambridge history of the English language*, Vol. 3, *1476-1776*. Cambridge: Cambridge University Press.

Nevalainen, Terttu 1994. Aspects of adverbial change in Early Modern English. In Dieter Kastovsky (ed.) *Studies in Early Modern English*, 243-59. Berlin, New York: Mouton de Gruyter.

Nevalainen, Terttu 1999. Early Modern English lexis and semantics. In Roger Lass (ed.) *The Cambridge history of the English language, Vol. 3: 1476-1776*. Cambridge: Cambridge University Press, 332-458.

Otsuka, Takanobu & Fumio Nakajima (ed.) 1982. *Shin eigogaku jiten* [The Kenkyusha dictionary of English linguistics and philology.] Tokyo: Kenkyusha.

Peters, Hans 1994. Degree adverbs in Early Modern English. In Dieter Kastovsky (ed.) *Studies in Early Modern English*, 269-88. Berlin, New York: Mouton de Gruyter.

Quirk, Randolph, Sidney Greenbaum, Geoffrey Leech & Jan Svartvik 1985. *A comprehensive grammar of the English language*. London, New York: Longman.

Sasaki, Akemi 2009. Plain infinitival constructions in John Evelyn's *Diary*. *Studies in Modern English* 25. Tokyo: The Modern English Association, 135-40.

Strang, Barbara Mary Hope 1970. *A history of English*. London: Methuen.

Wyld, Henry Cecil 1936. *A history of modern colloquial English*, Third Edition. Oxford: Blackwell.

The *Clerk's Tale*: Rewritten Griselda story

Hisayuki Sasamoto

Abstract

Chaucer's *Clerk's Tale* is the tale that the Clerk of Oxford narrates the story of patient Griselda, which was first put on Tenth tale (i.e. last tale) of Tenth day in the *Decameron* by Boccaccio. Petrarch was strongly impressed on this story written by his friend Boccaccio. He translated the story and placed it as the last letter of his *Epistolae Sentiles* (*XVII.3*) (*Historia Griseldis*, titled *De obedientia ac fide mythologia* (A Fable of Wifely Obedience and Faithfulness)), which was written in Latin prose for a wide audience. Afterwards Petrarch's tale became the model of the Griselda story, and then some versions of it were translated into French. J. Burke Severs established that Chaucer's principal sources for the *Clerk's Tale* were Petrarch's Latin *Historia Griseldis* and *Le Livre Briseldis*, an anonymous French translation of Petrarch.[1] The *Clerk's Tale* first seemed to follow Petrarch, but as the Clerk's narration advances, the borrowing from *Le Liver Griseldis* has increased. Chaucer adapted those sources so that the audience could feel pity to the miserable circumstances of gentle and submissive Griselda without any fault, although he portrayed her perseverance, too. Especially the expression of emotion of the characters is his original representation.

1. Introduction

The patient story of Griselda was well known in the latter period of the Middle Ages. Chaucer's *Clerk's Tale* is the first English rendering of the Griselda story, which exerted a great influence on many other writers and readers in the Western Europe by the end of the fourteenth century.[2] Especially it was paid attention by three main writers—Petrarch, Boccaccio and Chaucer—in those days.

Boccaccio raised this narrative from a folktale into a literary form. He wrote this narrative in his native Italian and put it on Tenth tale (last tale) of Tenth day (last day) in his *Decameron* (1353).

After twenty years since the *Decameron* was made public, Petrarch noticed and was strongly impressed on this story written by his friend Boccaccio. He translated this Boccaccio's version into a Latin prose

---

[1] Severs (1942: 251).
[2] Bronfman (1994: 7-22).

letter (*Epistolae Seniles XVII.3*) in turn. His first translation was in 1373; he revised it in 1374, and the revised version was used as Chaucer's primary source for the *Clerk's Tale*. And during the last 25 years in the fourteenth century, the Petrarch's version written in Latin was translated into French language.

There are two French prose translations from Petrarch. One is the anonymous *Le Livre Griseldis* (c.1390), which served as Chaucer's second source for the *Clerk's Tale*. This work is a straightforward translation of Petrarch's tale. The other French translation is in Philippe de Mézières's *Le livre de la vertu et du sacrement de mariage et du reconfort des dames mariees*, written between 1384 and 1389 for Jeanne of Chatillon. Philippe's version, which was translated from the version revised by Petrarch in 1374, became the source for a short prose retelling in *Le Menagier de Paris* (c.1393).

The Clerk in his Prologue of the *Clerk's Tale* acknowledged that the authority of the *Clerk's Tale* is from Petrarch.

> I wol yow telle a tale which that I
> Lerned at Padowe of a worthy clerk,
> As preved by his wordes and his werk.
> He is now deed and nayled in his cheste;
> I prey to God so yeve his soule reste!
>   "Fraunceys Petrak, the lauriat poete,
> Highte this clerk, whos rethorike sweete
> Enlumyned al Ytaille of poetrie,"   (26-33)[3]

Though Boccaccio had put the Griselda story in the *Decameron* before Petrarch, Chaucer not only did not mention it but also never told that the *Decameron* was written by Boccaccio. I do not know why he has never given even Boccaccio's name, although Chaucer has frequently made use of his other works, too.

Anyway, at least Chaucer knew the anonymous *Le Livre Griseldis*. He followed faithfully Petrarch's Latin version (1374) in the starting part of the *Clerk's Tale*. As the story advances, he made use of Petrarch's Latin version and the anonymous *Le Livre Griseldis*. But he did not change quite the plot and the tone of the story, though he made adaptation, expatiation and additions of his own.

---

[3] All quotations of the *Clerk's Tale* are from Benson (1987).

I am not sure when Chaucer wrote the story of Griselda, but probably he had already finished writing it before he began to write the *Canterbury Tales* about 1387. And it is presumed that he put this story as the *Clerk's Tale* into it.

For these reasons, first I would like to give consideration to their intentions: how each of three important writers in the fourteenth century wrote the story of Griselda. Next, I will examine characteristics of the Griselda story rewritten as the *Clerk's Tale*.

2. The background of Griselda story

The origin of the Griselda story is a version of Cupid and Psyche myth. Although the original story is told by Apuleius in *The Golden Ass*, the best known example of the story is probably the Scandinavian fairy tale, "East of the Sun and West of the Moon."

In "New Light on the Origin of Griselda Story" Bettridge and Utley hypothesize that a Greek-Turkish tale titled "The Patience of a Princess" is a far more likely candidate than Cupid and Psyche.[4]

As the story of this patient wife Griselda was developing the literary expression, the form of the story changed. One of the most important points it changed is that supernatural element was removed. Supernatural lovers turned into human lovers, so that the imbalance like the relationship of supernatural being and human being was dispelled. And the imbalance changed into that of the social class. It was Boccaccio that enhanced the Griselda story to narrative literature. While a version of this story that might have been known to Boccaccio has not yet been found, "The patience of a Princess" appears to be a more promising folk source for the Griselda story than the Cupid and Psyche myth. The written literary form of the Griselda story began with the final story of Boccaccio's *Decameron* (1353).

In the *Decameron*, the topic of the last day was about generosity, so the Griselda story should be an example of generosity. The narrator of the last tale of the last day was Dioneo, who was often giving the daily topics ironic twists. Before he began his tale, Dioneo told that his tale was not about 'generous virtue,' but was about 'matta bestialitade' (crazy brutality), and he warned that nobody should follow this example.

---

[4] Bronfman (1994: 11-13).

Boccaccio took up this Griselda story from the interpretation of novella, and dealt it with vulgar and somewhat obscene attitude. He also figured it out so that it could be consistent like novella. For example, Marquis Gualtieri went abruptly to Griselda's father at the day of marriage and did not offer him that he wanted to make her his wife. He had settled it with him beforehand. He had her new clothes made fitting a same girl in stature previously to put it on her.

On the contrary Petrarch wrote it as a parable and changed it to a kind of religious and moral tale. He took up this story from noble, moral, and mostly pious point of view. He regarded Griselda as an exemplary model not everybody can follow. Therefore he wrote it as the reading that encourages worldly women to be faithful to their chastity, in defiance of various temptations like Griselda.

Chaucer followed Petrarch in terms of the plot and the tone of the story, but he emphasized a happy conclusion like romance. He explained the poverty of Griselda in detail and laid emphasis on her virtue like saint, differing from Petrarch. And then he showed the dramatic validity, expressed the pity of Griselda with pathos, and recognized the unreasonableness of the story, namely, the unreality of it.

3. Comparison between Boccaccio and Petrarch

Comparing Boccaccio with Petrarch in a little more detail, they showed a difference of opinion when they draw a conclusion of the story of Griselda.

Boccaccio portrayed Gualtieri as a bad fellow of sheer nonsense and an unintelligent person, and treated him as if he were to blame. As he was unbearable of obvious insincerity of this story, he may have narrated what he felt through Dioneo, using ambiguous but obscene expressions.

When Petrarch finished the story of Griselda, he wrote with respect and words of praise that she endured patiently her distress.

He regarded her fortitude and chastity as an example how human should behave to God. His Griselda indicates the soul of human that sticks to its fortitude undergoing many ordeals, and his marquis Valterius suggests the agent of divine test.

Boccaccio concentrated the inhuman deed of the marquis Gualtieri,

The *Clerk's Tale*: Rewritten Griselda story   323

and portrayed him more strictly and cruelly than Petrarch's Valterius. Boccaccio emphasized the inhumanity of Gualtieri, but Petrarch showed Valterius to be somewhat more normal and kind person than Gualtieri of Boccaccio.

Boccaccio was conscious of no ordinary character of the marquis Gualtieri.

> Che si potrà dir qui, se non che anche nelle povere case piovono dal cielo de' divini spiriti, come nelle reali di quegli che sarien più degni di guardar porci, che d'avere sopra uomini signoria?[5]
> (What more needs to be said, except that celestial spirits may sometimes descend even into the houses of the poor, whilst there are those in royal palaces who would be better employed as swineherds than as rulers of men?)[6]

This remark that sounds sarcastic could be taken as a decisive conclusion of Boccaccio toward the marquis Gualtieri.

Petrarch used the first half of the story to admire Griselda, and omitted fairly his dissatisfaction about Valterius. Though Petrarch was not able to approve of the deed of Valterius, he did nothing but censure him suggestively, not clearly as follows:

> Cepit, ut fit, interim Valterium, cum iam ablactata esset infantula, mirabilis quedam quam laudabilis (doctiores iudicent) cupiditas, sat expertam care fidem coniugis experiendi âltius et iterum atque iterum retentandi.[7]
> (In the meanwhile, it so happened, when this little daughter had been weaned, that Valterius was seized with a desire more strange than laudable—so the more experienced may decide—to try more deeply the fidelity of his dear wife, which had been sufficiently made known by experience, and to test it again and again.)[8]

Surely the view of Petrarch is quite different from that of Boccaccio. Petrarch added the virtuous life of Griselda and especially her appearance of behaving filially toward her father that lacked in the *Decameron*, though she led her strict life. Petrarch's Grisildis engaged

---

[5] The *Decameron* X. 10, from Severs (1942: 13).
[6] McWilliam (1972: 824).
[7] Bryan and Dempster (1941: 310). Severs (1942: 268).
[8] Miller (1977: 144-5). It is mine that changed 'Walter' into 'Valterius.'

324   *Hisayuki Sasamoto*

in more dialogues with people, obeyed her husband's will more faithfully than Boccaccio. She showed stronger affections for both her husband and her children than Boccaccio's Griselda.

After all, there is a large difference in the literary style between
these two works. Boccaccio's work has the immediacy of the situation,
the conciseness, and the simplicity that concludes events more speedily and more effectively. The adapted story by Boccaccio seems to be
superior in narrative technique to Petrarch.

On the other hand, the interest of Petrarch was not the story itself
Boccaccio regarded as important, but was rather the disposition of
characters, especially that of Griselda, and the moral by experience.
He paid attention to her thought and her feelings, laid bare her heart,
and explained it fully.

4. Characteristics of the *Clerk's Tale*

When Chaucer tried to write the story of Griselda, I already told that
he made use of Petrarch's Latin version and anonymous *Le Livre
Griseldis*. For this reason the *Clerk's Tale* was naturally similar to
Petrarch's plot and expression. But he tried to create the Griselda story
of his own by adding and enlarging many important parts. As a result
it raised verisimilitude of the patient Griselda.

There are signs that Chaucer altered it so that his readers and his
audience could feel more sorrowful and have more gentle emotions
than Petrarch. He also brought it into sympathetic understanding of
ordinary people from the difficult religious and moral problem of
Petrarch.

The emotion arousing pathos is remarkable in the *Clerk's Tale*, even
if he must depend on the tendency of the age.

For example, when a sergeant first came to her, the account of
Griselda referred to the conversion to this emotion. In *Le Livre
Griseldis* after the heroine handed her child in silence except telling
him to bring it up carefully, she was apparently imperturbable.

> 'Et de plain front prist son enffant et le regarda un pou et le baisa et
> beneist, et fist le signe de la croix, et le bailla audit sergent.[9]
> (And with a calm face, she took up her child and looked at her for a little

---

[9]   Bryan and Dempster (1941: 313). Severs (1942: 271).

The *Clerk's Tale*: Rewritten Griselda story   325

while, kissed and blessed her, made the sign of the cross, and handed her over to the sergeant.)[10]

But Chaucer seems to treat this episode as important. The utterance of Chaucer's Griselda moves people to greater pity, and the Clerk describes in detail her sorrowful parting scene from her son, and he appeals to people's sympathy.

> "Fareweel my child! I shal thee nevere see.
> But sith I thee have marked with the croys
> Of thilke Fader—blessed moote he be!—
> That for us deyde upon a croys of tree,
> Thy soule, litel child, I hym bitake,
> For this nyght shaltow dyen for my sake."
>   I trowe that to a norice in this cas
> It had been hard this reuthe for to se;
> Wel myghte a mooder thanne han cryd "allas!"
> But nathelees so sad stidefast was she
> That she endured al adversitee,
> And to the sergeant mekely she sayde,
> "Have heer agayn youre litel yonge mayde."   (555-67)

Chaucer changed ordinary expressions of French version to her speech scene expressing her sentiment directly. Consequently the story became to take on more realistic touch.

In these stanzas Chaucer evoked sentiment of audience and induced them to feelings of pathos, and gave sophisticated atmosphere for the story of Griselda:

> "I wol no thyng, ne nyl no thyng, certayn,
> But as yow list. Naught greveth me at al,
> Though that my doughter and my sone be slayn—
> At youre comandement, this is to sayn."   (646-49)

And then he aroused emotions of pity by making Griselda say "Lat me nat lyk a worm go by the weye. / Remembre yow, myn owene lord so deere, / I was youre wyf, though I unworthy weere" (880-82).

These passages are Chaucer's additional parts. Thus every time Griselda undergoes many ordeals, he emphasizes her perseverance as well as her gentility and submissiveness, tingeing with pathos.

---

[10] Correale and Hamel (2002: 152).

The expression of such human emotions was what was incompatible with folk tale and what was not produced from both Petrarch and his French version. It became the important point of interest in Chaucer. Especially his comment that explains the inhuman treatment of Walter toward Griselda is applicable to it. This is the passage with which Chaucer enlarged French version.

> But now of wommen wolde I axen fayn
> If thise assayes myghte nat suffise?
> What koude a sturdy housbonde moore devyse
> To preeve hir wyfhod and hir stedefastnesse,
> And he continuynge evere in sturdinesse?   (696-700)

This Griselda story the Clerk narrates does not bear resemblance to either Petrarch or his French version. But the blame for Walter's behaviour and the unfavourable description of Walter's character resembles closely to Gualtieri of Boccaccio. You can see that there is some similar element at least between Chaucer and Boccaccio.

Besides, the Clerk narrates as follows:

> But ther been folk of swich condicion
> That whan they have a certein purpos take,
> They kan nat stynte of hire entencion,
> But, right as they were bounden to that stake,
> They wol nat of that firste purpos slake.
> Right so this markys fulliche hath purposed
> To tempte his wyf as he was first disposed.   (701-07)

Though marquis Walter possessed by an unreasonable fixed idea tries to test Griselda, he, as a condition for marriage, held Griselda to his promise that she would never complain whatever may happen and whatever trial she may undergo. Whatever unreasonable things he may think, she must always undergo these trials keeping his promise.

There was a close connection between them, but Chaucer appears to attach no importance of their promises. When they encountered each other, Walter forced Griselda to swear to obey him perfectly.

Chaucer portrayed Griselda as a wife not only protesting nothing but taking no way except enduring, and yet he depicted her as a gentle, discreet woman accepting quietly sorrow and humiliation, in spite of not having any rewarded hope. Although Petrarch may regard her as a symbol of soul enduring patiently worldly hardships as ordeals,

Chaucer rather made her a noble, courtly ideal lady of elegance, of good manners and with discretion as a living person. By changing like this, the climax of the *Clerk's Tale* became the moment deep human emotion floats, and it became to be portrayed as a gentle tale. The scene Griselda's children are taken away by a sergeant, the scene she requests one clothes when she leaves the court, and the scene she reunions with her children she gave up for dead, all excite audience's sympathy and make them sentimental. In the last scene she meets again her children, the Clerk exclaims with admiration:

> O which a pitous thyng it was to se
> Hir swownyng and hire humble voys to heere! (1086-87)

This phrase "a pitous thyng" is a crucial phrase for the Clerk. And when people standing beside Griselda saw her holding her two children tightly in a swoon, the Clerk narrates:

> O many a teere on many a pitous face
> Doun ran of hem that stooden hire bisyde;
> Unnethe abouten hire myghte they abyde.   (1104-06).

These passages show that he expects strongly that readers or audience affect their feelings. This will be the evident proof of Chaucer's trying to express characters more realistically and vividly than Petrarch and Boccaccio.

Chaucer did not portray Walter pleasantly, but he could not depict him as a bad person. In the beginning of the story he described Walter as a young and fine ruler, but showed that he had essentially egocentric character like a spoiled child.

Walter took Griselda to wife of his own accord and was proud that he was right in his choice by her popularity and graces. While he was proud of his noble wife, he wanted to try her ability. So he contrived rigorous tests to know the end of her tether how far she can undergo his trials. But he was not a nasty and cruel person by nature. When he took away their two children from his wife, he left her with a sad look. When he let her leave her family home, he felt it unbearable to remain there any longer out of pity. He, nevertheless, tried his wife. Though he loved her, he tried her as if possessed by something. He loved her as he please. Therefore even when everything went well, he did not suffer from his guilty conscience at all. Walter did not look like a surrogate of God, such as Marquis Valterius in Petrarch. Actually Griselda's father, Janicula, who is a poor and lowly person, looks to be more a dignified, fine-looking man than Walter. As Chaucer portrayed Walter as a mediocre person one often sees, it accelerated pity for Griselda all the more.

Chaucer rewrote newly to enhance her gentle obedience as well as her elegant behaviour. Her poor but honest and diligent life suggested the biblical background.

> A fewe sheep, spynnynge, on feeld she kepte;
> She wolde noght been ydel til she slepte.   (223-24)

There is the atmosphere of the Virgin Mary in Griselda's spinner or shepherdess. In those days the Virgin Mary was often portrayed as a spinner or a shepherdess.

The following passages are like the scene of the Annunciation and the Nativity.

> But hye God somtyme senden kan
> His grace into a litel oxes stalle;   (206-07)

This was sometimes taken up as an example which adapted Petrarch's version. Petrarch's version is as follows:

> sed ut pauperum quoque tuguria non numquam gratia celestis invisit,[11]
> (heavenly grace, which sometimes lights on even the poorest dwellings)[12]

This also reminds me of Boccaccio's somewhat sarcastic remark stated above (p. 323).

The fact that Chaucer inserted the image of 'litel oxes stalle' (i.e. the cow shed), which was never used by either Boccaccio or Petrarch, improved the effect of Griselda's nobleness and holiness despite her bred in the rustic and rude circumstances.

Griselda was a young woman of tender age with 'vertuous beautee' (211), but a mature and serious spirit was enclosed in the breast of virginity.

---

[11] Bryan and Dempster (1941: 302).
[12] Correale and Hamel (2002: 114).

Her beauty or her absolute discretion is what the Virgin Mary possessed. She was a person of firm character and a person of elegance of manners like Mary. Though she was poor, undereducated, and did never get a chance to come in contact with the refined society, she learned good manners and discretion, had truly ladylike elegance. As she did not lose these virtues, she was loved by all the people. She served her husband as faithfully and wholeheartedly as she did her old father, acted to him calmly, spoke to him softly and was true to him. She calmed people's grudges prudently, settled their disputes, and corrected their errors. She did not show her pride and gorgeousness for all her high rank of marchioness, but she had always plenty of prudence and discretion. She was extremely patient, and full of affection and modesty.

The Clerk narrated the story of Griselda using words of sympathy. He admired her virtue without criticizing a word, and had pity and compassion for her. He talked about her patience emphasizing pathos. Nevertheless he recognized that the story of Griselda was the unreasonable story of the situation that is improbable in real life. This story can be treated as the subject matter of fiction, but not as a real possible thing. As Griselda's patience is typical of patience, ordinary people cannot stand such patience. Her behaviour is unnatural. But these three writers in the fourteenth century did not think this story as unreasonable as nowadays. Petrarch was deeply affected by the narrative of Boccaccio. So he wrote the story in Latin so that it could be understood by not only people who were able to read Italian but a wide audience. Translation books from Petrarch's version appeared a lot in France afterward. Modern readers or critics will feel hatred toward this story, but it seems that people in those days were very interested in it. Probably one of reasons why Chaucer picked out this story would be the sentimental and religious tendency that was in a wide circulation about that time. Such a patience as Griselda experienced would be accepted as what belongs to the logic of normal things. In the middle ages it was necessary for religious teachings as well as many relations of society to endure obediently. Wives endured their husbands, subjects in fief did their feudal lords, and followers did their masters. Griselda was a subordinate as well as a wife to her husband. Her husband was a ruler of a country called marquis fief, even if it was a small country, and he was even an absolute ruler. He wielded absolute power over his subjects and the people of his land.

On the other hand, the society of Western Europe in Chaucer's age was beginning to flow. Although relations or connections between master and servant were still stronger, the parent-child ties and the marital ties were getting strong. So the absolute relation between master and servant was breaking down gradually. Therefore it is understandable that Boccaccio regarded this story as a special one, and also that Petrarch reached an idea that this was an example of abnormal patience we cannot repeat again. Chaucer recognized Walter's deeds like trying his wife to be unnecessary and out of date. And he regarded them as mistaken doings. So he inserted the following phrases unwritten in his authorities about Walter's behaviour.

> He hadde assayed hire ynogh bifore,
> And foond hire evere good; what neded it
> Hire for to tempte, and alwey moore and moore,
> Though som men preise it for a subtil wit?
> But as for me, I seye that yvele it sit
> To assaye a wyf whan that it is no nede,
> And putten hire in angwyssh and in drede.   (456-62)

The Clerk criticized and blamed Walter who tried Griselda only for the purpose of trying his wife, though he did not have any doubt about his wife.

But after he finished the story of Griselda and made somewhat comment on it, he changed from the cynical but serious manner of talking to the frivolous tone of voice. For example, he ironically compares women to coin as follows:

> It were ful hard to fynde now-a-dayes
> In al a toun Grisilidis thre or two;
> For if that they were put to swiche assayes,
> The gold of hem hath now so badde alayes
> With bras, that thogh the coyne be fair at ye,
> It wolde rather breste a-two than plye.   (1164-69)

His frivolous tone between lines 1163 and 1212, interestingly enough, bears a remarkable resemblance to the mood that Boccaccio changed to the frivolous note with obscene expression, immediately after he finished the story of Griselda. Boccaccio speaks thus:

The *Clerk's Tale*: Rewritten Griselda story   331

Al quale non sarebbe forse stato male investito d'essersi abbattuto ad
una che, quando fuor di casa l'avesse in camicia cacciata, s'avesse sì ad
un altro fatto scuotere il pelliccione, che riuscita ne fosse una bella
roba.[13]
(Who perhaps might have deemed himself to have made no bad invest-
ment, had he chanced upon one, who, having been turned out of his
house in her shift, had found means so to dust the pelisse of another as
to get herself thereby a fine robe.)[14]

And the same are the passages (ll. 696-707) Chaucer added of criticizing husbands for their obstinacy and bigotry, too. These manners
of talking are closer to Boccaccio than Petrarch. Perhaps Boccaccio
and Chaucer may have a command of frivolous note in common.

The conversion of mood is also characterized by that of verse form
(from rhyme royal verse <ababbcc> to six stanzas rhymed verse
<ababcb>) in the Lenvoy de Chaucer (ll. 1177-1212). The mood of his
sarcastic advice to the Wife of Bath as well as women who have same
opinions as she is far from the lyric mood in the story of Griselda.

The Clerk turns into satirical mood by changing to the popular way
of his talking.

Ye archwyves, stondeth at defense,
Syn ye be strong as is a greet camaille;
Ne suffreth nat that men yow doon offense.
And sklendre wyves, fieble as in bataille,
Beth egre as is a tygre yond in Ynde;
Ay clappeth as a mille, I yow consaille.   (1195-200)

The rhyme of the Envoy changes to the verse with colloquial vivid
style. Here there is a feeling that made a sudden change from the lyric
narration of the Clerk in the Griselda story that had still the atmosphere
of the fairy tale. Consequently the Clerk advanced from the verbal
description of a noble Griselda, who was one of the ideal women
believed by medieval church leaders and anti-feminists, to the ironical
controversy of the image of real women instructed by the Wife of Bath
that insists to dominate over his husband in marriage.

The *Clerk's Tale*—the story of the wife bearing up under heartless
treatment of the husband—is antithetical to the *Wife of Bath's Tale*—

---

[13] The *Decameron* X. 10, from Severs (1942: 12).
[14] Rigg, vol.2 (1930: 343).

332 *Hisayuki Sasamoto*

the story that the domination of wife over husband leads to happy marriage life.

5. Conclusion

The unbelievable submission of Griselda will be able to gain a better understanding from medieval point of view. But even in the fourteenth century, as the Clerk admits, a person like Griselda was one in thousand. The story ending with her sudden restoration of happiness appealed strongly to medieval audience as means of remedy to the ominous action of Fortune. Griselda gave great impression on even suspicious people as a symbol of womanly nobility and fortitude. Chaucer enhanced this impression by his good power of expression and the power of description which excites pity.

References

Baugh, Albert C. (ed.) 1963. *Chaucer's major poetry*. New Jersey: Prentice-Hall.

Benson, Larry D. (ed.) 1987. *The Riverside Chaucer*, 3rd edn. Boston: Houghton Mifflin.

Bronfman, Judith 1994. *Chaucer's Clerk's Tale: The Griselda story received, rewritten, illustrated*. New York & London: Garland Publishing.

Bryan, W.F. & Germaine Dempster (eds.) 1941. *Sources and analogues of Chaucer's Canterbury Tales*. Chicago: University of Chicago Press. Reprint. New York: Humanities Press, 1958.

Chadeayne, Lee & Paul Gottwald (trans.), Francis Lee Utley (intro.) 1970. Max Lüthi: *Once upon a time: On the nature of fairy tales*. Bloomington: Indiana University Press 1976.

Cooper, Helen 1983. *The structure of the Canterbury Tales*. London and Athens, Ga.: University of Georgia Press.

Cooper, Helen 1989. *Oxford guide to Chaucer: The Canterbury Tales*. Oxford: Clarendon Press.

Correale, R.M. & Mary Hamel (eds.) 2002. *Sources and analogues of the Canterbury Tales I*. D.S. Brewer: Cambridge.

Ellis, Steve 2005. *Chaucer: An Oxford guide*. Oxford: Oxford University Press.

Frank, R.W., Jr 1986. The *Canterbury Tales* III: Pathos. In Piero Boitani & Jill Mann (eds.), *The Cambridge Chaucer companion*. Cambridge: Cambridge University Press.

French, R.D. 1947. *A Chaucer handbook*, 2nd edn. New York: Appleton-Century-Croft.

Huppè, B.F. 1967. *A reading of the Canterbury Tales*. Revised. New York:

State University of New York.

Kellogg, A. 1972. *Chaucer, Langland, Arthur: Essays in Middle English literature*. New Jersey: Rutgers University Press.

Kirkpatrick, Robin 1983. The Griselda story in Boccaccio, Petrarch, and Chaucer. In Piero Boitani (ed.), *Chaucer and the Italian Trecento*. Cambridge: Cambridge University Press.

Kolve, V.A. & Glending Olson (eds.) 2005. *The Canterbury Tales: Fifteen Tales and the General Prologue: Authoritative text, sources and backgrounds, criticism*. 2nd edn. New York and London: W.W. Norton.

Mann, Jill (ed.) 2005. *The Canterbury Tales*. London: Penguin Books.

McWilliam, G. H. (trans.) 1972. *The Decameron*. Harmondsworth: Penguin.

Miller, Robert P. (ed.) 1977. *Chaucer: Sources and backgrounds*. New York: Oxford University Press.

Pearsall, Derek 1985. *The Canterbury Tales*. London: Unwin Hyman.

Rigg, J.M. (trans.) 1930. *The Decameron,* 2 vols. (Everyman's Library) London: J. M. Dent & Sons.

Severs, J. Burke 1942. *The literary relationships of Chaucer's Clerkes Tale*. Yale University Press. Reprint. Hamden Conn.: Archon Books, 1972.

Whittock, Trevor 1968. *A reading of the Canterbury Tales*. Cambridge: Cambridge University Press.

Winny, James (ed.) 1966. *The Clerk's Prologue and Tale*. Cambridge: Cambridge University Press.

Authenticity and consciousness representation in Defoe's *Moll Flanders* and *Roxana*

Eri Shigematsu

Abstract

Authentic writing was expected in the early eighteenth century, and therefore Daniel Defoe presents all of his autobiographical narratives not as "stories" but as personal "histories." There also was a growing interest in individual minds in this period, and indeed, Defoe is more interested in his characters' psychology than in their social and economic milieu (Novak 2000: 248). This paper aims to demonstrate how Defoe makes his narratives *seem authentic* in terms of representation of consciousness. As a case study, it focuses on the discourse depicting some crucial psychological experiences of the heroines in *Moll Flanders* (1722) and *Roxana* (1724), which were actually believed to be real "history" until 1775 (Downie 1997: 257). There is a critical view that Defoe's free indirect style is restricted to the rendering of utterances (Fludernik 1996: 171). This paper challenges this view, showing that Defoe uses free indirect thought as well as other categories of thought representation to represent the consciousness of the heroines. It consequently reveals that Defoe's narratives seem authentic through a formal distinction in consciousness representation between mimetic categories (e.g. free indirect thought) and diegetic categories (e.g. thought report).

1. Introduction

As is well known, all Daniel Defoe's fictional narratives are presented as records of facts (Mullan 1996: xii). Defoe's fictions except for *Robinson Crusoe* (1719) and *Colonel Jack* (1722), according to Downie (1997: 257), were believed to be genuine autobiographies until the late eighteenth century. The editors in Defoe's fictions always claim that they are presenting a true history. In the preface to *Moll Flanders* (1722), for example, the editor says "it will be hard for a private History to be taken for Genuine" (Defoe 2011 [1722]: 3), and yet emphasises that the author, that is the heroine Moll, is "suppos'd to be writing her own History" (Defoe 2011 [1722]: 3). Likewise, in the preface to *Roxana* (1724), the editor presents it as "*the History of this* Beautiful Lady" (Defoe 2008 [1724]: 1, the italics here as well as in the later examples from Defoe's texts are original), and clearly states that it is *"not a Story, but a History"* (Defoe 2008 [1724]: 1). In both prefaces, the editor emphasises the factuality of the narrative. Why should it be a true "history"? As Segel puts it, "men have always tended to divide experience into the real — life — and the unreal — art —" and only the real is considered to be valuable (1972: 50). This seems very much to hold true in the early eighteenth century. Fabricated stories cannot be taken seriously because they are not improvable or instructive (Segel 1972; McKeon 1987). In point of fact, in the sequel to *Robinson Crusoe*, which is titled *Serious Reflections During the Life and Surprising Adventures of Robinson Crusoe* (1720), the protagonist Crusoe argues that inventing a story is a crime and "it is a sort of Lying that makes a great Hole in the Heart" (Defoe 1720: 113). Therefore, "story" is regarded as invented human art, whereas "history" is supposed to be representation of real life. More specifically, in the case of *Moll Flanders*, for example, if the authorship is ascribed to Defoe, it is a made-up story, but if it is ascribed to Moll, it becomes a true account of her life. This implies that male authorship signifies "artifice" and "verisimilitude," but female authorship signifies "naturalness" and "authenticity" (see Bray 2003: 30-31). The term "authenticity" refers to the truthfulness or factuality of the narrative, and "verisimilitude" to an *air* or *effect* of truthfulness in this paper.

It is also important to note that "Defoe was surely interested in rendering the social and political milieu in which his characters moved, but he was always more interested in what went on in his characters' minds" (Novak 2000: 248). In his seminal book *The Rise of the Novel* (1957), Watt insists that what he calls the "formal realism," which Defoe and Richardson applied "much more completely than had been done before" (1957: 33), is based on an "immediate imitation of individual experience" (1957: 32). Defoe creates "an illusion of the real" (Novak 2000: 248), depicting the contemporary period from the point of view of his individual characters. Defoe's realism has often been associated with the depicted details of the external world in which his characters live. According to Novak (2000), however, Defoe's formal realism is also evidently visible in the representations of his characters' consciousness. Kawasaki (2007) and Konigsberg (1985) similarly point out that Defoe intentionally uses revolutionary narrative techniques for representing individual psychology to capture realistic images both objectively (from outside) and subjectively (from within). Defoe's ability to render images of the real and represent his characters' consciousness by using new narrative techniques is the principal reason why he has been regarded as one of the most important figures in English literature.

With these points in mind, this paper looks into the effect of authenticity in Defoe's fiction in terms of representation of consciousness. It aims to reveal the ways in which Defoe makes his narratives *seem authentic*. In order to present his narratives as "histories," Defoe used some narrative techniques to make his stories verisimilar, which will be explored and illustrated in the following sections.

2. Authenticating device: representation of consciousness

Authentication has been associated with a kind of realism in narratives. In his study of the realism in Chaucer, Bloomfield (1964) suggests a type of realism called "authenticating realism." This kind of realism is used "to avoid the accusation of lying," and is "fundamentally concerned with the truth-claim of the narrative" (Bloomfield 1964: 338). He further argues that "the suspension of disbelief is a fundamental process" for the reader "to know that the story is true or presumably true" (1964: 339). Disbelief is suspended with various narrative techniques of realistic representation, such as titles, prefaces, first-person narrators, actual names and localities, and so on, which he calls "authenticating devices" (1964: 340-41). These devices are used at different levels of the narrative structure: the author authenticates the narrative by putting the truth-claim of the narrative on "the level of the real world" or "the authenticating level," when he/she chooses authenticating devices such as titles, chapter headings, prefaces and first-person narrators outside the storyworld (Bloomfield 1964: 340). Once the author hands over the role of putting forward the narrative to the narrator, however, different authenticating devices begin to function as narrative techniques for making it seem authentic. The narrator manipulates both *what* details in the storyworld are to be represented and *how* they should be represented. At the authenticating level, one of the important authenticating devices in Defoe's narratives is the first-person autobiographical form, which was a common way to present an invented story as a true history in the early eighteenth century (see Konigsberg 1985: 21).

Defoe's authentication is also artistically achieved at the level of the narrator's discourse. What this paper focuses on is the ways in which fictional consciousness is represented in narrative in order to make what is represented seem authentic. In other words, this paper deals with internal realism or "psychological verisimilitude" (Fludernik 1996: 38) rather than external realism. Consciousness can be represented in various ways in narrative. Figure 1 below shows Leech and Short's thought representation sliding scale based on form and shift in point of view between narrator and character. Note that in the case of first-person autobiographical narratives, narrator and character are the same person and they are expressed in the same pronoun "I." Stanzel (1984) calls these two I's — that is, "I" as narrator and "I" as character — "the narrating self" and "the experiencing self." Although these two selves are the same person, "they do not share the same knowledge and they do not share the same time and space" (Galbraith 1994: 125), because they are the different phases of the self. As Cohn (1978: 143) argues, the narrating self's relationship to the experiencing self corresponds to a narrator's relationship to a character in third-person narratives. In first-person autobiographical narratives, therefore, point of view shifts between the two selves.

Narrator's point of view			Character's point of view		
N	**NRTA**	**IT**	**FIT**	**DT**	**FDT**

N	Narration	I was with her.
NRTA	Narrator's Representation of Thought Act	I wondered about her feelings.
IT	Indirect Thought	I wondered if she was happy with me.
FIT	Free Indirect Thought	Was she happy with me?
DT	Direct Thought	I wondered, 'Is she happy with me?'
FDT	Free Direct Thought	'Is she happy with me?'

Figure 1. Leech and Short's (1981) thought representation model[1]

---

[1] The example sentences are mine. They represent first-person examples of each category. See Leech and Short (2007 [1981]) for the prototypical examples of each category in third-person narratives.

In Leech and Short's sliding scale, point of view gradually shifts from the narrating self to the experiencing self towards the right end of the scale. In other words, at the left end, consciousness is represented *indirectly* or *mediately* through the narrating self's language, and more *directly* or *immediately* through the experiencing self's language with each step to the right. How are these categories which reflect different points of view in narrative used in Defoe's narratives to enhance the effect of authenticity? Close investigation into psychological scenes in *Moll Flanders* and *Roxana* will illustrate his narrative techniques for making the psychological experiences of his heroines seem authentic.

3. Psychological experiences in *Moll Flanders* and *Roxana*

This section now turns to consciousness representation in *Moll Flanders* and *Roxana*, focusing especially on the change in consciousness representation categories. According to Fludernik, Defoe's free indirect style "only represents *utterances*" (1996: 171, italics original). Contrary to this claim, I will show that the narrating selves in *Moll Flanders* and *Roxana* use varied categories of thought representation, including free indirect thought, in order to represent their past consciousness. The first example is taken from *Moll Flanders*. The passage represents Moll's agony in Newgate:

I was now fix'd indeed; 'tis impossible to describe the terror of my mind, when I was first brought in, and when I look'd round upon all the horrors of that dismal Place: I look'd on myself as lost, and that I had nothing to think of, but of going out of the World, and that with the utmost Infamy; the hellish Noise, the Roaring, Swearing and Clamour, the Stench and Nastiness, and all the dreadful croud of Afflicting things that I saw there; joyn'd together to make the Place seem an Emblem of Hell itself, and a kind of an Entrance into it.

Now I reproach'd myself with the many hints I had had, *as I have mentioned above*, from my own Reason, form the Sense of my good Circumstances, and of the many Dangers I had escap'd to leave off while I was well, and how I had withstood them all, and hardened my Thoughts against all Fear; it seem'd to me that I was hurried by an inevitable and unseen Fate to this Day of Misery, and that now I was to Expiate all my Offences at the Gallows, that I was now to give satisfaction to Justice with my Blood, and that I was come to the last Hour of

340   *Eri Shigematsu*

my Life, and of my Wickedness together: These things pour'd themselves in upon my Thoughts in a confus'd manner, and left me over-
whelm'd with Melancholly and Despair.

Then I repented heartily of all my Life past, but that Repentance
yielded me no Satisfaction, no Peace, no not in the least, because, *as I
said to myself*, it was repenting after the Power of farther Sinning was
taken away: I seem'd not to Mourn that I had committed such Crimes,
and for the Fact, as it was an Offence against God and my Neighbour;
but I mourn'd that I was to be punish'd for it, I was a Penitent as I
thought, not that I had sinn'd, but that I was to suffer, and this took away
all the Comfort, and even the hope of my Repentance in my own
Thoughts.

I got no sleep for several Nights or Days after I came into that wrech'd
Place, and glad I wou'd have been for some time to have died there, tho'
I did not consider dying as it ought to be consider'd neither, indeed noth-
ing could be fill'd with more horror to my Imagination than the very
Place, nothing was more odious to me than the Company that was there:
O! if I had but been sent to any Place in the World, and not to *Newgate*,
I should have thought myself happy. (Defoe 2011 [1722]: 228-29)

At the beginning of this passage, the narrating self says "'tis impossible to describe the terror of [her] mind." Such explicit inexpressibility,
according to Hardy, "articulates intensity of [emotional] experience"
(1985: 12, 22-23). The following analysis shows how the narrating self
articulates the strong and unutterable terror in the past. In the first paragraph, the psychology of the past self is represented through the
indirect representations of consciousness, such as psycho-narration
and internal narration. What is interesting here is that the proximal
deictic *now* co-occurs with the past tense at the beginning of this paragraph ("I was now fix'd indeed"), while the distal deictics *that* and
there are used to signify Newgate ("that dismal place," "there"). This
inconsistent use of deictic expressions implies that the two selves are
temporally close, but spatially distant. In other words, while she gradually enters into the consciousness of the past self, the narrating self
still cannot help but have a strong aversion to Newgate.

In the next paragraph, Moll's affliction continues to be represented
indirectly. However, the proximal deictics *now* and *this* are again used
in the indirect representations of consciousness ("Now I reproach'd
myself," "I was hurried by an inevitable and unseen Fate to this Day
of Misery," "now I was to Expiate all my Offences at the Gallows," "I

Authenticity and consciousness representation 341

was now to give satisfaction to Justice with my Blood"), which implies that the narrating self continues to stay psycho-temporally close to the experiencing self. The narrating self approaches the experiencing self more psychologically in the subsequent paragraph: the thoughts of the experiencing self are parenthetically introduced by the clauses, "as I said to myself" and "as I thought," which means that they are represented free-indirectly. The epistemic verb *seem* ("I seem'd not to Mourn that …") and the word *such* ("I had committed such Crimes") also reflect the point of view of the past self, signifying the fact that the narrating self is gradually and hazily remembering the traumatic psychological experiences in Newgate.

In the last paragraph, Newgate is again expressed with distal deictics ("that wrech'd Place," "to have died there," "the Company that was there"). What is different from the earlier part is that this time the deictic verb *come* is used as in "I came into that wrech'd Place." This means that the point of reference is in Newgate, and so the narrating self is psycho-spatially in Newgate, but at the same time, she is distant from Newgate as the use of distal deictics indicates. This contradicting use of spatial deictic expressions shows the even stronger aversion to Newgate that Moll still has in her mind. The repetitious use of negation ("nothing could be fill'd with," "nothing was more odious") indicates the inexpressibility of the terror, and finally, Moll's agony is represented through free indirect thought in the last sentence: "O! if I had but been sent to any Place in the World, and not to *Newgate*, I should have thought myself happy." This expresses her thought which might have been on the "threshold of verbalization" (Cohn 1978: 103), or in other words, the terror which Moll referred to as "impossible to describe" in words at the beginning of the passage. As such, the psychological tension between the two selves is represented through various forms of thought representation and also enhanced by the contradicting use of deictic expressions. This illustrates the natural shift in point of view in autobiographical memory as in real life. The imitation of "the temporal continuity of real beings, an existential relationship" (Cohn 1978: 144) in first-person narratives helps to make the representations of Moll's consciousness seem real, natural and hence authentic.

342   *Eri Shigematsu*

A similar authenticating effect is technically achieved in *Roxana*. In the passage below, the younger Roxana asks herself why she continues to be a whore even after she does not need to:

> ... yet the Sence of things, and the Knowledge I had of the World, and the vast Variety of Scenes that I had acted my Part in, began to work upon my Sences, and it came so very strong upon my Mind one Morning, when I had been lying awake some time in my Bed, as if somebody had ask'd me the Question, *What was I a Whore for now?* It occur'd naturally upon this Enquiry, that at first I yielded to the Importunity of my Circumstances, the Misery of which, the Devil dismally aggravated, to draw me to comply; for I confess, I had strong Natural Aversions to the Crime at first, partly owing to a virtuous Education, and partly to a Sence of Religion; but the Devil, and that greater Devil of Poverty, prevail'd;
> ...
> But not to dwell upon that now; this was a Pretence, and here was something to be said, tho' I acknowledge, it ought not to have been sufficient to me at all; but, I say, to leave that, all this was out of Doors; the Devil himself cou'd not form one Argument, or put one Reason into my Head *now*, that cou'd serve for an Answer, no, not so much as a pretended Answer to this Question, *Why I shou'd be a Whore now?*
> It had for a-while been a little kind of Excuse to me, that I was engag'd with this wicked old Lord, and that I cou'd not, in Honour, forsake him; but how foolish and absurd did it look, to repeat the Word Honour on so vile an Occasion? As if a Woman shou'd prostitute her Honour in Point of Honour; horrid Inconsistency; Honour call'd upon me to detest the Crime and the Man too, and to have resisted all the Attacks which from the beginning had been made upon my Virtue; and Honour, had it been consulted, wou'd have preserv'd me honest from the Beginning.
> For HONESTY and HONOUR, are the same.
> This, however, shews us with what faint Excuses, and with what Trifles we pretend to satisfie ourselves, and suppress the Attempts of Conscience in the Pursuit of agreeable Crime, and in the possessing those Pleasures which we are loth to part with.
> But this Objection wou'd now serve no longer; for my Lord had, in some sort, broke his Engagements (*I won't call it Honour again*) with me, and had so far slighted me, as fairly to justifie my entire quitting of him now; and so, as the Objection was fully answer'd, the Question remain'd still unanswer'd, *Why am I a Whore now?* ... but as Necessity first debauch'd me, and Poverty made me a Whore at the Beginning; so excess of Avarice for getting Money, and excess of Vanity, continued me in the Crime, not being able to resist the Flatteries of Great Persons; being call'd the finest Woman in *France*; being caress'd by a Prince;

Authenticity and consciousness representation 343

and afterwards I had Pride enough to expect, and Folly enough to believe, tho' indeed, without ground, by a Great Monarch. These were my Baits, these the Chains by which the Devil held me bound; and by which I was indeed, too fast held for any Reasoning that I was then Mistress of, to deliver me from.

But this was all over now; Avarice cou'd have no Pretence; I was out of the reach of all that Fate could be suppos'd to do to reduce me; now I was so far from Poor, or the Danger of it, that I had fifty Thousand Pounds in my Pocket at least; nay, I had the Income of fifty Thousand Pounds; for I had 2500 *l*. a Year coming in, upon very good Land-Security, besides 3 or 4000 *l*. in Money, which I kept by me for ordinary Occasions, and besides Jewels and Plate, and Goods, which were worth near 5000 *l*. more; these put together, when I ruminated on it all in my Thoughts, as you may be sure I did often, added Weight still to the Question, as above, and it sounded continually in my Head, what's next? *What am I a Whore for now?* (Defoe 2008 [1724]: 200-03)

In the first paragraph, the question is represented through free indirect thought when the experiencing self first asks herself. The past tense and the proximal deictic *now* co-occur in the question "*What was I a Whore for now?*" She tries to justify herself in the subsequent part, insisting that it was the devil of poverty that drew her into the crime ("the Misery of which, the Devil dismally aggravated, to draw me to comply," "but the Devil, and that greater Devil of Poverty, prevail'd"). In the second paragraph, however, her justification is counter-justified, because she is not poor any more. Here, the point of view of the experiencing self becomes gradually stronger, which is reflected in the co-occurrence of the past tense with the proximal deictic *now* ("But not to dwell upon that now," "or put one Reason into my Head *now*"). Because she cannot justify herself, the experiencing self questions herself again with a confused mind, which is reflected in the use of the auxiliary verb *should* ("*Why I shou'd be a Whore now?*"). It expresses her inability to formulate any reason for still being a whore. As the tense of the auxiliary verb *should* cannot be shifted further to the past here (it is not the back-shifted tense of *shall*), it is ambiguous whether it is free indirect thought and free direct thought, though it is more likely to be the former because the word order conforms to that of an indirect question.

In the next paragraph, the past self again tries to justify herself, explaining that honour was the reason for her crime. And then, her justification is duly objected to again. The experiencing self's thoughts are represented through free indirect thought with the past tense ("but how foolish and absurd did it look, to repeat the Word Honour on so vile an Occasion? ..."). After the gnomic expression "For HONESTY and HONOUR, are the same," however, the tense is shifted to the present ("shews," "pretend," "suppress," "are"). This indicates not only that these verbs are used gnomically, but also that the narrating self is entering more deeply into the consciousness of the past self. In the subsequent paragraph, though the tense is shifted back to the past, the point of view continues to be aligned with the past self, which is reflected in the use of the proximal deictic *now* with the past tense ("But this Objection wou'd now serve no longer," "and had so far slighted me, as fairly to justifie my entire quitting of him now"). She cannot help but completely admit that she has no reason to be a whore any more. This is reflected in the following question, *"Why am I a Whore now?"* Not only the temporal deictic adverb ("now"), but also the tense becomes proximal ("am"). The narrating self psychologically identifies with the experiencing self, and the unanswerable question becomes realistic to her in that she can never give a reasonable answer to the question.

Even though she cannot justify herself any more, the younger self still strives to make an excuse, saying that avarice and vanity were the causes of the crime. This is of course counter-justified again, because she is literally very rich when she asks the question. With the detailed information about her financial account ("for I had 2500 *l.* a Year coming in, upon very good Land-Security, besides 3 or 4000 *l.* in Money, which I kept by me for ordinary Occasions, and besides Jewels and Plate, and Goods, which were worth near 5000 *l.* more"), it becomes even more difficult to justify the crime. This naturally leads to the final question "what's next? *What am I a Whore for now?*," which is represented through free direct thought as in the previous question. What is different from the previous one is that another question, which is directed to the future, "what's next?," is added before the main question. This implies her secret willingness to continue the crime in the future as well as the impossibility of giving convincing justifications for it.

In sum, the question is represented more immediately towards the end of the passage. The change shows the process of her recognizing the problem realistically, and also that the narrating self cannot give an answer to the question even in retrospect. The psychological and existential relationship between the two selves shown by the change in thought representation categories promotes the effect of authenticity in this passage.

4. Summary

Defoe's internal realism or "psychological verisimilitude" (Fludernik 1996: 38) at the level of narrator's discourse is important for the embodiment of the subjective reality. It encourages the reader's involvement into the narrative by rendering immediate experiences of the character. Unlike authenticating realism which directly gives a truth-claim at the authenticating level, psychological realism does not directly claim the authenticity of the narrative, but enhances the effect of authenticity in that realistic representations of consciousness give credibility, plausibility and contemporaneity to the narrative. Although Defoe's psychological realism has been emphasised by some critics, his narrative techniques for representing characters' psychology do not seem to have been fully explored. As the analyses have shown, the effect of authenticity can be examined in terms of representation of consciousness. The narrating self can enhance the sense of authenticity by using various consciousness representation categories. The change in modes of consciousness representation linguistically embodies the existential continuity between the two selves. This internal tension between the two selves increases the impression that it is a true account of the life of the "I."

References

Bloomfield, Morton 1964. Authenticating realism and the realism of Chaucer. *Thought* 39(3): 335-58.

Bray, Joe 2003. *The epistolary novel: Representations of consciousness.* London and New York: Routledge.

Cohn, Dorrit 1978. *Transparent minds: Narrative modes for presenting consciousness in fiction.* Princeton: Princeton University Press.

Defoe, Daniel 1720. *Serious reflections during the life and surprising adventures of Robinson Crusoe.* London: W. Taylor.

Defoe, Daniel 2011 [1722]. *Moll Flanders*. Oxford: Oxford University Press.

Defoe, Daniel 2008 [1724]. *Roxana*. Oxford: Oxford University Press.

Downie, Alan 1997. The making of the English novel. *Eighteenth-century Fiction* 9(3): 249-66.

Fludernik, Monika 1996. *Towards a 'natural' narratology*. London: Routledge.

Galbraith, Mary 1994. Pip as "infant tongue" and as adult narrator in Chapter One of *Great Expectations*. In Elizabeth Goodenough, Mark A. Heberle & Naomi B. Sokoloff (eds.), *Infant tongues: The voice of the child in literature*, 123-41. Detroit: Wayne State University Press.

Hardy, Barbara 1985. *Forms of feeling in Victorian fiction*. London: Peter Owen.

Kawasaki, Ryoji 2007. *Robinson Crusoe* no katari [Narrative technique in *Robinson Crusoe*]. *Annual Report, Faculty of Human Cultural Studies* 9: 68-80.

Konigsberg, Ira 1985. *Narrative technique in the English novel*. Hamden: Archon Books.

Leech, Geoffrey & Mick Short 2007 [1981]. *Style in fiction: A linguistic introduction to English fictional prose*. Harlow: Pearson Longman.

McKeon, Michael 1987. *The origins of the English novel 1600-1740*. Baltimore: Johns Hopkins University Press.

Mullan, John 1996. Introduction. In John Mullan (ed.), *Roxana*, vii-xxvii. Oxford: Oxford University Press.

Novak, Maximillian 2000. Gendered cultural criticism and the rise of the novel: The case of Defoe. *Eighteenth-Century Fiction* 12(2&3): 239-52.

Segel, Elizabeth 1972. Truth and authenticity in Thackeray. *The Journal of Narrative Technique* 2(1): 46-59.

Stanzel, Franz Karl 1984. *A theory of narrative*. Cambridge: Cambridge University Press.

Watt, Ian 1957. *The rise of the novel: Studies in Defoe, Richardson and Fielding*. London: Chatto & Windus.

Palaeographical researches into the Macregol Gospels: The scribe of folio 126r, marginal notes and drawings

Kenichi Tamoto

Abstract

I made transcription from Oxford Bodleian Library, MS Auctarium D.2.19, edited and published it under the title, *the Macregol Gospels or the Rushworth Gospels*, from John Benjamins Publishing Company in 2013. In its introductory part, comprising CXXXIX pages, a palaeographical description of the manuscript is given. However, it seems that my explanation requires some more accurate accounts in several points, which concern the identity of the scribe who wrote the Latin text of folio 126r, which is the last page of St Luke's Gospel, marginal notes and drawings of figures which occur on the pages glossed by Farman and Owun. Concerning the Latin text, scholars have agreed on recognizing two scribes, Macregol and an anonymous scribe. I have proposed that Macregol wrote folio 126r. I also suggest that it is highly probable that OE and Latin marginalia occurring on pages glossed by Farman and Owun were written by these glossators, and finally that those glossators also drew the sketches of figures, fingers, and animals on the lower margins. I would like to express my appreciation firstly to Dr Houghton of the University of Birmingham for his kind suggestion concerning a research into the forms of ampersand, and secondly to the Bodleian Library for permission to use the copies of the following pages of MS Auctarium D.2.19 (all b/w): fols 5r, 21r, 36r, 36v, 113r, 125v, 126r, 127v, 147v, 148r.

1. The scribe of folio 126r

It seems that the discussion on identity of the scribe of folio 126r should begin with the observation about the quire which includes the leaf. The MS contains 169 vellum leaves,[1] which are gathered into 16 quires. Concerning those quires, Ker (1957: 352) makes a brief statement that they are normally comprised of ten leaves, that one quire is missing after folio 94, one leaf after folio 99, and two leaves after folio 109, and that probably 13 leaves are missing with the text and gloss of

---

[1] Leaves 132 and 133 make a single leaf.

Lk 4^{29}-8^{38},[2] 10^{20-38},[3] 15^{13}-16^{25}.[4] This observation is further clarified by McGurk's detailed description of the quires, as is shown below:[5]

Quires

1-5	foll.	1-50		all of 10
6	foll.	51-61	(MK. begins. Leaf cut out after f. 61)	11(+1)
7	foll.	62-72	(Leaf cut out after f. 65)	4(+1)+7
8	foll.	73-84	(Leaf cut out after f. 73 and after f. 74. Last quire of MK.)	1(+1)+1(+1)+10
9	foll.	85-94	(LK. begins) 2 quires, perhaps of 10 leaves each, and containing IV.29: civitas—VIII. 38: viri, are missing	10
10	foll.	95-103	(Leaf, containing X. 19: nocebit—X.38: quedam, is lost after f. 99)	5(+1)+4
11	foll.	104-113	(Leaf cut out after f. 106, 2 after f. 109 and 1 after f. 111)	3(+1)+3(+2)+2
12	foll.	114-126	(Leaf cut out after f. 113. Last quire of LK.)	(1+) 13
13-14	foll.	127-147	(JN. begins)	2 of 10
15	foll.	148-159		12
16	foll.	160-169	(Leaf cut out after f. 166. Position of f. 169 not clear)	? 7(+1)+2+1

The above analysis apparently shows that St Luke's Gospel comprises four quires, that is to say, quires 9, 10, 11, and 12, and that folio 126 is included in the twelfth quire. At this point our attention should be directed to the fact that the recto side of the folio is the last page of St Luke's Gospel and on the verso side of the same folio is drawn the portrait of St John, which relates to one of the arguments of the present article. It is generally admitted that the Latin text on those four quires, that is to say, the whole of St Luke's Gospel, was written by an anonymous scribe (Scribe B hereafter), who also wrote the first half of St

---

[2] The omission begins with Lk 4^{29} (illorum erat aedificata) and ends with Lk 8^{38} (et rogabat illum).

[3] The omission begins with the whole verse of Lk 10^{20} and ends with Lk 10^{38} (factum est autem dum irent et ipse intravit in quoddam castellum et mulier).

[4] The omission begins with Lk 15^{13} (longinquam et ibi dissipavit substantiam suam vivendo luxuriose) and ends with Lk 16^{25} (et dixit illi Abraham fili recordare quia recepisti bona in vita tua et Lazarus similiter mala nunc autem).

[5] McGurk (1961: 40-41).

John's Gospel (quires 13 and 14; folios 127-147v; Jn 1[1]-9[16], custodit); the rest, the Gospels of Saints Matthew and Mark, the latter half of St John (quires 1-8, 15 and 16; folios 1-84, 148-169; Mt 1[1]-28[20], Mk 1[1]-16[20], Jn 9[16], alii-21[25], the Latin colophon) was written by Macregol (Scribe A hereafter).[6] If we follow the view mentioned above, we could deduce that the Latin text on folio 126, the last leaf of the twelfth quire, might be ascribed to Scribe B. However, on the verso side of folio 126 is drawn the portrait of St John; scholars have attributed all the coloured portraits of the Saints and the first illuminated page of each Gospel to Scribe A, or Macregol, who worked both as a scribe and as an illustrator.[7]

Here occurs a contradiction concerning the scribe and the illustrator of folio 126. According to the conventional view, it follows that Scribe B might have written the recto side of folio 126, that is to say, the last page of St Luke's Gospel, and that Scribe A was the illustrator of the portrait of St John on the verso side of folio 126 because Scribe A, or Macregol, worked both as a scribe of his part of the Latin text and as an illustrator of all the coloured portraits of the saints, which include folio 126v, and the illuminated first page of each Gospel. However, with regard to the scribe who wrote the Latin text on the recto side of folio 126, I have proposed, as the result of calligraphical researches into the forms of letters,[8] that folio 126r was written not by Scribe B, but by Scribe A. Folio 126r is composed of only ten lines in Latin and seven lines of the OE interlinear glosses, as shown below (with my transcription):

---

[6] Liuzza and Doane (1995: 21).
[7] Barker-Benfield in Brown (2006: no. 59: 296-97). Tamoto (2013: XXVI-XXVII).
[8] Tamoto (2013: XLV-LXXV).

7 a-hæfnum hondum his bletsade
& eleuatis manibus suis benedixit

hiæ 7 aworden wæs miððy gibletsade hiæ
eis 51 & factum est dum benedicer& illis

eftfoerde from him 7 wæs gi-fered on heofnas
recessit ab eis & ferebatur in cælum

7 ða gi-gi-worðadun hine eft-færende werun
52 & ipsi adorantes eum regressi sunt

in mið glædnisse micler 7 werun
in hirusalem cum gaudio magno 53 & erant

symle on temple herende 7 blet-
semper in templo laudantes & bene-

sadun god
dicentes deum   Explicit

euangelium secundum lucam

INcipit euangelium

secundum Iohannem

In order to reinforce the above proposal with new evidence, it would be highly effective to compare the form of the ampersand between the two hands, which Dr Houghton of the University of Birmingham revealed in his criticism on Tamoto (2013).[9] The following table shows the first six examples of the ampersand occurring in folios 5r, 126r, 125v, 127v, 147v, and 148r.

Table 1. Occurrence of the ampersand in folios 5r, 126r, 125v, 127v, 147v, and 148r.

Folio 5r (Scribe A)	Folio 126r (Scribe A?)	Folio 125v (Scribe B)	Folio 127v (Scribe B)	Folio 147v (Scribe B)	Folio 148r (Scribe A?)
(line 3)	(line 1)	(line 1)	(line 1)	(line 2)	(line 2)
(line 4)	(line 2)	(line 2)	(line 3)	(line 3)	(line 6^1)
(line 5)	(line 3)	(line 3^1)	(line 4)	(line 4^1)	(line 6^2)
(line 9)	(line 4)	(line 3^2)	(line 5^1)	(line 4^2)	(line 6^3)
(line 11)	(line 5)	(line 3^3)	(line 5^2)	(line 5)	(line 7)
(line 13)	(line 6)	(line 4)	(line 5^3)	(line 6)	(line 9)

Note: line 3^1, line 3^2, line 3^3, line 4^1, line 4^2, line 5^1, line 5^2, line 5^3, line 6^1, 6^2, and 6^3 signify that the ampersand occurs twice or three times on lines 3, 4, 5, and 6.

---

[9] Houghton (2015: 91-97).

As shown in the above table, a clear distinction can be observed between the two scribes. The form of this sign in folios 5r, 126r, and 148r, the folio numbers of which are shaded and written in bold type at the top of the table, tends to slant to the left, whereas an upright vertical stroke is carried on in folios 125v, 127v, and 147v, where the horizontal upper stroke is rather thin. Furthermore, in folios 5r, 126r, and 148r, something like a serif can be recognised on the right-hand side, which may be a deciding factor. What can be concluded from the above analysis is that although folios 125v and 126r are included in the same quire, which as a whole used to be ascribed to Scribe B, there is a discrepancy in the form of the ampersand between those two pages, and therefore folio 126r should be discussed independently of the other leaves of the twelfth quire. The form of the ampersand in folio 126r is almost the same as that of folio 5r, which was written by Scribe A (Macregol), but that of folio 125v looks like that of folio 127v, which is the third page of St John's Gospel and is ascribed to Scribe B.

Incidentally, a brief mention should be made of quires 13-16, which used to be regarded as written by Scribe B. Calligraphical researches have confirmed that these quires should be divided into two groups, quires 13-14 (folios 127-147) and 15-16 (folios 148-169).[10] In this case also, the research into the form of the ampersand is effective at discriminating the scribes. Folio 147v is the last page of the first group (quires 13-14) of Saint John's Gospel, and folio 148r is the first page of the second group (quires 15-16). The above table shows that the form of the ampersand in folio 147v is that of Scribe B, but its form in the adjacent page, that is to say, folio 148r, is that of Scribe A. The first group of the quires except for folio 127r, which is the illuminated page drawn by Scribe A, was written by Scribe B, and the second group (folios 148-169) should be ascribed to Scribe A (Macregol).

2. Marginal notes

The Latin text of all the four Gospels is interlinearly glossed in Old English of the late tenth century.[11] Two glossators have been identified by the colophons in folios 50v, 168v and 169r; one is Farman,

---

[10] Tamoto (2013: XLV-LXXV).
[11] Liuzza and Doane (1995: 20). Tamoto (2013: XXX).

352   *Kenichi Tamoto*

who wrote in Mercian, and the other is Owun, whose English is close
to the Northumbrian dialect, or more specifically, the dialect used by
Aldred, the glossator of the Lindisfarne Gospels.[12] As early as 1702,
Wanley suggested partial charge of the glossators, observing that
Farman glossed the whole of Saint Matthew and Saint Mark 1^1-2^{15},
and all the rest was executed by Owun.[13] This observation by Wanley
was made more accurate by Waring (1856: cvii), who succeeded in
separating John 18^{1-3} from Owun's partial charge, and proposed that
Farman glossed the whole of St. Matthew, St. Mark 1^1-2^{15}, and St. John
18^{1-3}. This proposal has been supported by later scholars. Farman's
gloss has been discussed from various viewpoints. Concerning the
originality of Farman's gloss, it seems that the theory developed by
Menner (1934: 27) is highly persuasive. Menner concludes his argument as follows:

> Farman's independence as a transcriber, except for the rare lapses of
> which even careful scribes may be guilty, must be conceded, and the Old
> English Matthew considered, not a careless mixture of two discrepant
> dialects, but the Mercian dialect of Farman himself.

Menner also states that "Mr. John C. Pope, who has kindly examined
the MS. for me at the Bodleian, writes that the Latin corrections in
Matthew are almost certainly by Farman," and that "both the ink and
the handwriting (when minuscule) are the same as Farman's."[14] It
seems that these statements may attract the attention of the researchers
who have been interested in the marginal notes and drawings of figures.
    Concerning the marginal notes, which are mostly Latin corrections
with OE glosses, Ker (1957: 352) states that both hands, that is to say,
Farman's and Owun's, appear in correction to the Latin text on folios
19v, 21, 52v, 112, and 113. This statement is confirmed by Liuzza
(1995: 21), who comments that "both glossators correct the Latin text,
using majuscule for Latin and minuscule for OE," enumerating two
more examples on folios 26 and 26v. Further researches have revealed
that there should be about forty more instances of corrections into the

---

[12] Skeat (1878), St John, pp. xii-xiii. Brown (2006: 297). Tamoto (2013:
   XXX-XXXI).
[13] Wanley (1705: 82).
[14] Menner (1934: 27, note).

Latin text with OE glosses. As space is limited, one instance of Latin corrections by Farman and another by Owun are shown below.

Folio 21r of the MS contains the following verses:

The correction occurs in the right margin, and Mt 13[17] is transcribed as follows:[15]

```
soþ      ic sæcge   eow     forþon   monige  witgu      ⁊    soþfeste
Amen     dico       uobis   quia     multi   profetae   &    iusti
wilnadun þ geseon   þa þe   ge-seoþ  ⁊       ne         gesegon
cupierunt uidere    quae    uidetis  &       non        uiderunt
"⁊       gehera    þa þe   ge hoe[res]  ⁊    ne         gehe[rdon]"
"et      audir[e]  que     audi[tis]    et   ñ          audi[erunt]"
```
(For amen I say to you, that many Prophets and just men have desired to see the things that you see, and have not seen them; "and to hear the things that you hear, and have not heard them.")

In the above transcription the marginal addition is shown within double quotation marks. It seems that the correction in the margin cannot be easily recognized and, therefore, requires enlargement. The following image is the enlarged part of the addition.

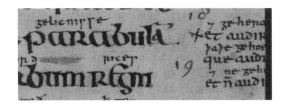

---

[15] The italicized parts in the brackets cannot be discerned in the MS, and they are restored in emulation of Skeat (1887) and the Vulgate (1969). Modern English translation given in the parentheses is based on the Douay Version of 1582 with a few but necessary alterations in accordance with the readings of the Latin text of the Macregol Gospels.

The addition is the last part of Mt 13[17], which reads "et audir[e] que audi[tis] et ñ audi[erunt]" with OE gloss "⁊ gehera þa þe ge hoe[res] ⁊ ne gehe[rdon]." The hand of the OE gloss in minuscule and its ink are Farman's. The ink of the Latin correction is not Macregol's but Farman's, and the forms of the majuscules 't,' 'a,' 'u,' 'q,' 'e,' and 'd' are obviously different from Macregol's—they must be Farman's. It is apparent that a decisive factor is Farman's employment of 'et,' which occurs as ampersand in Macregol's hand. Here the Lindisfarne MS reads "et audire quae auditis et non audierunt" with the gloss "⁊ gehera ða ilco ge heres ⁊ ne herdon." Farman's gloss is different from that of Aldred, who glossed the Lindisfarne Gospels, in "þa þe" / "ða ilco," "ge hoe[res]" / "ge heres," "gehe[rdon]" / "herdon." Farman is independent of Aldred's gloss.

The following image, with its transcription and translation, includes a correction which is added to Lk 19[2] on folio 113r.

⁊ heono   wer   "wæs ðæs"   noma   zacheus   ⁊   ðæs   wæs
& ecec[16] uir   "erat quidem" nomine iacheus[17] & hic   erat
aldormon beor-swinigra ⁊   he   wæs   weolig
princeps pulicanorum   &   ipse diues
(And behold "there was certainly" a man named Zachæus; and this was a Prince of the Publicans, and he was rich.)

The correction occurs in the right margin, and its enlarged image is as follows:

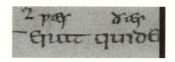

---

[16] Sic.
[17] Skeat points out that the word is altered to 'sacheus' in pencil, which is true. Here 'i' is altered to 's' by adding a curved ascender and a short descender. 'Zacheus' in the Vulgate (V hereafter). 'saccheus' in the Lindisfarne Gospels (Lind hereafter) .

The addition reads "erat quide*m*" with its gloss "wæs ðæs," which is meant to be palced after 'uir.'[18] As Ker (1957: 352) and Liuzza (1995: 21) point out, this correction with its OE gloss was written in by Owun. It must be noted that the Latin phrase "erat quide*m*" does not occur in V and Lind, and that the gloss "wæs ðæs," therefore, seems to be original to Owun.

3. Drawings of figures, fingers, or animals in the lower margins

The MS contains several pages which have small human figures or animals drawn in black ink in the lower margins. They occur in folios 4r (human fingers), 8r (a bird's head), 10r (an animal head), 19v (a bird's head), 27v (human fingers), 29r (a lion), 30r (a half-length figure), 31v (a bird's head), 35r (a lozenge), 36r (a half-length figure holding a book), 46r (a bird's head), 49r (a bird's head), and 122r (a human head). Scholars disagree as to the date and the illustrators of those drawings. Alexander (1978: 77) and Ohlgren (1986: 53) take the position that those drawings were added by a later artist presumably of the twelfth century, whereas Lowe (1972: No. 231), Hassall (1978: 4) and O'Neill (1984: 12) propose that the tenth-century glossators, that is to say, Farman and Owun, drew those sketches. Taking the latter scholars' opinion into consideration, Owun was in charge of only one drawing which occurs on folio 122r, and it follows that all the other sketches were drawn by Farman. The following drawing of a half-length figure holding a book occurs in the lower margin of folio 36r.

What is the aim of the illustrators' drawing the figure? What kind of document is he reading? What does the illustrator mean to convey by the perplexed look of the figure? It seems that these puzzles may be

---

[18] Skeat (1874: 246).

solved by a careful analysis of the text. Mt 22[13], beginning at the end of folio 36r, is continued at the top of folio 36v. Mt 22[13] of the MS reads as follows:

> þa   cwæþ   "se cyning"   to þægnum   gebindað him   foet   ⁊
> tunc dixit   "rex"   ministris   ligatis   pedibus &
> honda ⁊ sendeþ hine   in   ðiostre   þ ytmæst ł yterræ   þær
> manibus mitate   eum   in   tenebras   exteriores   illic
> bið   wop   ⁊   gristbitung   toþa
> erit   fletus &   stridor   dentium
> (Then "the king" said to the waiters, Bind [his] hands and feet, and cast him into the utter darkness: there shall be weeping and gnashing of teeth.)

It is apparent from the following enlarged image of the beginning of Mt 22[13] that "rex" and the OE gloss "se cyning" were added above the line by the same hand, that is to say, by Farman. The gloss for "rex" is "ðe cynig" in Lind, and therefore Farman is independent of Aldred's gloss in Lind.

The rest of Mt 22[13], beginning with "pedibus" and its gloss "foet," occurs in folio 36v of the MS, which reads as follows:

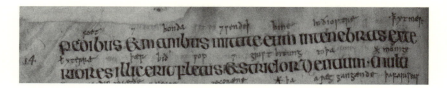

The above image shows that the pronoun *eius*, which occurs in V and Lind, is missing after "pedibus" in the Macregol Gospels, that "mitate" in the Macregol Gospels is an error for "mittite," which occurs in V and Lind, and that "illic" (there) is used in the Macregol Gospels instead of "ibi," which occurs in V and Lind.

At this stage, with due consideration for the above-mentioned correction, omission, error, and different reading, all of which occur in one verse, we might conjecture that it would be possible to speculate relevance between them and the drawing of a half-length figure (a scribe?) holding a book (a Gospel Book?) with a perplexed look. Would it be hasty to suppose that the scribe, by drawing the figure, possibly reading another Gospel Book, is trying to attract the readers' attention to the verse with a correction, an omission, an error, and a different reading?

4. Conclusions

Palaeographical discussions on 1) the scribe of folio 126r, 2) Marginal notes, and 3) drawings of figures in the lower margins have been developed in the present article.

The first point of the discussions is concerned with the form of the ampersand which is another factor affecting identification of the scribe of the Latin text in folio 126r. With regard to the problem of the scribe of folio 126r, which is the last page of St Luke's Gospel, Scribe A, that is to say, Macregol has recently been proposed as its scribe after calligraphical researches into the forms of letters. In the present discussion, which is based on analysis and comparison of the forms of the ampersand, it has been found that the result of the research on the new factor advocates the recent proposal for identifying Macregol as the scribe of the Latin text of folio 126r.

The second point is a graphological discussion devoted to the marginal notes, which are mostly corrections of the Latin text with the OE glosses added in the margins: 47 of them have been recognised. The marginal notes discussed in the present article are those occurring in folios 21r and 113r. They are corrections to the Latin text with the OE glosses at Mt 13^{17} and Lk 19^2, which are considered to have been added by Farman and Owun, respectively. The ink and the calligraphy of majuscules and minuscule of the marginal notes testify to execution by those two glossators.

The third argument is developed on drawings of figures, fingers and animals. Such drawings occur thirteen times exclusively in the lower margins. Twelve of them are found in the pages to which Farman added the interlinear OE glosses, and only one drawing occurs in Owun's part. The drawing which is taken up for discussion in the present article is a sketch of a half-length figure holding a book, which occurs on folio 36r, Mt 22[13], in Farman's part. After textual research into Mt 22[13], it has been proved that the verse contains a correction, an omission, an error, and a different reading. It seems that the figure is drawn there in order to attract the readers' attention to those matters.

References

MS. Auctarium D.2.19, Bodleian Library, Oxford (c. 800).

MS. Auctarium D.2.19, Bodleian Library, Oxford. A microfilm version.

MS. Auctarium D.2.19, Bodleian Library, Oxford. An electronic version in the Digital Image Library <http://bodley30.bodley.ox.ac.uk:8180/luna/servlet/detail/ODLodl~24~24~127350~142891>.

Biblia Sacra Vulgata 1969. Stuttgart: Deutsche Bibelgesellschaft.

Alexander, J.J.G. (general editor) 1978. *A survey of manuscripts illuminated in the British Isles, Volume I: Insular manuscripts from the 6th to the 9th Century*. London: Harvey Miller.

Brown, Michelle P. (ed.) 2006. *In the beginning: Bibles before the year 1000*. Washington, DC, Freer Gallery of Art & Arthur M. Sackler Gallery, Smithsonian Institution, 21 Oct. 2006—7 Jan. 2007. Washington, DC: Smithsonian, Freer Gallery & Arthur M. Sackler Gallery.

Drogin, Marc 1980. *Medieval calligraphy: Its history and technique*. New York: Dover Publications, INC.

Hassall, W.O. (introduction) 1978. *The Macregol or Rushworth Gospels*. Oxford: Oxford Microform Publications Ltd.

Houghton, Hugh A.G. 2015. Book review: Kenichi Tamoto (ed.), *The Macregol Gospels or the Rushworth Gospels: Edition of the Latin text with the Old English interlinear gloss transcribed from Oxford Bodleian Library, MS Auctarium D.2.19*. (Amsterdam & Philadelphia: John Benjamins, 2013). *Novum Testamentum* 57, 91-97. Leiden: Brill.

Ker, Neil R. 1957. *Catalogue of manuscripts containing A-S*. Oxford: Clarendon Press.

Liuzza, Roy M. and A.N. Doane (eds.) 1995. *Anglo-Saxon Gospels*. Philip Pulsiano & A.N. Doane (eds.), *Anglo-Saxon manuscripts in microfiche facsimile*, vol. 3. Medieval and Renaissance texts & studies, vol. 144. Binghamton, New York: Medieval and Renaissance Texts & Studies.

Lowe, E.A. 1972 (first edition 1935). *Codices Latini Antiquiores, Part II*, second edition. Oxford: Clarendon Press.

McGurk, Patrick 1961. *Latin Gospel books from A. D. 400 to A.D. 800. Les Publications de Scriptorum*, vol. V. Paris-Bruxelles: aux Éditions 'Érasme.'

Menner, Robert J. 1934. Farman Vindicatus: The linguistic value of *Rushworth I*. *Anglia* 58, 1-27. Tübingen: M. Niemeyer.

Ohlgren, Thomas H. 1986. *Insular and Anglo-Saxon illuminated manuscripts: An iconographic catalogue, c. A. D. 625 to 1100*. New York and London: Garland Publishing Inc.

O'Neill, Thimothy 1984. *The Irish hand, scribes and their manuscripts from the earliest times to the seventeenth century with an exemplar of Irish scripts*. Portalaoise: The Dolmen Press.

Skeat, Walter W. 1871, 1874, 1878, 1887. *The holy Gospels in A-S, Northumbrian, and Old Mercian versions, synoptically arranged, with collations exhibiting all the readings of all the MSS.; Together with the early Latin versions as contained in the Lindisfarne MS, collated with the Latin version in the Rushworth MS*. Cambridge: Cambridge University Press.

Stevenson, Joseph 1854. *The Lindisfarne and the Rushworth Gospels, now first printed from the original MSS in the British Museum and the Bodleian Library*. *Surtees Society*, no. 28. Durham: George Andrews/ London: Whittaker & Co.

Tamoto, Kenichi (ed.) 2013. *The Macregol Gospels or The Rushworth Gospels: Edition of the Latin text with the Old English interlinear gloss transcribed from Oxford Bodleian Library, MS Auctarium D.2.19*. Amsterdam/ Philadelphia: John Benjamins Publishing Company.

Tite, Colin G.C. 1997. Sir Robert Cotton, Sir Thomas Tempest and an Anglo-Saxon Gospel book: A Cottonian paper in the Harleian Library. In James P. Carley and Colin G.C. Tite (eds.), *Books and collectors 1200-1700: Essays presented to Andrew Watson*, 429-39. London: The British Library.

The Vulgate New Testament, with the Douay Version of 1582 in Parallel Columns. 1872. London: Samuel Bagster and Sons.

Wanley, Humphrey 1705. *Librorum Veterum Septentrionalium, qui in Angliae Bibliothecis extant, nec non multorum Veterum Codicum Septentrionalium alibi extantium Catalogus Historico-Criticus, cum totius Thesauri Linguarum Septentrionalium sex Indicibus*. Vol. II of George Hickes' *Linguarum Veterum Septentrionalium Thesauri*. Oxford: Sheldonian Theatre.

Waring, George 1861. *The Lindisfarne and the Rushworth Gospels, Part II, now first printed from the original MSS in the British Museum and the Bodleian Library*. *Surtees Society*, vol. XXXIX. Durham: Frances Andrews/ London: Whittaker & Co.

Waring, George 1863. *The Lindisfarne and the Rushworth Gospels, Part III, now first printed from the original MSS in the British Museum and the Bodleian Library*. *Surtees Society*, vol. XLIII. Durham: Frances Andrews/ London: Whittaker & Co.

Waring, George 1865. *The Lindisfarne and the Rushworth Gospels, Part IV, now first printed from the original MSS in the British Museum and the Bodleian Library. Surtees Society*, vol. XLVIII. Durham: Frances Andrews/ London: Whittaker & Co.

How Caxton translated French verbs of composite predicates by their English equivalents in *Paris and Vienne*: A study on the semantics of verbs along with their collocability with nouns

Akinobu Tani

Abstract

This study examines the correspondence of verbs (especially *avoir, gaigner, have*, and *get*) in composite predicates between the Middle French original and William Caxton's English translation of *Paris and Vienne*. The aim of the present study is to give a better understanding of how Caxton translated French verbs in composite predicates by their English equivalents, and of how he perceived semantic differences of those verbs between French and English. The study also treats the composite predicates that have traditionally been less studied, i.e. those with *get* and *bear*.

The results give a more subtle, rather than a simple one-to-one, correspondence between French and English verbs; the difference in the semantic contents of the same verb, even when it is employed in the same framework of composite predicates, depends on the noun collocates. At the same time, Caxton is found to have chosen translation equivalents rather cautiously, even if there is some interference involved in the translation, despite the fact that he is known to have made his translations rather quickly.

1. Introduction
1.1. Composite predicates

Composite predicates (CPs, henceforth) are phraseological items like *have a talk* which consists of a verb "light" in meaning and a deverbal noun which carries most of the meaning of the construction, and which has (almost) the same meaning as its corresponding one-word verb (*to talk* in this case).[1] Studies on CPs, including historical research, have been conducted mainly focusing on those with the following "light verbs": *have, take, do, make* and *give*. The reason for this probably lies

---

[1] Jespersen's (1942: 117) original formulation of CPs specifies a construction made up of a "light verb" and a noun "derived from and identical in form with" a verb. But in studies on CPs, especially historical ones, the restriction has been relaxed to include CPs with other deverbal nouns.

362   *Akinobu Tani*

in the fact that these light verbs are most frequent and neutral in meaning. It is, however, clear that CPs containing other verbs exist. The most typical would be the ones with *get*, which has been neglected probably because it collocates more freely with any kinds of objects than the aforementioned verbs. Actually, Jespersen (1942: 118), in one of the earliest studies of CPs, gives examples of CPs with *get* as in the following: *get a move on*, *give (get) the push*, *have (get) the bulge on*, *to get a remove,* and *he has not got his remove*. Cattell (1984) also dedicated a chapter to discuss the CPs with *get,* especially in relation to those with passive *give,* because these constructions are semantically similar. Given these treatments, it should be safe to say that studies on CPs should also give due attention to CPs with other less frequent verbs, such as *get,* as well. Thus, this study examines CPs with *get*. In the examination, the correspondence between these verbs and the original Middle French (MF, henceforth) verbs are investigated in order to analyse how Caxton dealt with the original French CPs in translation.

Tani and Osaki (2018) examine CPs with the aforementioned five verbs in Caxton's *Paris and Vienne* (*Paris,* hereafter) as a type of loan translation by comparing them with those in its MF original. They find that CPs were a convenient means of translation for Caxton, who is known to have translated in haste for business (Blake 1969: 146).

In addition to historical studies of CPs such as those by Gárate (2003) and Matsumoto (2008), which focus on the structure of CPs, there is another type of study which emphasises French influence on English phraseology: i.e. Sykes (1899), Prins (1952), Orr (1962) and more recently Iglesias-Rábade (2000). This type of study pays attention to the interaction of French and English in medieval times, which fits a recent surge of interest in language contact. These studies, however, demonstrate only an indirect relation between French and English phrases because they do not treat French and English translations, which most evidently show the direct relationship between such phraseology.

In this respect, Tani and Osaki (2018) is unique in dealing with the CPs in Caxton's *Paris* and its MF original, and in demonstrating the direct translation equivalents between the MF and Middle English (ME, henceforth) versions. The study, however, treats only the CPs with major verbs. Therefore, the present study, a sequel to the former one, complements it by discussing the CPs with less major light verbs, and at the same time, attempts to better clarify Caxton's translation method with a focus on the subtle correlations between the French original and Caxton's English translation.

1.2. *Paris and Vienne*

Paris belongs to a new kind of stories which came into being at the end of Middle Ages as "a reaction against earlier romance and a reflection of new culture patterns that were replacing those of the Middle Ages" (Leach 1957: v). Caxton translated a MF version into English, and printed it at Westminster in 1485. Among several manuscripts and incunabula of the MF story, Leach (1957: xxii) points out the close affinity between Caxton's version, Leeu's French text as printed in Antwerp in 1487, and a French manuscript B.N. Fr. 20044, and determines that Caxton used "a closely allied text rather than B.N. Fr. 20044" (for details and for the stemma, see Leach (1957: xxii-xxvi)), suggesting the affinity of Caxton's translation to the two French texts.

The present study quotes from Leach's (1957) EETS edition of Caxton's version and from Babbi's edition of B.N. Fr. 20044. The French manuscript, though not the direct source of Caxton's, but known to be close to Caxton's version, is employed since the direct source is not known. The citation from Leach (1957) is made in the form of page/line.[2]

2. CPs with *get* in *Paris* and the MF equivalents

As already pointed out, the CPs with *get* have been less studied. I searched for such examples in *Paris*, and found twenty examples of CPs with *get*. The nouns which the verb *get* takes are as follows:[3]

---

[2] I would like to express my gratitude to the late Professor Hisao Osaki from Osaka University and to the former Professor Tadamasa Nishimura from Osaka Gaidai Junior College for preparing the English-French parallel electronic edition employed in the present study.

[3] Among twenty examples of CPs, four examples do not have the corresponding CPs in the original MF version.

fame and honour (1x), *honour* (6x), *honour & prys* (1x), *honour and worshyp* (1x), *lordshyp* (1x), *maundement* (1x), *prys* (1x), (*the*) *prys and thonour* (1x), *renomee worshyp ne the praysyng* (1x), *worshyp* (5x), *worshyp and prys* (1x)

It is evident from the list that the verb collocates most frequently with two nouns: *honour* and *worship*. In fact, if we count their occurrences in binomials as well, the former amounts to ten and the latter eight. Furthermore, *honour*, *worshyp* and *prys* are synonymous, so they sometimes combine to form binomials such as *honour & prys*, *honour and worshyp*, (*the*) *prys & thonour* and *worshyp and prys*. The noun *prys* numbers four if we count the examples in binomials. This means that the verb co-occurs with very limited types of nouns to form CPs. Some examples are given here together with the corresponding original MF ones:[4]

(1) by cause they had not goten the honour of the feste   (18/6)
     pour ce qu'il n'avoyent eu l'onneur de celle feste

(2) & yf she gete the worshyp of the feste by a knyght   (12/28-29)
     et, se elle a l'onneur par ung chevalier

(3) And the knyght that shal gete the prys and thonour of the Ioustes shal haue all the thre baners and the thre Iewels   (14/19-21)
     Et le chevalier qui avra l'onneur de chevalerie avra toutes les .iii. banieres et les .iii. joyes[5]

(4) And whan vyenne herde speke of these tydynges / & sawe the grete honour & prys that she had goten   (19/3-5)
     Et quant Vienne ouyt parler de ceste noble feste et ouyt tant de grant pris et tant de honneur qu'elle avoit

All the examples from (1) to (4) above show a correspondence between *get* in Caxton and *avoir* in its French original. Example (3), however, should be noted since the French phrase "avra l'onneur de chevalerie" is translated with *get* as "shal gete the prys and thonour of

---

[4] Emphases in the examples are added by the author.
[5] In this part, Babbi's text does not correspond to Caxton's version, which has a binomial NP. Here, however, Leeu (1487), though it was created after Caxton's version and cannot be its original, shows a closer parallel to the English version:

Et le cheualier qui aura le pris & lhonneur de la iouste/ aura toutes les trois banieres & les trois ioyaulx   (f22)

How Caxton translated French verbs of composite predicates   365

the Ioustes" while the French phrase "avra toutes les .iii. banieres et les .iii. joyes" is translated with *have* as "shal haue all the thre baners and the thre Iewels," even though the verb *have* in the latter phrase signifies "to get or obtain." These examples point to the ambiguity of *avoir* and *have* in having both stative and dynamic meanings.[6] The correspondence should be said to be inconsistent because the English verb *get* is normally considered to have a more dynamic meaning while its counterpart *avoir* has a more stative one.

In contrast, the following examples with *get* translated from *gaigner* and *conquer,* are considered to exhibit the expected parallel in that these MF and ME verbs, when compared to *avoir* and *have*, involve a more dynamic meaning:

(5)   & there shall we do armes / by which we may gete fame and honour
                                                                  (20/30-31)
      et ferions chevalerie: de quoy nous gaignerions fame et honneur

(6)   where as they dyd grete feates of chyualrye & Ioustes wherof they
      gate grete honoure and worshyp   (21/1-3)
      et y firent maintes joustes et chevalleries de quoy il gaignerent
      honneur grant

(7)   and as two brethern of armes wente euer to gyder there as they
      knewe ony Ioustyug or appertyse of armes to be had for to gete
      honour   (2/31-33)
      et tousjours aloient ensemble aulx joustes et tournoyemens qui se
      faisoient par le monde ou ces deulx chevaliers conqueroient
      tousjours grant fame et grant renommee

(8)   Fayr sone Parys I am in a grete malencolye & in a thought for you
      that ye be not so Ioyeful ne mery as ye were wonte to be / here
      afore tyme I sawe you euer redy to the Ioustes and to al maner
      faytes of chyualrye for to gete honour   (10/14-19)
      Mon doulz filz, moult me suis esmerveillé de vous qui soulliez
      estre joyeulx et faisiés chevaleries et joustes et conqueriés grant
      honneur et renommee

In addition to the dynamic meaning of the verb *gaigner* itself, examples (5) to (8) have some features to prompt dynamic interpretation: examples (5) and (6) accompany the phrases which signify a means *de*

---

[6] Quirk *et al.* (1985: 177-78) discuss that the English verb *have* has a dynamic as well as a stative meaning.

quoy (translated into ME with *by which* and *whereof*), both of which cue a more dynamic interpretation; examples (7) and (8) involve CPs as purpose clauses in ME, different from the original constructions. Such contextual cues might be factors which made Caxton choose the verb *get* rather than *have* in contrast to examples (1)-(4).

Thus far, we have confirmed a subtle discrepancy between MF and ME verbs in translation of CPs: there is no clear one-to-one correspondence. The ME verb *get* is translated from the MF verbs *avoir* or *gaigner/conquer*. Does this signify a lack of correspondence between the MF and the translated ME verbs? This question is addressed by Tani and Osaki (2018). In fact, the following table, quoted from Table 7 in Tani and Osaki (2018), shows a fairly clear correspondence between French and English verbs:

Table 1. Correspondence of verbs in CPs between Caxton's and MF versions

	don	*yeven*	*haven*	*maken*	*taken*	total
avoir	3		104		3	110
faire	50	2	6	46	1	105
prendre			2		21	23
doner	2	14	4		1	21
porter			5			5
tenir				2		2
others	1	2	6	1		9
total	56	18	127	49	26	276

(quoted from table 7 in Tani and Osaki (2018))

Tani and Osaki's (2018) study finds the general pattern Caxton used to translate verbs of CPs into a set of fixed English verbs. In particular, they find regularity in correspondence between *avoir* and *haven*, though other verbs like *prendre-taken* and *faire-don/maken* also show a close parallel. Out of 110 examples of *avoir*, 104 examples are translated with *haven*, accounting for 94.5%. Given this close connection between *avoir* and *have* in *Paris*, the above examples where *avoir* is translated as *get,* seem inconsistent, as pointed out before. Despite such apparent correspondence, there exists a subtle discrepancy in terms of the MF verbs of CPs and their ME equivalents, as discussed above.

How Caxton translated French verbs of composite predicates   367

One question which arises from these observations is: to what extent do the examples of CPs with *get* correspond to *avoir* in the original? In order to answer this problem, the CPs with *get* are compared with the corresponding French verbs, which is summarised in Table 2:

Table 2. French verbs corresponding to *get*

Fr. verb	*avoir*	*gaigner*	*conquer*	none	total
#	12	2	2	4	20

Note: "None" in the table designates the examples where the verb *get* has no corresponding expressions in the MF original.

The results demonstrate that Caxton more often than not employed the English verb *get* to translate *avoir*, while there are two examples each of CPs with *get* translated from *gaigner* and *conquer*.[7] The French verb *avoir*, however, is normally translated with *have* in Caxton, as seen in Table 1. These two observations mean that the French *avoir* is translated both with *have* and *get* in Caxton's version, exhibiting the semantic elasticity of the verb *avoir*. *Gainer* and *conquer* in Table 2 are considered as having a more dynamic meaning than *avoir*; likewise, *get* has a more dynamic meaning than *have*. Despite these facts, however, Caxton employed *get*, as has been seen in the above, when translating twelve French CPs with *avoir*.

3. CPs with *have* as verb and *honour, worshyp,* and *prys* as nouns

To better understand Caxton's employment of the verb *get* to translate the French *avoir*, here I focus, for comparison, on a parallel type of CPs: those consisting of *have* as verb and *honour, worshyp,* and *prys* as nouns. I searched for such CPs, and counted their occurrences. The occurrences of such nouns in such CPs are:

> *honour* (5x), *honour & fame* (1x), *the prys and thonour* (3x), *the prys & the worshyp* (1x), *worshyp* (1x)   (eleven in total)

All of them, except for one example of *honour*, that is, nine examples of the CPs with the following nouns (i.e. *honour, honour & fame, the*

---

[7] The loanword *gain* from French *gaigner* lagged behind in adoption into English until 1548 (s.v. *gain* v.[2], *OED2*). As we will see later in section 4, the French *gaigner* is often translated with *win* in Caxton's version.

prys & the worshyp and *worshyp*) correspond to the MF ones with *avoir*. The verb *have* in the CP with *honour & fame* corresponds to the French verb *gaigner*, and that with *the prys & the worshyp* to *enporter*, while one example of *honour* and *worshyp* each have no corresponding parts in the MF original. Therefore, the English verb *have* in these CPs corresponds to *avoir* in seven examples, and to *enporter* and *gaigner* in one example each, the distribution of which resembles that of the CPs with *get*. At the same time, presence of the two verbs *gaigner* and *enporter* (cf. *porter* "bear") found along with *avoir* strongly suggests the ambiguity of *have,* like its French equivalent *avoir,* since the former verb *gaigner* has a dynamic meaning and the latter *enporter* a stative one. This ambiguity of the verb *have* in CPs does not seems to have been noticed in the previous studies of CPs.

(9) & alwaye he demaunded tydynges of the Iustes that were made in fraunce and who had thonour of the Iouste (17/28-29)
et toujours demandoit nouvelles des joustes qui se estoient festes en France, ne qui avoit l'onneur

(10) & the bruyt & renomme was that mylady constaunce shold haue thonour of that feste (12/11-12)
Et fust ung grant bruit que madame Constance avroit l'onneur de ceste feste

(11) And he that shal wynne the felde shal haue the prys and thonour of the feste (14/9-11)
et, celluy qui gaignera le champ, avra l'onneur de celle chevalerie

(12) and they that shold do best in armes at that day they shold haue the prys & the worshyp of the feste (11/20-22)
et que ceulx qui feroient plus vaillamment armes et chevaleries qu'il enporteroient l'onneur de celle belle feste

(13) I see wel that the grete amytye & loue that ye haue to my sone / and knowe ye for certayn that I haue in my hert grete melancolye whan I remembre that Parys hath had grete honour & fame of chyualrye (19/36-20/3)
Je voy bien la grant amour que vous avez avec mon filz, saichés que en mon cuer ay grant merancolie quant me souvient que joucques ycy Paris avoit gaigné grant honneur et fame de chevalerie

These examples with *have* in the above, i.e. (9) and (10), seem to have a dynamic meaning. This interpretation is partly supported by example (11), where the act of *gaignera le champ* results in that of *avra l'onneur de celle chevalerie*, suggesting the synonymy of the two verbs involved. Actually, the phrase in Caxton's version, i.e. *wynne the felde*, is very interesting as well because, although the phrase itself is not recorded in *OED2*, its parallels are listed as "*To get, have the field*" (s.v. *field* n. 8a. *OED2*), showing the elasticity of the verb *have* approaching the semantics of *get* in this phrase. This phrase shows the ambiguity of the meaning of the verb *have*, and the synonymy of *get*, *win* and *have* in these types of CPs.

4. Correspondence of *gaigner* with English verbs

Since we have seen several examples in which the MF verb *gaigner* is translated with *get* and *have*, the MF verb *gaigner* is here examined in the French text in comparison with Caxton's ME one. Thirteen examples of *gaigner* were found in the French text, among which five examples constitute (semi-)CPs: two examples are translated with *get* as in examples (14) while one example with *have* as in (13), and the other two related examples with *win* as in (15):

(14) et ferions chevalerie: de quoy nous gaignerions fame et honneur
& there shall we do armes / by which we may gete fame and honour
(20/30-31)

(15) et en ceste maniere Paris moult noblement gaigna l'onneur du champ.
and moche nobly & valyauntly he wanne thonour of the Iustes and of the felde   (17/13-14)

Therefore, this French verb, dynamic in meaning, tends to be translated into English with more dynamic verbs like *get* and *win*, although it should be also noted that it is translated with a more stative verb *have* in one example.

Furthermore, the other examples of *gainger,* which do not constitute CPs but are related to them, co-occur with *champ* (1x) and *joustes* (4x). The verb *gaigner* in all these examples is translated with *win*, a more dynamic verb:

(16) aussi vueil que deissiés se gaagnastes les joustes le viiie jour de septembre en la cité de Paris
After I wyl that ye say to me / yf ye wanne the Iustes the xviij day of septembre   (28/30-31)

(17) et luy sembla que fust celle que porta le chevalier qui gaigna les joustes
And hyr semed that it was the same that the knyght bare that wanne the prys of the Ioustes   (22/18-20)

(18) qui estoit celuy qui tant notablement avoit gaigné l'onneur
who was he that so valyauntly & so nobly had wonne the Iourneye & the honour of the Iustes   (17/31-33)

In contrast to *avoir*, the MF verb *gaigner* can take nouns (related to a fight) like *champ* and *joustes* (as in (16) and (17)) without adding *honeur* or *prys* which is necessary in the case of *avoir* as in examples from (9) to (11). In (17), the ME example inserts *prys* which does not exist in the MF original, forming a kind of CP, which is normally not included in that category because of the semantic richness of the verb. Example (17) should be also noted in that the phrase *wanne the prys of the Iouste* is parallel to that in the following example using the verb *get*:

(19) How Parys gate the prys of the Ioustes in the cyte af Vyenne   (7/16)

Examples (17) and (19), therefore, demonstrate the synonymy of *win* and *get* in these parallel phrases.

5. Correspondence of *porter* with English verbs
In this connection, there is another verb which has been neglected in studies of CPs: *bear* and its French equivalent, *porter*. Prins (1952: 75-77) gives some English phrases with the verb which he claims to be influenced by French phraseology:

> *to bear arms ~ porter les armes; to bear company ~ porter compaignie; to bear faith ~ porter foi; to bear honour ~ porter honneur; to bear rancour, etc. ~ porter rancune; to bear reverence ~ porter reverence.*

Both of the French and English verbs have more stative meaning than *avoir* and *have*. Therefore, examples with *porter* are examined together with those in Caxton's version.

(20) voyant la grant amour que tousjours m'a portee
consydered the grete loue that he hath alway had toward me
(39/20-21)

(21) Paris, voyant qu'il n'osoit dire l'amour qu'il portoit a la belle Vienne

Parys seyng he durst not say nor shewe the grete loue that he had to the fayr vyenne   (6/32-33)

(22) Paris, bien congnois la grant amour que vous me portés et, puis que ainsy est,
Parys my frende I knowe well the grete loue that ye bere to me / & sythe it so is   (34/15-16)[8]

Four CPs with *have* were found as in (20) and (21), and three CPs with *bear* were found, all of which have *loue* (< *amour*) as their object. Example (20) clearly shows a stative meaning of the verbs *porter* and *have* because of the presence of the adverb *tousjours* and *alway*. Therefore, in contrast to the verb *have* in the CPs with *honour*, *worshyp* and *pry* as nouns, the verb *have* in these examples of CPs with *loue* is more stative in meaning. This means that, even in the same CPs with *have*, the meaning of the verb varies depending on the object noun in the CP. Therefore, it can be said that even in the same framework of the CP, the semantics of the same verb in the CP can expand and contract, depending on the characteristics of its object noun. Example (22) is to be noted because it accompanies *bear* instead of *have* in English, and because the clause *sythe it so is* "since it is so" with the stative verb *be* suggests that the preceding clause with the CP, described as a state, clearly shows the stative meaning of the verb (of course this applies to *portés* as well).

Another example of an English CP with *have* translated from *porter* can be found:

(23) j'ay porte malveillance a ung homme de ceste cyte pour grant desplaisir
I haue wrath & rancour to a man of thys toune for certayn desplaysyr   (35/3-4)

This is an example with nouns of emotion, which diverges a little from the topic of the present discussion. Such nouns of emotion, however, can be taken by *porter* and *bear* as in the following:

---

[8]   As for this phrase, see the following quotation from *OED2* (s.v. *love* n.[1] 7.), the earliest citation of which should be antedated at least by this example (22) in *Paris*:

†***to give, bear love to***: to be devoted or addicted to. ... 1611 Bible *Transl. Pref.* 2 For the loue that he bare vnto peace.

(24) et toy, Vienne, en porteras la cruelle penitance
and also bothe ye tweyne shal suffre therfore grete penitence
(42/15-16)

(25) se Paris scavoit que pour luy portasse tant de mal
yf parys knewe it / þᵗ for his loue I suffre thus moche sorowe
(57/8-9)

(26) O, sire Dieu toult puissant, fais moy ceste grace que moy toult seul
porte la payne de ce fait
O god almyghty do to me that grace þᵗ I onely may bere the payn
of this fayt   (38/30-31)

These examples have nouns *paine* (1x), *penitance* (4x), and *mal* (1x) with their English equivalents like *penytence* (1x), *payn* (1x), *punycyon* (1x), *penaunce* (1x), *sorrow* (1x) and one non-corresponding example. In these examples, the meaning of the MF and ME verbs in question seems to shift from "suffer" to "endure," suggesting their belonging to the periphery in the cline of CPs. This kind of semi-CPs shows the gradience of the construction called the CP, which needs to be addressed in a future study.

6. Conclusion

The present study has surveyed Caxton's translation method by examining the correspondence of verbs between the MF original and Caxton's translation of *Paris*. In a previous study, Tani and Osaki (2018) found a regular pattern of correspondence between French and English verbs in CPs. Despite the general appropriateness of such findings, however, this study has found a more subtle correspondence between MF and ME verbs. This suggests that Caxton did not necessarily translate mechanically, and rather that he, even though he was known to have been quite rash in translating, thought well of the quality of translation even if there remained some interference from the MF original. At the same time, this study has found that the semantics of the same verb, even in the same framework known as CPs, can vary depending on its noun collocates, which seems to have been neglected in previous studies. This finding also reveals the elasticity of the verbs in question.

The results of this study concerning the correspondence between French and English verbs can be tabulated as follows:

Table 3. Correspondence of French and English verbs of CPs

porter		avoir		gaigner/conquer	
bear	have		get		win
3	5	7	12	2/2	2

This demonstrates the ambiguity and semantic elasticity of the verbs, both French and English, in the CPs, and a subtle correspondence between MF and ME verbs. At the same time, we can perceive the possibility that the MF *avoir*, having been translated more with *get* than *have* in Caxton's version, could have a more dynamic meaning than the ME *have* in this type of CPs. But this table, in a way, simplifies the overall picture, as it does not show the collocability of the verbs with the nouns. Therefore, the information on the correspondence is reformulated and schematised in Figure 1 to demonstrate the more subtle and complex picture of the correlation of the verbs and the nouns in the CPs:

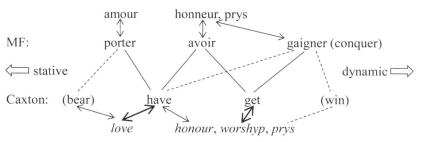

Figure 1. Correspondence between English and French verbs and their noun collocates in the CPs

The figure shows the interaction of the verbs and the nouns in the choice of the verbs: the noun collocates influence the choice of the verbs in the CPs. In other words, Caxton paid attention to this complex interaction in the process of translation.

The present study is not systematic in that the research began with examining the CPs with the verb *get* in comparison to its French counterpart, and proceeded to study the relevant French verbs and their relation to the English ones. As already pointed out, the noun collocates in the CPs influence the choice of verbs. Therefore, a more systematic study is needed, which surveys all the relevant verbs of CPs in comparison with their noun collocates between the MF and Caxton's version. Despite such limitations, the present study has demonstrated findings not discussed before.

References

Babbi, Anna Maria (ed.) 1992. *Paris et Vienne: Romanzo cavalleresco del XV secolo*. Milan: FrancoAngeli.

Blake, Norman 1969. *Caxton and his world*. London: André Deutsch.

Cattell, Ray 1984. *Composite predicates in English*. Sydney: Academic Press.

Gárate, Teresa Moralejo. 2003. *Composite predicates in Middle English*. München: LINCOM GmbH.

Iglesias-Rábade, Luís 2000. French phrasal power in late Middle English: Some evidence concerning the verb *nime(n)/take(n)*. In D.A. Trotter (ed.), *Multilingualism in later medieval Britain*, 93-130. Cambridge: D.S. Brewer.

Jespersen, Otto 1942. *A modern English grammar. VI. Morphology*. Copenhagen: Einar Munksgaard.

Leach, MacEdward (ed.) 1957. *Paris and Vienne: Translated from the French and printed by William Caxton*. OS 234. London: EETS.

Matsumoto, Meiko 2008. *From simple verbs to periphrastic expressions: The historical development of composite predicates, phrasal verbs, and related constructions in English*. Bern, Peter Lang.

Orr, John 1962. *Old French and Modern English idiom*. Oxford: Blackwell.

Prins, A.A. 1952. *French influence in English phrase*. Leiden: Universitaire Pers.

Quirk, Randolph, *et al.* 1985. *A comprehensive grammar of the English language*. London and New York: Longman.

OED2 = Simpson, John A. & Edmund S.C. Weiner prepd. 1989. *The Oxford English Dictionary*, Second Edition on CD-ROM (v. 4.0.0.3, 2009). Oxford: Oxford University Press.

Sykes, F.H. 1899. *French elements in Middle English: Chapters illustrative of the origin and growth of Romance influence on the phrasal power of standard English in its formative period*. Oxford: H. Hart.

Tani, Akinobu & Hisao Osaki. 2018. Chapter 5: Caxton ni okeru chu-furansugo composite predicats no honyaku ni tsuite [On the translation of Middle French composite predicates in Caxton's translation]. In N. Yusa (ed.), *Gengo kenkyu to gengogaku no shinten* III [*Evolution of linguistic studies and linguistics* III], 237-56. Tokyo: Kaitaku-sha.

On the adjectives modifying knights in Chaucer:
With special references to Troilus

Yue Zhou

Abstract

This paper aims to study the features of the knights in six of Chaucer's works through the perspective of adjectives. In the first section, the adjectives are divided according to the specific objects they modify. As a result, it is found that compared with the main characters, the outward appearances of the minor characters are more elaborately depicted with more adjectives. This is considered as a writing technique in this paper and its two functions are identified.

Next, in the second section "wyse" and "worthy" are discussed and their relation to the love of Troilus and Criseyde as well as the information they reveal is made clear. Moreover, "wo-bygon" which describes Troilus's state of mind is also examined in detail. Based on a study of 85 works which include Chaucer's, those of his contemporaries and those of previous authors, this study concluded that the adjective has two nuances.

1. Introduction

This study, which examines works of Chaucer and his contemporaries, as well as those of earlier authors, tries to make relatively comprehensive discussions of Chaucer's adjectives which are used to modify knights. Six of Chaucer's stories which have knights as their main characters are studied: *Troilus and Criseyde* (hereinafter referred to as *TC*), *The General Prologue, The Knight's Tale* and *The Tale of Sir Thopas* of *The Canterbury Tales* (hereinafter referred to as *GP, KnT, Thop* and *CT*), *The Book of Duchess* and *Anelida and Arcite* (hereinafter referred to as *BD* and *Anel*). Based on a database of the targeted adjectives in the six works, a comparison among the stories is made so that not only some of the features of Chaucer's writing but the characteristics of the knights may be manifested as well. In addition, a detailed analysis of some selected words is also conducted to discover either how they contribute to the contents of the stories or what kinds of nuances are hidden behind them.

Finally, with the results and discoveries obtained during the process, this study will hopefully help to cast some new light upon and contribute to a deeper understanding of the stories. However, since a detailed analysis of all the six stories would not be possible within the limited space available, only a closer observation of *TC* will be made after the general discussions.

There are many previous studies related to the vocabulary of Middle English. Room (1991) made a comprehensive study on the changes in meanings of more than 1,300 English words including adjectives, and compiled them into a dictionary. The author classified meaning changes into eleven different types and tried to quote actual examples to support them, yet the limited quotations are far from sufficient and the way in which he chose the 1,300 words remains unknown. Besides, although this book is convenient for a reader who wants to know the general changes in meaning of certain words, it will never be satisfactory for one who wants to know how a poet, such as Chaucer, used certain words and what kinds of nuances they have.

The next study on vocabulary to be mentioned is Mersand (1939). This work especially studied Chaucer's romance vocabulary and despite the fact that it was completed nearly 80 years ago, it provides incredibly detailed statistics. However, Hulbert (1947: 302) criticized it as follows:

> Dr. Mersand did not evaluate his evidence properly ... due to his misunderstanding of the results that lexicography obtains, and of the way in which to use such a dictionary as the *Oxford*. His method is to check Chaucer's Romance words with the *OED*, and whenever a quotation from Chaucer is earlier than any other given, to list it as an importation made by Chaucer. He states: "Chaucer used, at least in the opinion of the editors of the *New English Dictionary*, 1,180 Romance words for the first time." ... [While] the lexicographer hasn't "opinions"; he is merely doing the best he can with the evidence at hand.

Hulbert's words remind us that relying too much on dictionaries when doing a study on vocabulary is extremely dangerous.

Cannon (1998) improved Mersand's study and corrected some of his mistakes. This work features a wider range; for example, it does not focus only on the borrowed words as Mersand does, but also on the ones which Chaucer invented by using old elements that already existed in the English language. This book is definitely useful in understanding Chaucer's English in general, but it can hardly help deepen our understanding of certain works, such as *TC*.

On the other hand, we found Kanno (1996), which is a contextual and semantic study, more closely connected with the contents of stories. With *CT* and *TC* as its main sources, this study not only analysed some of Chaucer's keywords, including three adjectives, but also paid attention to his rhetoric. Nakao (2004) is also a helpful study on Chaucer. In this book the author discussed the ambiguities of *TC* with his sharp perspectives and illustrative examples, and made detailed analyses of adjectives such as "sely" and "weldy." Apart from all those mentioned above, we can also find Jimura (2005), which is a thought-provoking study on Chaucer's words and narratives. This book is mainly divided into four chapters, in which the author made careful investigations of four aspects: textual structure, dialects, collocations and grammar.

Despite all those previous studies mentioned above, the approach of comparing the adjectives which modify the same object in the six works of Chaucer as well as observing the targeted adjectives in the works of Chaucer, those of his contemporaries and those of earlier authors as the present study does is relatively new. Moreover, the words to be analysed in this paper, as far as the present study has discovered, have not yet been studied from the same angles.

2. A general view on the adjectives modifying knights in Chaucer

It has to be mentioned that the "adjectives modifying knights" are treated in a loose way, which means they do not refer only to the ones qualifying the knights themselves but also those which describe their countenances, builds, clothes, etc. Based on the detailed objects they modify, all the adjectives are subdivided into nine categories and their frequencies are shown in the following table.

Table 1. A frequency list of adjectives modifying each object

Objects / Knights	Whole[a]	Sorrow[b]	Face[c]	Heart	Dressing	Build[d]	Voice	Hair	Others
Troilus	152	57	34	30	1	3	13	0	59
Diomede	12	1	1	0	0	3	1	0	3

Arcita	41	9	5	10	1	5	0	0	17
Palamon	36	7	8	5	3	1	0	3	6
Other Kn's[e]	4	0	11	2	18	6	0	8	1
Arcita (A)[f]	10	0	0	0	0	0	0	0	2
Black Kn	10	6	8	3	1	1	1	1	17
Thopas	11	0	3	1	8	1	0	0	3
Squire[g]	7	0	0	0	5	1	0	1	1
Kn in *GP*	9	0	0	0	2	0	0	0	1
Total	292	80	70	51	39	21	15	13	110

Notes:
a. This category includes those adjectives which directly modify the characters, such as "*woful* Troilus" and "*false* Arcite."
b. Those adjectives which modify "tears" are also classified under this category.
c. Adjectives which modify the countenances of the characters as well as those which modify parts of their faces, such as eyes and noses, are classified under this category.
d. This category includes adjectives which directly modify parts of the body, except the head, such as "long" and "big" in "And therto he was *long* and *big* of bones" (*KnT* 1424) as well as those indirect ones such as "strong" in "This Diomede, as bokes us declare, / Was in his nedes prest and corageous, / With sterne vois and myghty lymes square, / Hardy, testif, *strong*, and chivalrous / Of dedes, lik his fader Tideus" (*Tr* 5.799-803).
e. "Other Kn's" stands for the knights who attended the duel together with Arcita and Palamon in *KnT*.
f. "Arcita (A)" refers to the character Arcita in *Anel*.
g. "Squire" stands for the squire described in *GP*, and the "Kn in *GP*" below in the table, stands for the knight in *GP*.

Since knights are closely related to warfare, it is supposed that there should be many adjectives qualifying their builds. However, it turns out that Chaucer used few adjectives on the builds of his main characters, especially Troilus, in whose data there are 349 adjectives in total but only three refer to his build. Moreover, of the three adjectives, one is "strong" which indicates his knightly shape, and the remaining two are both "lene" (whose modern spelling is "lean"), which shows that Troilus is more a lover than a knight in the story. The same thing can be said of Arcita, who also grew lean due to his love of Emelye. In addition, the table also shows that Chaucer did not lay much emphases on the other aspects of outward appearances of the main characters.

This paper uses the expression "main characters" above in order to make a distinction between the main characters such as protagonists of each story or story-tellers in *CT*, and those minor characters such as "other knights" in *KnT*. As to "other knights," the data show that the emphases of the descriptions of them are laid on their "dressings," "faces," "hair" and "builds," which are all related to their outward appearances. Why are descriptions of their appearances needed here? A hasty answer to this question may be that since it is impossible and unnecessary for the story-teller to enter the minds of all the minor characters and read their thoughts and feelings, he has to portray their outward appearances. However, this explanation belittles the portrayal of minor characters as a writing technique.

As a matter of fact, two functions of this writing technique are identified in this study. Firstly, the description of minor characters may set the main characters off in return and secondly the description may also form an indispensable part which makes the story substantial and logically right. *Guy of Warwick (stanzas)*, hereinafter referred to as *Guy (S)*, may be an illustrative example here. It is a story included in the Auchinleck MS by which, as Loomis (1965: 135) stated, "Chaucer was inspired... to write his parody, *Sir Thopas.*" In this story the minor character, Saracen, whom the main character, Guy, finally defeated, is portrayed as so undefeatable as follows:

(1)   Michel and griselich was that gome
       With ani god man to duelle.
       He is so michel and unrede
       Of his sight a man may drede
       …
       As blac he is as brodes brend,
       He semes as it were a fende
       That comen were out of helle.

"For he is so michel of bodi ypight
Ogains him tuelve men have no might
Ben thai never so strong,
For he is four fot sikerly
More than ani man stont him bi,
So wonderliche he is long.   (*Guy (S)* 737-40, 742-50)

He is dreadful and is so strong and mighty that even twelve people seem to be powerless in front of him. This Saracen doubtlessly sets Guy off in return. The more the author emphasizes his power and strength, the more formidable Guy will be.

Moreover, without the description here, the story will seem illogical. We should not forget that at the beginning of the story, Guy told his wife that he was so regretful for he was bound too much by his love to her and therefore failed to do good acts for Jesus. He was repentant because he has brought too many people to the ground and shed their blood with many a serious wound. Therefore, to atone for his sins he decided to go on a pilgrimage barefoot till the end of his life. Since Guy is regretful to have killed many of his foes, killing this Saracen will be illogical without the description above. As a matter of fact, the two lines in italics in (1) describe the Saracen as a "fiend from hell," which makes it reasonable for a pilgrim like Guy to kill him. As a result, on the one hand he can save Jonas and his fifteen sons and on the other, to kill this pagan "fiend" will be a good act he can do for Jesus as a redemption for himself.

In *KnT*, Chaucer also used the technique of portraying "other knights" to serve the main characters. On the one hand, Chaucer depicted the gorgeous clothing and nobility of "other knights" to remind us of the royal estate of Arcita and Palamon and of the fact that both of them are able to marry Emelye in terms of social status. On the other hand, since all those knights are brought by the two heroes to win the battle, the stronger and more powerful they are, the more ambitious the two heroes will seem to be to marry Emelye.

In addition, the data from the table above also show that adjectives used to describe the hair of Palamon are more numerous than those used in relation to other main characters. A closer reading found that Chaucer gave a close-up of his hair and clothing after the death of Arcita and used five of the six adjectives here.

(2)   With *flotery* berd and *ruggy*, *asshy* heeres,
       In clothes *blake*, ydropped al with teeres;
       ...
       But in his *blake* clothes sorwefully   (*KnT* 2883-84, 2978)

In fact, Palamon's fluttering beard and shaggy, ash-colored hair and his black clothes all sprinkled with tears are more effective and impressive in representing his woeful heart than any other adjectives and descriptions which directly express his inner feelings.

Arcita is described as the flower of chivalry in *KnT*; however, in *Anel*, which is a short and uncompleted story, he was depicted in a totally opposite way. *Anel* is found to be the work with the most monotonous adjectives in this study: seven of the twelve adjectives modifying Arcita are "fals." Readers can feel the anger of the story-teller towards the betrayer, Arcita, throughout the whole story. The repeated "fals" reminds us of *BD* whose protagonist, the Black Knight, repeated "fals" nine times when cursing Fortune.

3. A closer look at the adjectives modifying Troilus

This section makes special reference to the adjectives modifying Troilus and tries to analyse his personality in terms of them.

As Table 1 shows, there are 152 adjectives which directly modify Troilus and among them, there are ones expressing his states of mind, such as "woful" and "glad," which can hardly reveal his personality. Therefore, in the first part of this section, only those which are related to Troilus's personality are included. However, those excluded ones which mostly represent his states of mind, are also indispensable in the story, and therefore, one of them, "wo-bygon," will be examined in the latter half of this section.

3.1. "Wise" and "worthy"

A total of 28 adjectives which indicate Troilus's personality are found in the study and the following table illustrates how they are used by the four addressers, namely the narrator, Pandarus, Criseyde and Troilus.

Table 2. Adjectives reveal Troilus's personality and their addressers

Adjectives		N	Pandarus			Criseyde				Troilus		
			T	C	N (P)	C	T	P	N (C)	T	P	C
	benigne	1										
	(not too) bold								1			
	diligent											1
	discret								1			
	(beste) entecched	1										
	esy	1										
	fierse	1										
free	free			1								
	mooste fre	1										
frendly	frendly				1							
	frendlieste	1		1								
	fressh	1		2					1			
gentil	gentil			2			1					
	gentilest	1				2						
goode	goode			1								
	goodly	1										
	beste	2										
	hardy	1										
	humble											2
	knyghtly							1				
	konnynge	1										
	lusty		1									
	(not) malapert							1				
	pacient											1
	proude	1										
	secret							1				1
	subgit	1										
	thriftiest	1										
	trewe	1		2			1				1	2
	unworthi									1		1
	weldy							1				
	wyse		6	2		1		1	1			
worthy	worthy	2	1	3								
	worthieste			1		3						
	Total	**19**	**8**	**15**	**1**	**6**	**2**	**1**	**8**	**1**	**1**	**8**

Notes: N = narrator, P = Pandarus, C = Criseyde, T = Troilus. The letters under the names stand for the addressees. For example, "T" under "Pandarus" stands for the occasion when Pandarus is the addresser and Troilus is the addressee. Besides, those lines which are in the narrative parts but are apparently written from the perspectives of Pandarus or Criseyde are treated as their speeches and marked as "N (P)" and "N (C)." Adjectives are shown in the leftmost column in alphabetical order and their frequency is on their right.

As is shown in the table, "wyse" is a keyword which has the highest frequency, it is used by Pandarus eight times and by Criseyde three times. The high frequency of this word is closely related to Criseyde. As depicted in the story, she is a widow who cares about nothing more than her reputation, and therefore, the fact that Troilus is wise and knows how to keep secrets may be counted as the most important reason why she accepted him.

(3)　The first two instances of "wyse" are used by Pandarus.
　　　For bothe yow to plese thus hope I
　　　Herafterward; for ye ben bothe *wyse*,
　　　And konne it counseil kepe in swych a wyse
　　　That no man shal the *wiser* of it be;　(*Tr* 1.990-93)

Pandarus repeated the word "wyse" twice here when he heard that Troilus loves Criseyde. He is so confident that their love will go smoothly, for Troilus is wise and in terms of keeping secrets no one is wiser than he and Criseyde. Conversely, he emphasized the word twice here also to remind Troilus not to forget to keep the secrets and maintain her reputation.

Later, when persuading Criseyde to accept Troilus, Pandarus again emphasized "wise" twice and indicated that Troilus knows how to maintain secrecy. The following instance is cited from Criseyde's monologue after Pandarus left. She seemed to have temporarily believed that Troilus is "wise" enough and will not expose their love to the public, for she also heard the rumours about him before, which say that he is not an "aventour" (boaster).

(4)　"And ek I knowe of longe tyme agon
　　　His thewes goode, and that he is nat nyce;
　　　N'avantour, seith men, certein, he is noon;
　　　To *wis* is he to doon so gret a vice;　(*Tr* 2.722-25)

Pandarus succeeds by telling her this crucial aspect of Troilus's personality. However, as the next quotation says, her worry was not dispelled until they exchanged several letters and met several times, when Criseyde found Troilus was so discreet, secret and obedient. He is just like a wall of steel and a shield to her, defending her from troubles. She eventually became no longer afraid, for she finally confirmed that he is wise.

(5) For whi she fond hym so *discret* in al,
     So *secret*, and of swich obëisaunce,
     That wel she felte he was to hire a wal
     Of stiel, and sheld from every displesaunce;
     That to ben in his goode governaunce,
     So *wis* he was, she was namore afered —   (*Tr* 3.477-82)

"Wise" appears again in the scene in which Pandarus persuades Criseyde to let Troilus come to meet her. Criseyde was afraid lest others should notice their love. However, when realizing she could not refuse, she said what follows in (6).

(6) And for the love of God, syn al my trist
     Is on yow two, and ye ben bothe *wise*,
     So werketh now in so *discret* a wise
     That I honour may have, and he plesaunce:
     For I am here al in youre governaunce."   (*Tr* 3.941-45)

She said that she had to trust that both of them are wise and know how to do everything in a discreet way so that her reputation could be preserved.

Ironically, Criseyde changed soon after she went to the Greek camp, probably because no one except her father knew her background there. She was no longer bound and constrained by the moral concepts of Troy and accepted Diomede who is not discreet at all. In the description of Diomede, Chaucer may have intentionally included the following line.

(7) And som men seyn he was of tonge *large*;   (*Tr* 5.804)

The *OED* cites the above line as the earliest one under the definition of the adjective "large" which says: "[o]f speech, etc.: [f]ree, unrestrained; (in bad sense) lax, licentious, improper, gross…" (s.v. *large*, adj. 13). Obviously, Diomede is not a prudent person, but he is helpful, or as Chaucer says "prest," and that probably was what Criseyde needed in the strange environment.

Next, a discussion will be made of the superlative degrees that Criseyde used. In Table 2 we can find that compared with the fact that Criseyde used no superlative degrees when talking to Troilus, she used "worthieste" three times and "gentileste" twice in her monologue, which is the most among the three characters. Specifically, "worthieste" is used twice before she betrays him, which means that she considers Troilus as the "worthieste" but never told him. This fact reveals that she may have tried to restrain her love in front of Troilus. On the other hand, the remaining examples of "worthieste" and "gentileste" are used in her monologue after her betrayal.

(8)   She seyde, "Allas, for now is clene ago
      My name of trouthe in love, for everemo!
      For I have falsed oon the *gentileste*
      That evere was, and oon the *worthieste*!
      ...
      "But, Troilus, syn I no bettre may,
      And syn that thus departen ye and I,
      Yet prey I God, so yeve yow right good day,
      As for the *gentileste*, trewely,   (*Tr* 5.1054-57, 1072-75)

Criseyde sighed: "Alas, now my name of truth in love is completely and forever gone! Because I am unfaithful to the gentlest and worthiest person!" The superlative degrees obviously reveal her remorse and her guilty conscience: Troilus is the best, but she betrayed him. However, she also tried to find an excuse for herself: since they are apart, she cannot do better.

3.2. "Wo-bygon"

Troilus is not only wise and worthy, he is also woe-begone. "Wo-bygon" is an adjective used to express Troilus's grief. This section makes a detailed analysis of "woe-begone" and tries to clarify on what occasions it is used and what nuances are hidden behind it.

The form "wo-bygon" in which a hyphen was inserted between "wo" and "bygon" is borrowed from the *Riverside Chaucer*. However, this is no more than a practice of the editor, for no such hyphens are found in the manuscripts. Moreover, even textual editors do not seem to have reached an absolute consensus on where to insert the hyphen and

386   *Yue Zhou*

where not to.[1] Besides, this study found that in Chaucer, "wo-bygon" and "wo bygon" coexisted and therefore to ensure a more comprehensive result, both of the two forms are included in this study.

The present study examined "wo-bygon" and "wo bygon" as well as their variations in a total of 85 works, including the those of Chaucer and his contemporaries (Gower's *Confessio Amantis* and Langland's *Piers Plowman*), 44 works included in the Auchinleck MS, works of Breton Lais: *Emare, Sir Cleges, Sir Gowther, Sir Launfal, The Earl of Toulouse,* works of early Middle English: *Dame Sirith, Floris and Blauncheflour, The Fox and the Wolf, The Land of Cokaygne, The Owl and Nightingale* and one alliterative poem: *Sir Gawain and the Green Knight.*

As a result, only 33 instances are found, which means "wo bygon" is not an expression of high frequency. Fifteen of them are used by Chaucer, twelve are found in the works of Auchinleck MS, four in the *Confessio Amantis,* one in *Emare* and one in *The Fox and the Wolf.*[2]

Except the one in *The Fox and the Wolf,* the remaining 32 instances with the reasons why the characters feel woe-begone are illustrated in Table 3.

---

[1] With the aid of Jimura et al. (1999: 170) it is found that Windeatt (1984: 440) did not insert a hyphen in "That so bitraised were or *wo-bigon*" (*Tr* 4.1648). The *OED* explains that "woe-begone" comes originally from "me is wo bigon," and "[s]ubsequently a change of construction took place, parallel to the passing of *me is woe* into *I am woe..., woe* and *begone* becoming consequently so indivisibly associated as to form a compound" (s.v. *woe-begone,* a. (n.)).

[2] However, as to the instance in *The Fox and the Wolf,* which is quoted below, although the form is similar, this "wo bi-go" is actually not the one which express sadness. Instead, it is used as a curse: "(may) woe bego you." Therefore, this instance is excluded from the discussions.

    I do þe lete blod ounder þe brest,
    Oþer sone axe after þe prest."
    "Go wei," quod þe kok, "*wo* þe *bi-go*!
    Þou hauest don oure kunne wo.
    Go mid þan þat þou hauest nouþe; (*Fox and the Wolf* 51-55)

Table 3. A compendium of "woe-begone" and their reasons

WORKS		LINES	REASONS	WORKS		LINES	REASONS
Works of Chaucer	TC	3. 117	Due to love	Works included in the Auchinleck MS	Guy. (S.)	7189	Feel regretful
		3. 1530	Due to love			7507	Life is threatened
						7568	Life is threatened
		4. 464	Due to love		Guy (C.)	172	Due to love
		4. 822	Feel pitiful		Amis & Amil	968	Life is threatened
		4. 1648	Due to love / Be betrayed			1214	Be betrayed / All the possessions are lost
		5. 34	Due to love			1499	Betrayed/ All the possessions are lost
	MilT	3372	Due to love			2098	Feel pitiful / Feel regretful
		3658	Due to love		Tars	587	His child is malformed
	Ml	918	Be raped			644	His child did not get better
	Fk	1316	Due to love		Beues	3867	Life is threatened
	LGWF	1487	Due to natural calamity			4232	Life is threatened
		2409	Lives are threatened	Gower	Confessio Amantis	1. 1762	Against his will
		2497	Due to love / Be betrayed			4. 3394	Feel regretful
	RR.A	319	UNKNOWN			5. 4348	Life is threatened
		336	UNKNOWN				
Lai	Emare	697	Due to love			5. 4826	Against her will

Note: *MilT = The Miller's Tale, Ml = The Man of Law's Tale, Fk = The Franklin's Tale, LGWF = The Legend of Good Women* (Text F), *Guy (C) = Guy of Warwick (couplets), Amis & Amil = Amis and Amiloun, Tars = The King of Tars, Beues = Sir Beues of Hamtoun.*

As we can see from the table, in works other than Chaucer's, the adjective is most frequently used when the character's life is threatened or on other occasions such as when the character's newborn child is malformed or when the character is betrayed and has lost all his possessions. Therefore, in these works the adjective is mostly used to express such woe that is extremely intensive. However, in most instances in Chaucer, nine out of fifteen, the expression is used to represent the woe of love. Especially in *TC* and *MilT*, the adjective is almost restricted to love. This does not mean that Chaucer did not know or forgot the above-mentioned nuance of the word, for in *LGWF*, which is thought to have been written after the *TC*, he also used "woe begone" once when the characters feel their lives are threatened. Most probably, such as in quotation (9) below, Chaucer intentionally used "woe begone" to express Troilus's grief in love, indicating that this grief is extremely intense and may therefore even threaten his life.

Apart from those mentioned above, this study also tried to find some words which usually coexist with "woe begone." As a result, in nine instances, "forlore" and "forlorn" which are variations of the verb "forlesen" meaning "to lose or to abandon" as well as its synonyms such as "lese" are found near "woe begone." Cited below are two instances from *TC* and *Guy (S)* respectively. Other instances are marked with black in Table 3.

> (9) This Troilus, withouten reed or loore,
> As man that hath his joies ek *forlore*,
> ...
> So *wo-bigon*, al wolde he naught hym pleyne,
> That on his hors unnethe he sat for peyne.   (*Tr* 5.22-23, 34-35)

> (10) Y trowe in þis warld is man non,
> Ywis, þat is so *wo bigon*
> Seþþen þe world made was,
> For alle min sones ich haue *forlorn* —
> Better berns were non born —
> Þerfore y sing allas.
> For bliþe worþ y neuer more
> Alle mi sones ich haue *forlore*   (*Guy (S)* 7506-13)

Since "forlesen" and "lese" are not words with high frequency in these works, the fact should not be dismissed as an accidental phenomenon, but treated as an important hint that "woe begone" may contain the nuance that something is lost (or to be lost), or someone is abandoned (or to be abandoned). Actually, to look at the instances in Table 3 with this nuance again, we can find that most of them, even those not marked with black, have something to do with "lose."

4. Final remarks

The first section found that compared with the main characters, Chaucer laid much more emphases on the portrayal of the outward appearances of the minor characters. This is a writing technique which may not only set the main characters off in return, but is indispensable to make the story logically right as well.

Next, in the first half of section two, adjectives which reveal Troilus's personality are examined. The results show that "wise" has the highest frequency. This adjective is closely connected with the fact that Criseyde cares about her name excessively. On the other hand, it is found that the two adjectives of superlative degrees "worthieste" and "gentileste" used by Criseyde reveal firstly her intention to restrain her love in front of Troilus, and secondly her remorse and guilty conscience.

"Wo-bygon" is examined in the second half of section two. The results show that in works of Chaucer's contemporaries and those of earlier authors, this adjective is most frequently used when the character's life is threatened as well as on other occasions when the character's woe is severe. Chaucer most probably had this nuance in mind. Moreover, it is also found that "forlesen" as well as its synonyms such as "lese" often appear near "wo begone." This fact is considered to be directly connected with the second nuance of the adjective: something is lost (or to be lost), or someone is abandoned (or to be abandoned).

Room for further studies remains, for many of the adjectives collected are yet to be analysed.

Texts

Anne, Laskaya & Eve Salisbury (eds.) 1995. *The Middle English Breton lays*. Michigan: Medieval Institute Publications.

Bennett, J.A.W. & G.V. Smithers (eds.) 1966. *Early Middle English verse and prose*. Oxford: Clarendon.

Benson, Larry D. (ed.) 1987. *The Riverside Chaucer*, 3rd ed. Boston: Houghton Mifflin Company.

Burnley, David & Alison Wiggins (eds.) 2003. *The Auchinleck manuscript* <http://auchinleck.nls.uk/>. Last accessed July 2017.

Macaulay, G.C. (ed.) 1901. *The complete works of John Gower.* Oxford: Clarendon.

Schmidt, A.V.C. (ed.) 1978. *The vision of Piers Plowman*. New York: E.P. Dutton & amp; Co. Inc.

Tolkien, J.R.R., E.V. Gordon & Norman Davis (eds.) 1967. *Sir Gawain and the Green Knight*. New York: Oxford University Press.

390 *Yue Zhou*

Windeatt, B.A. (ed.) 1984. *Troilus and Criseyde: A new edition of 'The Book of Troilus.'* New York: Longman.

References

Benson, Larry D. 1993. *A glossarial concordance to the Riverside Chaucer*, vol. 1. New York & London: Garland Publishing, Inc.

Cannon, Christopher 1998. *The making of Chaucer's English: A study of words*. Cambridge: Cambridge University Press.

Davis, Norman, Douglas Gray, Patricia Ingham & Anne Wallace-Hadrill 1989. *A Chaucer glossary*. Reprinted. Oxford: Clarendon.

Hubert, J.R. 1947. Chaucer's Romance vocabulary. *Philological quarterly*, 26, 302-06.

Jimura, Akiyuki 2005. *Studies in Chaucer's words and his narratives*. Hiroshima: Keisuisha.

Jimura, Akiyuki, Yoshiyuki Nakao & Masatsugu Matsuo (eds.) 1999. *A comprehensive textual comparison of* Troilus and Criseyde*: Benson's, Robinson's, Root's, and Windeatt's editions*. Okayama: University Education Press.

Kanno, Masahiko 1996. *Studies in Chaucer's words: A contextual and semantic approach*. Tokyo: Eihosha.

Kittredge, G.L. 1951. *Chaucer and his poetry*. Cambridge, Massachusetts: Harvard University Press.

Kurath, Hans et al. (eds.) 1952-2001. *Middle English dictionary*. Ann Arbor: The University of Michigan Press.

Loomis, Roger Sherman 1965. *A mirror of Chaucer's world*. New Jersey: Princeton University Press.

Mersand, Joseph 1939. *Chaucer's Romance vocabulary*. New York: Kennikat Press, Inc.

Nakao, Yoshiyuki 2004. *The structure of Chaucer's ambiguity*. Tokyo: Shohakusha. [In Japanese]

OED=Oxford English dictionary. 2nd ed. [CD-ROM] Ver. 4.0. Oxford: Clarendon.

Room, Adrian 1991. *NTC's dictionary of changes in meanings*. Illinois: National Textbook Company.

Curriculum vitae of Akiyuki Jimura

Born:
Adogawa, Shiga Prefecture, Japan, in 1952

Education:
Takashima High School, Shiga Prefecture, 1971
Hiroshima University, B. A., 1976
Hiroshima University, M. A., 1978
Hiroshima University, PhD., 2002

Studies abroad:
Simpson College, USA, 1974 – 1975
St Peter's College, University of Oxford, UK, 2003 – 2004

Academic positions:
Lecturer, Otani Women's University, April 1979 – March 1984
Associate Professor, Otani Women's University, April 1984 – March 1986
Associate Professor, Mie University, April 1986 – March 1992
Associate Professor, Hiroshima University, April 1992 – March 2004
Professor, Hiroshima University, April 2004 – March 2016
Professor, Okayama University of Science, April 2016 –

List of publications
Books:
2005: *Studies in Chaucer's words and his narratives*. Hiroshima: Keisuisha.
2011: *The World of Chaucer's English*. (in Japanese) Hiroshima: Keisuisha.

Jointly-written books:
2000: N. Harano, *et al. Cross-cultural contact in medieval Europe*. (in Japanese) Hiroshima: Keisuisha.

392   Curriculum vitae of Akiyuki Jimura

2002: N. Harano, *et al. Multiplicity in medieval European culture.* (in Japanese) Hiroshima: Keisuisha.

2003: N. Harano, *et al. Cultural symbioses in medieval Europe.* (in Japanese) Hiroshima: Keisuisha.

2004: N. Harano, *et al. Travels through space and time in medieval Europe.* (in Japanese) Hiroshima: Keisuisha.

2005: N. Harano, *et al. Exclusion and toleration in medieval Europe.* (in Japanese) Hiroshima: Keisuisha.

2006: H. Mizuta, *et al. Death and life in medieval Europe.* (in Japanese) Hiroshima: Keisuisha.

2007: H. Mizuta, *et al. Women and men in medieval Europe.* (in Japanese) Hiroshima: Keisuisha.

2008: H. Mizuta, *et al. Laughter in medieval Europe.* (in Japanese) Hiroshima: Keisuisha.

2009: H. Mizuta, *et al. Tradition and innovation in medieval Europe.* (in Japanese) Hiroshima: Keisuisha.

2010: H. Mizuta, *et al. Feasts in medieval Europe.* (in Japanese) Hiroshima: Keisuisha.

Jointly-edited books:

1995: A. Jimura, Y. Nakao, and M. Matsuo (eds.) *A comprehensive list of textual comparison between Blake's and Robinson's editions of* The Canterbury Tales. Okayama: University Education Press.

1999: A. Jimura, Y. Nakao, and M. Matsuo (eds.) *A comprehensive textual comparison of* Troilus and Criseyde*: Benson's, Robinson's, Root's, and Windeatt's editions*. Okayama: University Education Press.

2001: A. Jimura, Y. Nakao, and M. Matsuo (eds.) *A comprehensive textual comparison of* The Parliament of Fowls*: Benson's, Robinson's, Brewer's, and Havely's editions. The Hiroshima University studies*. Graduate School of Letters 61, Special issue 3.

2001: Y. Nakao and A. Jimura (eds.) *Originality and adventure: Essays on English language and literature in honour of Masahiko Kanno.* Tokyo: Eihosha.

2002: A. Jimura, Y. Nakao, and M. Matsuo (eds.) *A comprehensive textual comparison of Chaucer's dream poetry:* The Book of the Duchess, The House of Fame, *and* The Parliament of Fowls. Okayama: University Education Press.

2002: A. Jimura, *et al.* (eds.) *A comprehensive collation of the Hengwrt and Ellesmere manuscripts of* The Canterbury Tales*:* General Prologue. *The Hiroshima University studies*, Graduate School of Letters 62, Special issue 3.

2008: A. Jimura, Y. Nakao, and M. Matsuo (eds.) *"General Prologue" to* The Canterbury Tales*: A project for a comprehensive collation of the two manuscripts (Hengwrt and Ellesmere) and the two editions (Blake [1980] and Benson [1987]). The Hiroshima University studies*, Graduate School of Letters 68, Special issue.

2009: Y. Nakao, M. Matsuo, and A. Jimura (eds.) *A comprehensive textual collation of* Troilus and Criseyde*: Corpus Christi College, Cambridge, MS 61 and Windeatt (1990).* Tokyo: Senshu University Press.

2016: K. Nakagawa, A. Jimura and O. Imahayashi (eds.) *Language and style in English literature*. Hiroshima: Keisuisha.

Articles:

1979: Aspects of adjectives in *Beowulf. Bulletin of Ohtani Women's College* 14 (1).

1980: Chaucer's depiction of characters through adjectives: *Troilus and Criseyde*. (in Japanese) *Bulletin of Ohtani Women's College* 15 (1).

1981: The Anglo-Saxon poem 'The Seafarer' and Ezra Pound's 'The Seafarer': Similarities and differences. *ERA*, ns, 1 (2).

1982: Was she unsexed?: An essay on Lady Macbeth. *Ohtani studies in English language and literature* 9.

1983: Chaucer's use of impersonal constructions in *Troilus and Criseyde*: by aventure yfalle. *Bulletin of Ohtani Women's College* 18 (1).

1987: Chaucer no yakata no hyogen. *Hito no iye kami no iye*. Kyoto: Apollon-sha.

1987: Chaucer's depiction of courtly manners and customs through adjectives in *Troilus and Criseyde*. *Philololgia* 19.

1989: Chaucer's use of "hous" and its synonyms: With special reference to *Troilus and Criseyde*. *Jinbun ronso* 6.

1990: Chaucer's use of northern dialects in "The Reeve's Prologue and Tale." *Ogoshi Kazuso sensei taishoku kinen ronshu*. Kyoto: Apollon-sha.

1990: Some notes on hypocritical vocabulary in "The Reeve's Prologue and Tale": With special reference to the Miller and his family. *Philololgia* 22.

1991: *Koshaku Fujin no Sho* ni okeru kotoba asobi ni tsuite. In H. Tsuru (ed.), *Reading Chaucer's* Book of the Duchess. Tokyo: Gaku Shobo.

1991: Chaucer's use of "soth" and "fals" in *The House of Fame*. *Philololgia* 23.

1991: Chaucer's use of "herte" in *The Book of the Duchess*. In M. Kawai (ed.), *Language and style in English literature: Essays in honour of Michio Masui*. Tokyo: Eihosha.

1992: *The House of Fame* ni okeru taisho goho to sono yoho. In T. Saito (ed.), *Eigo eibungaku kenkyu to computer*. Tokyo: Eichosha.

1992: A historical approach to some determiners of English: Notes on hiatus. In Y. Niwa, Y. Nakao, and M. Kanno (eds.), *Theoretical and descriptive studies of the English language*. Tokyo: Seibido.

1993: Word-formation of Chaucer's English (I): Collected data. *Bulletin of the Faculty of School Education, Hiroshima University, Part II* 15.

1993: The language of Criseyde in Chaucer's *Troilus and Criseyde* (I). *Essays on English language and literature in honour of Michio Kawai*.

1993: The language of Criseyde in Chaucer's *Troilus and Criseyde* (II). *English and English teaching*.

1993: A comparative study of *Beowulf* and Yamato Takeru. *In Geardagum* 14.

1994: The language of Criseyde in Chaucer's *Troilus and Criseyde* (III). *Bulletin of the Faculty of School Education, Hiroshima University, Part II* 16.

1995: Negative expressions in "The Clerk's Tale." *Bulletin of the Faculty of School Education, Hiroshima University, Part II* 17.

1995: Chaucer's use of 'un'-words in "The Clerk's Tale": With special reference to "unsad," "untrewe," and "undiscreet." In M. Umeda (ed.), *Kotoba no chihei: Eibei bungaku gogaku ronshu*. Tokyo: Eihosha.

1997: Textual comparison between Blake's and Robinson's editions of *The Canterbury Tales*. In M. Kanno, M. Agari, and G. K. Jember (eds.), *Essays on English literature and language in honour of Shun'ichi Noguchi*. Tokyo: Eihosha.

1997: Chaucer's description of nature through adjectives in *Troilus and Criseyde*. *English and English teaching* 2.

1998: Metathesis in Chaucer's English. In M. Kanno, G. K. Jember, and Y. Nakao (eds.), *A love of words: Philological studies of the English language in honour of Akira Wada*. Tokyo: Eihosha.

1998: Notes on the word order in Chaucer's English. *Bulletin of the Faculty of Letters, Hiroshima University* 58.

1998: An approach to the language of Criseyde in Chaucer's *Troilus and Criseyde*. In J. Fisiak and A. Oizumi (eds.), *English historical linguistics and philology in Japan*. Berlin: Mouton de Gruyter.

1999: Notes on word forms in Chaucer's English. *Bulletin of the Faculty of Letters, Hiroshima University* 59.

2000: Chaucer's description of God and pagan gods through adjectives in *Troilus and Criseyde*. In H. Tsuru (ed.), *Fiction and truth: Essays on the fourteenth century English literature*. Tokyo: Kirihara Shoten.

2000: An introduction to a textual comparison of *Troilus and Criseyde*. In L. C. Gruber (ed.), *Essays on Old, Middle, Modern English and Old Icelandic*. New York: The Edwin Mellen Press.

2000: A heterogeneous culture in Chaucer's English. (in Japanese) In N. Harano, *et al. Cross-cultural contacts in medieval English*. Hiroshima: Keisuisha.

2001: Notes on French elements in Chaucer's English. In Y. Nakao and A. Jimura (eds.), *Originality and adventure: Essays on English language and literature in honour of Masahiko Kanno*. Tokyo: Eihosha.

2002: Metathesis in Chaucer's English. (in Japanese) *The bulletin of the Japanese Association for Studies in the History of the English Language* 7.

2002: Multiplicity in Chaucer's English. (in Japanese) In N. Harano, *et al. Multiplicity in medieval European culture*. Hiroshima: Keisuisha.

2003: Chaucer's experiment of language. In M. Kanno (ed.), *Eigo goi ronshu*. Tokyo: Eihosha.

2003: Chaucer and his proverbial expressions: An approach to oppositional thinking. (in Japanese) In N. Harano, *et al. Cultural symbioses in medieval Europe*. Hiroshima: Keisuisha.

2003: A historical approach to English: Notes on word forms in Chaucer's English. *Studies in Modern English: The twentieth anniversary publication of the Modern English Association*. Tokyo: Eichosha.

2004: Metathesis in Chaucer's English. (in Japanese) In Y. Tagaya and M. Kanno (eds.), *Words and literature: Essays in honour of Professor Masa Ikegami*. Tokyo: Eihosha.

2004: On Chaucer's imagination: With special reference to nature. (in Japanese) *The Hiroshima University studies, Graduate School of Letters* 64.

2004: Chaucer and Mandeville's travels: Travels and pleasure in medieval world. (in Japanese) In N. Harano, *et al. Travels through space and time in medieval Europe*. Hiroshima: Keisuisha.

2004: A project for a comprehensive collation of the Hengwrt and Ellesmere manuscripts of *The Canterbury Tales: General Prologue*. (by Y. Nakao, A. Jimura, and M. Matsuo). In J. Nakamura, N. Inoue, and T. Tabata (eds.), *English corpora under Japanese eyes*. Amsterdam: Rodopi.

2005: Manuscripts and texts in Chaucer's works: An approach to exclusion and tolerance for texts. *Proceedings of international research conference*, 23-24 March 2005, Hiroshima University.

2005: On Chaucer's imagination: With special reference to nature. (in Japanese) *Essays on poetry* 21.

2005: Manuscripts and texts in Chaucer's works: An approach to exclusion and tolerance for texts. (in Japanese) In N. Harano, *et al*. *Exclusion and toleration in medieval Europe*. Hiroshima: Keisuisha.

2006: Shoho no eigoshi. In M. Tajima (ed.), *Ways with words: Beyond east and west*. Tokyo: Nan'undo.

2006: Death and life in Chaucer's *The Book of the Duchess*: With special reference to "herte." (in Japanese) In H. Mizuta, *et al*. *Death and life in medieval Europe*. Hiroshima: Keisuisha.

2007: Women governing men in Chaucer's works: With special reference to Griselda and Wife of Bath. (in Japanese) *Chusei Europe ni okeru ai no shoso*. (Report of the Grant-in-Aid for Scientific Research by Ministry of Education, Science, Sports and Culture.)

2007: Chaucer's multiple ways of thinking: With special reference to proverbial expressions. In M. Sawada, L. Walker, and Sh. Tara (eds.), *Language and beyond: Festschrift for Hiroshi Yonekura on the occasion of his 65th birthday*. Tokyo: Eichosha.

2007: Settoji *y*- tsuki kakobunshi no suitai ni tsuite. *The rising generation* 153 (1).

2007: Women governing men in Chaucer's works: With special reference to Griselda and Wife of Bath. (in Japanese) In H. Mizuta, *et al*. *Women and men in medieval Europe*. Hiroshima: Keisuisha.

2007: Eigoshi ni okeru ikei no ikkyokuka ni tsuite. *The rising generation* 153 (7).

2007: Manuscripts and texts in Chaucer's works: An approach to exclusion and tolerance for texts. In Y. Nakao, *et al*. (eds.), *Text, language and interpretation: Essays in honour of Keiko Ikegami*. Tokyo: Eihosha.

2008: Laughter and Chaucer's English. (in Japanese) In H. Mizuta, *et al*. *Laughter in medieval Europe*. Hiroshima: Keisuisha.

2009: A project for a comprehensive collation of the two manuscripts (Hengwrt and Ellesmere) and the two editions (Blake [1980] and Benson [1987]) of *The Canterbury Tales*. (by Y. Nakao, A.

Jimura, and M. Matsuo) *Hiroshima Studies in English Language and Literature* 53.

2009: Chaucer no shahon to kanpon ni okeru "settoji y- tsuki kako-bunshi" oboegaki. *IPSHU research report series* 42.

2009: A historical approach to variant word forms in English. In Sh. Watanabe and Y. Hosoya (eds.), *English philology and corpus studies: A festschrift in honour of Mitsunori Imai to celebrate his seventieth birthday*. Tokyo: Shohakusha.

2009: Tradition and innovation of Old English language and literature: "The Seafarer" revisited. (in Japanese) In H. Mizuta, *et al*. *Tradition and innovation in medieval Europe*. Hiroshima: Keisuisha.

2010: Kotonoha to chinona: Kotoba kara mita eibei to nihon no chimei ni tsuite no oboegaki. In M. Kosako, *et al*. (eds.), *Eigokyoiku heno aratana chosen: Eigokyoshi no shiten kara*. Tokyo: Eihosha.

2010: Chaucer's alcoholic drink and *The Canterbury Tales*: With particular reference to wine and ale. (in Japanese) In H. Mizuta, *et al*. *Feasts in medieval Europe*. Hiroshima: Keisuisha.

2010: Impersonal constructions and narrative structure in Chaucer. In O. Imahayashi, *et al*. (eds.), *Aspects of the history of English language and literature*. Frankfurt am Main: Peter Lang.

2011: Idiom no hensen: Chaucer kara Dickens he. In M. Hori, *et al*. The Dickens Lexicon Project to riyoho. *Osaka Ohtani University studies in English language and literature* 38.

2011: On the decline of the prefix *y-* of past participles. In T. Matsushita, T. Matsushita, A. V. C. Schmidt, and D. Wallace (eds.), *From Beowulf to Caxton: Studies in medieval languages and literature, texts and manuscripts*. Frankfurt am Main: Peter Lang.

2013: Chaucer's imaginative and metaphorical description of nature. In Y. Nakao and Y. Iyeiri (eds.), *Chaucer's language: Cognitive perspectives*. Osaka: Osaka Books.

2014: Some notes on idiomatic expressions in the history of English: With special reference to 'meat and drink.' In Y. Iyeiri and J. Smith (eds.), *Studies in Middle and Modern English: Historical change*. Osaka: Osaka Books.

2015: Choice and psychology of negation in Chaucer's language: Syntactic, lexical, semantic negative choice with evidence from the Hengwrt and Ellesmere MSs and the two editions of *The Canterbury Tales*. (by Y. Nakao, A. Jimura, and N. Kawano) *Hiroshima studies in English language and literature* 59.

2015: Kan'yoteki eigohyogen no tsujiteki imihenka no kenkyu-ronbun ni miru kyoikuteki igi: Akiyuki Jimura "Some notes on idiomatic expressions in the history of English: With special reference to 'meat and drink.'" (by K. Morinaga, A. Jimura, and N. Kaneshige) *Gakushu system kenkyu* 2.

2016: A computer-assisted textual comparison among the manuscripts and the editions of *The Canterbury Tales*: With special reference to Caxton's editions. (by A. Jimura, Y. Nakao, N. Kawano, and K. Satoh). In Y. Yanase and T. Nishihara (eds.), *Kotoba de hirogaru chisei to kansei no sekai*. Hiroshima: Keisuisha.

2016: *Kantaberi Monogatari* no shahon to kanpon ni okeru gengo to buntai. (by Y. Nakao and A. Jimura) In M. Hori (ed.), *Corpus and English stylistics*. Tokyo: Hitsuji Shobo.

Translation:

2016: A Japanese Translation of Geoffrey Chaucer's *The Legend of Good Women* (1). (by A. Jimura and H. Sasamoto) *The bulletin of the Okayama University of Science*. B. 52.

Reviews:

1991: M. L. Samuels and J. J. Smith, *The English of Chaucer and his contemporaries* (Aberdeen: Aberdeen University Press, 1988). *Studies in English literature* 67 (2).

1996: Jennifer Potts, Lorna Stevenson, and Jocelyn Wogan-Browne (eds.), *Concordance to* Ancrene Wisse*: MS Corpus Christi College Cambridge 402* (Cambridge: D. S. Brewer, 1993). *Studies in English literature* (English number 1996).

2001: N. Harano, *et al.*, *Cross-cultural contacts in medieval Europe* (Hiroshima: Keisuisha, 2000). *The bulletin of the Japanese*

Association for Studies in the History of the English Language 5.

2002: H. Sasamoto (tr.), *The Canterbury Tales* (Tokyo: Eihosha, 2002). *Shukan dokushojin*, 4 October.

2005: Akiyuki Jimura, *Studies in Chaucer's words and his narratives*, (Hiroshima: Keisuisha, 2005). *The bulletin of the Japanese Association for Studies in the History of the English Language* 14.

2009: J. Terasawa, *Eigo no rekishi: Kako kara mirai heno mono-gatari* (Tokyo: Chuo Koronsha, 2008). *Web eigo seinen*, June.

2010: Lynda Mugglestone (ed.), *The Oxford history of English* (Oxford: Oxford University Press, 2006). *Studies in Modern English* 26.

2013: Jacek Fisiak and Magdalen Bator (eds.), *Foreign influences on medieval English*. (Frankfurt am Main: Peter Lang, 2011). *Medieval European studies* 5.